From Henri she learned that by the middle of March they would be gone. The bakery would stand empty, the fire would be unlit, and grass would grow up between the stones of the floor. Strangers would walk the floors and peer at what remained of their vanished way of life. No doubt they would steal what little they could before the Provost's men learned of the Luyons' flight and commandeered the property in the name of the king.

In spite of her longing to be in England Solange was saddened by this picture and in the silence of the night woke on more than one occasion to whisper her apologies to their soon to be abandoned home, 'I'm sorry but we must go. We must.'

Sweet Sally Lunn

PAMELA OLDFIELD

SPHERE BOOKS LIMITED

For Mike and Angela
with every good wish

A *Sphere* Book

First published in Great Britain by Michael Joseph Ltd, 1990
Published by Sphere Books Ltd 1991

Printed in Great Britain by
BPCC Hazell Books
Aylesbury, Bucks, England
Member of BPCC Ltd.

ISBN 0 7474 0873 4

Sphere Books Ltd
A Division of
Macdonald & Co (Publishers) Ltd
Orbit House, 1 New Fetter Lane, London EC4A 1AR
A member of Maxwell Macmillan Pergamon Publishing Corporation

Sally Lunn was well known in Bath in the late seventeenth century for the delicious teacakes she sold in her coffee-house. Facts about her life, however, have been hard to find and harder still to verify. I have, therefore, relied heavily upon my imagination in my attempt to bring this fascinating character to life.

Chapter One

A HOT FRENCH SUN burned down upon the fair head of a small girl making her way through a field of tall grasses. High above her a skylark sang and higher still the sky arched blue and cloudless but Solange was oblivious to the beauty that surrounded her as she cut a path through the grass with strong blows of Grandpère's stick. She tried not to think of the old man, recently laid to rest in that cold, deep grave.

A fat spider appeared on a trembling web in front of her, barring her path, but she disposed of it with an impatient jab of her stick and marched on undeterred. Solange was not afraid of spiders, snakes, bats or beetles, nor was she troubled by the mice that hid among the flour sacks in the bakery which was her home. Within her plump, eight-year-old body her heart was bold and her spirit indefatigable. Solange Luyon feared only one thing, and that was the power of King Louis XIV who hated her because she was a Huguenot.

He hated her with a grand passion – she had heard Grandpère say so on numerous occasions and since no one had ever contradicted him Solange knew it must be true. He hated La Rochelle, too. All the kings did.

Jean had told her that not so long ago one of them had besieged the city walls with a huge army so that no food could reach the people inside. The English king had tried to help the people of La Rochelle and had brought ships full of soldiers, but the French king's army drove them away. Most of the people in the town starved to death. Perhaps that would happen again! Solange thought it very likely, and just in case she made a point of eating every scrap of food on her plate.

'A grand passion'! These words alone had the power to make her shudder with a dreadful foreboding. He might even come to La Rochelle in search of her. If he did she would hide, but if he found her she knew he would wreak a most terrible vengeance upon her.

Solange knew that the king was no respecter of persons. Men, women and children had suffered at his hands. Some nights she dreamed that he strode into her tiny bedroom wearing his best velvets, his sword clanking at his side. She saw the candlelight reflecting on the gold of his jewelled crown, highlighting the red rubies and green emeralds which winked like evil eyes. His long hair curled over his shoulders with wild abandon and his fingers were covered with rings as they reached out for her. Behind him, in the narrow doorway, his soldiers jostled for a better view and laughed cruelly as the king fastened a cold hand around her wrist and dragged her from the bed.

Always in the dream his hands were cold. That was because he had no heart, she thought. He was 'a cruel, heartless monster', according to her brother Jean, who knew almost everything about everything and would

2

sometimes take the time to explain things to her. This did not happen as frequently as Solange would have liked but that was because Jean was much older than her and had to work for his living.

While Solange slept in her truckle bed he made the dough for the *pain* as her mother was busy with the *brioches* and *gâteaux*. While Solange attended her classes Jean and Maman slept and Grandmère cleaned the house, washed the clothes and shopped in the market.

Solange came to an abrupt halt as a crouching hare sprang into life at her feet and leaped away to safety through the long grass. A broad smile lit up her face as she waited, hoping it would reappear, but after a moment she gave up and carried on through the field.

Yes, if the king caught her he would undoubtedly take her away and lock her up in a convent where the Ursuline nuns would somehow turn her into a papist, and then she would never see Jean or Maman or Grandmère or the cats ever again. Because they were all Huguenots. The prospect was too awful to contemplate but the dream persisted to spoil her sleep and the fear lingered to trouble her waking mind.

According to Grandmère none of these terrible things would happen to her as long as she had faith in God, but she could not entirely believe this. Her father had surely had faith, she argued, yet he had been driven out of France a few months after Solange was born and now lived somewhere in England.

'But why?' she had asked on countless occasions and in her opinion the answers had been less than satisfactory.

Maman had said sharply, 'Don't ask me, child. The less said about your father the better!'

Grandmère had said, 'Papa has fled the king's wrath, Soli. 'Tis best you forget all about him.'

Grandpère had said, somewhat mysteriously, that he had seen it coming (whatever 'it' was) and was not surprised. Only Jean had made any attempt to explain the reason for her father's sudden disappearance, and he had hinted at an excess of wine which had led him to make certain disrespectful remarks about King Louis and his papists, which had later reached the ears of the king's representatives. Flight, according to Jean, had been the only solution.

Every night when Solange said her prayers she reminded God that her father was in England and was bound to be lonely without his family, and she asked Him to arrange for the rest of the family to join him as soon as possible. Once, long ago, they had received a letter from her father and Maman kept it in the Bible next to her bed. In the letter (parts of which Maman had often read aloud) her father told them in his unlovely handwriting that he was living in a village called Bideford and was looking for work.

Bid-e-ford. Solange loved the name of that village and would sometimes repeat it a dozen times or more like a chant. In her mind she equated Bideford, England, with all that was good in the world – with a warm bed, plenty of food, friendly neighbours and freedom from fear. In Bideford they would be reunited with Papa and would live happily ever after. She was certain of it.

Now she stopped again in her tracks and turned to admire the path she had cut through the meadow. Beyond it she could just make out, among the trees, the warm red tiles which formed the roof of her tutor's house.

'Dear Monsieur Dulain,' she whispered, 'I do love you.'

She loved him because he was part English (on his grandmother's side) and because he was teaching her the language – teaching her secretly, because it would never do for the king to know that she was one day going to join her father in Bideford. Fortunately the tutor lived outside the town on the northern side, and by going through the fields Solange could attend her classes unobserved.

He was also teaching her to read and write, but Solange considered these subjects of little interest although she was showing considerable talent in both. She loved Monsieur Dulain although he was fat and unlovely and smelled almost as bad as his four mangy cats. She did not always call him Monsieur. Sometimes she called him Master Dulain because he had told her that somewhere in England people were calling her father Master Luyon and she thought it sounded rather grand.

'Master Luyon!' she said aloud and thought how wonderful it sounded. Screwing up her face she began to recite her verbs in English:

'I am
You are
He is, she is
We are
You are
They are.'

It was a difficult language but Solange never doubted

that she would one day speak it as well as Papa, who by now would undoubtedly speak it like a true Englishman. She herself spoke it with the broad native vowels of the west coast of France and it sounded clumsy even to her eager ears, but she persevered, earning Monsieur Dulain's praise for her efforts.

She continued through the field with the verb 'to have', timing her strokes of the stick to match her words, her blonde curls bobbing with each stroke.

'I have.' A swing to the right. 'You have.' A swing to the left. The rhythm pleased her.

From somewhere nearby a cow lowed mournfully for a lost calf and the scent of wood smoke drifted on the air but Solange was oblivious to anything but the verbs.

To her surprise Grandmère was waiting for her outside the town walls, an anxious expression on her face. 'You're late today, Soli,' she said. 'I was worried and came to look for you.' Grandmère was small and plump and her eyes were dark as currants.

Solange fell cheerfully into step beside her as they passed through the gateway into the city itself.

'We started late,' Solange told her. 'Monsieur Dulain was out when I got there. He had been to buy fresh hay for his bed. He came back puffing like a pig!' She laughed at the memory. 'He had been running –'

Grandmère gave her a sharp look, 'Running? From whom?'

Solange shrugged plump shoulders. 'He didn't say.'

'Hm!' After a moment's deliberation Grandmère asked suddenly, 'And who said you could take your grandfather's stick?'

They both looked at the well-worn stick with its duck's-head handle and narrow silver band.

Solange looked up at the familiar face and said coaxingly, 'No one said I shouldn't take it, Grandpère wants me to have it. He came to me in a dream and said, "Solange, I want you to have my stick with the duck's-head handle."'

Grandmère was unimpressed with this lie. 'He said no such thing!'

'Oh, but he did!' Solange's large blue eyes were bright with apparent innocence.

'Jean might want it,' her grandmother suggested.

'He doesn't want it. He told me so.' She nodded firmly and almost believed it herself.

Grandmère glanced down at the curly head and warned, 'Soli! What have I told you about telling lies? God knows what is in your heart.'

'Jean *will* say that if I ask him,' Solange amended.

'Then you ask him.'

A stubborn tightening of the childish mouth did little to detract from the beauty of the small heart-shaped face. Solange, who took after her absent father, had the features of a cherub and her grandmother feared for her soul. Life for the beautiful was far too easy, she prophesied gloomily on more than one occasion. Temptations would await her round every corner and the Devil himself would mastermind her downfall!

Solange asked hopefully, 'What is for dinner today?'

'Rabbit stew.'

Grandmère pretended not to notice the expression of distaste on the girl's face and her thoughts reverted to the hastily penned letter in her pocket which had arrived that morning from her only surviving brother who lived in Poitou. So far she had not shown the letter to anyone else, aware that the contents would drastically affect their lives. The decision to leave La Rochelle would have to be taken and that meant flight to England with all its attendant dangers. To Grand-mère it meant a new and difficult life in a foreign country in which they would never truly feel at home; where they would always be looked upon as strangers. It meant also abandoning the grave of her husband.

She sighed deeply. Ever since her son's flight she had resisted the idea of following him and had hoped that she might live out her last years in her own country and be buried beside her husband in La Roch-elle. Now things had changed. The threats against the Huguenots were growing and the king's hostility had increased dramatically since the death of his mother in 1666. It was rumoured that he had made her a deathbed promise to rid France of all Protestants.

With the arrival of her brother's letter she felt bound to accept the inevitability of a sea journey which (pro-vided that they did not drown on the way over) would be followed by an uneasy sojourn in a foreign land. The young people might adapt to English ways but at her age she never would. Her mouth twisted unhappily at the prospect. True, she would be reunited with Pierre, her only surviving child, but she had to admit that he was weak and unreliable – a disappointment to them all with his irresponsible ways. She sighed. He had been such a beautiful child but now he had fled to England and she did not want to join him there. She was too old to learn a new language and too set in her own ways to welcome any changes.

8

The alternative, however, was to remain behind in La Rochelle and what could she then expect from life? Even if it was possible to keep the bakery she would have to train new people. And how empty her days would be without her daughter-in-law, Marie, and her two grandchildren. It was unthinkable that she should remain in La Rochelle.

She could not even pretend that they could correspond for she found reading difficult and could barely write, and this morning she had been forced to ask a neighbour for help. More to the point, perhaps, was the possibility that the letters from England would never arrive. Pierre had promised to write but they had received only one letter in seven long years. Not that she was surprised by this. She had lost confidence in him years ago. After his marriage to Marie he had become lazier than ever and had spent much of his time in the little inn round the corner. Even now she found herself wishing that he had been a son she could be proud of instead of a handsome idler. With the birth of his first child he had made a renewed effort but he had soon lapsed back into his bad habits. By the time Solange was born there were frequent quarrels as well as the occasional infidelities which the family tried unsuccessfully to hide from Marie.

Sometimes in the still of the night Grandmère awoke convinced that her son had met with some misfortune in England – had been arrested for drunkenness, perhaps, or lay dead somewhere, unacknowledged and unmourned. She kept these fears to herself, however, aware that her daughter-in-law suffered already from Pierre's absence and that her increasing sharpness hid a deep unease and a growing sense of dread which matched her own.

'Will we have to have rabbit stew in England, Grandmère?' Solange asked. 'Perhaps there are no rabbits there?'

'Who knows?'

Solange sighed noisily to express her deep disappointment at this answer and then changed the subject.

'Monsieur Dulain's house was horribly dark today,' she confided. 'His shutters were closed. He says he won't open them ever again.'

Grandmère stopped abruptly. 'Why not?' she demanded, her voice sharpened by fear. 'What has happened? Tell me at once!'

'The papists threw burning reeds into his bedroom and the bed caught alight. They called him names and said, "Death to the Huguenots!"'

'Mon Dieu!' gasped Grandmère. Her face had paled and she gripped the child's arm. 'Burning straw, you say? Oh, but that's terrible. The poor man! And he told you all this?'

Solange nodded. 'The house smelled funny and I asked him why. His mattress was in the yard, drying in the sun.'

'He might have been burned alive!' cried Grandmère. 'God in heaven!'

Her heart raced with fear. Monsieur Dulain lived only a few metres outside the town walls. So the atrocities of which her brother had written were virtually upon them. La Rochelle, with all its fortifications, could not save them from the wrath of the papists. The king wanted a Roman Catholic nation and he would

10

brook no resistance. The Huguenots must give up their faith or suffer the direst consequences.

The little bakery, on the edge of La Rochelle, had been in the Luyon family for five generations and stood in the rue des Deux Moulins. It consisted of the bakery itself, an adjacent storeroom and living quarters above. Its fortunes had varied depending on the mood of the monarchy, for when the king was tolerant Roman Catholics would also buy from them, but in time of persecution only Huguenots would support them and even these were becoming less numerous as the various families gave up the unequal struggle and fled abroad to seek a more tolerant environment in America or England. To Solange the bakery, with its warm, rich smells, was the nicest room in the house.

After the hated rabbit stew, while Grandmère dozed in her chair upstairs, Solange crept down as usual to curl up among the empty flour sacks with whichever of the cats could be persuaded to settle on her lap. Today it was the tabby and as it purred Solange hummed to herself and watched the motes of dust which swirled in a narrow shaft of sunlight that came through the open doorway. As always her drowsy thoughts turned towards England and today, for the first time, it suddenly dawned on her that going to England would mean leaving the bakery behind. The idea startled her and she sat up abruptly. Somehow she had never imagined them living in a different house and it had certainly never occurred to her that the family might have to follow a new line of business. How stupid she had been!

She began to consider her surroundings. Slowly her eyes roamed over the familiar room with its stone floor, rough walls and shadowy corners. To her right stood the huge lidded trough where Jean would labour over the dough, up to his elbows in flour and water. Two empty buckets beside the trough waited to be filled with fresh water from the pump in the yard. There were two large well-scrubbed tables, one for the bread, the other for the preparation of a variety of pastries. Nearby stood a violin-shaped table with a long flexible arm which was used for making *brioche*. Solange knew a lot about baking and had always known that one day she would become a baker. Would that still happen if she went to England, she wondered uneasily. Was Papa a baker now? If only he would write to them again!

Her reverie was suddenly interrupted by a small scuffling sound which came from somewhere in the half-empty wood store, and at once the cat leaped from her lap and streaked across the room. There was a brief skirmish among the twigs and then the cat reappeared with a large mouse dangling from its mouth. It sat down in the middle of the floor and began to play with it.

Solange watched cat and mouse half-heartedly, her mind teeming with insoluble problems. Could they take all the cats with them to England? Did the English king approve of cats? She had been told he was a kind, tolerant man, loved by all his subjects, but she had heard also that he favoured small spaniel dogs. Still, a man who allowed Huguenots into his country would surely not object to a few well-behaved cats. Good mousers, too.

She gave a small nod and said, 'But of course he will!' To the cats she said, 'Then you will have to learn how to miaow in English! Did you know that, Minou? Did you? Eh?'

The cat turned towards her voice and the mouse, taking its chance, ran desperately in the direction of its home. The cat, however, moved swiftly, a striped paw extended to prevent the escape of its plaything. Solange knew she should feel no compassion for the helpless mouse (because mice ate flour and flour cost money which they could not afford to waste) but she decided to give the mouse a chance. Taking up a rush basket from the nearby pile she rolled it across the floor so that the cat was once again distracted. As the cat hesitated the mouse fled thankfully to the safety of a dark corner and was seen no more.

'Serves you right,' Solange told the disappointed cat. 'You should keep your mind on your work!' After a puzzled glance around the floor, the cat sat down and, wrapping its tail neatly around its feet, yawned widely with apparent indifference.

Solange stretched out her short legs and eyed her wooden clogs severely as though they might somehow be held responsible for the family's predicament, then impulsively she covered her face with her hands and with tightly closed eyes whispered urgently, 'Write to us, Papa! Please write to us! Send for us and we will come at once.'

He still loved them, she was sure, and would never deliberately abandon them, but perhaps of late he had become very busy and the family had somehow slipped his memory. Peeping between plump fingers she saw the peel, the long-handled shovel which later on would slide the dough into the oven and draw out the newly-baked bread. Another hour or so and Jean would rouse himself and go out into the yard and wash his face under the pump. She made up her mind to ask him again about the long delayed trip to England. If he was in a good mood he would say something comforting, for he alone had patience with her obsession whereas Maman would merely snap at her and Grandmère would sigh gloomily and shake her head. Solange tutted to herself for, since Grandpère's death, the old lady had ceased to smile and no longer told Solange funny stories or taught her rhymes. Jean had explained that Grandmère was grieving, and Solange must be patient.

Now Solange allowed her gaze to drift past the oven to the wooden shelves cluttered with earthenware pots and half-filled sacks and on to a huge basket full of utensils. What little bread remained from the previous night's baking was still in the basket in the corner. With a deep sigh Solange rose to her feet and stretched her arms above her head. She had work to do before Jean appeared. It was her job to fetch in faggots from the store and to sweep the floor free of crumbs and ash and broken twigs.

Just then a shadow blocked out the light and Solange saw old Madame Marais silhouetted in the narrow doorway. The toothless old woman mumbled something.

Solange smiled and said, 'I'll have a look, Madame.' She crossed to the basket and fetched a few stale rolls which she slipped into the old woman's hands.

'Bless you, child,' said the old woman and patted Solange's curly head. 'And God knows we could do with His blessing,' she added. 'He has turned His beloved face from the Huguenots and what's to become of us now? That's what I ask myself. What's to become of us now?' Ignoring Solange's shocked expression, she turned and shuffled noisily away over the cobbles.

Turned His face away from us? Solange watched her go with a worried frown. Such disloyal talk was not allowed in the Luyon family. Grandpère had taught them that hardships were sent from God to test their faith. Turned His face, indeed! But the old woman's words had made her anxious and she decided to speak to Jean later on the subject. Turned His face away from them? She sincerely hoped not.

Later that day, while Solange was at the house of a neighbour, Grandmère produced the letter from her brother and handed it to Jean to read aloud. It was dated August 4th, 1680.

My dearest sister,
The writing of this letter grieves me sorely as I imagine the fear it will instil in your heart but I believe I would be failing in my duty if I did not acquaint you with certain facts of a most severe nature.

Marie's right hand fluttered to her lips apprehensively. 'I don't want to hear this!' she whispered. Jean glanced at his grandmother, who nodded grimly, and he read on:

> Yesterday our revered pastor was arrested by the archers while on his way to a prayer meeting. He offered no resistance but beseeched God to help him.

'Much good that will do him!' said Marie bitterly, and Jean continued:

> They tied him to the tail of a horse and dragged him away. He has been taken to an undisclosed place and all enquiries as to his whereabouts are rejected. His unfortunate wife was taken with a seizure from the shock and cannot yet be roused from it. You can well understand our alarm and only our prayers sustain us in this most dreadful hour.

He paused to decipher the next hastily scribbled word and Grandmère shook her head.

'He will never be seen again!' she prophesied. 'Mark my words, it is the end of him, poor fellow!'

Jean glanced up at her. 'Why do you abandon him to his fate so quickly? You should be ashamed of such pessimism.'

Marie said automatically, 'Don't speak to your grandmother that way.' But her reprimand bore none of her usual sharpness as she struggled to overcome the fear which the letter had inspired.

'It isn't pessimism,' Grandmère protested, ''tis the truth and you know it.' She looked round at them blankly. 'Why should we pretend to ourselves? If the Provost's men have arrested him then only a conversion will satisfy them and we all know a Huguenot pastor

16

can never become a papist simply to save his life. You know that as well as I do.'

Jean said stubbornly, 'He could be rescued. He could escape. He could –'

The old lady's mouth tightened with annoyance. She dearly loved her grandson (who fortunately took after his mother) but he had reached the age when he liked to challenge his elders and she frequently lost patience with him. Now, although she knew he wanted to believe that the pastor stood a chance of survival, she could not allow him that luxury. The family had pretended for too long. Her brother's letter had finally convinced her that they must flee and the sooner it was done the better.

'Don't talk such nonsense!' she told him. 'No one will ever see him again. If he did renounce the Protestant faith he could never live with the shame of it. He is as good as dead!'

Marie said coldly, 'I'd like to hear the rest of the letter when you two have finished squabbling.'

For a moment it seemed from the expression of Jean's face that he had more to say, but reluctantly he turned his attention once more to the crumpled page and read on:

In view of this event I feel bound to urge you once again to consider that course of action we spoke of at such length during my last visit to you. For fear this letter falls into the wrong hands I will say no more than to beg you to take the family and rejoin your son.

Jean's voice faltered slightly.

Here in Poitou we are aware that the net is tightening. Act now before it is too late. For myself I am too old and ill to think of flight but it would greatly ease my mind to know that you and Marie and the children are safe.

He looked up irritably. 'Does he think I am still a child?'

No one answered him.

Marie said, 'So! 'Tis come at last.' Her face was pale and her expression bleak. She did not look at either of the others but said dully, 'We must go.'

Jean crumpled the letter and threw it on the ground. 'I will not leave Louise,' he told them. 'Never! You know we are to be wed.'

'You *will* leave her,' said Marie, 'because we will not leave La Rochelle without you and we have to go.' He began to interrupt but she held up a hand to silence his protests. 'I know you care for each other but you are young and there will be other girls. You are still much too young to think seriously of marriage.'

His face flushed angrily. 'Just because I am young I have no say in the matter? Is that what you mean? Because I am young I have no feelings? Is that it? And Louise? How about her? Doesn't it matter that we love each other?'

Grandmère reached down for the letter and picked it up and began to flatten it out so that it was readable once more. Jean's feeling for Louise was a matter for Marie to deal with.

She said, 'I simply said you would meet other girls –'

18

'I have no wish to meet other girls! I want to marry Louise Rey!' His voice was shrill. 'You cannot force me to go to England! What if I refuse? What then?'

Marie said, 'Suppose you remain here. What future is there for you and Louise and the children she will give you? You will be waiting each day for the Provost's men to beat a tattoo on your door!'

Grandmère, anticipating a protracted argument, decided to intervene and touched his arm gently. 'Would you let us go without you, Jean? Two women and a child, all that way? Think, lad, before you speak.'

'Then Louise must come with us!' he cried. 'She will leave her family if I ask her. She will come to England with us. I know she will.'

'No!' said Marie. 'She is only sixteen, Jean, a mere child. We cannot take her away from her family. Suppose we do not reach England? Suppose the boat founders? Her parents would never allow her to take such a risk and who can blame them?'

Grandmère said quickly, 'Finish the letter, Jean. We will talk then.' For a moment she thought he would refuse but then his lips moved soundlessly as he searched for his place in the letter:

I know it will be hard to leave the bakery but you will make a new life for yourselves in England with Pierre.

Jean looked up. 'If he is still alive!' he said bitterly.

Marie refused to be side-tracked again. 'The letter, Jean,' she prompted.

He glared at her rebelliously for a moment but then went on:

Do not answer this letter unless you can be sure that your messenger can be trusted. No one is safe today. Go, for God's sake, before it is too late. My love and prayers will go with you all. Your devoted brother.

'He hasn't signed it,' said Jean.

Marie sighed heavily. 'If he did and it fell into the wrong hands they would learn of our intention to escape! He would be a fool to put his name to such a letter.' She looked at her mother-in-law. 'You will come, then? You are sure?'

The old woman shrugged, 'Do I have a choice?'

'Thank God we have the money,' said Marie.

Jean asked, 'Money? What money?'

'From my brother,' Grandmère told him. 'He sent it two years ago when things looked black for us. 'Tis to pay for our passage to England. He sent us his life savings, God bless him. Now he has nothing for his old age.' Her lips trembled and Marie leaned across and touched her hand in sympathy.

Jean said defiantly, 'We do not need his money! When have we ever accepted charity? When we sell the bakery we shall –'

Grandmère shook her head. 'Think, Jean, before you speak! Selling the bakery would be a clear signal to the authorities that we meant to flee the country. We would find the Provost and his men waiting at the quayside and the Lord knows what would happen to us. You would most likely be sent to prison or be put to work as a galley slave. Is that what you want? Eh?'

He did not answer and the two women exchanged

exasperated glances. The hazardous undertaking that was being forced upon them was terrible enough but a resentful Jean would make it that much harder to deal with.

Jean looked up suddenly. 'How do we know that it will be any better in England?' he demanded. 'They have a Protestant king now, but for how long? He has no sons – no legitimate sons anyway – and his brother James is staunch for the Roman Catholic faith.'

Marie said, 'But King Charles cannot be more than fifty.'

'He could still die,' Jean insisted. 'Many men die before they reach sixty. If we move to England and find ourselves with James where will we run to then? I say we should stay with the devil we know. At least we belong here. We speak the language. We have roots.'

Marie said, 'For pity's sake, we have talked about this often enough times! Must we go all over it again? We are only welcome to remain here if we are prepared to denounce our Huguenot faith and adopt the Roman Catholic religion. Are you prepared to do that, Jean?' She stared at her son who sat with his hands clenched angrily in his lap.

'Of course not!' he told her. 'But will it be any better over there? How will you and Grandmère make friends if you cannot speak the language? Are we only to talk with our own sort?'

'We'll learn English,' said Grandmère. 'We'll pick it up as we go along. Soli will help us. And you, Jean – you've had lessons.'

He snorted disdainfully, 'Lessons! From that old fool Dulain! Soli has learned a little, I grant you, but I

21

learnt next to nothing, and you know it.' Jean had indeed proved a most inept linguist and the two women could not argue with his statement.

There was a long silence. Marie, knowing that the burden of the preparations would fall on her, felt a niggle of doubt in the face of his determined resistance. Grandmère hesitated also and Jean was quick to follow up his lead.

'Our own King Louis might fall sick and die,' he suggested. 'His successor might well be more tolerant towards the Huguenots. Everything could change for the better in France. Have you thought of that?' He turned towards Grandmère and added mockingly, 'Eh? Eh?'

Incensed by his rudeness Marie leaned forward and slapped his head and he at once sprang to his feet, his face furious.

'I'm not a child to be slapped!' he shouted. 'I'm a grown man.'

'You have the manners of a child!' cried Marie. 'Apologize to Grandmère at once.'

'I won't!' He slammed his fist on the table so that the crockery jumped noisily.

Marie snapped, 'And is this how a grown man behaves then?'

'I tell you, I won't leave France!' he told her. 'Not without Louise.'

'We must go, Jean.'

'Then go without me!' he shouted. 'Turn your back on La Rochelle if it means so little to you. Go, and see if I care! But don't expect me to come with you for I won't!' And before either of them could remonstrate further with him he ran from the room, swearing under his breath and slamming the door behind him.

They heard him clatter down the stone steps on his way out and looked at each other in growing dismay.

Grandmère said, 'Let him be, Marie. He's afraid but can't own to it. I understand how he feels. I'm terrified, too, and not ashamed to say so. The very thought of leaving France churns my stomach. If only Pierre would write! Mon Dieu! What will become of us?'

She began to cry soundlessly but Marie made no effort to comfort her. Her own eyes were dry but her jaw was set as she struggled to quell the panic that was rising steadily within her. If only Jean was with them on this issue she felt she could cope but without him — she was so afraid. Her resolve wavered. Suppose Jean was right? Suppose it would be wiser to stay?

She looked around at the familiar room with its meagre furniture and the few knick-knacks that were the sum total of all they possessed. A crude but serviceable table carved by her grandfather many years before she was born; four stools which Pierre had bought from a neighbour the first year they were married; a chest with iron hinges, which he had won in a card game. On the wall a sampler stitched by herself at the age of ten; and a small mirror in a wooden frame which her father had given her on her eighteenth birthday. There was nothing of value but without them what did she have?

She closed her eyes wearily. Here they led a frugal existence but the bakery kept them from starvation and provided a roof over their heads, though it was a constant struggle to make ends meet. Could it possibly be any better in England?

At the thought of her absent husband she shook her head in despair. He had given her two fine healthy children and in the early days of their marriage she had worshipped the ground he walked on. Later the doubts had set in but in spite of his faults she still tried to love him. But did he still love her? Or had he found himself another woman in England? One of her nightmares was that they would arrive in Bideford to find him nicely set up with a new wife and family! Yes, she would cheerfully hang for him if he had betrayed her. She sometimes wished she had never married him.

At other times her mood changed and then she thought that if he would only write she could forgive him anything. An encouraging letter from Bideford would make all the difference. Wearily she shook her head. 'I don't know,' she whispered. 'I just don't know.'

At the sight of Marie's tears Grandmère's courage was also evaporating. She said hesitantly, 'Perhaps we *should* think it over a little more carefully. Wait a few more weeks –'

Her daughter-in-law clutched at the straw thankfully. 'Yes, yes! That might be best,' she agreed. 'A few more weeks. Then maybe Jean will come round to our way of thinking. Yes, that's the way.'

Grandmère looked at Marie who would not, or could not, meet her eye. Once again the daunting prospect of change had defeated them and they had chosen delay.

By March of the following year the Luyon family were bitterly regretting their decision to remain in France for conditions had worsened considerably and many families, including the Reys, had fled the town. In the streets houses stood empty and familiar faces were seen no more. Here a cobbler had gone, there a weaver. One by one the merchants and skilled craftsmen were departing, slipping away at dead of night to brave the sea voyage, carrying only the possessions the skipper was willing to accept – a few clothes, tools, a few cooking utensils and a blanket or two. Sometimes a whole family disappeared, sometimes only the younger people, and the mood of the remaining Huguenots was one of deepening despair. It was becoming increasingly difficult to escape the watchful eyes of the Provost's men who had spies everywhere so that carefully laid plans were suddenly revealed to the authorities and the would-be fugitives exposed to a nightmare of cruel retribution.

On the last day of March Solange was sitting in the bakery with a black cat on her lap when she was startled by the appearance of a strange man who staggered through the narrow doorway from the street and collapsed on to the floor. As she sprang to her feet the cat was thrown from her lap and rushed to hide itself below the trough, spitting angrily, while Solange stared in dismay at the crumpled figure on the floor. One quick glance convinced her that the man was a stranger and she stared at him curiously. He was younger than her grandparents but older than Jean – perhaps the same age as Maman, she thought. His face was thin and his body spare and his dark hair was beginning to turn grey at the temples. His hands, she noticed, were smooth – not the hands of a labouring man. Suddenly it occurred to her that possibly her nightmare was about to become reality – this man might have come to warn her that the King was coming for her! With a gasp of fear, she ran to the door to peep cautiously out in search of any possible pursuers but seeing no one she returned to kneel beside the unconscious man.

'Monsieur, are you dead?' she asked in a quavering voice and was answered by a groan.

At any moment she expected to hear the clatter of horses' hooves in the road outside but still she hesitated to wake the adults. Previous experience had taught her that they valued their sleep and that a scolding was the most likely reward she could expect for disturbing their slumbers. Another look out into the road re-assured her. If her unexpected visitor *was* being chased then he had obviously given his pursuers the slip, for there was no one to be seen except the old organ-grinder at the far end of the street where a small group of children danced to his raucous music.

Solange took one of the buckets out to the pump, half filled it with water and staggered back. From the bucket she filled a bowl and, turning back to the stranger, saw to her relief that he was now struggling to sit up. His eyes were open and she saw that they were brown.

'Drink, Monsieur,' she suggested. He took the bowl with trembling hands and drank from it noisily.

'Food!' he whispered hoarsely and she nodded and hurried to fetch a stale roll.

She scrutinized him carefully while he ate and realized from the cut of his clothes that he was not a vagrant as she had half suspected but a traveller of some kind. His clothes were dusty but good and his boots were scuffed but not down at heel.

'Are you the Luyon child?' he asked at last, and when she nodded he shook his head in dismay. 'So you are still here in La Rochelle. Paul hoped you had gone to England long since.'

Solange frowned. 'Paul?' she echoed.

'I'm a friend of Paul Dubois,' he told her, wiping his sweating face with a grimy handkerchief. 'You know him, of course?'

She shook her head dubiously.

'Of course you do,' he insisted. 'He was your great uncle. The brother of your Grandmère. He was my neighbour in Poitou, God rest his soul! A better man never lived. We played chess together. We walked and talked in the cool of the evening and shared a glass of wine at midday. He was like a father to me and now –' He broke off and Solange fancied she saw tears in his eyes.

'My great uncle?' she repeated, unconvinced.

'He was a good man. He was one of the best.'

'Is he a bad man now?' she asked, puzzled.

'A bad man? No, no, but he's –' He stopped in mid-sentence again. 'I must speak with your mother,' he said, 'or Grandmère or your brother Jean.' Solange was reassured by this catalogue of names. This stranger obviously knew their family.

'They are sleeping,' she said. 'Later they will –'

He took hold of her wrist. 'Not later – now!' he told her. 'There is no time to lose or we shall all perish. Go and rouse them at once, child.'

She hesitated, having seen the way he gobbled the roll. 'Would you like more to eat?' she asked.

He shook his head although he had eaten nothing for three days. 'By and by,' he said, 'but for now go quickly!'

'I'll fetch them,' Solange told him and, flushed with importance, she hurried up the stairs to rouse the rest of the family.

As soon as they were all safely assembled in the kitchen the stranger introduced himself as Henri Sautreau and apologized for being the bearer of bad news.

To Grandmère he said gently, 'Your brother Paul is dead, killed by one of the dragoons billeted upon him by the authorities. It is a new instruction authorized by the governor of the province.'

Grandmère drew in her breath and then let it out in a rush of tears. Solange hurried to her side and threw her arms round the old woman's waist. She heard Jean curse and saw that her mother stared at the newcomer in horror. While the old lady struggled with her grief they waited patiently but at last she nodded her head and the stranger went on.

'I was Paul's friend and neighbour for many years,' he told them. 'More than that, I am greatly in his debt for once he saved my life. I was stricken with a strange fever and the physician himself despaired of my recovery. Paul Dubois nursed me for eight days, feeding me on a recipe of his own made from sunflowers.'

Marie said, 'You have no wife then?'

'No, I have never married. Paul and I – we were two dull old bachelors.'

Grandmère smiled. 'Paul was very knowledgeable,' she said, 'and herbs interested him. Flowers too. But go on, monsieur.'

Henri shrugged. 'Two weeks later I was myself again.' He fell silent and they waited patiently for him to continue. As he remained deep in thought, Jean prompted him.

'But this new instruction you spoke of?'

Henri said, 'Ah, that! Last week it was announced that to "aid" the conversion of the Huguenots in our town the dragoons would be billeted upon us. Seven came to my little house and nine to your brother's. They had been encouraged to make our lives as miserable as possible and the bullies could not wait.' He shook his head at the memories. 'They behaved like animals. Animals! They insulted me, spat upon me, pushed and jostled me so roughly that I am black and blue. One slept in my bed, others defaced the walls and broke up my possessions. It was the same all over the town.'

Jean cried, 'The bastards! May they burn in their own hell!'

Grandmère began to weep afresh.

Henri swallowed and then said shamefacedly, 'I have to tell you that in the face of such persecution many people renounced their faith in order to protect their loved ones from their torments. Others for fear of their own lives. It takes an exceptional person to choose death, but I believe they are still Huguenot in their hearts and God will forgive them.'

Marie said dully, 'We must go to England.'

Jean clenched his fists. 'If I had been there –' he began boastfully but was silenced by a look from his mother.

Henri continued quickly, 'One old woman was suffocated with a pillow in her own bed because they claimed her sobbing distracted them from their cards! For my part –' He shrugged. 'They burnt my beautiful books! I had collected them all my life – some of them were very valuable. They threw them into the fire and made me watch them burn! Still, I was one of the lucky ones.' He covered his face with his hands and drew a long shuddering sigh.

When he lowered his hands he said to Grandmère, 'Your brother tried to save a portrait which they were threatening to run through with their sabres.'

Grandmère raised her hand. 'The portrait of our father,' she said softly, 'painted on his fortieth birthday!'

He nodded. 'It seems they wrestled at the top of the stairs and either Paul fell or they pushed him down the stairs. He broke his neck. It must have been very quick, very merciful.'

After a long silence Jean said, 'And you have come all this way, Monsieur Sautreau, just to tell us this?'

Henri shook his head. 'I am on my way to England,' he told them. 'I have endured enough. If I have to choose between my country and my faith then I renounce France. She is no longer the France I knew and loved where honest men could live out their lives in peace. I am not too old to start again. I can work hard.'

'What do you do?' asked Marie.

'I am a tailor,' he said. 'I can ply my trade anywhere in the world.'

'Anywhere but France!' said Grandmère with a sorrowful shake of her head. 'Oh Paul! My poor, dear brother. What a way to die!'

Solange had not missed any of this conversation and had understood most of it. She turned to her mother. 'So will we go now, Maman? To join Papa?'

Marie looked at Monsieur Sautreau, and he said, 'Why don't we go together?'

And before the day was over it had been agreed.

For the next few days Henri Sautreau remained out of sight in an upstairs room. Solange learned that Maman had forbidden him to set foot in the street outside for fear of attracting attention to himself as a stranger in the town. Interest in the Luyon family was to be discouraged at all costs and it was imperative that everything should appear as normal as possible. They continued to bake bread and cakes and to chat with their customers as though nothing out of the ordinary was happening, and Solange was warned not to speak to any of her friends about their visitor and threatened with a sound smacking if she defaulted. She was kept mainly in the dark about the details of the planned escape and her pleas for information were met by the inevitable, 'No, Solange, it is for your own good that you know nothing at all.'

Although in her heart she acknowledged this to be sensible could not resist trying to trick information from the rest of the family by artful questions.

'Oh, but we shall still be here on Sunday,' she would say in the hope of receiving an unguarded answer.

Her mother grew angry with her constant questions, Grandmère (busy with her own griefs) largely ignored them and Jean, patient as ever and pretending to know very little about their plans, grumbled that he, too, was eager for information. Only Henri Sautreau fell into

31

her traps. He was a bachelor and unused to children and quite unprepared for the subtleties of what he imagined to be Solange's innocent mind. From Henri she learned that by the middle of March they would be gone. The bakery would stand empty, the fire would be unlit, and grass would grow up between the stones of the floor. Strangers would walk the floors and peer at what remained of their vanished way of life. No doubt they would steal what little they could before the Provost's men learned of the Luyons' flight and commandeered the property in the name of the king.

In spite of her longing to be in England Solange was saddened by this picture and in the silence of the night woke on more than one occasion to whisper her apologies to their soon to be abandoned home, 'I'm sorry but we must go. We must.'

One night she dreamed that the king's own baker moved in to bake a special bread for his royal master. Solange saw him turn in triumph from the oven with a delicate circle of *brioche* in his outstretched hands.

'My liege,' he said humbly, 'you are well rid of Solange Luyon. Now you must celebrate.'

The king took it and held it up so that the gleaming circle framed his face. The *brioche* was baked a fine golden brown and the cherries gleamed rich and dark where the points of the dough spread outward like the petals of a giant flower.

But the king's face was contorted with rage. 'So she is fled!' he roared. 'Solange Luyon has escaped me!' And with large powerful hands he crumbled the *brioche* and flung the pieces into the air so that a thousand crumbs pattered down like fine rain.

In her waking moments Solange was concerned that the king, hating her as he did with a grand passion, might learn of their escape and send his archers after her to sink their boat. Could an arrow pierce the side of a fishing boat, she wondered, aware that none of the family could swim.

She lay sleepless one night in the moonlit room, trying to convince herself that if the boat foundered they might somehow *float* to England. Suddenly the door opened and her mother entered the room. She had a finger to her lips and at once Solange sat up in bed, her stomach fluttering with a mixture of excitement and dread.

''Tis tonight!' Marie told her. 'Dress quickly, Soli, and for God's sake don't make a sound. Everyone else is ready to go. The boat will be waiting below the fairway. Put on as many clothes as you can, one on top of the other. You see why? No one must guess we are leaving. Now hurry.'

Surprised, Solange repeated, 'One on top of the other? But –'

'You heard what I said. There's no time for questions. Just do it, for the love of God! And hurry.'

With trembling fingers Solange pulled on her two pairs of drawers, tugged her everyday dress and her going-to-church dress over her head and, from habit, slipped on her pinafore. As she dressed she spoke urgently to her absent father, 'We're coming, Papa! We're truly on our way. Please be there.'

She imagined that he would learn of their escape and visualized him waiting to greet her on the quayside. The sun would glint on his fair hair, his arms would be outstretched in greeting as she stumbled ashore. There would be tears of joy in his eyes and he would gather her into his arms and hug her half to death.

Jean's head appeared round the corner of the curtain to interrupt this daydream.

'Make haste, Soli! We're waiting for you!'

'I am nearly ready.' She thrust her feet into her clogs but by now her heart was thumping and she felt sure the watchful eye of the Provost would catch the sound as she crept through the darkened streets! Solange began to ask about the cats but for once Jean had no time for her questions. Impatiently he caught hold of her wrist and hurried her down the stairs and into the bakery where Grandmère, Maman and Henri Sautreau waited.

'At last!' cried Maman. Her face was pale in the candlelight and Solange thought she had been crying.

Grandmère's face was half-hidden by her best shawl and she carried a small bundle beneath her voluminous apron. The pockets of Henri Sautreau's coat bulged alarmingly. Maman carried a basket on one arm and Jean carried a bundle wrapped in a blanket.

'The cats!' Solange repeated.

Her mother whirled round. 'Cats? Mon Dieu! We are risking our lives and you ask about cats! The cats stay here, Soli. Now let me see . . .' Her eyes travelled slowly round the room.

'Have we forgotten anything? Oh yes! The doll! I shall forget my own head next!' She thrust a rag doll into Solange's arms and said, 'Don't let it out of your sight, Solange – not even for a moment.'

Solange stared at the doll which she had never seen

34

before. It had frayed string for hair and its body bulged. Its dress reminded Solange of the curtains in Grandmère's bedroom. It was very heavy indeed. It was an ugly doll and Solange regarded it resentfully.

'But why –' she began.

'No buts,' snapped her mother. 'Just do as you are told.' Solange opened her mouth to protest further but Jean caught her eye and closed his own in a broad wink which meant he would explain later and Solange, satisfied, fell silent.

Grandmère said in a trembling voice, 'We should pray.'

Maman said, 'One quick prayer then, but make haste.'

They all closed their eyes as Grandmère prayed and the familiar words encompassed them. Solange muttered an impatient 'Amen' and opened her eyes. They looked at each other in disbelief. It was happening. They were leaving. They would never see their home again. No one spoke and the seconds passed.

The tabby cat awoke and stretched loudly. Solange's lips quivered. 'Maman –' she began.

But Maman said harshly, 'Time to go.'

Incredibly Solange found herself out in the cold dark street, hurrying over the cobbles beside Jean, with the doll under one arm and Grandpère's stick under the other.

Solange looked back and said loudly, 'We have left the candles burning!'

'Hush!' said Jean. 'We have to leave them burning. People have to think we're still in there, making bread for the morning.' His voice was low and it shook slightly.

Grandmère and Henri Sautreau walked ahead – arm in arm, Solange noted with surprise. Marie followed, walking alone with her eyes downcast. Fortunately, it was not yet midnight and the loud singing and uncouth behaviour of a few late-night revellers masked the sound of their footsteps as they made their way stealthily through the streets.

Luck was with them and the only alarm they suffered was a meeting with a strange dog that flew at Jean's ankle and was sent howling into the darkness with a well aimed kick. In a fever of apprehension they walked on until they reached the sloping quay where a variety of boats rode at anchor, their outlines vague in the darkness, their rigging in constant motion.

Solange's eyes had now become accustomed to the dark and she was able to look around her. The area below the two towers was a familiar one in daylight but now it was alien to her. Bales of hay, tubs of salt, barrels of wine and crates of fish awaited the next tide, and the refugees concealed themselves among these and waited for Maman to make contact with the skipper they had hired. To their great consternation he was discovered deep in conversation with one of the Provost's men and they were forced to remain in hiding until at last the two men parted company with a burst of bawdy laughter from the Provost's man and with a cheery 'Adieu!' from the fisherman. As he went his way the Provost's man passed within feet of the Luyons' hiding place but luck was with them and his attention was elsewhere.

When they were sure he had gone the little party of Huguenots emerged into the moonlight and made themselves known. The skipper was a rough, grizzled man in his sixties whose wife had died several years earlier. He had no family and no one to care if he lived or died. He had made the hazardous trip to England three times already and was growing wealthy on the proceeds, but this was to be his last trip. He, too, was a Huguenot and he fancied his luck was running out. This time he would stay in England.

He helped them down into the boat which was much smaller than Solange had expected it to be. It smelt strongly of tar and wet ropes and fish and she wrinkled her nose in disgust as they were led to what was to be their hiding place for the duration of the voyage. It consisted of a shallow box-like area where in normal times the fish would be stored and the little party looked at it incredulously. Solange could not imagine how they would all fit into such a small space.

'Get in!' growled the skipper. 'And no talking until we're on the open sea. Voices travel across water at night, and God knows where King Louis' frigates will be. If they see us they'll board us and you'll all be done for – and I'll dangle at a rope's end! And I'll thank you to hand over the money we agreed on. 'Twill be safer with me!' He laughed as though he found this humorous.

'Soli,' whispered Marie, 'give him the doll.'

Solange stared at her in astonishment. Give a sailor a *doll*? Had Maman taken leave of her senses? As she hesitated, Jean whispered, ''Tis stuffed with gold, Soli – the money from Grandmère's brother to pay for our passage to England.'

Solange handed it to the old man, who stuffed it

unceremoniously inside his shirt as the refugees struggled to wedge themselves into the space provided, and almost immediately a couple of large wet sails were thrown over them. Solange shivered in spite of all the clothes she was wearing, but by now her natural optimism was reasserting itself and her earlier fears had subsided. With her knees up under her chin and her arms pressed uncomfortably to her sides she was cramped between Maman and Grandmère who were similarly doubled up.

Henri Sautreau whispered, 'Packed like pickled herrings in a tub!' But only Solange was kind enough to laugh at his little joke. She was glad Monsieur Sautreau was with them. She liked the way his eyes crinkled at the corners when he smiled, and she liked his voice and the way he asked her opinion and listened to it gravely. He made her feel very grown up and that was a good feeling.

As they waited for the skipper to cast off they felt the small boat rock beneath them and as Solange crossed her fingers for luck she heard Grandmère resume her prayers.

Without warning a rough voice hailed them from the shore and they froze into immobility. They recognized the voice. It was the Provost's man again!

'Skipper! You still here?' he shouted. 'You're going to miss the tide! Your lady friend won't like that.'

The skipper laughed, 'I'll get my marching orders, like as not!'

Greatly daring, Solange peeped from her hiding place and saw the skipper pushing against the harbour wall with a boat hook. The boat rocked more violently and Grandmère's lips moved feverishly.

'Give her my regards!'

The skipper laughed again and suddenly Solange was aware that the movement of the boat had changed. It was smoother and lighter. From somewhere above them the refugees heard the snap of a sail as the wind filled it.

'Mon Dieu!' whispered Maman. 'We're on our way!'

Chapter Two

SOLANGE WATCHED AS the lights of the town receded and the familiar towers that guarded the entrance grew gradually smaller. With a churning of the stomach she realized that she would never see La Rochelle again and she tried desperately to commit it to memory. In her mind's eye she conjured up the tall timber-framed houses and the squat building with its single tower where once the Huguenots had dared to worship. She thought of the Lantern Tower and the Big Clock and then her memory failed her. The harder she tried the less she could remember and at last she gave up the struggle and obeyed her mother's urgent command to cover herself with the sail.

For the best part of an hour the fugitives remained in their cramped quarters, whispering encouragement to one another in the darkness, but at last the skipper finally decided it was safe for them to emerge. When they did so, they stumbled out thankfully, stretching their cramped limbs, to find themselves surrounded by dark waves whose breaking crests curled white and faintly ominous in the moonlight. It was not an encouraging sight but they hid their fear as well as they could, assuring each other that they had chosen a fine skipper and that with his skill and a following wind they would soon be on dry land again. The small boat wallowed alarmingly, however, and Solange's excitement was slightly subdued by a growing feeling of nausea which she did her best to ignore. The skipper, however, with a total disregard for their feelings, assured them rather unkindly that the sea was as still as glass.

After a very few minutes Grandmère declared she had seen enough of the sea to last her a lifetime and decided to return to the comparative safety of their cramped hiding place and pray for their deliverance.

Marie and Henri Sautreau stood at the rail together, staring fearfully out into the gloom while Jean and Solange prepared to explore the boat. They took care to keep out of the skipper's way as much as possible for, although he had been well paid for the risks he was taking, his manner was surly and Jean did not altogether trust him. He had heard rumours of unscrupulous skippers who accepted passage money and then threw their luckless passengers overboard.

Eventually exhaustion overtook them all and they rejoined Grandmère beneath the sails and made themselves as comfortable as they could. They were cold and hungry but they settled themselves without complaint for their first night at sea, grateful for the fact that the first part of their adventure had gone according to plan.

Solange listened as one by one her companions fell asleep while she remained wide awake and queasy, aware of every creak of the boat's timbers and the monotonous splash of waves against her hull. Countless questions filled her mind as she pondered their present predicament. What would they eat, she wondered? Had Maman's basket contained provisions? If not, raw fish seemed the only probable source of nourishment and although she shrank from the prospect she promised God that she would force it down without a murmur if only He would see them safely through the voyage.

Suppose He sent a storm to test their faith? Then she would be brave. She would accept the horrors of seasickness and would not mention Grandmère's snoring. Earnestly she assured God that as long as He kept His eyes on them until they stepped safely ashore at Bideford she would be His loyal servant for the rest of her life.

She wondered if news of their escape had reached King Louis and imagined the look of fury on his face as a timorous Provost admitted the facts to him. He would grind his teeth in a rage and almost certainly he would utter terrible profanities for which God would punish him at a later date. Perhaps the king would snatch off his golden crown and hurl it across the room in a fit of temper.

Jean had done that once, only he had thrown a pot of honey instead of a crown and it had smashed against the wall. The sight of the honey trickling down was still vivid in Solange's memory. Maman had tried to beat him but Jean had wriggled from her grasp and fled to the woods. Instead of the beating he had been given bread and water for a whole day but Solange had smuggled a piece of cheese to him and a handful of currants. Then he was only twelve but now he was a man. Perhaps he would find Louise in England and they would be married. Solange did hope so for then they would set up home and perhaps they would produce a child. Then she would become an aunt which was a very important thing to be. She frowned into the darkness. It had depended on the sort of gooseberry bush they planted, for Jean had explained that babies were found under some of them but that others produced only berries.

A niece would be almost as good as a sister, she thought with a yawn and her eyelids fluttered. Would they give the child an English name, she wondered, and would that make her English? It would surely be a most enviable thing to be aunt to an English niece.

As she yawned again she heard the skipper's footsteps approaching and braced herself for conversation but he passed by without pausing and his steps faded again. At least he was still awake and steering the boat, she thought sleepily, and then her eyelids closed once more and she slid into a dreamless sleep.

It was accepted in La Rochelle that the crossing to England could take as little as a week with following winds but when they blew from the west or north it was possible to be at sea for the best part of a fortnight. The Luyons started their journey with a favourable but light wind, but after three days it strengthened and swung round until it came from the north east and then the small craft bobbed and rolled unmercifully. The passengers tried to convince themselves that they were making some progress but the skipper informed them with apparent relish that they were making little or none at all.

Four days out from La Rochelle they were still

within sight of Ushant on the coast of Brittany and growing daily more anxious. The skipper had smuggled a little food on board – a few apples, hard biscuits, cheese and onions – but although Marie insisted that everyone should eat something each day they were so seasick that for the most part they could not keep the food down long enough for it to sustain them. Only Solange gained her 'sea-legs' and she spent much of her waking hours ministering to the less fortunate members of the party.

On the seventh day when they were finally out of sight of land the wind dropped away to nothing and they found themselves becalmed. The food that remained now had to be eked out and the water strictly rationed. To make matters worse, the skipper was rarely sober and became coarse and insulting. He threatened more than once to turn the boat round and head back to La Rochelle, but Henri Sautreau hinted at possible reprisals and he evidently thought better of it.

Eventually, however, their prayers were answered and a wind sprang up which blew them steadily northwards. A few vessels passed them incuriously and gulls wheeled incessantly over their heads but apart from these distractions the days passed interminably. When the sea was rough they were too ill to care, and when they were well they bickered among themselves, their nerves jangled with alternate hopes and fears. It was grim but just tolerable.

On the eleventh day disaster struck. Jean had just helped Grandmère to the rail when a particularly large wave struck the boat so violently on the starboard side that it lurched suddenly, throwing them both to the deck which tilted alarmingly. They both began to roll and Jean grabbed desperately at a nearby rope and managed to hold on, but the old lady was not so lucky and began to slide towards the rail, screaming frantically for help as she did so. Jean made a desperate attempt to reach her but just as his outstretched hand touched her foot the boat shuddered under the impact of a second wave and, sick with horror, he saw her slide under the rail and over the side. Her thin scream of fear ended abruptly and as the boat righted itself he pulled himself to the rail in time to catch a brief glimpse of her head and arm before the next wave hid her from sight. When it passed she was nowhere to be seen.

For a few seconds the suddenness of the disaster froze him but then he shouted for help and began to climb over the rail. He became aware that his mother was clinging to his arm, shouting to remind him that he could not swim. Monsieur Sautreau had appeared at his side.

Marie cried, 'He can't swim. They will both drown!'

'I can swim,' he said and before anyone could stop him he had plunged over the side.

The captain shouted, 'Don't be a fool, man. You'll never find her in this. She's gone for good!' But the wind bore his words away and he began to lower the sail in an attempt to stay as near as possible to the spot where the old lady had fallen in.

Marie knelt at the rail, gazing at the churning grey water, her hands clasped in urgent prayer while Jean, beside her, sobbed with frustration. Solange, who had been dozing, emerged to find Jean shaking the skipper furiously by the shoulder, insisting on a rescue attempt.

'What's happening?' she asked, rubbing the sleep from her eyes. She saw Maman at the rail but glancing quickly round the ship she saw no sign of Grandmère or Monsieur Sautreau, and a cold finger of fear touched her. As Jean caught sight of Solange another huge wave burst over the boat and she lost her footing with a cry of panic. Fortunately she rolled towards Jean and he caught her by the arm.

'Get back in the sail locker,' he told her fiercely.

'But Jean —' she began.

'And don't argue or I'll beat you!' Something in his pale face made her bite back the protest that sprang to her lips and she moved to obey him with a sense of impending disaster. As she did so she heard Jean say, 'A rope-ladder, then, or a rope, you murderous bastard, or do you want to see them both drown?'

She heard Maman sobbing, 'Father in heaven, be merciful, I beseech you. Have pity on us and save them. Oh God!'

When Solange reached the security of the sail locker she curled up in a corner and put her fingers in her ears in an attempt to shut out the tragedy that was taking place.

A rope-ladder was finally produced and lowered over the side but it seemed impossible that anyone could have survived the rolling waves. As the skipper struggled at the wheel Marie and Jean searched the sea with despairing eyes.

Suddenly Jean cried, 'I see someone! See, there! To the right! Mon Dieu! 'Tis Monsieur Sautreau!'

'Just Monsieur Sautreau?' Marie tried to hide her disappointment. He had risked his life and if he alone had survived she must not begrudge him his safety. 'Can he reach us?' she cried. 'We must save him!'

'The skipper's lowering a rope-ladder,' Jean told her. 'If he can reach that there is still a chance.' Marie, anguished, still searched the waves for a glimpse of the old lady although she knew in her heart that there could be no hope.

Slowly, painfully, Henri Sautreau drew closer, urged on by hoarse cries of encouragement. At the last moment it looked as though his strength would fail him but to everyone's relief he managed to reach the rope-ladder and willing hands reached down to help him. Slowly he clambered back up the ladder until Jean and Marie could pull him back on board. Choking and gasping for air he lay on the deck in a state of utter exhaustion.

When at last he could speak he looked up at the sky. 'I'm so sorry, Paul,' he whispered. 'I didn't see her – not once. I was too late. You must forgive me.' To Marie he repeated earnestly, 'I didn't see her. Not once. Forgive me.'

Maman leaned over him with tears streaming down her face. 'Forgive you?' she said. 'For what? For risking your own life? You did all you could and more! Forgive you? Why, we can never thank you enough!'

As he struggled into a sitting position she took him in her arms and wept anew while Jean watched wordlessly. Then, remembering Solange, he made his way unsteadily back to tell her as gently as he could that Grandmère was no longer with them.

She listened white-faced as he explained what had happened. 'God has called Grandmère to him,' he said finally. 'Her body is in the water but her spirit is in heaven among the angels.' He watched her face for the release of tears but the large blue eyes remained dry and wary.

'Did she want to be called?' she asked at last.

'Maybe she did.' He nodded, 'Yes, I dare say she did. She didn't want to go to England, did she, Soli? Maybe she wanted to be with Grandpère and that was God's way of letting them be together. I think she's happy now. They both are.'

She eyed him suspiciously, 'Then why are you crying?'

He sniffed loudly and drew a deep breath. 'I'm crying for myself because I shall miss her. She's always been with us. Always. You'll miss her, too, Soli.'

'Yes.' Solange looked thoughtful. 'Will she miss us?'

'I dare say. Aren't you going to cry for her?'

'You said she was happy.'

He wondered if he would ever understand his small sister.

Solange tried to imagine her grandparents together in heaven, chatting cosily together on a fleecy cloud. Grandmère would be telling him about the family's decision to leave La Rochelle while the old man tut-tutted doubtfully. She thought he might pat Grandmère's knee with his gnarled old hand and then, convinced by her explanation, he would nod his head approvingly. After a moment or two the picture was quite clear in her mind and she began to see that in fact Grandmère had exchanged a very uncomfortable life on the boat for one of enduring comfort and luxury.

She smiled suddenly at Jean and said, 'Yes, Jean, she *is* happy.'

To reinforce this positive opinion he said quickly, 'She was nearly sixty. She had a good long life, a happy life. Do you remember the stories she used to tell us about her childhood?' Trying to blot out the thought of her final struggle in the cold sea he rushed on, 'Do you remember how she ate the toadstool instead of the mushroom and nearly died – and how she found her mother's ring in the bread dough.' He swallowed hard. 'And how she climbed the tallest tree that even her brothers dared not climb.' He smiled to cheer himself a little.

'And how she broke her aunt's mirror,' cried Solange, 'and stole the apples from the tree next door!' Her voice trembled, and uncertainty returned to her face. 'They *are* happy together, aren't they, Jean?'

He hugged her fiercely and then kissed the tip of her nose. 'Of course they are, Soli,' he said.

Grandmère's death cast a profound gloom over the family and Henri Sautreau suffered also – from a conviction that if he had acted a moment sooner or had searched more diligently, the outcome might have been happier. Useless for the Luyons to assure him that he had done all that was humanly possible. He felt very deeply that he had failed in his duty as a friend; if he could have saved Grandmère he would have repaid the debt he owed to Paul Dubois.

The tragedy did, however, have the effect of putting their other problems into perspective. Lack of food and water, absence of basic sanitation, seasickness and the dangers of their predicament all paled into insignificance beside the loss of a dearly-loved member of the family. Even the skipper appeared to have been affected by the event and his excesses with the bottle were not so frequent nor his tongue so sharp.

Fourteen days out from La Rochelle they woke at dawn to wonderful news – they were within sight of England's south-westerly coast. Huddled together at the rail they gazed out at the smudged and unfamiliar shoreline. Feelings of hopeful anticipation replaced grief and despair. Outwardly they had recovered from the shock of Grandmère's death and were gradually coming to terms with her loss.

As the captain pointed out Land's End a subdued cheer went up from the Luyons and Henri Sautreau nodded his head in silent approval. Overhead a weak sun shone and the land of England lay green and inviting.

Jean tweaked Solange's hair and asked, 'Well, Soli, what do you think of England? Is it what you expected?'

Solange's expression was rapturous as she nodded. 'I knew it would be beautiful,' she told him with a beaming smile. To Marie she said, 'And we are going to Bideford, aren't we, Maman? We are going to find Papa?'

Maman exchanged a glance with Jean before answering carefully, 'We hope so, Soli, but Papa is bound to be very busy and he may not be on the quayside to meet us. You must not expect miracles. We have reached England safely and that must be enough for now.'

Seeing the child's face darken Jean added quickly, 'You see Papa doesn't know we are here yet. 'Twill be a wonderful surprise for him. We couldn't write to him because he moved and we don't know his new address but we'll soon track him down, you'll see.'

This news came as a bitter disappointment to Solange who had pictured the rapturous quayside reunion for so long that she now felt cheated. Her jaw tightened and her lips became one thin line as she struggled to hold back angry words of reproach.

Jean said, 'We'll find him, Soli, I promise you.' She stared at him, sick with disillusion, not trusting herself to speak.

In silence they watched the shoreline sharpen as the little boat rounded the point and headed east towards the Bristol Channel. As they watched the approach of all their future hopes they were filled with a sense of gratitude and wonder that after the terrors of the past two weeks they were now within sight of their destination and one by one, without any prompting, they closed their eyes in a prayer of thanks for their delivery.

Hours passed and the wind lessened so that they made slow progress but nobody complained of thirst or hunger as the north Cornish and then the Devon landscape unfolded before them. The captain was noticeably more cheerful now that he knew he would live to spend his hard-earned gold and he even relaxed sufficiently to invite them to follow their progress on his chart.

With a stab of a grimy finger he said, 'That back there was Hartland Point and now we're crossing

Bideford Bay.' He spoke the foreign names awkwardly, but no one was inclined to be critical. With a jerk of his thumb he added, 'Wales is that way but a few miles off and we won't see it.'

Solange whispered, 'Bid-e-ford! Bid-e-ford!' And added, 'Be there, Papa! Please be there!'

As the boat hugged the shore they passed a few hamlets too small to be marked on the chart and then they were leaving the bay and changing course for the estuary where the land stretched for miles, low and marshy on either side. With some difficulty the captain negotiated a broad sand bar before steering them between a salt marsh and sand dunes.

A little further on two rivers met, the Taw and the Torridge, and here there was plenty of activity as boats of all sizes and shapes plied to and fro. Solange waved excitedly at every one that passed but her efforts were rewarded for the most part by unsmiling curiosity although once or twice someone would return her greeting with a word or two. Hearing the English tongue Marie grew suddenly nervous and clutched Solange by the arm.

'I hope you remember your verbs, Soli,' she said. 'We are going to need them shortly.'

Solange faced her with shining eyes and began in English, 'I am, you are, he is –'

'Well done!' Marie interrupted her and Solange positively glowed with pleasure and importance.

By the time they reached the village the tide was falling rapidly and a great many boats lay stranded on the mud or bobbed at anchor in the deeper water in the middle of the river. The skeleton of a large ship rose, half completed, from its stocks, and further along there was an air of leisurely activity as the day's catch of fish was unloaded from the boats in baskets and dumped unceremoniously on to the strand. Here and there bales of wool were stacked precariously and casks of wine stood among coils of rope; tubs of salt could be glimpsed through piles of multi-coloured fishing nets. There was no quay but about twenty yards back from the river's edge a row of white-washed houses faced out across the water to softly rolling fields on the opposite bank. A group of men watched the approach of the French fishing boat and muttered among themselves; behind them a woman also watched, her shawl drawn tight across her chest to protect her from the cold breeze.

Behind the houses the ground rose steeply and more houses and narrow cobbled streets climbed the slope. The Huguenots were embarrassed to find themselves the centre of so much attention but the skipper remained unperturbed. As he nosed the boat on to the mud he shouted, 'Bid-e-ford?'

The men shook their heads and some smiled. 'Appledore,' said one, 'App-le-dore!' He pointed further up the river and said, 'Bid-e-ford.'

'*Merde!*' muttered the skipper.

'What are they saying?' Marie demanded.

'This isn't Bideford,' the captain told her with a scowl. ''Tis called Appledore or some such, but I'm going no further so you must make the best of it.'

A short, sharp argument ensued which was won by the skipper who now grew increasingly eager to be rid of his passengers, and he urged them in unchivalrous terms to get themselves ashore as quickly as possible and leave him in peace.

Ten minutes later the little group of Huguenots found themselves standing on English soil at last, clutching their pathetic bundles, and staring at each other, quite at a loss to know what to do next. True, they were in England, the sun was shining and they had escaped the wrath of the French king, but, for the adults, the moment they had anticipated for so long failed to live up to expectations. Doubts and uncertainties filled their minds and the future remained a frightening blank. They were exhausted from their journey and desperately hungry and they had very little money. Friendless in a strange country where no one would understand their language, they gazed around them with anxious expressions not knowing what to expect.

Only Solange relished the moment. She was in England, she told herself, and her beloved Papa could not be far away. Soundlessly, but with quiet earnestness, she hugged Grandpère's stick and began to practise her verbs.

Chapter Three

BY NIGHTFALL THAT EVENING their situation was a little more comfortable. A trace of cautious optimism had crept into their conversation and a small flicker of hope glowed in their hearts. They had found temporary lodgings with a widow, Mistress Webbe, who lived in New Street. The house was small but she gave up her own bedroom to accommodate Marie and Solange while Monsieur Sautreau and Jean were given makeshift beds in the attic. For the time being Mistress Webbe would sleep in her sister's house next door. Large and shapeless and constantly racked by a chronic cough, Mistress Webbe was yet a cheerful soul who made light of her difficulties. She earned a precarious living in a variety of ways – from taking in washing to laying out the dead – and she also made and sold perry from the pears in her garden. She was a kind-hearted soul and a good cook and that evening they sat down together to enjoy their first hot meal for two weeks – a boiled hog's cheek with parsnips followed by a batter pudding, the whole meal washed down with small beer. Conversation was inevitably a stilted affair but they managed to communicate with plenty of hand-waving and even more goodwill and the Huguenots went to bed later that night with feelings of confidence.

The following day Monsieur Sautreau offered to remain with them until they were safely reunited with Marie's husband and Marie accepted gratefully. His own plan was to make his way to Bristol and there to set up in business as a tailor but he could not find it in his heart to abandon Paul's family at such a critical time. During the shared hardships of the journey he had developed an affection for them all and wanted to satisfy himself that their future was secure before he attended to his own needs. Bachelor that he was, he did not own even to himself the growing attraction he felt towards Marie and had he been challenged on the subject would have denied it most indignantly. Marie, however, in the way women are, was aware of his interest and might in other circumstances have encouraged him. She had a husband, however, and her first priority was to find him. Until she had solved the mystery of his disappearance from their lives she could make no plans at all for the future.

The following day, while Solange remained with Mistress Webbe to help her with the washing, Jean, Marie and Henri Sautreau began to make enquiries as to the whereabouts of Pierre Luyon. Armed with a scrap of paper bearing his name Jean set off to ask in Appledore. Marie and Henri hired a horse from a friend of Mistress Webbe, rode the few miles into Bideford and began their search there. The village was twice the size of Appledore and in addition to a large fishing fleet, it boasted a thriving shipyard, numerous lime kilns and an extensive rope works.

Their enquiries met with a variety of responses, from an impatient shake of the head from those unwilling to cope with the French tongue, to those who were sympathetic and genuinely wished to help but could tell them nothing. It was dispiriting work but late in the afternoon the first hopeful contact was made when they approached an elderly man outside a tavern. He had spent many years as a wine shipper and had travelled to and from France regularly. He proved to have a reasonable grasp of the French language and introduced himself as Jack Sterne. Then he listened intently as Marie explained in French what their circumstances were and that she was looking for her husband.

'Luyon!' he murmured when Marie showed him the name she had written on a scrap of paper. 'Let me see. That name rings a bell for some reason ... Pierre Luyon? What was he like, your husband? Describe him to me if you will, madame.'

Thankful to be able to converse in her mother tongue, Marie launched into a detailed description. 'He is about your height, monsieur,' she told him, 'but with fair curly hair and light brown eyes and a tiny scar on his left temple. He is, was, a baker by trade. He came to England seven years ago and we have had only one letter which came from this town.'

'And his age?'

'About my age which makes him nearly forty-one years old.' She looked at Jack Sterne hopefully. 'Do you think you know of him, monsieur? We must find him.'

'And you have tried all the bakers' shops?'

She nodded. 'We started with them. No one has heard of him.'

'That's most strange.' He stroked his beard thoughtfully. 'And you are sure he is still in Bideford?'

Marie exchanged an anxious glance with Henri Sautreau before answering reluctantly, 'We know nothing for sure but if he isn't here then we are in serious trouble. He *must* be here.'

Sterne shrugged. 'Leave it with me, I will do what I can. I would like to help you for I too am a Protestant. You Huguenots are unfortunate people for your king is a harsh man. I know our own Charles is a foolish man with his spendthrift ways and his many lovers but he is tolerant and rules us well enough. He is well loved by most of his subjects. You will do well enough in England if you are prepared to work hard.'

'Oh, we are, monsieur!' Marie assured him. 'We have worked hard all our lives.'

Henri Sautreau who had so far remained silent said, 'I am a tailor by trade. I left a flourishing business because I did not choose to renounce my faith.'

Their new friend smiled wearily. 'Life is a vale of tears, my friend, so it behoves us to help one another.' To Marie he said, 'I will make some enquiries, madame. When will you come to Bideford again?'

They arranged to allow him two days for his enquiries and promised to meet again outside the tavern at three o'clock. As they rode home they were full of hope and looking forward to supper when they would be able to compare notes on their progress.

Over supper Jean listened to his mother's report on Jack Sterne before volunteering his own information.

'One of the fishermen is a Huguenot like ourselves,' he told them. 'He says his cousin works in the rope works in Bideford and this brother spoke of a Frenchman who worked with him for a time. He insists the man's name was Linn or maybe Lunn, he can't recollect which. It was a few years ago now.'

Solange cried, 'In a rope works? Oh, but Papa was a baker –'

Marie silenced her with a look. 'You eat your supper,' she told her, 'before it gets cold.' To Jean she said, 'Linn or Lunn, you say. I wonder.'

'Either the fisherman has the wrong name or Papa has changed it,' Jean suggested. 'If it is him,' he added.

'Changed his name!' Marie cried indignantly. 'Why on earth should he do that? What's wrong with Luyon? It's a good Huguenot name and nothing to be ashamed of.'

Henri Sautreau saw the worried look that crossed Marie's face and guessed something of her doubts on that subject. He said gently, 'He may have good reasons, Marie, we don't know. We shouldn't judge too harshly.'

Marie flashed him a brief look of gratitude and impulsively he reached across the table and touched her hand. Jean, busy with his boiled plaice, missed the small exchange but Solange did not. She registered the gesture with a sense of profound shock and lowered her eyes immediately so that no one should recognise her anger. How dare Monsieur Sautreau behave in such a way! If Papa were here he would not touch Maman's hand. And how could Maman allow it? She seemed to enjoy it! Solange's confusion was so great that her mouthful of food went down the wrong way and she began to cough and splutter.

'Soli!' cried Marie as fish and potato spattered on to the table. 'Where are your manners?' and she apologised to their hostess.

Mistress Webbe said, 'Bless you, the child meant no harm.'

Solange said nothing, but inside she was seething and it suddenly became imperative to her that they find Papa as quickly as possible.

From that moment she vowed to keep a careful eye on Monsieur Sautreau for her father's sake. Her admiration for him had vanished totally. It was true he had tried to save Grandmère's life but Solange could no longer see him as a hero. In her eyes Monsieur Sautreau had become a threat.

Two days later it was Marie, Jean and Solange who went to Bideford to meet Jack Sterne while Monsieur Sautreau remained in Appledore. Since they could not pay for their lodgings with money, it had been agreed that they should contribute in other ways and today Monsieur Sautreau had offered to make alterations to Mistress Webbe's Sunday clothes which no longer fitted her. The neighbour's horse was not available on this occasion so, warmly wrapped against the cold and with high hopes, the family set off to walk the six miles into Bideford.

There Jack Sterne greeted them kindly. It appeared that his enquiries had also pointed in the direction of the rope works but first, however, he insisted on taking them to his own home to meet his elderly sister who offered them hot punch and a slice of caraway cake. The sister spoke no French at all but she smiled and nodded approvingly as Solange tried out her verbs. Then she taught them all to say 'Good morning, mistress' and 'Good morning, master'. She waved them farewell with a cheerful smile on her face but when they had gone her expression changed and she shook her head sadly, knowing that the information her brother had unearthed was likely to dash their spirits.

On the way to the rope works Jack Sterne explained as gently as he could that a Peter Lunn had once worked there but had not been seen for some years.

'It might not be the same man,' he warned. 'I don't think you should raise your hopes too high.'

Solange refused to be dismayed. ''Tis Papa!' she cried excitedly. 'I know it!'

Marie said sharply, 'You know nothing of the kind, child, so hold your tongue.'

The rope works was a large bustling concern surrounded by rows of posts around which a cat's-cradle of ropes was stretched. Here they waited as Sterne went inside the main building to find their informant. Joe Bysshe was a small swarthy man with dark, close-set eyes. He spoke no French but using Sterne as translator, he soon convinced the Luyons that he had indeed worked with Marie's missing husband.

'He called himself Peter Lunn,' he told them, 'and he spoke English passably well but he was definitely a Frenchman in spite of his straw-coloured hair. He had been in a spot of bother with the law on several occasions.'

'That sounds like my husband!' said Marie, but there was no bitterness in her voice. If only she could find him, she told herself, she would forgive him his drinking and brawling and they could make a fresh start.

'Did he have a small scar — here?' She touched her left temple.

Jack Sterne translated her question but Mr Bysshe shrugged his shoulders.

'Ask him if Peter Lunn spoke of his family at all,' Marie suggested. 'His wife, Marie, or his parents; his children Jean and Solange. Did he come from La Rochelle? Was he a baker by trade?'

Solange said, 'Ask him if he had four cats.' She turned a glowing face to Jean. '"Tis Papa, I *know* it!' and she gave a little hop of delight.

Jean patted her shoulder and said, 'Maybe, Soli. But you must be patient.'

To their intense delight, however, the man answered all Marie's questions in the affirmative but there the good news ended. It appeared that after a few months Peter Lunn had fallen in with a group of men whom Mr Bysshe described as 'ne'er-do-wells', with whom he had fallen foul of the law on more than one occasion. He had boasted to his workmates of the money he made gambling, yet he had run up various bills which he insisted he was unable to pay.

'Apparently,' Jack Sterne explained, 'he told Mr Bysshe that Bideford was getting too hot for him and that he might move on to Bath. It seems that large numbers of Huguenots had already settled there.'

'And did he?' Jean asked. 'Did he move on to Bath?'

'No one knows. It seems he disappeared, quite literally, overnight.'

'Disappeared?' cried Marie, turning to Mr Bysshe. 'But how could he just disappear?' Disappointment mingled with fear in her voice as she tried to prepare herself for whatever might follow. 'I don't believe it! He couldn't just disappear.'

Jean put an arm across her plump shoulders and whispered, 'Let him finish, Maman. It may not be as bad as it sounds.'

Sterne conferred with Mr Bysshe and his expression changed. He continued, 'It seems that one morning he failed to arrive for work. The next morning he was also absent and the next day the body of one of his feckless friends was washed up on the fore-shore below Appledore – they call it Northam Burrows.'

'But how does that –' Marie began.

'A small boat was also missing. It seemed possible that Peter Lunn was with them and that they may have been smuggling. Nobody knows.' He hesitated. 'At any rate, he was never seen again. Presumed drowned. I'm so very sorry.'

The ensuing silence was broken by a stifled sob from Marie as her hands flew up to her face to hide her grief. Mr Bysshe shuffled his feet uncomfortably and when a coin had been slipped into his hand, took the chance to hurry back to his work bench.

Solange stared up at them, her eyes dark with misery, her face pale. 'Papa is *not* drowned!' she stammered. 'He's not dead. He can't be dead. I want to see him.'

No one answered her.

Aware of his mother's distress Jean said, 'But his body was never found?'

'No.'

'So he *might* be alive? There's a very small chance that he might have gone to Bath?'

Jack Sterne shrugged without replying.

'He might *not* have been smuggling,' Jean insisted and hugged his mother who was now weeping openly.

Solange rarely saw her mother cry and she hurriedly averted her eyes from the dreadful sight. If Maman was crying then maybe Papa *was* dead but that was too awful to think about. Solange turned quickly away from them, walked to the nearest post and laid a hand on the rope. Slowly she walked its length, allowing it to run loosely through her fingers, taking comfort from its rough feel. When she reached the far post she sat down with her back to it and watched Maman fumbling with a handkerchief while Jean and Jack Sterne talked together. Solange felt illogically that Jack Sterne had betrayed them: they had trusted him to help them and now he had made Maman cry and had said terrible things about Papa. If those things were true then life would never be the same again. She felt her whole future stretching ahead, grey and disconsolate, and could not bear it.

Jean began to walk towards her but as she watched him her throat constricted. He would speak kindly to her and then she would cry and Maman would lose patience with her and scold. As tears pricked her eyelids Solange jumped to her feet and ran from her brother, ducking beneath the strands of drying rope, desperately trying to distance herself from that mournful group.

As she ran her heart pounded within her chest as she dodged this way and that, ignoring Jean's warning shout. Though her eyes were blurred with tears she cast an anguished glance behind her and saw that he was gaining on her. In her efforts to escape she did not see the neatly coiled rope ahead of her and, running into it, was thrown violently forward. She sprawled on the hard ground, aware of a sour taste in her mouth and the fact that her hands were torn and her knees bleeding. With a cry of fury she dragged herself to her feet and spat blood while her probing tongue discovered a loosened tooth which had pierced her lower lip.

'Soli, wait!' cried Jean.

But she was off again, running and sobbing distractedly, oblivious of her wounds.

'Soli! Come back here!'

She shook her head and ran on, glad she was hurt for now she had an excuse for the scalding tears which she could no longer hold back.

Jean caught up with her at last and swung her up into his arms. 'Don't cry, Soli,' he told her. Mistaking the reason for her grief he added, 'If Papa truly is dead I will take care of you and Maman. I swear it. You have nothing to fear.'

Solange did not acknowledge this generous promise but struggled so fiercely in his arms that he was forced to put her down again. She drew a long shuddering breath and accepted the handkerchief he offered without thanks, afraid to speak in case her voice trembled and revealed the extent of her misery.

'My knees,' she said at last, pronouncing the words with great care. 'I've hurt my knees.'

She stared straight into his eyes without blinking. It was important that he should understand that she was not crying for Papa. Why should she? Papa was not dead. He could not be dead.

She simply would not allow it.

*

For Solange the first few weeks in England were very difficult, and the next month passed in a bewildering succession of events which left her confused and rebellious. To her dismay the long family conference that followed the abortive trip to Bideford ended in the general acceptance that Pierre Luyon, alias Peter Linn or Lunn, was almost certainly dead. Even if by some remote chance he was still alive and living in Bath, that town was miles away and the family had no resources. The advisability of travelling such long distances in the faint hope that they would find him was questionable and after much debate it was decided that they would settle in Appledore. If at any time they happened to have a little spare capital they might reconsider and extend their enquiries.

Solange's loud and bitter protests fell on deaf ears and on more than one occasion she was rebuked kindly but firmly by Monsieur Sautreau which infuriated her.

'Don't speak to your mother like that, Solange,' he said one evening, and her furious, 'You're not my father!' earned her a spanking from Maman.

It was not the spanking which worried her, however, for it was a half-hearted affair and she had had worse in her time. It was the unguarded look that passed between her mother and Monsieur Sautreau which frightened her – a look that denoted a special under-standing; a look that hitherto Maman had only ex-changed with Jean or Grandmère.

The next day Solange approached Jean. 'When is Monsieur Sautreau leaving us?' she demanded without preamble.

Jean avoided her eye as he explained that Monsieur Sautreau was looking after them for a few weeks until they were comfortably settled.

'But we *are* settled,' she insisted.

'No, Soli. We're not comfortable. We are simply surviving.'

'I don't like him,' Solange insisted. 'He is old and ugly and I want him to go away.'

'But what would we do without him?' Jean asked, ignoring her unkind description which was so patently untrue. 'Maman earns very little and I still have not found work. His tailoring is all that keeps us from the gutter. We need him, Soli. Try to like him. He is a good man.'

'I hate him!' she announced.

'How can you hate him? Have you forgotten that he risked his life to try and save Grandmère?'

After a brief hesitation, Solange replied, 'But he *didn't* save her, did he? He let her drown!'

'Soli!' cried Jean, genuinely shocked. 'That's most unjust and well you know it! He did his very best and he might have been drowned himself. We all owe him a great deal.'

'I wish he had drowned!' she muttered rebelliously.

'What was that?'

'Nothing!'

'I should hope not!'

But Solange remained unconvinced and the days passed uneasily with a state of undeclared hostilities developing between herself and Monsieur Sautreau. When he offered to pay for her lessons given by two elderly sisters, Solange at once resisted the idea, declaring that it was a plot to get her out of the house. When forced to acquiesce she retaliated by talking constantly about Papa whenever Monsieur Sautreau was present, reiterating her conviction that he was still alive and well and living in Bath.

At school, however, she proved an able pupil and surprised everyone by her progress. Surrounded by English-speaking classmates, her command of the language grew rapidly so that at home she soon proved invaluable in running errands for the rest of the family. They were still living with Mistress Webbe but Maman was looking seriously for other accommodation.

One day Jean returned triumphantly home with the news that he had found a job on one of the Bideford fishing boats. 'She's called *Venturer*,' he told them, his face alight with enthusiasm. 'That means she ventures or goes into foreign waters. And she does, too. She sails to Newfoundland for the cod. She's old but she's very big – I'll take you to see her, Solange. The son and father used to work together but now the son's wed a Bristol girl and is to work for her father on his boat.'

'But Bideford is miles away,' said Solange.

Jean hesitated. 'I could lodge with one of the crew – one John Petty and his wife. They would be glad of an extra shilling.' He looked anxiously at his mother. 'I won't go if you need me but 'tis a good chance. What do you say, Maman?'

Before Marie could answer Solange cried, 'I say don't go.' She saw at once that without her brother she would have no ally in the family. 'I don't want you to go away.'

Marie said doubtfully. 'I don't know, Jean. Splitting up the family so soon . . .'

'It might not be for long, Maman,' he told her quickly. 'There's a bonus sometimes for a very good catch. I could save up. Maybe you could join me later in Bideford.'

His mother was wavering, he knew.

'How much will they pay you?' she asked.

'Three shillings and sixpence a week.' He shrugged. 'Not much I know but it's —'

'How much is that in *French* money?' said Marie.

Jean laughed, 'But we're in England now, Maman!'

'But is it fair? Is it good money? Are they cheating you — you not understanding the language?'

''Tis quite fair, Maman,' he told her. 'Be thankful for small mercies.'

Solange, with vivid memories of their own fateful sea-crossing, said quickly, 'But you're a baker, Jean. And anyway you can't swim.'

Monsieur Sautreau bit off his thread and said, 'That's no problem. I'll teach you, Jean, as soon as the summer comes.'

Marie said, 'Would you? Oh, thank you, Henri!' and there was a brittle silence as the alien word registered in everyone's mind — Henri!

Solange's head snapped up. Maman had called Monsieur Sautreau by his first name! She stared at her mother who was biting her lip in vexation at the slip.

Then everyone looked anxiously at Solange.

She stammered, 'You called him Henri! You did!'

Jean muttered under his breath as Solange sprang to her feet. 'Wait, Soli . . .' he began hastily. 'You must

69

try to understand Monsieur Sautreau is a very good friend of ours now. We . . .'

'Henri!' cried Solange, trembling with an emotion she did not understand. 'He is not Henri! He is Monsieur Sautreau!'

Marie tried to brazen it out, 'Now you listen to me, Solange . . .'

But Solange, with a cry of anguish, fled from the room. There was a tense silence as the door slammed behind the hysterical child.

Henri said unhappily, 'Poor little Soli. I do wish we could be friends.'

Jean made as though to follow Solange but Marie shook her head.

'Let her go,' she said wearily. 'She is as stubborn as a mule. There is nothing any of us can say. We might as well let her cry.'

Henri said, 'She cannot face up to the fact that her Papa is dead. I can understand that.'

Marie shook her head in despair, 'After all you have done for us, Henri – I am so ashamed. She is an ungrateful wretch.'

Henri smiled. 'She is just a child. So young. How do we know what thoughts go through that curly head of hers? Do not be angry with her on my account, Marie.'

Marie snorted, 'You are too soft with her. She needs a good shaking!'

Jean said again, 'Let me go after her. She might listen to me.'

But Marie, as stubborn as her daughter, shook her head. 'No, Jean. We will not pander to her tantrums.

If she will not see how lucky we are to have Henri then let her cry.'

After Jean's departure to Bideford further changes took place. Monsieur Sautreau became 'Henri' (except to Solange) and his influence on their lives grew more significant. He was a very skilful tailor and his services were soon in great demand so that he quickly became accepted in the village. He worked hard and by the end of July he was able to rent a house at the northern end of the village. He then suggested that Marie should move in as his housekeeper (bringing Solange with her) and offered in exchange two rooms on the second floor. To Solange's chagrin Marie accepted this offer gratefully and the move was finally accomplished at the end of the month.

Marie and Henri made every effort to conceal their growing affection for one another, but Solange was not deceived and deeply resented the man who was attempting to replace her father. She felt unable to treat Monsieur Sautreau with even the barest courtesy because, in her mind, to do so would imply approval of his relationship with Maman. Worse still, that would indicate an acceptance of her father's death which would be a most terrible betrayal. It seemed to Solange that while she remained optimistic on Papa's behalf there was still hope. In her wildest daydreams she fantasized about the night when he would return and confront her mother and Monsieur Sautreau. The interloper would be revealed as the villain of the piece and sent away; Maman, in floods of tears, would confess her mistake and Papa would carry them off to a wonderful new life in Bath.

This hope, and her constant prayers to this effect, sustained Solange through her darkest hours which were unfortunately many. As the weeks passed, her exasperated mother was regularly forced to punish her for her rudeness to Henri but the child remained totally unrepentant and endured her bread and water and frequent slaps with an infuriating air of martyrdom. Had it not been for Henri's frequent interventions on her behalf, her punishments would have been even more severe, but this knowledge did nothing to soften Solange's attitude towards him. She interpreted all his friendly overtures as attempts to undermine her loyalty to her father and the gulf between them widened inexorably.

She missed Jean, too, with an intensity that was largely unacknowledged and Grandmère, also, had been taken from her. Maman had eyes for no one but Henri and Solange believed herself unloved and rejected.

Christmas was almost upon them when Jean returned briefly to Appledore with unwelcome news. Henri was setting in a sleeve and Marie was mending a tear in one of Solange's pinafores but they both listened in silence as he explained that he had met someone who recalled a man's body being washed up on the beach at Morte Bay, beyond Baggy Point. He had made further enquiries. Before he could say any more Marie put a finger to her lips to warn him that Solange was in the next room and might overhear what he had to say.

'But she'll have to know,' said Jean, surprised.

Henri glanced up from his stitching but made no comment.

'I'll decide whether she shall know or not,' Marie told her son. 'She is difficult enough already. What she doesn't know cannot harm her. There is no point in upsetting her for nothing so go on quietly with your story and let me worry about Solange.'

Jean continued, 'It seems the body was discovered a few weeks after the first man was drowned so nobody made the connection. They made a few enquiries in Woolacombe and Croyde as to missing persons but no further south than that.'

He hesitated, but Marie said, 'Don't hold anything back, Jean. I've imagined so much for so long – what you have to tell me cannot possibly be any worse than my nightmares.'

Reluctantly he went on, 'The body had been in the water a long time and they couldn't get a very accurate description but he definitely had fair hair.'

'Mon Dieu!' In spite of her brave words the truth hurt her and for a moment Marie hid her face in her hands.

Henri spoke up at last. 'But is there any real proof, Jean, or is this mere surmising? A half-truth is often harder to bear than the whole.'

But Jean was nodding his head. 'The ring his grandmother gave him before she died. They found it still on his hand. The finger was so swollen it . . .'

Henri held up a warning hand and Jean fell silent.

Marie was very pale. 'Of course! The ring!' she whispered.

'They buried it with him,' said Jean, 'or so they said. You cannot trust these fellows. They made a note of it. Gold with a single ruby. Dear Maman, I'm sorry but it must have been Papa.' He put an arm round her but she looked up at him dry-eyed.

'I knew he was dead,' she said. 'I knew it in my heart although I couldn't bring myself to admit it. Well –' she shrugged helplessly, 'so my poor Pierre drowned. What a way to die. First him and then Grandmère.' Sharply she looked up at Jean. 'See that you are not the third! If you go that would be the end of me!' She shook her head as though stupefied by the news. 'So – Pierre is dead.' Twisting her apron between her fingers, she did not look at Henri.

He said, ''Tis better by far to know for certain than to go on wondering, Marie.'

'I dare say,' she said, her voice flat and unemotional. A little of the colour was now returning to her face and she suddenly lifted her head to look imploringly at Henri; he smiled encouragement but made no effort to replace Jean who was kneeling at her feet.

'There's one more thing,' said Jean. 'I found his grave. He's buried in the churchyard in Braughton. It says "Male person unknown. Drowned".'

Henri said, 'Is there a headstone?'

'A stone of sorts with the inscription scratched upon it.' Marie drew a long breath and said, 'So, I am a widow. Why don't the tears come, I wonder? Can't I even weep for my poor dead husband? Even if I can do nothing else I should shed a few tears.'

Henri and Jean were silent, not knowing how to answer.

Jean said at last, 'What about Solange? What shall we tell her?' Marie's grief was replaced by a more prosaic exasperation and she groaned aloud. 'Solange!'

she said. 'Your little sister, Jean, grows more difficult with each day that passes. Every day 'tis, "When are we going to Bath to look for Papa?" or, "Is there a letter from Papa yet?" Yesterday it was, "Do I take after Papa?" "No!" I told her. "You take after the pedlar!" That child drives me crazy. Sometimes I think I shall take her by the shoulders and shake the life out of the little wretch!'

Henri said, 'She is so loyal to her father. This news will break her heart.'

Marie said stubbornly, 'She hardly knew her father — that is the joke! She has created this wonderful father for herself and we are all expected to believe in him! The truth is that if he walked up to her in the street tomorrow she would not know him from the man in the moon! She knows nothing about him because we have kept the worst from her. Maybe we were wrong. Loyalty to her father! So much for loyalty! I sometimes think she does it simply to annoy me.'

Henri said, 'We must make allowances.'

'Allowances? Oh, Henri! You make too many allowances for the girl.'

'You know I'm fond of the child, Marie.'

'And do you think I'm not?' she demanded. 'Not fond of my own daughter?'

He nodded gently. 'She is so much like you! You are both stubborn.'

Jean smiled faintly. ''Tis true, Maman. She may take after Papa in looks but in all other respects she is her mother's daughter. The question is — should we tell her?'

'Tell me what?'

They swung round in dismay to find Solange standing in the doorway, a look of deep suspicion on her face. She looked at her brother.

'Tell me what?' she repeated. 'I want to know, Jean. You shouldn't keep secrets. They'll eat into your soul!'

Marie said, 'Oh, Solange!'

Instinctively Jean looked towards Henri who in turn looked at Marie.

'Maman?' cried Solange. 'Jean? What is it? Is it about Papa?'

Henri said, 'She must be told, Marie.'

Solange had gone very pale and her hands were clenched tightly by her sides.

Jean said, 'Papa was drowned, Soli. We have found his grave, so we know for sure now that he is dead.'

'No!'

Nobody spoke.

''Tis a lie!' cried Solange and her voice was suddenly thin and desolate.

'Soli, 'tis God's own truth,' said Marie. 'You must believe it. There's no doubt now. None at all.'

'No! No! I won't listen!' Solange's voice was trembling. 'You want me to believe that because of *him*!' She pointed accusingly at Henri. 'Because you want him instead of Papa. Oh, yes you do.' She glared passionately at Marie. 'Well, I don't want him as a father. Not ever. If I can't have Papa then I don't want a father!'

Henri said, 'Please listen, Soli —' but Solange turned on him furiously.

'Don't speak to me! I hate, hate, hate you! You want Papa to be dead. You and Maman! I know you do.'

Marie, red-faced, shouted, 'Don't you dare speak to him that way! Are you a guttersnipe? Have you no manners? You'll apologize, Soli, do you hear me? You'll apologize to Henri, at once.'

Jean said, 'Maman is right, Soli. You must not say such dreadful things. Henri is a good man but you won't give him a chance. Please, Soli. For me. Say you are sorry.'

'But I'm not sorry,' she cried defiantly, 'and he's not a good man. Papa is a good man and –'

'Your Papa is *dead*!' cried Marie. 'Dead and buried. Why won't you admit it, you foolish child? Do you think you can bring him back to life by your stubborn ways? He is *drowned*, Soli.'

'And you don't care!'

'Of course I care,' Marie protested, 'but caring won't bring him back to life, will it?'

Jean said, 'Listen, Soli, poor Maman is lonely without Papa. All these years she has been alone. She –'

'So am I!' cried Solange. 'I am lonely too. I am lonely without Papa for years and years –'

Marie's patience finally snapped. 'Lonely? Oh, don't talk such nonsense! How can you miss someone you have never known? He was gone long before you were old enough to know him. You were still in your crib when your fine father took to his heels and left me with two children to feed and clothe. And why did he go?' Her voice grew harsh. 'Did you ever stop to ask yourself why your loving father left us? He went because he was in trouble as always. Too much drink, too many ne'er-do-well friends, too much gambling, too many debts!'

Jean said warningly, 'Don't, Maman! You'll be sorry later!'

She rounded on him, '*Don't*, you say? Don't tell her the truth, you mean? Must I listen to her abusing poor Henri who is twice the man her father ever was?' She turned back to Solange, 'Your precious father was a wastrel, Soli. Do you hear? My mother warned me not to marry him. Even Grandmère warned me that he was too wild to make any woman a good husband.'

Shocked, Solange stammered, 'Grandmère would never say that!'

'Oh, but she did, Solange!' cried her exasperated mother. 'But I loved him. I thought I could change him. Huh! What a fool I was. I got what I deserved.'

Henri reached out to touch her hand but she shook herself free and rushed on impetuously, 'So maybe when he ran away to England I was not too sorry. I managed to pay off his debts and I tried to forget. I told myself that if we found him again in England things would be different but in my heart I knew it would be the same old story! Now he's dead and I can make a fresh start.'

'Well?' she demanded. 'Don't you think I deserve a new start?' Her anger evaporated suddenly and she asked querulously, 'Don't I deserve a little happiness?' and began to cry.

Solange looked from one to the other, white-faced. The silence lengthened uncomfortably but no one knew how to break it. Solange tried to speak, swallowed and tried again but no sound passed her quivering lips. She turned with a sob and ran along the landing and they heard her clogs clattering down the steps and out into the street.

Jean shook his head despairingly and Henri, his face pale and troubled, took Marie into his arms and kissed her.

Blindly Solange ran down the street and round the corner to the left, colliding with someone and running on, still sobbing and almost breathless. She ran, without knowing why, to the little school house where the Tidden sisters lived. To Solange's surprise the front door was ajar and without a second thought she ran up the steps and into the familiar parlour which served as a schoolroom. One large table stood in the middle of the room with six chairs ranged round it. Today was Saturday. On weekdays the chairs would have been occupied by the school's six pupils but now it was empty and Solange slumped into her own chair, folded her arms on the table and laid her head despairingly on her arms. There was a smell of beeswax in the air and a pile of musty primers remained in the centre of the table where they had been left the previous day.

The Tidden sisters, orphaned at an early age, had been educated by their uncle who was a vicar in Glastonbury. He had taught them to read, write, add, subtract and multiply. He had thrown in a few Latin verbs for good measure and all these accomplishments (plus the learning by heart of several psalms) were passed on to the pupils in relation to their ability. For this tuition they each paid the sum of tuppence a week and were considered privileged.

As Solange sobbed she heard the steady ticking of the clock and opening her eyes a little saw the tall corner cupboard where the cane was kept along with the large brass bell which was rung each morning to hurry them into lessons. It felt strange to be sitting alone in a room which she usually shared with her classmates and with the teachers.

She sat there for perhaps a quarter of an hour trying to come to terms with what she had heard about Papa but when Emily Tidden finally discovered her, she was still in a state of acute shock and lifted a woebegone face when the teacher laid an enquiring hand on her shoulder.

'Why, 'tis Solange Luyon,' Emily said. 'What brings you here today, little maid?'

Solange said, 'Nothing!' and quickly slid from the chair, poised for flight.

Emily's fingers, however, had tightened slightly on her shoulder.

'Nothing, you say?' She stared down into the small anguished face with a compassion she normally preferred to hide from her pupils. 'Now let me see . . . How old are you, Solange?' she asked innocently. 'Is it seven or eight years?'

'Nine years,' Solange corrected her.

'Nine is it? Ah, then I think you are old enough for a small glass of my elderberry wine!' Emily told her. 'I don't care to sup alone. Will you join me?'

Solange was so surprised that she nodded meekly and followed her teacher along the passage that led to the kitchen at the rear of the house.

Emily was the younger of the two sisters, a widow with no surviving children. Her sister Mary was a spinster and they were very alike in temperament – kindly but firm and devoted to their pupils. As Solange studied her new surroundings Emily said, 'My sister Mary is out visiting a sick friend so we shan't be interrupted.'

Receiving no answer she busied herself at the dresser and soon laid a plate of biscuits on the table followed by a glass of wine for herself and another, suitably diluted, for Solange.

'Do try one of my biscuits,' she said. 'I made them this morning. Do you like cooking?'

This fortunate question opened the floodgates. Solange launched into a vivid account of her life in the bakery in La Rochelle and Emily listened and nodded encouragement. Before Solange realized what had happened she had also confessed the reason for her unhappiness and had dwelt at length on her relationship with Henri.

Emily said little – a word here and there – but nothing that was critical. She knew that if she was to earn the child's trust she must be seen to be impartial so she simply smiled and made no judgements. She was very experienced in the ways of children and she soon came to the conclusion that nothing that she or anyone else could say would change Solange's opinion of Henri Sautreau. Circumstances had conspired to sour the relationship and the damage was done. If she wanted to help the child, and she did, she could provide no more than a sympathetic ear and an occasional distraction.

Feeling rather grand Solange sipped the wine slowly, making it last, and nibbled the biscuits daintily, her mood brightening, her tears already forgotten.

When they had finished their refreshments Emily took her young visitor into the back garden where a few flowers bordered a tiny lawn and before long Solange was on her knees pulling up weeds and cheerfully laughing at the antics of Emily's kitten.

From that day onward Emily took a close interest in her 'little Huguenot' and was quick to recognize the child's potential and foster it in different ways. She made a point of talking to Marie about Solange's ability and told her that her daughter had a quick mind and an aptitude for figures that was rare in a girl. Marie was surprised but unimpressed. Secretly she hoped that her difficult daughter would marry young and produce a brood of children that would keep her out of mischief. The teacher's tentative suggestion that Solange should learn a little Latin was met first with amusement and then with a firm refusal. What good would Latin do the girl, Marie demanded, when she would be cooking and cleaning from morning to night to care for a husband and children? No, as long as her daughter could read and write and speak English Marie would be well satisfied and Henri's money well spent.

Emily took the disappointment very well – she had not really hoped for anything else – but she continued to keep a keen eye on her pupil's progress. Solange was one of the most intelligent children she had ever taught and, had she been a boy, Emily would have forecast a very successful future. As it was she could only hope to stimulate Solange's mind and to this end she lent her books and encouraged her to read.

As the weeks became months Emily came to look upon Solange more as a daughter than a pupil and a bond of trust and affection deepened between them.

*

The most bitter blow for Solange came in the August of 1682 when Marie broke the news that she and Henri Sautreau were to be married. As everyone had predicted, Solange took the news badly. After an initial outburst of hysterical weeping she withdrew into a frozen silence from which no one, not even Emily Tidden, could coax her.

After a long argument on the morning of the wedding Solange announced that she would not attend the ceremony and Marie, exhausted and out of patience with her unyielding daughter, gave up the attempt to persuade her to change her mind. Solange spent the day wandering along the river bank, vowing all manner of revenge against the man who had supplanted her father, yet in a curious way she blamed her mother most. Somewhere deep within her Solange dimly recognized that what Marie had said about her errant husband might possibly be true but she did not allow this heresy to surface into her conscious mind. An impossible gulf therefore existed between mother and daughter, a fact which troubled Henri as much as anyone. Solange managed to find a little comfort in the certainty that with such guilty consciences they could not possibly 'live happily ever after', for God would find a way to punish them.

As the weeks passed, however, Solange's white-hot resentment cooled marginally and occasionally she managed a few polite words for Henri, but towards her mother she maintained an aloof silence. There were moments, too, though rare and fleeting, when she was aware of a seditious longing for Henri's approval and actually envied her mother the affection he gave her;

but whenever these treacherous thoughts surfaced, she was quick to suppress them, reluctant to admit, even to herself, that Henri might not fill the role of ogre for which she had cast him. She had also cast herself in a part which did not suit her affectionate nature and the daily performance of this role occasionally plunged her into a deep depression. These moods served to alienate her even further from Henri and her mother, and inexorably the strain began to undermine her health.

By the time her eleventh birthday arrived she had changed from the impetuous, happy child she had once been to a morose and lacklustre shadow of her former self.

Marie, despondent in her turn, tried to convince herself that Solange would eventually 'come to her senses', but Henri was not reassured and finally suggested that they discuss the child with Emily Tidden. Emily told them bluntly that in her opinion a complete change of environment was the only solution and after much heart searching it was agreed that Solange should be placed somewhere nearby as a servant. To everyone's surprise and relief this suggestion met with Solange's immediate approval and not long afterwards a position became vacant on a farm a few miles west of Abbotsham. The farmer's name was John Gadbury and although he considered an eleven-year-old too young for the job he agreed to see her to please Emily Tidden who had once taught his cousins.

Marie was unwell on the day of the interview so to Solange's dismay it was Henri who accompanied her in the donkey cart specially hired for the occasion.

At three o'clock on a bleak January afternoon they

arrived at the farm, cold and windswept from their journey, and while Alice Gadbury led Henri into the parlour for a hot toddy, Solange was shown into the farmer's untidy kitchen. She gave a little bob as Henri had instructed and stared at the man who might become her employer.

John Gadbury was an ox of a man in his late fifties with broad shoulders and a weather-beaten face best described as ruddy. His hazel eyes were small but humorous beneath shaggy grey hair but his hands, clenched on the table, were enormous. Solange thought doubtfully that she would not care to cross such a man.

John Gadbury saw a pale child with a pinched face, large blue eyes and a cautious expression. Her body, about to begin the change from child to woman, was unattractive and her movements lacked grace. Her shoulders drooped unhappily and she looked tense and ill at ease. She wore what were obviously her Sunday best clothes and her fair hair was mostly tucked out of sight beneath a serviceable bonnet.

He regarded her sternly from beneath lowered brows and said, 'So you are Solange Luyon? What have you to say for yourself? Are you a hard worker? Do you get up in the morning without being called twice? Do you argue with your elders and betters? Well?'

Solange bristled visibly. Then she said, 'Yes. Yes. And sometimes.' He regarded her blankly so she explained, 'I *do* work hard and I *do* rise when I'm called and I *do* sometimes argue but I will try very hard not to.'

They stared at each other, he surprised by her

honesty and she already repenting her forthright manner. Maman had warned her to watch her tongue.

'Hmm!' He drummed on the table with sausage-like fingers. 'Your teacher tells me you are a clever girl, Solange. What do you say to that?'

Solange searched for a suitable answer. 'I take after my father,' she said pointedly.

'If I showed you a cow would you know which end the milk comes out?'

Taken by surprise she smiled and a little of the tension went out of her face as she added, 'Yes, I would.'

Encouraged by the smile he asked, 'Could you cure a ham if it was sick?'

She laughed outright and said, 'I could learn.'

So, he thought, she had a sense of humour. He could not abide serious women.

'Your English is good,' he said. 'A bit Frenchified maybe, but that will fade in time. Do you like England?'

Her eyes lit up. 'England is the finest country in the whole world!' she declared unequivocally. 'And King Charles is the finest king!'

'Oh, you think so?' He leaned forward, amused by her answers and rapidly revising his original opinion of her. Emily Tidden had said she was unhappy at home but had a naturally sunny disposition. Plenty of wholesome food would help, he thought. He was a great believer in the restorative properties of food. And plenty of fresh air would put colour in her cheeks.

'Don't you think the king a trifle foolish with his frills and flounces?' he asked. 'A little too much lace, perhaps?'

'Oh no!' she cried. 'He has to look kingly. He has to look more handsome than the rest of us or how would we pick him out in a crowd?'

He hid a smile and said, 'Maybe there's something in what you say.'

After a few more questions Alice Gadbury came in and asked a few of her own which Solange answered to her satisfaction. Because of her youth it was agreed that she would retire to bed at eight instead of nine and that an hour each afternoon would be devoted to studying her letters and reading the Bible under Alice's eagle eye. Her duties would be varied and she would sometimes work on the farm as well as in the kitchen. Her meagre wages were agreed, she would be fed and clothed by the Gadburys and she would have two whole days off once every eight weeks when she would return home.

As they drove back to Appledore Solange's face was radiant.

Life on the farm proved very different from anything Solange had known previously and she threw herself into it wholeheartedly. She rose at five-thirty. Her new mistress was kind but strict and her master, though irascible on occasions, was a just man and she greatly admired them both. She found the work hard but interesting and within a few months she could milk a cow and churn butter, bake bread and smoke ham. She learned to sew and make candles and could mix a toothpaste which Alice generously claimed was even smoother than her own.

To Marie and Henri's delight the move brought about the desired improvement in Solange's disposition and on her infrequent visits home they marvelled at the change in her. Her sullen expression was gone and there was a refreshing eagerness about her manner which, combined with a growing confidence, boded well for the future. She grew taller and her body began to develop pleasingly and although her hands and arms were roughened by her work her face bloomed with a healthy colour and her eyes sparkled.

'Thanks be to the Lord for small mercies!' Marie remarked after one of her daughter's visits. 'Soli is greatly improved and becoming quite personable.'

And Henri, smiling, said, 'Amen to that! The age of miracles is not yet past!'

Chapter Four

SOLANGE PUT HER fingers in her ears as the pig in the yard squealed long and lustily, and imagined the large knife in her master's hand and the quick, purposeful thrust of his arm. In spite of Alice's repeated warnings Solange had allowed herself to grow fond of the amiable animal and now she tried unsuccessfully to shut out the memories of the one killing she had witnessed. Last year curiosity had got the better of her and she could still recall with a shudder how the blood had gushed from the pig's pale throat.

She had watched the present victim grow from a small piglet to a huge beast more than five feet long and had foolishly treated it as a pet instead of looking upon it as a source of food. Now it was being slaughtered and she was sorry it had to suffer such an ignominious fate. Later today the carcass would be cleaned out with hot water and hung up to dry. Tomorrow, while Alice cut the meat into manageable portions, Solange would mix salt, black sugar, salt-petre and soda. Then together they would rub the mixture into the meat until their fingers were red and sore. It would take most of the morning but Solange was looking forward to it because she knew her mistress would tease her about Jess.

Jess Criswell was the son of the Gadburys' shepherd and he also worked for John. Three weeks ago he had sent Solange a beribboned twig on Valentine's Day and Alice still joked about it. Solange insisted that she 'could not abide him', but it made Alice laugh to see how the hot colour rushed into the girl's cheeks whenever Jess was present and she constantly referred to the tall, gangling youth as 'Solange's beau'.

Now, cautiously, Solange withdrew her fingers from her ears and listened. The squealing had ceased and she was relieved to know that the pig's agony was obviously over. She picked up the scrubbing brush and returned to the half-scrubbed table, humming cheerfully as she did so and thinking about Jess.

'Calf's eyes!' she said aloud. 'He's got durned great calf's eyes! Big and brown and silly as they come!'

'Durned' was one of Alice's favourite expressions and was one of many which Solange had appropriated for her own use. She giggled at the comparison. Jess was her first Valentine and though she knew he was courting the daughter of a neighbouring farmer and had sent the twig only in fun she was secretly thrilled by the gesture and considered herself almost a woman. Despite her loud assurances that she would 'throw the silly twig away' it remained hidden in the bottom drawer of her chest and she took a quick peep at it every night before she went to bed to remind herself that she had an admirer.

When the table was scrubbed to her satisfaction she carried the pail out into the yard and threw the soapy water across the cobbles with a practised swing of her arm.

It was now November in the year 1685 and Solange was twelve, rising thirteen. She stood five feet two in her bare feet and was trying desperately to gain a few more inches. Her face had lost its childish plumpness and a fine bone structure was just discernible. Her eyes were as blue as ever and Alice never tired of commenting on the fact that she 'looked more English than the English' which Solange took as a great compliment. She now spoke very passable English, could read with reasonable fluency, could add a lengthy column of figures correctly and could divide and multiply. She knew the Lord's Prayer by heart and several psalms and, each Sunday when the family went to church, she held a prayer book which made her feel very superior.

Now as she turned back towards the kitchen she heard the sound of approaching hooves in the lane and waited curiously to see who was approaching.

She heard her master call a greeting, 'Hello there, Master Benn. What brings you out here at such a time?'

So it was the miller. Solange paused to listen, the empty bucket over her arm.

'Bad news, Master Gadbury,' said the miller. 'Bad news indeed.'

Intrigued, Solange moved a little nearer to the gate, trying to avert her eyes from the body of the pig which was hanging head downward from the chestnut tree beside the stable.

Master Benn slipped down from his horse. 'They say the king's dying!' he cried breathlessly as he came into the yard through the gate which John held open for him. 'Took with an apoplexy on Monday, so they say, and lost the use of 'is senses for a full hour or more.'

The farmer stared at him in consternation, stunned by the suddenness of the disaster. 'Dying?' he stammered. 'Our king dying? Oh, never say such a dreadful thing! He's still with us, surely?'

'So far, but who can tell?' The miller shrugged unhappily. 'Who can tell what will happen?'

'An apoplexy, you say? Poor fellow.' John shook his head and whistled his dismay at the news. 'But the physicians will save him, won't they? God's truth! If they can't save the king of England, who *can* they save?'

He looked at the miller for reassurance but Master Benn was not to be robbed of his moment. 'I wouldn't gamble on it,' he said gloomily. 'Not a penny, I wouldn't. They've bled 'im, of course — sixteen ounces, so they say, and applied hot pokers to 'is head.'

John tutted in disapproval. 'Bleeding, yes, but I never did go a lot on hot pokers,' he said. 'Does a man more harm than good, I reckon.'

The miller shrugged. 'How else are they to keep 'im conscious?' he demanded. 'If they let 'im doze off he'd slip away. 'E'd be lost for certain sure, then. A necessary evil, pokers are, though I shouldn't fancy 'em myself!'

John took out a handkerchief and blew his nose while they both considered the problem of their ailing monarch.

John said at last, 'But he's not above fifty, is he? He's not of a dying age! Surely he —' He broke off as he caught sight of Solange and beckoned her forward. The miller murmured a polite greeting.

'King Charles is taken ill,' John told her, 'and like to die, according to the miller.'

Solange asked, 'Who told you, Master Benn?'

'I had it from the coach driver come straight down from London,' said Master Benn. 'Mind you, he was smirking fit to burst and all cock a hoop, damn 'is eyes! A papist through and through, that one, and bragging how much 'e would welcome a Roman Catholic king to put the country to rights as 'e called it. I'd like to put '*im* to rights, cheeky bastard! A king's a king, I told 'im and you show a bit of proper respect!'

Solange felt her heart skip a beat. 'A Roman Catholic king?' she repeated.

'Oh aye! James is full of popery nonsense and so is that scrawny wife. There'll be a regular how-d'you-do if 'e gets on the throne, you'll see.'

'A how-d'you-do?' she repeated shakily.

John, seeing the colour drain from Solange's face said quickly, 'But 'tis of no account to the likes of you, Soli. Never you fear. Our English kings are civilized men, not like your Louis. You'll come to no harm here, in England, be it Charles or James!'

'I'm glad on it,' she said, unable to hide the slight tremor in her voice.

John turned to the miller who was looking puzzled and said, 'Huguenot,' by way of explanation.

The miller said, 'Huguenot?'

'French Protestant.'

'Ah!' said the miller. 'Good thing you left France then,' he said to Solange. 'Things are bad there, so they say.'

She nodded wordlessly, still shaken by the news. Dear King Charles with his beautiful curls and his dogs and his fancy clothes! Poor, poor man! She could not bear the thought of him at the mercy of such heartless physicians. Bleeding and purging, maybe, but hot pokers! God would never let such a good man die, she told herself. Or would he?

John turned back to Solange and said, 'Where's your mistress? She'd best know the bad tidings.'

'In the dairy skimming milk,' Solange told him and was sent at once to fetch her.

Alice, humming cheerfully, was not inclined to leave the dairy but Solange hinted that the news, though bad, was worth hearing. So, throwing her shawl over her head and shoulders she reluctantly followed Solange across the yard.

'King Charles is a-dying!' Master Benn called quickly, determined to get in the first word. 'Struck down with an apoplexy and like to die at any moment!'

'Like to die? Oh Lordy, no!' cried Alice, her kindly face crumpling in dismay. 'I can scarce believe it. Oh,' she clapped a hand to her mouth as a fresh thought struck her, 'his poor wife! What must she be going through? We must pray for him! We must pray for them both. Oh Lordy! What a catastrophe that would be! England without King Charles? It wouldn't seem right, somehow. Oh Lordy, no!'

Gratified by this emotional response to his news the miller added gloomily, 'His very life hangs by a thread. He could slip away at any moment.' He shook his head and sighed.

'He *might* live,' Solange suggested hopefully. 'He might surprise the physicians. They don't know everything.'

'He might live,' the miller agreed without much enthusiasm, 'but then again he might not.'

He gave Solange a severe look. He had ridden four miles to deliver these bad tidings and he did not want a tuppenny servant girl to go looking on the bright side.

John said, 'It'll be a sad day for England if he doesn't. A very sad day.'

Alice began to cry and he laid a hand awkwardly on her shoulder.

'Now don't take on so, Alice. Tears won't help him.'

'But I'm knocked all of a heap,' she protested. ''Tisn't every day you hear your king's like to die!' She looked through her tears at the miller who silently nodded his approval of her state of mind.

'Aye!' he agreed quickly. 'Fair knocks the heart of you, doesn't it. For all 'is faults 'e was better than most and you can't say fairer than that. Poor old Charles, we shall miss 'im and that's a fact.' He sighed deeply and with a baleful glance at Solange said, 'England without King Charles. Just can't imagine it no-how.'

John said, ''Twill be a very sad day for England if he goes.'

Alice's sobs increased and her husband put an arm round her plump shoulders. 'Now don't take on so, my dear,' he said.

Alice looked up at him tearfully. 'I've no heart for the skimming,' she whispered.

'Naturally not,' he told her. Unaware of the extent of Solange's distress he added, 'Solange will finish off for you.' He gave Solange a nod and she turned dutifully in the direction of the dairy. 'You have a bit of a sit down,' he told his wife. 'We don't want you to have one of your turns.'

The miller shook his head and tutted again. 'Took my old mother the same way when she 'eard,' he confided. 'All of a tremble she was and 'ad to take a sip of brandy to pull 'er around.'

As Alice trotted obediently back to the house and into the comforting warmth of the kitchen Solange took her place in the cold dairy. Her eyes were dry but as she swept the wooden spoon over the surface of the milk her hands were trembling.

Despite the fervent prayers of his loyal subjects, King Charles II lost consciousness in the early hours of Friday morning and died at noon. His body, accompanied by a small cortege, was taken to Westminster Abbey during the hours of darkness, and was eventually laid to rest with a minimum of display.

The majority of his erstwhile subjects mourned him sincerely, the Roman Catholics rejoiced openly and the whole country waited to see what sort of monarch James II would prove to be.

Aware of this James stepped very carefully for the first year of his reign. He had inherited a Protestant country but he was eager to show his Roman Catholic supporters that he had their interests at heart. His followers knew that in Ireland he had restored a great deal of land to the Catholics and had appointed many of them judges. Surely, they argued hopefully, he might follow the same pattern in England.

These hopes were soon realized as dismissals began to be made among the Protestant clergy and the army. England's Protestants began to grow uneasy and with good reason, for James sent some of their bishops to the Tower. Worse was still to come, however, and in 1687 rumour gave way to certainty. The queen was expecting a child. With the official announcement the fears of the Protestants suddenly crystallized. If the child was a boy then the next king would also be a Roman Catholic, and his sons after that. Protestant England would have a Catholic monarchy! To the majority of the people the prospect was unthinkable and they turned, in their hour of need, towards Prince William of Orange whose wife Mary was James's daughter. They were both Protestants and William was naturally eager for his wife to inherit the English throne which should rightfully be hers on James's death, provided that he had no sons.

In June the church bells were rung to announce the birth of James's child. It was a son and England could wait no longer.

Messengers were sent secretly to Prince William of Orange to inform him that if he decided to invade England many powerful men would rally to his cause to remove James and to ensure the throne of England for Mary. The offer was accepted, preparations were set in hand and in the summer of 1688 more than six hundred ships set sail for England. Strong contrary winds, however, caused havoc among them and the attempt had to be abandoned.

They tried again in November and by the third day of the month lay off Calais while sixty English warships waited in the Thames . . .

Solange came downstairs one morning to find Jess Criswell waiting for her at the back door.

Hiding her excitement at this early visit she hastily

rubbed the sleep from her eyes and unbolted the door to let him in. She put a warning finger to her lips for Alice was still asleep in the room above them.

'What brings you here, Jess?' she asked, 'and looking so pleased with yourself. Found a shilling, have you?'

She glanced at him curiously. His face was flushed and he laughed importantly as he tossed back a slick of dark hair.

'Got a bit of news might interest you,' he told her. 'Prince William's landed an army at Torbay –'

'Jess Criswell!' she exclaimed. 'He landed days ago. Everybody knows that!'

Ignoring her he ploughed on, 'He's on his way to –'

'To Exeter,' she finished for him, with a smile. 'Tell me something new, Jess.'

There was a pained expression in his brown eyes which she ignored. He ran a hand through his unruly hair as she put a light to the fire for the first kettle of the day and began to collect cups and saucers for her mistress's breakfast tray. John Gadbury had been up almost an hour and was out in the milking shed.

Jess said, 'They reckon he's got ten or eleven thousand men with him and wagons full of money!'

'Never!' she scoffed. 'Nobody has wagons full of money.'

'Well, he does, so they say. And what's more he wants more soldiers for his army. He wants Englishmen and there's hundreds flocking to enlist.' He waited until she paused in her work. 'So that's where I'm going. What d'you say to that, Soli?'

She stared at him, thunderstruck. 'You? Going for a soldier? You never are!'

'I am so!' he laughed, pleased by her reaction. 'Thought you might want to give me a goodbye kiss – for luck, like.'

Ignoring the invitation Solange said, 'Have you lost your wits, Jess? You're no soldier.'

He was hurt by her lack of faith. 'I can learn, can't I?' he protested. 'Same as any other man. I can carry a pike. Soldiering's easy. There's nothing to it – and I've read they pay well.'

She looked at him helplessly. 'But you might get yourself killed!'

Jess shrugged and went on, '"Course, James has more soldiers, a sight more, so they say, but they've gone north.'

'Gone north?' She frowned. 'Why would they do that?'

'Because James thought William was headed for the Humber and so he was but the wind blew him east along the channel. If I move fast I'll catch up with them before they reach Salisbury.'

'Salisbury!' said Solange. 'You'll have to run all the way!'

'Well, I won't then,' he told her triumphantly, 'because I'm going with Ted Burrows and he's going to take his father's horse. We'll ride it together.'

'Does his father approve?'

Jess grinned, 'He won't know 'til it's too late! We'll slip away tonight while everyone's asleep. So – what about that kiss? You're my girl, aren't you, Soli? A lad ought to get a farewell kiss from his girl when he's off soldiering.'

'I don't remember saying I was your girl,' she told

him. 'Just because you quarrelled with Meg Styles. Oh, yes! I heard all about it.'

'Meg Styles!' He looked puzzled as though he hardly recalled such a person. 'Oh, Meg Styles!' he laughed. 'To tell you the truth I was never that struck on her but she did pester me so. Eyeing me that way and blowing me kisses. Threw herself at me she did and that's a fact. 'Twas always you, Soli, as I really fancied.'

Solange gave a scornful toss of her head and carried the ashes outside but when she came back she gave him a long look from beneath her lashes.

'Fancied me, did you, Jess Criswell,' she challenged. 'Then how come you never said?'

'I sent you Valentine twigs!' he protested. 'Trouble was you was young and I've been biding my time, like. But now I'm off to be a soldier and might not come back . . .' He left the rest to her imagination.

Flattered, she asked, 'So what am I now then, Jess? Aren't I a child?'

''Course not, Soli. You're a woman growed, near enough.'

Distractedly she looked from Jess to the fire, and with a muttered grumble she knelt to blow on the latter. Neglected, it was threatening to go out.

'So what about it?' Jess insisted. 'Going to kiss me, are you? A real kiss, I mean, between man and maid, not a peck. You'd like it a lot.'

Solange stood up again and smoothed her skirts, trying to hide her growing excitement. He had said 'a real kiss between man and maid'! The phrase had a magical ring to it but kissing led to all sorts of other

100

things of which she knew very little. Did Jess know about them, she wondered, and if so would he expect her to do whatever it was? And was she willing? She thought not – but then she reminded herself that he was off to be a soldier in William's Protestant army, fighting for the faith, fighting for the Huguenots. Fighting for *her*!

'Just a kiss?' she asked tentatively and saw his expression brighten. 'Maybe one kiss,' she said, feeling very strange, 'but only if I'm your girl. Not otherwise.'

Solange prayed eagerly that her mistress would not take it into her head to come downstairs early. Jess was grinning in delighted anticipation and she thought that he was more handsome than she had realized. Her heart began to beat faster and her throat felt dry. So this was courting, she marvelled silently – this pleasurable, breathless, yearning feeling!

Jess tossed his cap on to the table but she made no move towards him. He reached out and took hold of her hands.

'Sweet sixteen and never been kissed,' he murmured softly.

'I'm only fifteen,' she contradicted, feeling both wary and eager as he bent his head towards her. She wondered suddenly how it was that she had never appreciated the beauty of the large, roughened hands which held her own so gently. She looked into his eyes which were deep and mysterious and was ashamed to have likened them to calves' eyes.

'You're a bonny lass!' he murmured and at once his lips were brushing hers. Startled she stepped back and gazed at him in alarm.

'I won't hurt you,' he told her. 'Swear to God I won't! Just a kiss. That's all.'

She leaned forward and kissed him abruptly. 'There you are then,' she said, stepping back immediately and withdrawing her hands.

'Soli!' He rolled his eyes in mock despair. 'What sort of kiss was that for a soldier to remember when he's away?'

As Solange laughed at his rueful expression she had a sudden mental picture of him lying dead on the battlefield with blood oozing from a gash on the head. He might give his life for her and she had not even given him a worthwhile kiss! Feeling contrite she flung her arms round his neck with such force that he almost lost his balance.

'Kiss me then, Jess!' she cried. 'Any way you will!'

His arms went round her waist and then he clasped his hands and there was no escape. His mouth closed greedily over hers as he held her close and she was soon struggling for breath and half swooning with an excitement that bordered on ecstasy.

When at last he tried to release her she clung to him in a desperate bid to burn into her memory the bewildering sensations that filled her being. He was going away, she told herself dramatically – maybe forever, just as she had learned the meaning of love!

Slowly she let her hands fall to rest on his shoulders and her expression was anguished.

'Jess! Oh, my dear Jess!' she whispered. 'Do you have to be a soldier?'

Overcome by her reaction he said, 'Yes, leastways I reckon so. They can't win the war without me and Ted

Burrows. But I'll be coming back, Soli. Will you wait for me?'

Her eyes widened. 'Wait for you? Oh, Jess, you know I will. Oh, Jess, that was wonderful, that kiss. I never guessed how it would be! I feel so – so different! Did you feel that way too, Jess?'

'I've felt that way before,' he confessed. With more candour than tact he added, 'With Meg Styles up in the cornfield.'

'Ah! Yes, I forgot.'

Solange suddenly remembered that there was more than kissing and her legs grew weak at the thought of whatever it was. She knew about the animals on the farm so she was not entirely ignorant and occasionally Alice had taken her to the market where she had heard the men outside the taverns boasting of their prowess with women. The phrase 'willing mare' came back to her. Was that a good thing to be, she wondered. And the red-faced farmer who 'wanted his oats'. Was that what Jess wanted? His oats? She hoped not. It was all happening too fast and she had had no breakfast, and never did think well on an empty stomach.

Recalling Meg Styles Solange tried to imagine her in the cornfield with Jess, and to her surprise a fierce wave of jealousy struck her so that she had to bite back a spiteful comment. Her Jess with that horrible, pasty-fasced Meg! Big fat face and eyes like currants – whatever had he seen in a girl like that? Another terrible thought struck her. Suppose on his wanderings with the army he met someone else? Suppose he was unfaithful to her? Already she saw him as her future husband.

She said, 'Jess, if you love me, I mean really love

me, couldn't you stay and be my beau? There's plenty of other lads as'll join the army. Lads that have no women waiting for them. Lads that are fancy-free. They won't miss you.'

His face fell. 'Not join the army?' he stammered. 'Oh, but I must. What about Ted Burrows?'

'Never mind Ted Burrows!' she cried. 'What about *me*?'

'But, Soli, he won't go without me,' Jess argued. '"Tis all agreed between us. Being friends we shall watch out for one another. In the thick of battle we shall have someone to rely on. If he's in trouble, I'll be there to help him out. He'll do the same for me!' His eyes glowed at this romantic vision of the closeness of comrades but seeing Solange's expression he added, '"Tis our duty, Soli. Our solemn duty. Would you have me called a coward?'

'No, but –'

'Well then, I must go. But I'll come back. It won't take long.'

'They might kill you!' she protested.

'They won't kill me,' he laughed at the very idea, 'nor Ted. We'll come back heroes! How's that?'

She sighed. 'How long will you be gone, then?'

'A month or so, maybe. I don't know, do I?'

Dismayed, she regarded him with exasperation. What was the good of a declaration of love if he was now going to leave her?

She tossed her head. 'Someone else might come courting me while you're gone! Did you think of that, Jess Criswell?'

'You'd have to say you was promised.'

'You'd stay if you really loved me,' she repeated, her expression reproachful.

Jess looked at her, perplexed. 'I thought you'd be proud to have a soldier for a sweetheart,' he said. 'There's not many girls round here can say that.'

She hesitated, considering this point. Perhaps it would be rather grand. She could moon about the house looking sad and pensive and everyone would treat her kindly and whisper behind her back that her sweetheart had gone to the wars and might never come back. She suddenly saw herself weeping silently over one of his letters while Alice made her a cup of posset and tried to give her courage.

'Would you write to me?' she asked. 'Proper letters, I mean?'

He shook his head. 'I'm not one for putting pen to paper,' he said, unwilling to admit that he could not write, 'but I'd think of you every day – and you could pray for me, Soli. Pray for my safe deliverance.'

Now she saw herself in church, kneeling at the altar, praying earnestly while the congregation watched, their eyes full of unspoken sympathy. It would be rather romantic.

She nodded. 'And you will be faithful to me?' she asked.

'On my honour!' he cried. 'Cross my heart and hope to –' He clapped a hand over his mouth.

'You didn't say it,' she consoled.

'So, what do you say, Soli?' he asked. 'Is it settled between us?' Solange nodded slowly and he kissed her again but halfway through it the bed creaked overhead and they sprang apart guiltily.

''Tis the mistress!' cried Solange recalling all the

chores that awaited her — the bread to be cut and buttered and the egg to be boiled for Alice's breakfast. There were sheets to be soaked for the wash, the table to be scrubbed and the floors to be swept, not to mention the hens waiting to be fed and a duck waiting to be plucked and stuffed.

'I must get on!' she told him. 'You'd best be gone, Jess, before the mistress comes down though I'd rather you could stay.'

He nodded and picked up his cap. 'So you do love me, Soli?'

'I do, Jess. With all my heart!' she told him.

He grinned radiantly, but just then there were footsteps on the stairs and he snatched a last hasty kiss before making for the back door.

She cried, 'Jess! Will I see you again before you go?'

'No, you won't but I'll be back.' He hurried to the door and she followed him as far as the step.

'Take care, Jess!' she cried. 'God go with you!'

He nodded gallantly and waved his cap and bade a jaunty 'Good morning' to John who was coming across the yard.

Alice entered the kitchen in search of her breakfast and John wiped his boots on the scraper.

Clutching her secret to her Solange began to rush around the kitchen while both master and mistress made unflattering remarks about gossiping servants. Solange accepted these criticisms with unwonted meekness. Nothing so trivial could ever distress her again, she told herself dramatically, for she now had a beau and for the first time in her life she was in love.

*

The next day, however, all thoughts of Jess were temporarily driven from her mind for it was market day and on this occasion both John and Alice had decided to attend, unwittingly providing a chance for which Solange had long been waiting. She had decided to pay a secret visit to an old woman who lived a few miles away from the farm and she could only do this when both mistress and master were engaged elsewhere. The woman's name was Charity Becket and rumour had it she was a witch. It was said that she could cast spells and foresee the future and some even went so far as to claim that she could influence the weather and communicate with the dead. Solange wanted to know whether the un-named man in the graveyard at Braughton was indeed her father as Jean had alleged, and it seemed that Charity Becket might be the only person who could tell her.

In spite of all the evidence to the contrary, Solange still clung to the image of her father as a reformed character, flourishing somewhere in the West of England, unaware that his beloved daughter was nearby. She still cherished the idea that they would be reunited and live happily ever after and it was this hope that now drove her across the two miles of rough country that separated the Gadburys' farm from the old woman's cottage. In fact the cottage turned out to be no more than a hovel – a wooden lean-to under a dilapidated slate roof, in a serious state of disrepair. It was surrounded by waist-high nettles, and Solange found it a depressing sight but she fought down her disappointment and gingerly pushed her way through to the half-open door.

'Mistress Becket!' she called, rapping as loudly as she dared on the ancient door. 'Is anyone home?'

A lean grey cat appeared suddenly in the doorway and eyed her solemnly with large golden eyes.

'Minou! Here, Minou!' whispered Solange but at the sound of her voice the cat arched its back and hissed at her and withdrew as abruptly as it had come.

A 'braget' cat! thought Solange, with a thrill of fear. This, she had been told, was a sure sign of a witch. A braget cat and a magpie in the window. Apparently the devil himself often took on the disguise of a bird. Nervously, she glanced at the gaping window and was secretly relieved to see the sill devoid of birds of any kind. A rush of doubts filled her mind. Perhaps after all it had been a mistake to come here. Suppose her father really *was* dead – did she want to know? Wasn't it more pleasant to believe that he lived?

Undecided, she called again but received no answer. Greatly daring she pushed the door open further and peeped into the gloomy interior. It was very dark and it took a moment or two for her eyes to accustom themselves to the lack of light. When at last she could see she gasped with dismay for the muddle that met her startled gaze was incredible and the place was undeniably filthy. At the far end of the room a smouldering fire supported a blackened kettle and the grey cat she had seen a moment earlier now shared the hearth with a scruffy dog of indeterminate breed, and both animals stared fixedly into the glowing coals. Cobwebs and a withered ham decorated the ceiling and the smell was overpowering.

'Mistress Becket?' she repeated.

108

Solange's nervousness was giving way to curiosity. She had come this far, she told herself, and she could not turn back. At the far end of the room she saw a table on which bottles of all sizes and shapes jostled for space with a huge bundle of dried leaves and grasses which were crammed into an earthenware jug. As Solange took a step towards the table a voice startled her.

'I'm Mistress Becket. What do you want with me?'

An old woman lay on a bundle of rags in the corner beyond the table. Her face was grey and deeply lined with age, her body was shrunken and she clutched a tattered shawl to her neck with bony hands. As Solange watched, her throat suddenly dry, the old woman struggled to her feet.

'I seek news of my father,' Solange stammered. 'They say he is dead and buried and —'

The old woman cried harshly, 'Do you expect me to raise him from the dead? If he's dead, he's dead. Let him rest in peace.' Solange began to protest, but she went on unheeding, ''Twill come to all of us soon enough. The Grand Reaper —' She broke into a cackle of laughter which turned into a cough as she shuffled slowly towards the fire. She removed the lid from the kettle, peeped inside it and replaced the lid without comment. Then she made her way to a stool and sank heavily on to it.

Solange cleared her throat and tried again. 'I know you can't bring him back if he's dead,' she said, 'but I don't believe he is dead. Can you tell me? There's a grave they say is his but it has no name on it.'

'What's his name?'

'His name is Luyon, Pierre Luyon. It's a French name. We're Huguenots.'

The Mistress Becket closed her eyes and Solange waited. For a long time the old woman sat still and silent until Solange began to fear she had fallen asleep.

Solange said loudly, 'He might have a new name. He might be called Lunn.'

There was a long silence. Charity Becket appeared not to have heard; if she had she made no acknowledgement. Ignoring Solange she crossed to the table and selected a handful of dried twigs from the jug. These she stared at for a long minute, then turned abruptly and tossed them into the embers of the fire. Solange saw her lips move soundlessly and then the twigs flared with a sharp crackle, giving off a greenish smoke. They both stared at the burning twigs and the dog whined softly. The old woman turned from the fire.

'I can't see him,' she said. 'Not a sign of him.'

'Is that good or bad?'

'Good.' The old woman yawned and scratched her matted head. 'Neither hide nor hair of him!' she went on. 'Satisfied, are you?'

Solange hesitated. Then she said, 'His name – it might even be Peter Lunn.'

'His name doesn't matter,' said the old woman. 'If he was dead I'd see him by his given name and I don't. That means he's not dead. He'd come to me if he was.'

'Come to see you?' Solange felt her spine tingle.

Charity Becket waved a vague hand. 'His ghost would be near me. I'd feel his presence.'

Solange drew a deep breath. 'My father *is* alive then? You're certain of it?'

'I've said so, haven't I, time and again!'

'Oh, thank you!' cried Solange. 'You can't imagine how happy it makes me to know that Papa *is* alive!'

The old woman raised a bony hand and pointed at Solange. 'You've a sweetheart, I see. You'll be wanting a love potion.'

Startled by the change of subject, Solange was slow to answer.

The old woman went on, 'A few drops in his ale and he'll be forever faithful. Never fails.' She reached for one of the bottles on the table and carefully poured a few drops into a small phial.

Solange said, 'He's gone for a soldier in William's army.'

'He'll return.' She wiped the drips from the bottle and thrust in a cork, then held it just out of Solange's reach.

'Oh yes,' said Solange. 'How much is it?'

'How much have you got?'

'Threepence.'

'That's how much it is then.' She grabbed the money from Solange's hand. 'And now I'll bid you good-day,' she said and sank once more on to the stool.

The grey cat sprang into her lap and the dog growled jealously. As Charity Becket stroked the cat, Solange began to back away.

'Thank you,' she began. 'About Papa, I mean.'

The old woman paid her no attention and Solange slipped thankfully through the doorway. Once outside she drew a deep breath of fresh air.

'So you *are* alive, Papa!' she whispered exultantly. 'And I shall find you. We shall prove them all wrong!'

She turned her face southward and hurried home, so full of plans for the great reunion with her father that poor Jess was quite forgotten. She would say nothing about her visit to Charity Becket to Maman but she would tell Jean and enlist his help in another search. In the face of her new evidence he surely would not refuse. She ran the last half-mile back to the farm and full of fresh hope set about her work with renewed energy.

Chapter Five

WHILE SOLANGE WAS trying to decide the best way to contact Jean he solved the problem by turning up at the farm one day with news of his own. As Solange sat with her head pressed into the side of one of the cows he crouched beside her; watching the milk spurt into the pail he launched into his story. It appeared that by dint of exhaustive enquiries Louise Rey had found out where he was living and had written a letter to him. Her father, a highly-skilled weaver, had established himself in Bath and was planning to expand his business. He was offering Jean a chance to learn the craft and possibly to inherit the business.

'But only *if* I become his son-in-law,' Jean explained. 'I have written back that I shall give up the sea at once and travel to Bath. Since it is already two weeks from Christmas I shall travel early in the New Year.'

'And you will wed Louise?'

'I will.'

'And Maman? Does she know this? Does she approve?'

'Of course. She is delighted.'

'So Louise has been searching for you all these years! How romantic, Jean! Shall I like her for a sister, do you think?'

113

'Most certainly, Soli. You will love her.'

'And will she love me?'

He grinned, 'I dare say – *if* you behave yourself!'

'Jean!' She glared up indignantly.

'I mean it, Soli. You can be very difficult.'

'Not any more,' she told him earnestly. 'I'm not a child, remember.'

'True enough!' he marvelled. 'I can't believe it.' He shook his head. 'Henri says –'

'Henri! Huh! Don't speak to me of that man!' cried Solange but without real rancour. 'He has no right to be married to Maman, you know – Papa is still alive! Oh yes, Jean! I know it for certain now so don't look at me that way.'

She stood up and patted the cow affectionately before carrying her pail and stool to the next animal and settling herself once more. Jean stood watching her, his hands on his hips.

'Not all that nonsense about Papa again!' he said with a shake of his head. 'I thought you said you had grown up!'

Solange launched into her account of the visit to Charity Becket, adjusting the story a little as she went in order to render the old woman more credible in Jean's eyes – referring to Charity Becket as a 'wise woman' instead of a witch, and omitting to mention the state of squalor in which she lived.

'So you see,' she concluded breathlessly, 'if Papa was dead she would have seen his ghost but as he is alive she couldn't make contact. So he *is* alive, Jean, and I am going to find him. I thought I would leave the farm and find work in Bath because that's where he is, mark my words. And now you are going to Bath and I can travel with you. You will help me, Jean, won't you?'

But Jean said hastily, 'Maman will never allow you to leave the farm. It is a good position for you here. The Gadburys are good to you and you are well fed. You would be crazy to give it up for a search that will only end in heartache and disappointment.'

Solange tugged at the cow's teats and her mouth tightened. 'I don't *need* Maman's permission. I'm nigh on grown. In fact,' she added with a flash of her blue eyes, 'I have a beau and might even be wed in a year or two!'

She hoped he would be impressed but instead he merely laughed.

'A beau? This is news, Soli.'

''Tis true, Jean,' she told him, incensed by his attitude. 'His name's Jess Criswell and he's gone for a soldier in William's army but he's my beau right enough. You ask Mistress Gadbury. She'll tell you.'

'Jess Criswell? Well I never!' Jean shook his head. 'Just fancy our little Soli with a sweetheart! How old is this Jess?'

'Nineteen and a fine man. He's taller than you, Jean, and he thinks the world of me. He's handsome and brave and . . .'

'He'd have to be brave to consider you for his wife!' said Jean. 'Has he kissed you?'

She raised her head from the cow's side and gave him a withering look. 'Kissed me? He certainly has! He has a wonderful way with kisses!'

Jean frowned suddenly. 'Has he now? Then you take care, Soli, that kissing is all he does.'

Flattered by his concern Solange smiled. 'I'll watch him. Don't you fret, Jean.'

'So what will this Jess have to say if he comes home from his soldiering and you are gone to Bath? He won't be too pleased. Had you thought of that?'

Solange considered the problem for a moment. 'I shall write him a letter from Bath,' she said at last, 'and send it to his mother to wait on his return. Then he can come and find me.'

'And if he doesn't care to come chasing after you?'

'He will.'

'But if he *doesn't*?'

'Then I'll find myself another,' she told him with a toss of her head. 'If he won't come after me then I shall know he doesn't truly care for me. I *must* go to Bath.'

She stood up and, carrying the brimming pail, moved carefully to the bench. She released the cows and sent them out into the yard, leaving them to find their own way back into the meadow. Thoughtfully, she led the way across the yard to the kitchen where Alice had promised the visitor a bite to eat.

Outside the back door Solange put a hand on her brother's arm. 'Please take me with you to Bath, Jean,' she begged. 'I could stay with you at the Reys while I look for –'

'No!' he said emphatically. 'No! No! No! I will not impose further on Louise's family, Soli. You cannot come with me. If you came to Bath you would be on your own in a strange city and you would have to fend for yourself.'

She shrugged. 'Then I will. I'll find work. You'll

see. Bath will be kind to me – I feel it in my heart. Only take me with you, I beg you. It's not much to ask.'

He regarded her uncertainly. 'If I thought you would behave yourself . . .' he began. 'I wouldn't want you to make a bad impression on Louise's family. This is a great opportunity for me – the greatest of my whole life.'

'I won't disgrace you, I promise. Please take me with you. If you won't, I – I shall make the journey on my own!' She was pleased to see that this suggestion horrified him.

'All that way alone?' he protested. 'Don't talk so foolishly. You would be set upon by footpads or waylaid by highwaymen before you had gone more than a mile, and well you know it. We should have to join up with other travellers – there's safety in numbers.' Seeing her expression he cursed his lack of caution and went on hurriedly, 'Now don't look at me that way, Soll. I haven't said I *would* take you, but only *if* I should take you . . .'

But recognizing the chink in his armour Solange flung her arms around his neck and kissed him.

'Oh, Jean, Maman will be so pleased that we shall be going together, and I swear you will never regret it. Not for a moment. I shall be a model travelling companion. I am so changed, Jean, from the wilful child I once was. I am quite grown up and – and *sensible*.'

'You? Sensible?'

'Yes, sensible, Jean. I shall be no trouble to you at all.' Unable to resist her enthusiasm Jean was coming reluctantly to the conclusion that it might be possible to take her with him.

'But you must look after yourself in Bath,' he insisted. 'I shan't impose on the family – not even for a moment.'

'They might need a maid,' Solange suggested hopefully.

'God forbid!' he cried with more honesty than tact. 'We must tell Maman as soon as possible.'

Marie, as Solange had anticipated, was firmly against the idea and a heated argument ensued. A full-scale quarrel was only narrowly averted by Henri's common sense but eventually Marie was won over, and mother and daughter finally parted with a friendly hug.

Within a short time it was all settled.

Jean's original plan had been to travel south to Tiverton with a family of seven who were moving to that area; from there he would await the chance to move eastward again. At the last moment, however, one of the party fell ill and their move was temporarily abandoned. Jean fumed at the delay but another opportunity came a few days later when Jean learned of three churchmen who were on their way to Glastonbury and looking for travelling companions. Contact was made and their plans finalized but by this time two brothers had asked to join them. The latter were in their early twenties and were on their way to a funeral in Wheddon Cross. The churchmen were middle-aged or elderly but to Jean's surprise they insisted that they would take the shorter route across Exmoor rather than go the long way round by way of Tiverton.

Solange's farewell to her mother and Henri was heartfelt and she parted from Emily Tidden with tears in her eyes. Two days after Christmas her parting from the Gadburys was also full of genuine regret, for the couple had been very good to her and she was properly grateful. She hugged Alice and shook hands with John and promised to write to them as soon as she reached Bath.

The seven travellers met on the strand at Appledore, very near to the spot where the Huguenots had first landed, and to Solange this seemed a most auspicious omen. It was not yet eight o'clock in the morning and was barely light as they shivered together in the raw air, peering through the river mist for a sign of the man who had agreed to ferry them across to Instow Quay where further transport had been arranged.

Solange examined her fellow-travellers with great curiosity, but found the churchmen uninspiring. The Reverend Meade was tall and very fat; Brother Thomas was short and ungainly and Reverend Goodfellow was elderly and very short-sighted. The brothers, Simon and James Pett, however, promised to be more congenial companions – Simon was tall with red hair, plain features and bold, grey eyes and James was shorter, better looking and with darker hair. To her delight she saw that they regarded her with undisguised approval and at the prospect of a few days in their company Solange's spirits rose accordingly.

It transpired that the brothers, having a relatively short distance to travel, were going to walk but the three churchmen had arranged the hire of a small pony cart which would seat two and in which they would ride in turn. Jean had bought what he referred to as 'a knock-kneed nag' which when necessary could carry him and Solange. The going would be slow, though only the Pett brothers, on their way to a family funeral, were in any real hurry — but, as Simon told Solange cheerfully, since the weather was cold the body of their uncle would last an extra day if necessary.

Waiting at the water's edge Solange shivered and stared impatiently across the river until finally her keen ears detected the splash of oars from an approaching boat. It grew gradually louder until at last the outline of the ferry boat and its single occupant appeared out of the mist and as the ferryman pulled the boat ashore she was already scrambling in, eager for the big adventure to begin. Apart from her stolen visit to Charity Becket and very occasional trips in to market with John, she had been confined to the farm and any excursion was a welcome event.

When everyone was safely on board they pushed off again and the ferryman settled himself to the oars.

For a moment he rowed in silence but then he said, 'You'll have heard about the king, I dare say.'

All heads turned his way. 'The king? No. What news?' they chorused.

'Why, he's fled the country, hasn't he. Gone, without a shot fired on either side.'

In the gloom the churchmen exchanged startled looks but said nothing. Officially they owed allegiance to James as the established monarch but privately they longed for a Protestant king.

'Gone?' echoed Jean. 'Gone where?'

The man paused to rest on his oars and peer over his shoulders into the gloom. As he resumed his rowing he said, 'Gone to France, so they say. Louis will accommodate him, you'll see. Rank papists, the pair of them and close as two fleas on a dog's leg! Well, as a God-fearing Protestant, I say good riddance to James. I'd rather see Mary on the throne or even William.'

Simon Pett said, 'What's happened to the queen then, and the new baby?'

'Sent on ahead, so they say, all secret like.' The ferryman shook his head. 'What a coward, eh? A whole army to do his bidding but he turned his back and ran.'

'But what of the army?' asked Solange.

'Disbanded, aren't they,' he told her. 'They say the streets of London are full of soldiers getting into all kinds of mischief. You know soldiers.'

'Disbanded!' said Jean. 'Whatever next!'

Somewhere up river a horn sounded eerily and the ferryman peered for a few seconds in the direction of the sound before continuing.

'Stole the Great Seal, didn't he, and threw it into the Thames! A fit of pique, like. I ask you!'

'What is the Great Seal?' asked Solange, wide-eyed at the news.

'Damned if I rightly know,' the ferryman admitted, 'but whatever 'tis they say you can't rule the country without it.'

The largest churchman leaned forward. ''Tis part of the Parliamentary procedure,' he said, pleased at the chance to air his knowledge. ''Tis necessary for the proper government of the realm. If what this fellow says is true –'

'Oh, 'tis true enough!' cried the ferryman. 'But they'll get it back. Some poor fisherman will be paid a penny or two to fetch it up from the mud for 'em.'

'We must hope so,' said the churchman with a hint of reproof in his voice.

'And where is William's army?' asked Solange, wondering about Jess. 'They can't be in London so soon.'

The ferryman laughed, 'Not unless they've got wings! Last time I heard he'd reached Windsor but they'll get to London before long and with James gone . . .' He finished the sentence with a shrug and they all began to talk at once.

All except Solange who hugged herself with joy at the news of James's departure. Ever since James's accession to the throne she had waited for the persecution to begin, but with Mary and her Protestant husband on the throne there would surely be nothing more to fear. Ever! She smiled up at the lightening sky and thanked God for his mercies.

By the time they reached the other side of the river the daylight had pierced the mist and they made haste to pay off the ferryman. With that part of the journey out of the way it was now time to look about them for their respective means of transportation and it took best part of an hour before everyone was ready to start out. The churchmen grumbled that their cart was smaller than they had been led to expect but the owner had sent his young son along to deliver it so they could not make any real headway with their complaint. Jean's horse was even worse than he remembered but there was little point in grumbling since it was too late to do anything about it.

They set off at last in high spirits, intending, if they could, to cover the five miles to Barnstaple before midday. The road soon petered out but a track of sorts was discernible and they found their way without too much difficulty to the River Taw. There they crossed the narrow stretch of water by means of an insubstantial bridge and shortly afterwards found themselves in Barnstaple. Delighted with their progress they stopped only briefly for a slice of venison pie washed down with small beer before continuing towards Brayford.

The way now lay along narrow winding tracks which led them up and down below bare trees which met overhead and dripped constantly upon them. It had rained in the night and the track was muddy and sodden bracken hemmed them in on either side. They reached a small hamlet just as night was falling and went their separate ways in search of food and lodgings that would suit their respective pockets.

When they met again next morning they learned that the Reverend Meade had been taken ill in the night with severe cramps in his stomach and it had been decided to leave him behind in the care of the inn keeper's wife who was well respected for her knowledge of herbs. If her remedies did not alleviate the symptoms a physician was to be fetched from Barnstaple and a purse had been supplied to cover this eventuality. When he recovered he would await the next party of travellers and eventually rejoin his colleagues in Glastonbury.

'So we are one less now,' Jean remarked.

'For the time being,' said Simon, 'but we may well find others waiting along the way who will swell our numbers. I confess I would feel happier if we were not so few.'

'We must put our trust in the Lord,' said the Reverend Goodfellow piously. 'He surely will provide.'

So they set off again and for much of the day Solange was glad to ride behind Jean with her arms round his waist. There was a cold wind now and she sat with her face pressed against his back to protect it from the worst of the weather but occasionally, to stretch her cramped limbs she would walk a mile or so, picking her way gingerly around the puddles. To cheer herself up she talked about Jess and the surprise he would get on returning home to find her gone on to Bath. She had left a short letter for him (which Alice had promised to deliver) in which she had promised to send word of her new address as soon as she had one. Her favourite daydream now was one in which he came at once in search of her: on finding her again he would declare his undying love and, desperate for her kisses, he would carry her to the altar without further delay.

Time passed quite pleasantly and in the afternoon they saw a few wild ponies but met no other humans until the ground began to rise towards the moor. Then they passed a farmer driving three cows, and half an hour later they reached Brayford. Here they discovered to their chagrin that it was scarcely larger than the hamlet where they had spent the previous night, and did not even boast an inn large enough to accommodate them. They were still discussing their predicament when a large pig raced past them followed by an even larger woman. She brandished a stout stick and was red-faced and breathless and her language was more than colourful. Solange, Jean and the two brothers joined in the chase and eventually the pig was cornered and driven back to its sty. Panting after her exertions the woman leaned against the gate.

'I'm a farmer's wife,' she told them, 'and I'm obliged to you all. That dratted animal has pulled that trick on me for the last time! I'll slaughter him before the week's out, or my name's not Maggie Tucker! Cunning as the devil that pig, but his hours are numbered.' She surveyed the travellers with a practised eye. 'Thought you'd find lodging hereabouts, I dare say.'

They nodded.

'They all do,' she replied. 'My husband says we should be running an inn instead of a farm. We've no rooms, I'm afraid, but plenty of folks sleep in the barn and you're welcome to it and no charge. 'Tis dry, at least, and there's some straw you could sleep on.'

Knowing they would find nothing better the travellers accepted gladly and were also able to buy some smoked ham and bread from her for their supper. The barn proved less than ideal as a dormitory. An owl, screeching loudly at regular intervals, ensured that sleep did not come easily to the occupants and they spent a cold and restless night. They rose next morning in subdued spirits but a modest breakfast of ham and eggs quickly restored their morale, and when they left Brayford just after nine o'clock they were in a cheerful mood. Their intention was to cross the moor, a distance of approximately sixteen miles, and reach Wheddon Cross on the far side by nightfall. The first miles passed pleasantly in desultory conversation enlivened from time to time by the Petts' renderings of one or two popular (if somewhat bawdy) ditties. The brothers also offered to teach the rest of the party the words and tune of 'Lili Bolero' which William's followers were singing on their march towards London but only

Solange accepted. She proved a quick learner and the three of them strode ahead of the others, their arms linked companionably.

> Though by my soul the English do prat
> The law's on their side and Christ knows
> what . . .

They sang lustily ignoring the disapproving glances of the two churchmen and Jean's obvious amusement.

> But if dispence do come from the Pope
> We'll hang Magna Carta and them in a rope.
> Lero lero, lili bolero, lili bolero bullen
> a-la . . .

Their voices rang out cheerfully and in this way the miles slipped by. Later a fine rain began to fall but it stopped again within the hour and before long they had reached and passed Exford. Soon they were only three miles from their destination and were beginning to congratulate themselves on their progress when, without warning, two mounted men appeared suddenly from the bushes ahead of them and turning their horses, effectively barred the travellers' way forward.

'Mon Dieu!' muttered Jean, coming to an abrupt halt. 'Highwaymen!'

The two churchmen crossed themselves hurriedly and Solange, Simon and James, who had been walking ahead, fell back hastily to join their companions.

One of the horsemen rode a black stallion and was fashionably dressed with a wide-brimmed hat which shaded his face – the upper half of which was covered by a black mask. He carried a pistol which he levelled at his intended victims. His companion was similarly armed but shabbily dressed and his mouth and nose were hidden by a red scarf. He was stocky with broad shoulders and his hatless head was covered with straw-coloured hair. His mount, a mud-spattered roan, was obviously past its prime and hung its head disconsolately.

In a quaking voice the Reverend Goodfellow cried, 'We've nothing of value. Nothing at all. I beg you let us pass in peace, good sirs.'

Jean put a protective arm round Solange but the masked man motioned him away from her with an imperative wave of his pistol.

'Let the maid step forward,' he said. 'She will come to no harm.'

'If you hurt a hair of her head –' Jean began, but the man laughed.

'And what is she to you? Your wife?'

Despite the gravity of their predicament Solange could not resist a smile at this suggestion as Jean said, 'Certainly not! She's my sister.'

'Then your sister is safe with me,' he was assured.

'But she has nothing of any worth,' Jean insisted. 'We are Huguenot refugees and poor as church mice.'

The man laughed, 'Every man tells me how poor he is, then we prove him a liar.'

He stared at Solange, waiting for her to step forward; but as she still hesitated the shabbily dressed man slid from his horse and seized her arm but his companion called, 'No, Tom! Let her be!' and he released her reluctantly.

Taking heart from this exchange Solange stepped

forward. Looking up at the highwayman she said, 'My brother speaks the truth. We have little but the clothes we stand up in.'

To her surprise he, too, dismounted and tossed the reins of his horse to his companion. Then he took off his hat and bowed courteously.

'Allow me to introduce myself,' he said with lightly veiled mockery. 'Richard Duke at your service. Well known on this wild moor for his willingness to relieve travellers of the burden of their valuables. Jewels or coins — we are content with either. Tom, my partner in crime, is a very rough diamond but I was raised to respect the opposite sex and I promise you will suffer no indignity at my hands.' His tone hardened slightly. 'Now, you will please show me your fingers.'

As Solange held out her hands he saw they were indeed bare of decoration and gave a small nod. Then, without lowering the pistol he reached forward and felt around her neck for a locket or necklace.

'I told you I have nothing,' she repeated.

'Apparently so,' he said. 'Then we shall have to investigate your companions.'

At these words the Reverend Goodfellow fell to his knees and began to pray earnestly with his eyes closed and his face turned heavenwards. With a gesture of impatience Richard Duke nodded to his companion who moved forward, still leading the two horses, and tugged a gold ring from the hand of each of the churchmen. He bit each ring and called triumphantly, 'Gold! They'll be worth a shilling or two!'

Richard Duke nodded his approval and then Jean was searched and his last shilling was taken from him.

Solange was allowed to rejoin him while Simon and James were searched, and here the robbers had better luck for James was carrying a sovereign intended for his recently bereaved aunt and Simon was wearing a pocket watch, a present from his uncle.

While this was happening Solange whispered to Jean, 'They are only two but we are six! We could overpower them!'

He looked at her aghast. 'Soli, are you mad? They have pistols!' he reminded her. 'Do you want to see me killed? They would shoot us as soon as look at us. Don't be fooled by Duke's good manners. I wager he has killed before and would do so again if needs be!'

'But if we could get the pistols –' Solange hissed but then Simon, on Jean's other side, interrupted her.

Leaning towards Jean he whispered, 'We outnumber them! Let's take them on! Just you, me and James. We can forget the churchmen.'

Jean still looked dubious. 'If only we had some kind of weapon –'

'But they won't be expecting it,' Simon argued in a fierce whisper. 'We shall have the element of surprise.'

He turned to repeat his suggestion to his brother who at once gave a slight but eager nod of his head.

Solange said, 'Oh Jean! We can do it! I know we can!'

'And if one of us dies?'

As she began to reply Tom became aware of the whispers and turning shouted, 'Hold your tongues or I'll silence you forever!'

Defiantly Solange muttered, 'Strange how a pistol makes a coward brave!'

129

He looked at her suspiciously. 'What was that?'

Jean dug her fiercely in the ribs and said, 'She said she is afraid.' And he gave Solange a look that dared her to repeat her rash remark.

As Tom's attention moved once more to his master, Solange whispered, 'I could distract their attention. I could fall in a swoon —' But at that moment, before they could perfect any plan, Richard Duke gave a cry of triumph and held aloft Grandpère's stick which he had found tied to the saddlebag of Jean's horse.

'A silver top! I shall keep this pretty piece for my —'

Before anyone could guess her intention Solange hurled herself forward.

'Give that to me, you thieving wretch!' she shouted. 'That belonged to my Grandpère, and you shan't have it!'

The highwayman began to laugh with delight at her reaction and raised the stick teasingly above his head.

At that moment Simon realised that unwittingly Solange had provided the perfect diversion and with a shout to the others he began to run after Solange who, with no thought for her own danger, was now trying desperately to retrieve her property. As she jumped furiously for the stick Duke's full attention was on her and Tom's warning cry came too late. Simon seized his right arm and Jean tried to prise the pistol from his grasp. Meanwhile, James had hurled himself upon Tom and the two of them were struggling wildly.

The two churchmen, still on their knees, watched in amazement as Solange gained possession of the stick and ran with it to help James. As she began to beat Tom with Grandpère's stick, Duke's pistol went off unintentionally. Everyone froze except Tom who gave a cry of pain and fell to the ground, clutching his right thigh and roaring obscenities. Simon had wrestled Duke to the ground when Jean managed to take the pistol and gasped, 'Let him up, Simon. I have him covered!'

James, who now held Tom's pistol, hurried towards them, grinning triumphantly but as soon as he did so Tom struggled back on to his horse and a moment later had disappeared into the trees.

'Damn!' cried Jean who was beginning to enjoy himself. 'We've lost one of the wretches.'

'Good riddance to him!' cried James. 'We still have our property.'

While Jean held the pistol they retrieved the watch, sovereign and rings and were then faced with the problem of what to do with their captive. They would soon be at Wheddon Cross but would anyone there be authorised to hold a highwayman? Did Wheddon Cross even boast a gaol? Nobody knew, but it seemed improbable.

Solange listened in dismay as they discussed their captive's future — a trial and eventual punishment which might well be a hanging.

'Perhaps we could let him go,' she whispered to Jean. 'He intended us no real harm.'

'No harm?' he cried indignantly. 'You have a very short memory, Soli! He robbed us, didn't he?'

'I meant no physical harm,' she amended. 'He was courteous — and he didn't kill any of us. We could keep his pistol and let him go. Without it he could not rob anyone else.'

Jean snorted disparagingly, 'He'd soon get himself another pistol. And how do we know that he hasn't killed some other unfortunate traveller? He may be a murderer ten times over. No, Soli, the man is an outright rogue and should stand proper trial for his misdeeds. You have too soft a heart, Solange. That's your trouble. The fellow is a criminal and deserves his fate.'

They were still arguing when Richard Duke took matters into his own hands by making a sudden dash for freedom. He ran towards his horse, leaped on to its back and was urging it into a canter as Jean took careful aim with the pistol.

Solange cried, 'Don't hit the horse, Jean!' and covered her face with her hands but the pistol shot failed to materialize.

Instead there was an empty 'click' and Solange watched in relief as the highwayman made good his escape. James and Simon cursed angrily and Jean, infuriated, threw down the useless pistol.

The two churchmen scrambled to their feet. 'Give me my ring!' cried Brother Thomas, holding out his hand. His face was flushed with relief but his voice trembled. 'It belonged to my dear mother, God rest her soul. And they did not find my money which is cunningly sewn into the lining of my coat!'

Simon said, 'Solange, you were superb! We could never have routed them without your intervention.'

Solange's smile broadened as the two churchmen also heaped congratulations upon her but Jean and James were too busy bemoaning the loss of their captives, insisting that they would cheerfully see them behind bars or swinging from a rope's end.

'But the one called Tom was injured,' Solange reminded him, 'and Richard Duke has lost his pistol. They haven't exactly escaped scot free.'

'Their pride has been hurt if nothing else,' James agreed. 'I think all things considered we have come out of it rather well. I vote we put it down to experience –'

'And keep the pistols for our own protection,' said Simon. He examined Duke's pistol which was made of walnut with a long barrel and intricately carved lock-plate. The other was crudely made and worth very little. 'We should at least report the incident when we reach Wheddon Cross,' he suggested, 'so that travellers going eastward will be on their guard.'

This was agreed and they eventually continued on their way in high spirits. The two churchmen, relieved but rather silent, rode together in the pony trap and Jean rode alone while Solange, Simon and James walked together.

Towards the end of the afternoon Simon and James held a brief whispered consultation from which Solange was excluded and James suddenly dropped back to strike up a conversation with Jean.

Almost immediately Simon told Solange that James was courting. 'But I am fancy-free,' he added.

He waited for her comment but she did not rise at once to the bait as she struggled with her conscience. She was promised to Jess Criswell, she reminded herself, but he was miles away and it was possible she might never see him again. Simon, meanwhile, had the boldest grey eyes she had ever seen.

'And you?' he prompted. 'You are definitely spoken for?'

'Yes and no,' she told him. 'He was my Valentine, though half in jest. But now he is gone for a soldier and I am off to Bath. No doubt he'll find another maid to kiss when he finds me gone.' She laughed lightly and gave him a provocative glance.

'I wish I was going on to Bath,' he told her with a deep sigh. 'I shall miss you.'

'Then come to Bath!' she said lightly, amazed by her own forwardness. 'Your uncle's funeral cannot last forever.'

'But I have to go home – I have my work,' he protested. 'I work in my father's mill. We both do.'

'Ah! Then we are doomed to part,' she said.

'Does that grieve you at all, Solange?'

'Most certainly it does.' She gave him another look from beneath her lashes and saw the indecision in his eyes.

'I could see you tonight,' he suggested. 'If I knew where you are lodged I could slip out from my aunt's house on some pretext or other. Would you meet me? Secretly, I mean.'

'Secretly!'

Her heart began to race in that unfamiliar, jolting way and her emotions tumbled rapturously. Surely being wooed by a handsome young man was the most wonderful excitement the world offered!

'I would try,' she whispered.

He lowered his voice and said, 'If we met would you let me kiss you?'

'On so short an acquaintance!' She tried to sound indignant but without much success. 'It all depends, doesn't it?'

'On what?'

'On a great many things. The way I feel. The way you feel.'

He lowered his voice and said softly, 'Did your soldier kiss you?'

'He did.'

'On your neck? Your shoulders?'

'Certainly not!' she gasped, genuinely shocked by the suggestion. 'And nor will any man who has not spoken formally for me.'

'You might want me to,' he suggested.

'Never, Simon Pett! I think you've taken leave of your senses!' she told him breathlessly, but he laughed at her confusion and wisely said no more on the subject.

Her imagination would do the rest.

Soon after ten o'clock Solange retired, with much exaggerated yawning, to her bed in the large room under the eaves which she was to share with four other women travellers. Three of these were already fast asleep in their truckle beds and one was snoring loudly. A fourth woman was undressing. A gaudy red satin gown hung from a hook in the wall and she was now removing layers of underclothes, folding each discarded garment neatly before laying it on a stool beside her bed. Solange hesitated. She had arranged to meet Simon Pett under the large chestnut tree on the green so it was pointless for her to undress.

She shivered in the cold unheated room and said firmly, 'Well, I shan't take off a single stitch! This room's as cold as ice. You'll catch your death, I shouldn't wonder.'

The woman protested that she must change her clothes. 'They'll be crumpled beyond wearing else!' she told Solange, 'and I should look a proper scarecrow.'

'I'll risk it,' said Solange cheerfully then, remembering she was supposed to be tired, she yawned widely again and said, 'Oh, I'm so weary. I could sleep on a log tonight!'

She laid her shawl over the bed and rolled herself under the threadbare blankets without even removing her cap or shoes. Closing her eyes, she wondered how long it would be before the woman fell asleep. Simon had promised to be by the tree 'soon after the church clock strikes the third quarter'. Solange meant to be there but it would not be easy if this woman proved talkative.

Peeping from beneath her lashes Solange watched her pull a voluminous nightdress over her ample form.

'I saw you at supper,' the woman said, ignoring Solange's silence. 'My name's Harriet. Harriet Warburn. I'm travelling with my second husband, Gilbert.'

Solange murmured indistinctly, trying to give the impression that she was already half-asleep in order to discourage further talk, but it seemed Harriet was not to be silenced quite so easily.

'If there's one thing I can't abide it's a snorer,' she said fretfully. 'My first husband snored for twelve years, yet when he died I couldn't get used to the quiet. Kept me awake for weeks. Do you snore?'

Solange made no answer, crossing her fingers beneath the bed clothes, and Harriet repeated the question.

When she still received no reply she went on regardless, 'And the other things I can't abide is bugs.'

By this time she was muttering to herself, apparently convinced by Solange's laboured breathing that she had fallen asleep. Solange half-opened her eyes and saw Harriet inspecting the bed, cautiously folding back each blanket and looking beneath the pillow.

Just as the clock struck the half-hour Harriet slid under the bedclothes but she was a large woman and obviously found the narrow, straw-filled mattress very uncomfortable. She was still fidgeting and grumbling to herself when the clock struck the last quarter and Solange could bear it no longer.

Sitting up in bed, she clutched at her stomach and groaned loudly. 'I'm going to be sick!' she moaned. 'Ooh! I feel terrible!'

Harriet sat up at once and said, 'Then get yourself downstairs, girl, and out into the yard. You can't be sick in here.'

Solange moaned weakly. 'Must have been the hog's cheek I ate at supper,' she muttered.

'The hog's cheek?' Harriet looked alarmed. 'Oh dear! I ate that too. I hope I shan't be ill.'

Solange gave another realistic groan and snatched up her shawl and, delighted with her subterfuge, hurried downstairs as quietly as she could. She had left Jean playing brag in the tap room and he might still be there. Luck was with her, however, and she reached the front door without meeting anyone. She closed it behind her and began to run along the street, stumbling awkwardly on the uneven cobbles and praying that Simon would wait for her. When she reached the green she hesitated, but then to her immense relief she saw him step out from beneath the large tree, his hands held out to her in welcome.

Breathlessly she recounted the problems she had had to overcome in order to meet him and he told her that he had been forced to bring his aunt's dog out for a last walk.

Solange looked around. 'Where is it then?' she asked.

He laughed, 'I chased it off. I didn't want it spoiling our fun!' He had taken her hand and was leading her back into the shadow of the tree and his arm around her shoulders was warm and full of promise.

When at last she stood with her back against the tree trunk he wasted no time but planted a kiss firmly on her unprotesting lips.

'That's the first course!' he told her slyly. 'Then there's the main course and pudding. I hope you're hungry, Solange.'

It was her turn to laugh. 'Maybe. Maybe not!' she told him, 'but don't you rush me, Simon Pett. I'm a slow eater. Always have been!'

She thought this a very witty thing to have said and was rather surprised at the ease with which it had slipped from her tongue.

'I won't rush you,' he told her. 'But nor will I let the food go cold! I've been waiting all my life for this moment!'

'All your life?' she began, but now he reached up and looped one of her curls round his finger.

'You've got bonny hair!' he told her huskily. 'If there's one thing I do love on a woman it's fair curls, and you've got more than your share. Oh, Solange! If you only knew what you do to me! Or maybe you do know!'

He leaned forward so that his weight pressed her back against the tree and his fingers began to explore her neck. She felt her knees buckle as his hands moved down over her shoulders.

'You've got beautiful shoulders,' he whispered. 'I've never seen such sweet shoulders!'

'You can't rightly see them in the dark,' she objected nervously, 'and don't lean on me so heavy, Simon. I told you not to rush me.'

She tried to wriggle free but his arms slid round her waist and her half-hearted efforts achieved nothing but a delighted chuckle from her admirer.

'Now what will you do?' he teased. He lowered his voice melodramatically. 'You're in my power, Solange. But tell the truth – you don't want to escape me, do you?'

'Yes, I do!' she protested. 'You're holding me too tight! I can hardly breathe! Let go of me, Simon Pett!'

Instead he kissed her again and whispered, 'Pretty shoulders and pretty hair. I'll warrant you've got pretty ankles too!'

'Simon Pett,' she cried, scandalized. 'You just forget about my ankles!'

'I bet they're as neat as any I've seen!' he suggested coaxingly. 'I reckon they're smooth and –'

'My ankles are my affair!' she told him. 'What sort of a girl do you think I am? Ankles, indeed!'

His right hand began to slide down her body and she was seized by a growing uneasiness. She dimly realized that for all his size, Jess Criswell had been a mere boy compared with this experienced young man.

How far was he hoping to go and what exactly should she allow? Her body was responding to his, betraying her in an alarming way, weakening her resolution. Is this how young women were 'taken advantage of', she wondered. Not forced against their will, as she had always believed, but surrendering willingly beguiled by their own emotions. If this was how women fell from grace then she could sympathize with them. Being tempted to say 'yes' might result in the most dire consequences and she had no desire to become a trollop. But saying 'no' to this persuasive man might soon become impossible! And suppose she said 'no' and he took no heed? He was so much stronger than she was.

'Let's sit down on the grass,' he suggested suddenly and before she could find the words to object he had swung her off her feet. Even as she cried out she found herself flat on her back with all the breath knocked out of her and with Simon on his knees beside her. The grass was cold and damp through her clothes and her cap felt crooked. She could see Simon's teeth whitely in the moonlight as he laughed down at her!

'Simon Pett! You rotten apple!' she cried, pummelling his shoulders in an effort to dislodge him. 'That was a mean, nasty trick. I'm surprised at you!' She tried to twist sideways but now he was kneeling astride her and she felt his fingers reaching down towards her ankle.

'Ah! 'Tis a beautiful ankle!' he cried. 'Just as I –'

But he did not finish his sentence because at that precise moment a large dog sprang upon them from the darkness and began to leap about barking hysterically. Solange screamed and Simon cursed loudly.

'Rollo! Get off, you stupid brute! Get away!' he

shouted, but the dog was delighted to have found him again and was eager to join in the fun. As Simon tried to subdue the dog Solange took her chance. She rolled free and hastily scrambled to her feet, brushing down her clothes and trying hard not to laugh at Simon's predicament. After a few moments he fought off the excited dog and pulled himself to a kneeling position but before he could stand up the dog pounced again, knocking him down, and then proceeded to worry at the toe of his left boot.

Grateful for the dog's timely intervention and unable to hold back her laughter any longer, Solange backed away. Eventually, Simon managed to stand up but the dog still circled him playfully, reluctant to relinquish the game.

'For God's sake keep quiet, you stupid animal!' cried Simon. 'You'll waken the whole village!'

But it was already too late. From the far side of the green a familiar voice rang out.

'Solange? Is that you?'

It was Jean.

The laughter died abruptly on her lips. 'Oh Lordy!' she groaned. 'Now I'll be for it! Worse than my mother, that brother of mine!' Desperately she looked around her but there was nowhere to hide.

'Damnation!' cried Simon petulantly, his romantic interlude in ruins. 'Rollo! Get away from me!' He lashed out with his foot and the dog's excited yapping changed to a howl of pain.

At once Solange's sympathies were with the dog. 'Don't you kick him, you great bully!' she told Simon. ''Tis your own fault for bringing him.'

'Solange!' cried Jean for the second time and she answered resignedly.

'I'm here, Jean!'

'Look Solange, tell him we just happened to meet –' Simon began, but before Solange could invent a convincing lie Jean strode up to them out of the darkness and without preamble punched Simon squarely on the jaw and knocked him down.

'Jean!' cried Solange. 'Oh, you shouldn't have done that! He didn't – I mean we haven't –'

'Don't speak to me!' he snapped, and he took her by the arm and began to drag her away across the green.

She stole a look at his face which was grim and unrelenting. She turned back to look and saw Simon still trying to fend off the excited Rollo. Despite the ignominy of being hauled away in disgrace, she burst out laughing again as a sneaking regret mingled with relief.

'What have you got to laugh about?' Jean demanded furiously. 'Just you wait until Maman hears about this. Feeling sick, were you? You lying hussy. Thought you could sneak away and make a fool of me, did you? So much for your fine promises, Soli!' She tried to slow down their progress but he jerked her forward at a breathless pace so that she had to run to keep up with his long strides. 'So much for "Please take me to Bath, Jean,"' he went on. '"I won't be any trouble, Jean!" Huh! What a dolt I was ever to agree to bring you with me! I should have left you in Appledore.'

His words sobered her instantly and her heart sank. Surely he was not going to send her back. She began to plead.

'Oh, Jean, I'm truly sorry!' she told him. 'I truly am. I know I did wrong – at least, I didn't do wrong with Simon. Not that sort of wrong but I did wrong to deceive you and I –'

'I don't want to hear any of your damned excuses!' he snapped. 'You have had your chance, Soli! I warned you from the start. Now back you go. How do you think I would feel if Louise or her family should get word of this, eh? My little sister with the morals of a she-cat!'

'But that's not true. I haven't *done* anything!' she protested. 'I swear to you . . .'

'I hope for your sake you haven't,' he told her, 'because if you have you might end up with a love-child. Did you stop to think of that?'

Solange pulled herself free of his grasp. 'You don't believe me!' she cried furiously. 'I tell you nothing happened. Don't you trust me?'

'Trust you? After this?' His laugh was incredulous. 'No, I don't trust you, you lying little baggage! Not any more. Feeling sick, indeed!'

For a moment they faced each other, glaring defiance, then suddenly Solange's anger evaporated.

'Oh, Jean, you're right and I'm wrong,' she said miserably. 'I did lie and I'm sorry. 'Twas very rash of me but I swear to you nothing happened. It might have if that dog hadn't come along – Oh, Jean!' Her laughter bubbled up again. 'It was so funny! I'm sorry to laugh, but if you had been there –'

Jean's common sense was also slowly reasserting itself.

'Well, at least I have taught Simon Pett a lesson he won't forget in a hurry!'

'Poor Simon!' she began but was silenced by her brother's expression.

Together they glanced back and saw Simon walking away across the grass with a subdued dog on a lead beside him.

Jean said grimly, 'I think the word hang-dog applies to both of them! Let's hope Master Simon has learned his lesson.'

Solange said, 'Did that fat woman tell you I was feeling sick? Harriet's her name.'

'Yes.'

'That was mean of her.'

'She was *worried*, Soli, when you didn't come back,' he reproved her. 'It was kind of her to be concerned. Don't blame *her*. The fault was all yours.'

They walked back to the inn without further conversation and went inside and up the stairs. On the landing they parted with a final warning from Jean and Solange slipped back into the bedroom.

Harriet said at once, 'Oh, there you are. Are you quite recovered?'

'Yes, thank you,' Solange answered guiltily.

'You were gone so long I thought perhaps you had fallen into a swoon and might lie there all night, unattended.'

'I – I went for a walk. I thought the fresh air . . .' Solange let the sentence trail away.

She took off her cap and shoes, slid under the blankets once more and sighed deeply. She knew she ought to feel sorry that Simon had been knocked down but perhaps he had deserved it. She wondered what would have happened without the dog's timely arrival and was glad it had appeared when it did. She lay wide awake feeling troubled and ashamed until the clock struck one but when at last she fell asleep she did so with a smile on her face.

Chapter Six

THEY MADE AN early start the following day – Jean, Solange and the two churchmen – and made their way in the direction of Watchet on the coast of Blue Anchor Bay, cutting through the woods below Dunster and following the coastline for several miles. The Bristol Channel in winter, however, was a cheerless sight and they soon tired of the rusty brown water with its angry white breakers and felt no desire to linger.

They reached Watchet around midday and found some refreshment and then set off again towards Nether Stowey, skirting the Quantock Hills and arriving in the village later than they expected. They found indifferent lodgings and a lukewarm welcome but now it was Jean who was taken ill. He went down with a fever and excessive lassitude and was obviously in no state to continue the journey and the churchmen were forced to travel on without them. Solange did her best to minister to her brother but it was three days later before Jean felt well enough to venture forth once more. They were able to join forces with a family of five who were heading for Glastonbury and these kindly people insisted that Jean ride in their wagon while their mother and Solange shared the horse.

They proved good companions and the two-day journey passed very pleasantly, but on the third day Solange and Jean were forced to part company with them and to head for Shepton Mallet unaccompanied. They were thankful to reach the town unmolested and without encountering anything worse than an abandoned stage coach overturned in a ditch.

Two days later, approaching Bath from the south, they finally caught their first glimpse of the town and Solange could not hold back a cry of delight. As they drew near to the bridge over which they must pass, a bright winter sun lit the warm stones of the encircling medieval wall and glinted on the waters of the broad river.

'The river Avon,' said Jean in answer to Solange's unspoken question.

''Tis all so beautiful!'

He smiled at the rapture in her voice.

The town itself lay in a broad and shallow valley – a small huddle of roofs topped to the east by a tall spire.

'The abbey church,' said Jean knowledgeably when Solange drew his attention to it. 'Don't look surprised, Soli. I learned a great deal about the place from the churchmen you so much despised. While you were flirting with the Pett brothers I was –'

'I was *not* flirting –' Solange began indignantly but then fell hastily silent as honesty prevailed.

'They used to have a large monastery,' he told her, 'and bishops lived there, but then there was a king called Henry the Eighth who broke with Rome and closed down most of the monasteries.'

She stifled her impatience and, mindful of her recent

fall from grace, gave Jean her full attention as he proceeded to air his recently acquired knowledge and enlarged earnestly on the town's history.

She said with apparent interest, 'Closed down the monasteries? Well I never!'

Jean looked at her suspiciously but her blue eyes were wide and innocent.

'So now the town has a mayor and a corporation,' he went on, 'and a church stands where the abbey used to be. It's quite a big wool town.'

When Solange asked him to elaborate, however, it seemed he knew little more than that.

'But they also have healing springs,' he told her, 'where the water comes hot from the ground. Doctors have written books about it and kings and queens have visited Bath to take the waters and improve their health.'

At last he had genuinely caught Solange's interest. 'Take the waters?' she repeated. 'How do you mean?'

He shrugged. 'They drink it and bathe in it.'

'But how does that make them healthy?'

'I'm not sure,' he confessed, 'but we'll find out soon enough.'

The extent of his knowledge of the town now appeared to have been reached and they made their way across the bridge in a state of eager anticipation. They walked between the wooden houses of Southgate Street, past a horse bath on their right and then reached the city wall which bore signs of recent repairs.

Finally, they passed under the arch and found themselves in the town itself. They walked slowly, admiring the tall houses which rose on both sides of Staules

Street. Here it was too narrow for a horse and carriage but instead they saw several sedan chairs – narrow upright boxes containing space for one seated person, which were carried by two chairmen.

Solange clapped her hands. 'Sedan chairs! Oh, what fun!' she cried. 'When I'm rich I shall ride in them all the time!'

'When you're rich!' laughed Jean. 'And when will that be?'

'Some day!'

'When pigs fly!'

Just then one of the chairs came to an abrupt halt nearby and was set down roughly on the cobbles. At once the face of an elderly woman appeared at the window.

'What is it?' she demanded querulously. 'Why have we stopped? This isn't number fourteen High Street.'

The two men exchanged sly grins and one of them said, 'This is as far as we go, unless we get our money.' His face was gaunt and unshaven and a clay pipe was clenched between his teeth.

'You'll get your money,' said the woman angrily, 'when I reach my house and not before.'

The second man laughed rudely, 'All we want is our proper due, mistress. A sixpence will see you safely home, I promise you.'

'A sixpence!' cried the woman. 'But that's out-rageous. I shall pay you the proper fee. You shall get twopence and not a penny more.'

'Sixpence for the likes of you!' he answered.

'I would rather walk!' she cried.

'Suit yourself, mistress. If you want to take a chill I won't stop you!'

Solange was watching this little drama with astonishment but Jean pulled her a few yards further along the street.

'Wait, Jean!' she protested and he released her reluctantly.

As they watched, the gaunt-faced chairman turned the handle on the outside of the door, effectively imprisoning his unfortunate fare.

'You rogues!' shouted the old woman furiously. 'Open this door at once and let me out. You shan't get a penny out of me for this impudence. Not one penny! Do you hear me?'

Solange said, 'Shouldn't we help her, Jean?'

Jean shook his head, 'Better not to interfere. 'Tis none of our business.'

'But that poor old woman!'

The two chairmen now strolled nonchalantly away, leaving the chair in the middle of the road. Three men on horseback were approaching from the far end of the street.

'We should help her,' Solange repeated uneasily.

As he passed, one of the riders thumped on the roof of the sedan chair with his fist and his two companions roared with laughter at the old woman's plight. Unable to stand idly by a moment longer, Solange rushed forward and before anyone guessed her intentions she had turned the handle of the door.

'Make haste and get out, mistress!' she cried.

The two chairmen, seeing what she had done, began to run back towards them. Unconcerned, the three horsemen had ridden on and so Jean was forced to take his place beside his impetuous sister who was helping the elderly lady from the sedan. To their surprise they saw that she was swathed in blankets and had pulled a large mob cap well down over her ears.

Seeing their surprised looks she said, 'I have just come from the King's Bath. My maid usually accompanies me but she is indisposed and my son is at work.' She smiled at Solange. 'I don't know how to thank you, my child. What is the world coming to?' She shook her head in despair. 'These chairmen get worse each year. Rogues and scoundrels, the lot of them! 'Tis nothing short of scandalous.' As the chairmen reached them she fumbled in her purse, withdrew two pennies and held them out.

'Take it or leave it!' she said fiercely. 'You won't get another penny out of me and I shall see to it that I never hire either of you again. The stocks would be too good for the likes of you but if I ever see you there I shall throw my rotten fruit with a good heart!'

One of the men spat disparagingly but the other snatched the money from her hand. They began to threaten and bluster, saying that she had swindled them but Jean, his fists raised, took a step forward. He was obviously much younger and fitter than either of them and exchanging glances they decided against a show of force. With a final oath and a rude gesture they took up the sedan chair and hurried away in search of further victims.

'Good riddance!' the old woman said forcefully, pulling her blankets closer.

Jean said, 'Perhaps we could accompany you to your home. Do you think you could ride the horse?'

The old lady eyed it dubiously and then shook her head.

'I'll walk,' she said. 'I am well wrapped up. But if you would accompany me I would feel much safer. Bath is no place for the weak although 'tis marginally better than it used to be. Most of the streets are lit at night now which is a great improvement. Are you two new to the town?'

'Very new!' laughed Jean. 'We have only just set foot in it! It certainly promises plenty of excitement.'

They introduced themselves and learned that the old lady's name was Cooper. They made their way towards her home, turning right into Cheap Street and then left again. As they went she learned from them the reasons for their presence in the town and in turn told them a little about the various buildings they passed.

Jean listened eagerly but Solange, marvelling at the sights, was lost in a world of her own. In spite of the rude behaviour of the chairmen and the old woman's critical remarks about Bath, she felt an immediate and overwhelming rapport with the city and its inhabitants. She was impressed by the tall buildings, but not awed; she had been incensed by the chairmen, but not dismayed. She felt towards the town like a mother with a naughty child – exasperated but still fond. From now on Bath was *her* town, she told herself gleefully, and felt that her life could start in earnest. All of her past had been no more than a prelude to this day. Choked with emotion she could find no words to explain how she felt.

She only knew that she had come home.

When they arrived at number fourteen High Street Solange was startled out of her reverie to learn that she was to lodge temporarily with the old woman.

'For a few days, maybe longer,' Jean told her.

'But suppose I don't –' Solange began but he hastily brushed aside her protests.

'Mistress Cooper is without a maid at present,' he told her. ''Tis the most fortunate coincidence.'

'Polly is sick,' said Mistress Cooper.

Jean nodded eagerly, 'So you can take her place, Soli, until she recovers and while you find something more permanent. I shan't be far away. Louise's family live in Cock Lane which is over that way.' He waved a hand vaguely.

Mistress Cooper smiled at Solange. 'Do say yes, Sally,' she urged. 'I shan't eat you, my dear, and it seems there is no room for you where your brother is going.'

Solange tried to hide her disappointment.

'None at all,' said Jean firmly in response to Solange's unspoken plea. 'I told you that when you first mooted the idea of coming to Bath.' He lowered his voice. 'Our meeting with Mistress Cooper is a godsend. You can help her in the house until her own girl returns to work and then we will think again. I have told her that you were highly thought of by the Gadburys in Devon and that should she want a reference they would supply one.' He leaned towards her and muttered, 'Look *pleased*, for pity's sake!'

Instead a stubborn look settled on his sister's face. 'And suppose I won't go?' she hissed. 'Suppose I say I shall –'

'Then you can go hang!' he snapped. 'Fend for yourself. I have done my part by bringing you to Bath. I have my own way to make. If you turn down this opportunity you are more foolish than I thought!'

Jean's patience was at an end. He was anxious to be reunited with the Reys and spoke more harshly than he intended.

Solange turned abruptly away from him, wrestling with her thoughts. She had no real objection to lodging with the old lady but she was mortified by the speed with which Jean had seized his chance to be rid of her.

Seeing her reluctance, Mistress Cooper said tactfully, 'Well, I must go in out of the cold or I shall most certainly take a chill. Follow me in, Sally, if you decide to stay. I'll leave the door ajar.'

As soon as she had gone Jean turned to Solange. 'Listen, Soli, you must not spoil things between me and Louise! After all these years I am longing to see her. You can't expect me to turn up on their doorstep with an extra mouth for them to feed. I will not do it and there's an end to it. They have been generous enough to me already. You said you would fend for yourself if I brought you to Bath but at least I have found you a bed for a few nights. 'Tis only until you can find somewhere better.' He pursed his lips despairingly. 'Oh, Soli! Look at you – what a long face! You truly are an ungrateful baggage!'

Seeing his wretched expression, Solange's resentment began to melt away. What he said was true, she reflected. He had agreed to bring her against his better judgement and she had already caused him some anxiety. It would not do to antagonise him further for she too was looking forward to meeting Louise and her family and was hoping to create a favourable impression with them. She certainly did not want Jean to speak unkindly of her to his future in-laws.

Reluctant to give in too easily she muttered, 'She keeps calling me Sally!'

'What of it?' he demanded. ''Tis a good English name. I thought you had a taste for all things English.'

Solange shrugged. Then with as good grace as she could muster she said, 'For a few nights then, Jean. Just to set your mind at ease.'

'Good girl!' he said with relief and stooped to kiss her briefly. 'I must be off to find Louise. 'Tis so long since we have met I admit I am a little nervous!'

'She should think herself most fortunate,' Solange assured him. 'If she doesn't want you as her husband, I will have something to say to her!'

He smiled. 'Your heart is in the right place,' he told her and kissed her again. Then he tugged at the horse's reins.

Solange watched him go with a sudden lump in her throat. Soon he would be lost to her, no longer her beloved brother but Louise's husband, he would be part of the Rey family. She tried to imagine Jean as a married man with a wife preparing his supper and a child bouncing on his knee but found it impossible. Would Louise make him a good wife, she wondered, and would he like being a weaver?

She had a sudden memory of the little bakery in La Rochelle and unexpectedly a wave of homesickness washed over her. For a moment she allowed the past few years to roll back and memories she thought were gone for ever returned with great clarity. She saw a younger Jean, bending over the trough, almost up to his elbows in flour and water; Maman was busy with the *brioche*, holding the dough while Grandmère –

poor, dear Grandmère — worked in the extra butter. She even saw herself in clogs and apron, pattering in and out of the picture, with her arms full of wood for the fire . . .

But now Jean had turned the corner and she shook herself free of the memories. She sniffed hard and wiped her eyes on the corner of her shawl. Then, with a scarcely discernible sigh, she set her mouth, straightened her back and went into number fourteen.

Mistress Cooper proved to be even older than Solange had at first thought — a small, bird-like woman who, widowed for the past ten years, had nonetheless raised three sons. Of these, the youngest was in the weaving trade, working in Broad Street, and was married to a 'flighty young wench' by the name of Lucy. The second boy had died of smallpox at the age of nine and Ned, the oldest, was employed in a nearby quarry.

'Twenty-eight, he is,' she told Solange as she prepared a hot toddy for both of them, 'and the first fifteen years engraved on my soul until the day I die. Oh, what a trial he was as a boy. Always ailing. You wouldn't think so to see him now. Nearly six foot tall and strong as a horse. Takes after his father, Ned does.' She smiled proudly at the thought of her son. 'But such a sickly child. I was at my wits' end. You have no idea what I went through with Ned.'

The old lady stirred a generous spoonful of honey into each bowl and handed one to Solange. 'The young women buzzed around him like bees but he wasn't interested. Too busy with his quarrying.' She sipped her drink and then smiled, 'You can't wed a quarry! That's what I used to tell him but he just laughed. There's nothing he doesn't know about mining stone. Nothing at all!'

Solange asked, 'And did he wed?'

'Lord bless you, no! But he came very near it. He fell in love with a girl called Rose but it wasn't to be. Poor Ned. He'll never wed now.'

'What happened?' asked Solange.

The toddy, a fragrant mixture of milk, rum and honey, was going to her head rather delightfully.

The old lady tutted. 'Why, the poor child died, that's what happened! She took ill and faded away. Her parents took it very hard, poor souls. An only child she was, you see, and they doted on her.'

'Did she love him back?' asked Solange blinking a little.

'Of course she did!' Mistress Cooper bridled a little at the idea that any woman could resist Ned. 'And would have wed him, too, but the good Lord had other plans. Rose took to having hysterical fits and the physician tried everything. Pumping and bucketing and . . .'

Solange gazed at her wide-eyed. 'What on earth is that?'

'Why, they're cures, of course.' She laughed at Solange's ignorance. 'No need to look so alarmed. The physician recommended daily attendance at the King's Bath. They poured the hot water over the afflicted part – in her case it was her head. They used buckets at first but then the doctor thought that wasn't hot enough so they pumped it over her as hot as she could bear it.'

'But it didn't work?'

'No, sadly not. The poor girl grew worse, with palpitations of the heart and terrible pains in her head and I don't know what else. They took a second opinion but it was too late. She went into a decline and that was the end of her. Broke my poor Ned's heart. He's never looked at another woman since. Not so much as a glance.'

'How sad,' said Solange and without warning two large tears rolled down her cheeks.

Startled, Mistress Cooper cried, ''Pon my soul, Sally, but you're a soft-hearted creature!'

She was handing Solange a handkerchief when there was a timid knock on the kitchen door and Mistress Cooper opened it to admit a large, shapeless woman with a covered basket on her arm. This, it appeared, was Polly's mother with the news that her daughter's 'sickness' was due to her 'condition' which in turn was the responsibility of a certain young soldier who had recently befriended her. This being so Polly would shortly be marrying the young soldier and would no longer be working for Mistress Cooper.

'So I've come for my daughter's Sunday clothes,' she told Mistress Cooper, 'and her comb and mirror, her second-best petticoat, and her knife and spoon.'

When these had been handed over she managed a brief apology for the inconvenience and disappeared as suddenly as she had come.

Mistress Cooper sat down heavily and looked at Solange. 'They come and go,' she said. 'And her barely sixteen. Oh, the silly girl! I sometimes despair. So, it seems there's a permanent job for you here if you would like it. We might suit one another – we might not. Will you give it a try, Sally?'

With the toddy warming her stomach Solange was finding it hard to concentrate.

She nodded slowly and said, 'Thank you and I will, mistress, but my name is Soli, not Sally.'

'Solly?' Mistress Cooper frowned. 'What nonsense! Solly is a man's name. No, no, that will never do. Sally is much more suitable. I shall call you Sally.'

Solange nodded sleepily, 'Whatever you say and thank you kindly.'

And then, to her new mistress's astonishment, she folded her arms on the table, rested her head on her arms and was immediately asleep.

Early next morning a freezing mist hung over the quarry set high above Bath and through this white haze a watery sun filtered through the branches of the bare trees. There was no breeze. Half-way up the track that led up the hillside a tall, well-built man was making his way towards the quarry, his feet searching unerringly among the frozen wheel ruts, his large hands thrust deep into the pockets of his coat. This had once seen better days but now the stout cloth was impregnated with the pale dust among which he spent most of his working life. He walked steadily, yet appeared unhurried and his head was bent a little as though he examined the ground over which he walked. His dark brows were drawn together in a frown of concentration, his face was set in quiet lines and his brown eyes were thoughtful.

At the top of the track he turned as he always did to look down at the town which lay five hundred feet below him. Today its outline was hidden by the mist and the river's strong curve had also blurred into the landscape. For a moment Ned Cooper stared around him, then he continued his way past the stables where the horse was kept and on to the shack which doubled as an office and implement store.

Taking a key from his pocket he let himself in and, without removing his coat, set about lighting a fire in the rusting iron stove on which Old Stanley would shortly be making the men's cocoa.

That done, he rubbed his cold hands together for warmth before turning his attention to the mass of papers on the large trestle which served as a desk. These papers had been separated into various piles, each one weighted down by a small sample of the stone which was mined at the quarry. The invoices were kept under a lump of ragstone, a coarse, brown limestone full of minute shells. This so-called ragstone formed the top layer of stone and extended to a depth of several feet.

A piece of Bath or free stone topped the pile of orders – a hard, white, finely textured stone which, many years ago, had been cream in colour. Over the years the sap had dried out of it changing its colour to a soft white. This stone lay beneath the ragstone in a broad deep layer which varied in thickness from twenty to thirty feet. A pile of drawings and plans was kept in place by an insignificant lump of crystalline spar.

Ned pulled a letter from beneath the fourth weight (a small knob of the pitching stone used to pave the streets) and read it thoughtfully. It concerned a request for advice from a local stonemason and with a slight sigh Ned took up a handy quill, dipped it into the inkwell and began to cover a sheet of paper with his large but well shaped handwriting.

He was half-way down the page when Old Stanley scuttled in. He was small and wiry and sixty-seven years old and had finally accepted a surface job after a lifetime spent underground. With a quick tug of his hair and a brief, 'Mornin', Master Cooper, sir,' he snatched up the kettle and took it outside to fill it from the rain butt.

One by one the quarrymen arrived, stamping their feet to warm them, their noses red with cold. Mr Bridges, the 'gaffer', would be in later – there was no early rising for the quarry's owner who was content to leave the management of the place in the capable hands of his foreman. He never let a day pass, however, without putting in an appearance and when he did arrive he would discuss the day's business with Ned. Later he would take a stroll, admiring the towering stacks of pale stone slabs which reached to twice a man's height. On some days he would stand for a few moments beside the horse crane watching critically as the men lowered the blocks of stone into the waggons. He would often walk a few yards down the carriage road with the loaded waggon, one hand resting on the leading horse's bridle as though, by his attentions, he could ensure the load's safe arrival in the town.

He was a portly man, puffed up with his own importance, who sincerely believed that his appearances at the quarry were vital to the men's morale and the proper functioning of the business. He was totally unaware that its success, modest though it was, was directly attributable to the skill of his foreman, Ned Cooper, and the respect in which the men held him.

Ned finished his letter, sanded, rolled and sealed it and reached for the next order. Outside the quarry was coming to life as the horse was led from its stable, its breath white in the cold air, its hooves sounding on the frozen ground. The men had finished their hot drinks and now came in to collect their tools, each one according to his own line of work — crowbars, mattocks, sledge hammers and lifting dogs. Ned had a cheerful word for each man as they made their way to the opening of the inclined shaft which, cut deep into the hillside, led down to the level on which they were working.

When he was once more alone Ned tried to focus his attention on a letter from a firm asking for extra time in which to settle an account for two tons of slab stone. His mind wandered, however, to the new servant his mother had engaged, with whom he had exchanged a few words the night before. Sally Something-or-other, of Huguenot extraction apparently — although she looked as English as they came with those large blue eyes and small straight nose.

'She made me laugh!' he said aloud as though to justify the time he was wasting on her. He stared at the letter with unseeing eyes. Yes, she seemed wholesome enough but was it right for his mother to employ the girl straight off the street without sending for her reference? She might be lazy or shiftless. She might even be light-fingered. They had only the brother's word that she had been successfully employed elsewhere. His mother was so impulsive. With a shrug of his shoulders he turned to concentrate on the letter.

'Lunn!' he said suddenly. That was the girl's surname. Sally Lunn. Not very French but the girl had explained earnestly that Lunn was her father's 'chosen' name and she wanted to share it.

He smiled at the memory.

'Sally Lunn!' he murmured, then shook his head in mock dismay. The girl was already installed and his mother, gullible as ever, seemed sure she would prove suitable. He would watch and wait. With a final effort, he returned to the letter and forced his wavering attention to the job in hand.

Chapter Seven

SUNDAY CAME WITH a flurry of snow, which did not settle, with attendance at church in the morning and with a sermon that Solange found interminably long. She had been invited to spend the day with the Reys but had turned it down in order to satisfy her curiosity about Ned Cooper. She considered him something of a challenge and was eager to know him better.

They sat down to a dinner of roast beef cooked above a batter pudding which was also shared by Mistress Cooper's elderly sister and her husband. At Ned's request Solange was allowed to join them at table instead of eating a solitary meal in the kitchen as she normally did.

After dinner they all played a game of charades at which Solange (or Sally as she now thought of herself) excelled. From time to time she amused herself by trying to flirt with Ned, but he would have none of it and persisted in treating her like a precocious child so that she went to bed feeling very put out and wishing she had accepted the invitation from Louise's family.

The following Tuesday Mistress Cooper prepared to attend the hot bath. Her physician had prescribed twice-weekly visits to the King's Bath (where the water was hottest) as a means of holding old age at bay and as she and Sally prepared for the visit the old lady explained the medical thinking behind the treatment.

'At my age,' she told Sally, 'the body shrinks and is less able to withstand the rigours of the climate or the onset of disease. The hot water plumps out the flesh, you see, and restores the vitality.' She held out her bony wrists as proof of this theory and Sally nodded obligingly. 'I feel so much better since following this regime. I can't tell you how weak I was before – nor how low in spirits. Doctor Bishop is my sister's doctor also and we both worship him. Gout has been the cross she has to bear and his treatment has given her wonderful ease. Some of the so-called doctors in this town are nothing more than quacks and 'tis a great relief to have a doctor you can trust.'

'So is that all there is to it?' asked Sally. 'Two hot baths a week?'

'Two baths and the elixir,' said Mistress Cooper. 'Didn't I mention that? Oh, that is most important. Three drops in water first thing in the morning. The elixir is the doctor's own secret recipe and he alone can prescribe it. I truly am a changed woman. Ask Ned. Ask anyone. They will vouch for my extraordinary recovery.'

Warmly dressed they set off to walk to the bath, a bundle of blankets for the return journey tucked under Sally's arm.

'You must watch me from the street above,' Mistress Cooper told her. 'You'll see me in the water and I will wave when my time is up so that you can come round to meet me at the door. No need to help me on with

165

my clothes. I can manage perfectly well with the cloth woman's help and it gets so crowded in there. I shall call a sedan and will ride home while you walk alongside as Polly used to do. Oh, that foolish girl! I wonder how she is faring with her soldier?' She frowned. 'What was I saying? Oh, yes. Those chairmen only play their pranks on the unaccompanied so we should have no nonsense from them today.'

They made their way at a leisurely pace past the bustling Market House where a surly-faced man of indeterminate age was locked in the stocks. For a moment they watched a group of bare-footed children who were tormenting him with mocking taunts and small clods of earth which they threw with unerring aim.

'Poor man,' said Sally. 'I wonder what he has done.' Mistress Cooper shrugged her thin shoulders. 'Skulduggery of some kind. They used to pin up a notice spelling out the crime but they don't seem to bother so much these days. There's talk of taking them down – the stocks and pillory I mean – but how shall we deter the wretches then? Don't waste your time on the wretch. He will serve as a warning to others. This town is plagued by his kind, rogues and tricksters who prey on gullible folk – Ned among them. They know he has a kind heart and take advantage of him most cruelly. "There but for the grace of God go I," he says, but I tell him he's a soft-hearted fool.'

Sally caught the man's eye and hastily looked away. 'He looks harmless enough,' she said.

'He *is* harmless, now,' retorted her mistress. 'You'd be harmless with your arms and legs in that contraption.' She stared. 'I've seen him there before. A regular, you might say. I recognize his hair, fair and curly, and those bright blue eyes.'

'He might have been handsome once.'

'Well, it must have been a long time ago! Miserable creature. The town is riddled with men like that. I blame the authorities.'

They walked on.

'Can't they do anything?' said Sally.

'Huh! You may well ask! A crowd of weak-kneed, lily-livered cowards. Couldn't say "boo" to a goose. Bath needs a firm hand but where are we to find such a man?'

They passed the Abbey church, dawdled past the tennis court watching the players for a while and finally reached the bath.

Ten minutes later Sally found herself leaning on the stone balustrade with a dozen other spectators, enjoying the antics of the bathers in the steaming water below them. Beside her a man waved and called out something to a woman bather. Solange did not catch what he said but the woman laughed and stuck out her tongue in return. A woman standing on Sally's left cupped her hands to her mouth and called down instructions.

'Move your arms, Oliver. Remember what the physician told you! Move them round and round!'

But Oliver merely waved a hand in acknowledgement and began to swim away across the bath. In the water a woman ducked her child repeatedly, ignoring its screams of fright. At the far end of the bath a blind man, accompanied by a sighted friend, leaned forward and splashed the water repeatedly into his sightless eyes. Immediately below her two women clung together, giggling like children as a young man floated past, his yellow regulation drawers clinging to his reed-like legs. Raised voices echoed from the damp walls, steam curled in the air and the noise was incredible.

Sally searched among the bathers for a glimpse of Mistress Cooper and suddenly recognised her. Dressed in a shapeless yellow bathing dress, her diminutive employer was wading resolutely through the steaming water which came up to her chest.

'I see you, mistress!' cried Sally, waving frantically, and receiving a cheerful smile in return.

A plump man pushed in between Sally and the woman next to her and his lurcher dog thrust its head through the stone balustrade and began to bark frantically, almost throttling himself in an effort to join someone he had recognised in the water below.

'Hold your noise, Jack!' his owner entreated. 'She's not drowning!'

The dog, however, remained unconvinced, and straining desperately against his collar, redoubled his efforts. Suddenly an urchin boy appeared beside them, his eyes fixed hopefully on the dog's owner.

'Chuck in a penny, Master Dalmer!' he urged. 'I'll fetch it for you quicker'n blinking!'

The man growled, 'Be off, you scamp! I've no penny about me today!'

Undeterred, the boy grinned up at him. ''Course you have!' he insisted. 'Just a penny, Master Dalmer. Just one.'

'I've told you, no! My purse is at home.'

To Sally's surprise the lad then clambered up on to the balustrade and snatched the man's hat from his head.

'Hey! You give that back this instant!' roared Master Dalmer and he made frantic efforts to retrieve it.

The dog, sensing further excitement, withdrew its head to see what was happening and, leaping up and down, added his voice to the din.

'Chuck in a penny,' the boy insisted, 'and the hat's yours!'

'Go to the Devil!'

'Then say farewell to your fine hat!' cried the boy and held it out over the steaming water.

Master Dalmer's dog now added to his problems, twisting his lead round the man's legs, apparently determined to pull him off balance.

Impulsively Sally drew a penny from her purse. 'Here!' she told the boy, holding it up for him to see. He made a grab for it but she was too quick and with a flick of her wrist dropped it into the water.

The boy tossed the hat back to its owner and then, with a disregard for the winter weather, slipped deftly out of his tattered clothes and climbed on to the balustrade as naked as the day he was born. Passers by watched, either amused or scandalised, but before anyone could make a move towards the boy he had pinched his nose, shouted a warning to those below him and jumped into the water. He disappeared with a loud splash and the spectators leaned over to watch as enraged bathers shouted for the Sergeant of the bath to apprehend him. The boy, however, was making his way underwater and suddenly reappeared by the exit, redfaced but triumphant, holding aloft his penny. Despite the cold, he ran up the steps and, dodging his pursuers, disappeared into the interior of the building to re-emerge a moment later in the street.

Scampering back to Sally he gave her a 'thumbs up' sign and then wriggled back into his tattered clothes.

Impressed, Sally said, 'That was very good!'

'Nothing to it!' he assured her. 'I should have been born a fish!' And he winked cheekily and ran off along the street to spend his hard-earned penny.

Master Dalmer smiled at Sally. 'It seems I owe you a penny and I must thank you for the return of my hat. May I know your name?'

''Tis Sally Lunn,' she told him. 'And think nothing of it. I couldn't see so fine a hat drowned before my eyes.'

He laughed and for a moment they regarded each other curiously. He saw a trim young woman with a thick shawl over her faded blue dress, whose fair curls were mostly covered by a neat white cap. She saw a plump man in his early middle age with shrewd eyes in a humorous face.

'I'm newly come to this town,' she told him. 'I work for Mistress Cooper, there.' She pointed out the diminutive figure of her employer who now rested in one of the alcoves along the wall of the bath.

'And I am a master baker and have lived in Bath all my life,' he told her, 'like my father and grandfather before me.'

'Was it your wife you were calling to?'

'My sister. This noisy animal is her beloved Jack.'

Sally began to tell him about the Luyons' bakery in La Rochelle but at that moment his sister called up to him and pointed towards the exit.

'Ah, the session is finished,' he told Sally. 'Please excuse me but I must find her a sedan. It has been a pleasure meeting you.'

As though aware that he was soon to be reunited with his owner, the dog began to tug at his lead and Sally watched man and dog for a moment before turning her attention once more to the fascinating scene below her. Time passed very quickly and, before she knew what was happening, it was time to help Mistress Cooper into a sedan chair for the journey home. On this occasion, to Sally's secret relief, the chairmen proved to be honest men and they arrived at number fourteen without incident.

'So what did you think of it?' Mistress Cooper demanded, as Sally ran the warming pan over the sheet and helped her mistress into the bed.

'I was very impressed!' Sally admitted with a smile. 'It looks great fun. With a remedy like that I should never want to be cured!'

A few days later Sally made her way up the path towards the quarry in search of Ned Cooper. After much deliberation and in spite of his mother's insistence that he was a confirmed bachelor, Sally had decided he was worthy of her attention.

With this in mind she had told her mistress a lie and this pricked her conscience a little as she staggered up the final incline, one hand held to her painful stitch in her left side. Mistress Cooper believed that Sally was spending her day off at the Reys. Although this was not true Sally had almost convinced herself that the lie was justified on the grounds that it would cause Mistress Cooper less anxiety than the truth.

Sally had given Ned a great deal of thought of late and had convinced herself that he was a tragic figure – a man for whom a solitary life stretched interminably ahead; a man who, left to his own devices would never betray the memory of his beloved Rose and would passively accept the loveless future which Fate had allotted him. His mother, it seemed, had resigned herself to her son's misfortune. Only Sally could avert the disaster and save him from the miserable existence which would be his after the death of his mother.

She stopped outside the shack to catch her breath and plan her opening sentence but at that moment the door opened and Ned was staring at her, a look of amazement on his face.

'Sally!' he said. 'Whatever brings you up here?' His expression changed. 'I trust there's nothing wrong at home. My mother –?'

'No, no!' Sally assured him. 'All's well.'

Taking her by the arm, he led her into the smoky warmth inside where she pulled off her gloves and held her hands over the stove, rubbing them briskly while she strove to remember her little speech.

'So, to what do I owe this honour?' he asked. 'And why are you not at the Reys as planned?'

She took a deep breath, thankful that they were alone together and aware that to anyone else her words would sound precocious.

'I thought it was time I inspected your beloved

quarry,' she said, her tone deliberately light and teasing. 'I thought if I asked you would most certainly refuse me so I thought I would take you by surprise. Take the bull by the horns, so to speak.' She gave him a sideways glance and laughed, 'And here I am.'

For a moment he regarded her in silence and she thought he was annoyed but at last the corners of his mouth twitched with amusement and she breathed with relief.

'But the Reys must be wondering where you are,' he said and she felt her cheeks redden slightly.

'They weren't expecting me,' she told him. 'Not really. Oh, Ned, please don't be angry. You talk so often about the quarry that I . . .'

She faltered to a stop. His expression was impossible to read – was he aware of the true purpose of her visit? If he was would he be angry or flattered? A new thought occurred to her. Perhaps it would be good for him to know that another woman was interested in him.

'I thought you might be kind and show me round,' she suggested boldly, 'unless it's bad luck or somesuch. Do any women work in the quarry?'

'Not one.'

'Would the men mind?' He shrugged without answering and she sensed that he was considering her proposition. 'I wouldn't cause any trouble. I'd behave myself,' she added.

His gaze was disconcerting and she could not decide if he thought her a wilful child or, as she hoped, a young woman with initiative.

'Do say something, Ned!' she protested at last when

she could stand the uncertainty no longer. 'Will you show me your quarry or have I walked all this way for nothing?' Suppose he refused? Suppose he told his mother of her deception? For the first time she began to doubt the wisdom of the undertaking.

''Tis hardly the place for a woman,' he said and she saw the uncertainty in his eyes.

'You'd be with me,' she answered. 'I'd come to no harm. Please, Ned.'

He was wavering.

Slowly he said, 'Those shoes are hardly suitable for a trip underground.'

So he was going to take her. Her heart leaped.

'They are stout enough,' she said quickly. 'At least, they are the stoutest I have.'

'You will need a stout heart as well,' he told her. ''Tis dark as pitch except for the candles and there are puddles and —'

She interrupted him, 'Don't try to frighten me. I really want to see it.'

'Frighten you?' He shook his head. ''Twas a friendly warning, nothing more. A quarry is no place for the faint hearted.'

She bristled. 'Do you think me faint-hearted then?'

He laughed. 'Indeed I don't. I doubt you have ever been that in your whole life! I will take you down if you wish. Give me a few moments to finish what I was doing.'

While he fussed with the papers on his desk Sally inspected the room, trying to hide her disapproval of its untidy appearance and imagining how it could be improved with a good spring clean and a pair of decent curtains. A strange picture pinned to the wall attracted her attention and she moved to examine it. It appeared to be a haphazard collection of irregular star shapes.

'What an odd picture!' she exclaimed. 'Is it a mosaic?'

Ned smiled. ''Tis no picture but a map of the quarry,' he told her. 'A plan of the workings underground.' He moved to stand beside her and she fought to keep her eyes on the map as his finger traced one of the shapes. 'It shows us which areas have been worked and where the stone columns remain. It has to be updated at the end of each week.'

He went to a cupboard and slipped a candle and a tinder into his pocket. Then he picked up a ring of keys. As he did so there was a knock at the door and Ned called out, 'Come in!'

A small man entered, roughly dressed, his fingers blue with cold. He might have been any age between forty and sixty and looked very ill at ease. He gave one brief glance at Sally then turned back to his superior.

'What is it, Mackley?' Ned asked.

''Tis that new man, Stubbs,' he blurted out. 'I'm not a one to grouse about any man – there's good and there's bad and I've worked with all of them – but, begging your pardon, master, my men's not happy about him. Not happy at all. And not only mine, there's others feel the same way but won't speak up. Useless he is – Stubbs, I mean – and that's a fact. Can't stay off the drink, sir, and we turned a blind eye at first but 'tis getting beyond a joke. He can't be trusted to do anything without someone stands over him all the time.'

175

Ned said, 'You did right to tell me, Mackley. If he can't pull his weight –'

'Oh, but 'tisn't only that. He's like to cause an accident. Careless as well as useless and that's the truth of it. They set him to collecting up the gob for the wall but he dropped a rock on Turner's foot and you know Turner's temper when he's riled. Turner went for him and would have killed him if the men hadn't held him back. There'll be violence done, begging your pardon, if you don't get rid of him.'

Sally saw Ned's mouth tighten. 'He shall go at the end of the day,' he promised. 'Let the men know that but don't tell Stubbs. I'll do that myself.'

The man's expression changed to one of relief. 'Thank you, master! Thank you. That'll be welcome news, I can tell you.' He smiled, briefly revealing a few discoloured teeth. 'I'll be getting back below then – and thank you again.'

When he had gone Sally looked enquiringly at Ned.

He shrugged. 'I thought he was worth a chance,' he told her. 'The poor wretch came asking for work and I took pity on him. Thought he might make himself useful doing odd jobs for the men. Seems I was wrong.'

'What's gob?' she asked.

'Gob? 'Tis just our name for the lumps of scrap stone. When the block is freed from its bed 'tis an irregular shape and the rough masons have to trim it. There's a lot of waste.'

He locked the store and pocketed the key before leading the way towards a rectangular entrance in the steep face of the hill. Sally pulled her shawl more closely around her shoulders. In front of her the entrance to the quarry sloped steeply and led down into darkness. There might be rats down there or bats but whatever she encountered she would not complain, she told herself. She was with Ned and that was the main thing. He was enjoying the pleasure of her company (at least she hoped he was) and she would make every effort to impress him with her intelligent grasp of the subject. If he thought of her as a featherbrain she would disillusion him.

'Shall I take your arm?' he said.

'No, thank you, I can manage,' she replied but then immediately regretted it. In her effort to appear self-reliant she had lost the chance to be closer to him. She walked a little further and then pretended to trip.

'Oh dear!' she laughed. 'Perhaps I spoke too rashly.'

To her relief his strong fingers closed around her arm and he kept her close to him as they proceeded down the steep slope which grew muddier with every step.

The daylight was gradually left behind and she stared round somewhat fearfully as Ned released her arm to light the candle. They moved on and, twenty yards further in, the ground levelled but now there was no light at all except the pale wavering gleam from the candle which threw shadows over the walls and roof and gleamed in the water that lay over much of the ground. The steady drip of water accompanied them and their voices echoed eerily. Ahead of them voices murmured and the sound of metal on stone came clearly to their ears. It was impossible to avoid the puddles and Sally could already feel water seeping coldly into her shoes.

Ned said, 'Are you sure you want to go on? You can change your mind, you know. It really isn't –'

'I want to go on,' she insisted.

The sounds of activity grew louder and suddenly they rounded a corner and found themselves in a vast cavern-like area. Here several small groups of men worked by the light of their tallow candles which either jutted from the muddy ground or were wedged into crevices in the rock walls. Each group consisted of four or five men.

'One man in each group is the ganger,' Ned told her in a low voice. 'He employs the others. I pay him for the work they do and he pays them out of the money.'

They watched the nearest group in silence as they toiled at their separate tasks, illuminated in the glow from the candle, isolated from the other groups by the darkness, apparently oblivious to everything around them.

Ned had blown out his candle and he no longer held her arm but Sally stood as near to him as she could, hoping he might notice the lavender water which she had sprinkled lavishly over her person before dressing. He leaned down to explain something and as she turned towards him she thought how near their lips were and how easily, under different circumstances, they might have kissed.

She tried hard to concentrate on what he was telling her.

'The rock lies in horizontal beds,' he was saying, 'and there are natural faults in it which run vertically. When they can, the men make use of a fault, treating it as the end of a block. Then they have less cutting to do. They scrape out a space above the rock, that's called "jadding", then cut downwards to the bottom of it. That's the stage these men have reached with this block.'

'Can we stay until they finish it?' Sally asked, becoming interested in spite of herself.

He shook his head. 'It would take too long. The stone is hard to cut, but we'll find a group that are more advanced.'

He moved on through the darkness and Sally followed demurely at his heels. Her own feet were wet and cold and she resigned herself to the knowledge that her shoes were ruined. The visit was proving expensive, she reflected, but if it prompted Ned to take an interest in her it would be well worthwhile.

The darkness deepened and then eased again as they rounded another corner and came upon a gang of men, intent upon their work. Ned pointed out the outline of the block they were removing from the rock wall.

'See the bottom edge of it? That is resting on a natural bed where it parts from the layer of stone beneath it. The stone they are working on is the middle section and when that one is removed it will be easy for the men to climb into the space it leaves and work on the blocks on either side. The middle stone is called the wrist.'

Surreptitiously Sally withdrew her left foot from a puddle and searched unsuccessfully for a drier place to stand.

'Why the wrist?' she asked.

Ned shrugged. 'I can't tell you that. It has always been the wrist as long as anyone can remember. 'Twas so-called in my father's time and his father's. Most likely the Romans called it the wrist also.'

Seeing her surprise he said, 'Oh yes, they quarried the golden oolite as long ago as that. 'Tis a beautiful stone and the masons love to work it because of its adaptability. It can be cut in any direction, you see, without splitting, and it throws off very little dust because it contains sap.'

'Sap?' Sally echoed. 'Like a tree, d'you mean?'

'Sap is moisture – water in other words. The stone has to be left to dry out before being cut. We call it green block until it dries out and hardens.' He sighed. 'I doubt we make as good use of the stone as we should. Builders are so old-fashioned. They still choose wood when they could choose stone. Still, one or two of the new houses going up in Bath are being built in stone, I'm pleased to say, and hopefully other people will follow their example. We have this wonderful building material on our doorstep – enough to rebuild Bath and half of London! Wood is so much more vulnerable – it reacts to changes of temperature and can be eaten away by insects.' He sighed again. 'Wood was good enough for our grandfathers, I grant you, but this is the seventeenth century, for heaven's sake!'

Sally smiled. 'Your mother told me that you were wedded to your quarry; that you love the stone more than you love her! I can well believe it!'

Ned's laugh rang out. 'She said that? I hope she exaggerated! She makes me sound very dull.'

'Oh no!' Sally protested. 'Not dull. Passionate, perhaps. You are passionate about your work and that is a great compliment, surely.' He made no answer and she wondered how passionate he might be in other circumstances. Had he been passionate with Rose? She felt a pang of jealousy which she smothered hastily as she once more gave him her full attention.

He went on with his explanation. 'You see how they have driven wedges into the gap at the bottom?' He pointed. 'When the side cuts have been made they will lever up the block until it splits from the wall behind it. Do you understand?'

She nodded. She did not fully understand his explanation but could hardly tell him that she was content merely to stand beside him and listen to his voice. In the concealing gloom she took the opportunity to study him as she had not been able to do before. He seemed a quiet almost withdrawn man but had Rose found him so or had her death changed him? Was Ned the sort of man with whom she, Sally, could live for the rest of her life? Could she ever love him? Would he ever give her the chance? If she compared him with Simon Pett, she must admit that Simon had excited her whereas Ned intrigued her. Suppose she took hold of his hand and kissed it? How would he react? She dared not risk a rebuff.

With an effort she tried to concentrate upon the information he was giving her, telling herself sternly that she had insisted on this tour of inspection and had professed an interest. The least she could do was to listen.

Ned's enthusiasm was infectious. As he warmed to his theme his voice grew eager and Sally began to appreciate the depth of feeling he felt for the stone which was so much more than his livelihood. Generations of Coopers had spent their lives in these gloomy vaults, wresting the precious stone from its dark home and carrying it into the light of day to beautify the world. The words 'to the glory of God' entered her head and she did not think them excessive.

'Did you ever work down here,' she asked, 'like these men?'

'Most certainly I did,' he assured her. 'My father saw to that. He was foreman here for the last ten years of his life and I never considered working anywhere else. He was determined that I should follow in his footsteps and educated me accordingly. But he insisted that I start at the beginning and learn the hard way and I'm pleased that I did. Oh yes! I can wield a pick with the best of them.' He laughed briefly but then became serious again. 'You have to work with the material to know its true potential.'

They proceeded with the tour until Sally suddenly stumbled and almost fell. When Ned put an arm round her to steady her he realized that she was shivering and chided himself for his neglect.

He at once set down the candle and pulled off his jacket. When Sally realized what he was doing she protested that it was not necessary, but was nevertheless glad when he insisted. The jacket was much too big for her, but it was still warm from Ned's body, and she felt as though his arms were round her.

'Is that better?' he asked.

'Much better, thank you.'

'You should have told me you were cold. I'm a thoughtless wretch!'

'But I wasn't. Or if I was, I scarcely noticed. There was so much to see.'

'We'll go back to the surface now,' he said. 'You've seen enough.'

This time he held out his hand for her. She took it gratefully, and they made their way back to the surface hand in hand, saying little. Once above ground they blinked in the bright sunshine and faced each other uncertainly. In spite of her muddy shoes Sally had enjoyed the experience and told Ned so.

'I did too,' he confessed. 'You are the first lady I have ever taken into the quarry and I was in two minds whether to agree or not.'

He had called her a lady! 'I'm glad you said yes,' she told him. She took off the jacket and returned it to him. 'Walking will warm me,' she assured him.

He caught sight of her ruined shoes and his expression changed.

'Oh please!' she protested untruthfully. 'They were old ones. They don't matter at all.'

'I should buy you another pair.'

'Oh no! I hated them. They pinched my toes.'

Immediately she wished she had kept silent. Together they could have visited the shoemaker and Ned could have seen her slim ankle as she stretched out her foot for the shoemaker's measurements. She cursed her stupidity in refusing his generous offer but now it was too late. He put on his jacket and smiled uncertainly and she realized with regret that the intimacy they had so recently shared in the quarry had been largely brought about by the darkness and was not going to survive the harsh light of day. Up here they were once more uneasy with each other. Or perhaps she had imagined their closeness. Or had imagined that Ned felt something, too.

'Well, Ned,' she said reluctantly, 'I must go. You must have plenty of work to do.'

A sudden thought occurred to her. 'Oh – do you think we should tell your mother that I came here instead of . . .' She fell silent, looking at him appealingly.

'I dare say I shall forget to mention it,' he said with the slow smile she found so attractive.

Surprising herself she said suddenly, 'Rose wouldn't want you to remain single, you know. Not if she really loved you.'

Then, seeing the surprise on his face, she once more cursed her runaway tongue and hurried down the path before he could answer.

Winter took its usual grip on the land. Time passed uneventfully but in February the people of England learned that the throne had been accepted by William of Orange and his wife Mary. After this flutter of excitement had died down life went on again much as before. For Sally, however, the winter had been enlivened by a determined and systematic search for her father which took her to the most unlikely parts of the town. In her spare time (which was little enough) she visited every inn and tavern in Bath; she mingled with the onlookers at bear-baitings and cockfights and lurked on the fringes of wrestling matches. She even attended a dogfight without catching so much as a glimpse of anyone who remotely fitted her father's description.

She scanned the congregation in church each Sunday to no avail and asked at every bakery with no better luck. To every street-seller she met she repeated the vague details which were all she had, but was met invariably with a shake of the head. Whenever she was sent on an errand she went by way of the hot baths so that she could scrutinize the bathers but still she saw no one who could possibly be her father. Very occasionally someone would suggest a further line of enquiry but these proved equally unproductive and she bore her disappointments as well as she could. She remained buoyed up by the hope inspired by her visit to Charity Becket and told herself that her father was living somewhere in Bath and that sooner or later she was *bound* to find him.

On several occasions she was invited to take tea with the Rey family but unhappily these occasions proved somewhat of a trial for all concerned since the Reys did not approve of Sally's fervent enthusiasm for all things English. Although grateful for the new life that England had given them, they chose to remember their birthplace with nostalgia and remained staunchly Huguenot in outlook. They made little effort to learn English and spoke it only when necessary, and they chose their friends from a small circle of fellow refugees with whom they could converse in French and with whom they shared so many memories. Sally's blunt rejection of France wounded their sensibilities and her obsession with her adopted country tried their patience. Only Louise's good-natured interventions prevented a serious rift developing between them.

Louise was a timid girl but for Jean's sake she often spoke up in support of Sally and as the weeks went by a cautious friendship sprang up between the two young women.

In early April, however, a formal betrothal was agreed between Jean and Louise and all other considerations were immediately set aside as preparations were put in hand for the approaching wedding. At the top of the Reys' house a room was being prepared for the newly-weds to share until such time as they could afford a separate home of their own. Louise and her mother began to sew sheets, pillowcases and table-cloths, and Sally spent as much time as she could at the Reys' house, sharing in the excitement.

To her delight Jean decided that her Sunday-best dress would not do justice to the occasion and he bought her a length of blue silk. With the help of Mistress Cooper this was transformed into a new dress, with a close-fitting bodice and full skirt which divided in the front to reveal a striped petticoat.

Two weeks before the wedding Sally and the Coopers attended St Michael's church to hear the banns read and Sally, sitting between Ned and her mistress, was proud to see her brother in the Reys' private pew. She felt that, knowing such fine people, she was at last moving up in the world.

That evening as she paraded her new dress for the first time she was pleased to note that Ned was properly appreciative of her charms.

'You look very fine, Sally,' he told her. 'Don't you agree, Mother?'

Sally twirled gracefully and Mistress Cooper said, 'Very handsome, Sally, but do stand still. You make me dizzy with all that turning.'

'Louise's dress is rose-pink,' Sally told her. 'It suits her complexion admirably. She has a most delicate skin. I think this blue silk goes well with my eyes.'

She glanced hopefully towards Ned but he said nothing.

In the weeks that Sally had been with them Ned had learned something of her excitable nature and understood how easily she could be swept off her feet by a few careless words.

'I shall wear my curls bunched at each side,' Sally told him, 'and your mother is lending me a feathered fan.'

To her disappointment he merely nodded approvingly but made no further comment and after a little more preening Sally felt obliged to retire to her attic room and take off her finery.

The next morning as she peeled apples she asked Mistress Cooper if she didn't think it a 'terrible great shame' that her son would one day be all alone in the world.

'After you are gone,' she pointed out, 'he will have no one to care for him.'

Mistress Cooper, recognizing the ploy, hid a smile and said, 'Don't you fret, Sally, I intend to live for many years yet.'

'But when you *are* called.'

'The Lord will provide.'

'But no wife,' Sally went on, 'and no children! Poor man. My heart fair aches for him!' She sighed elaborately. 'Grandmère always used to say that there is no sadder sight than a lonely old man!'

In fact, to the best of her knowledge, Grandmère had never made such a comment in her life but Sally felt that the old lady's endorsement lent a little weight to the opinion.

'Ned's too set in his ways,' said Mistress Cooper, 'but he's happy enough. Poor dear Rose was the only woman for Ned and I wouldn't encourage him to look for a wife. We live very comfortably together and I doubt he would want to set up home elsewhere. I certainly hope not — Oh, do look what you're about, child! You're dropping the peel on the floor.'

As Sally retrieved it she searched her mind for any other telling remarks which Grandmère might have made but failed to think of any.

Desperately she went on, 'Old men are so helpless. They don't feed themselves properly and —'

'Fetch me some cinnamon, Sally,' the old lady interrupted, 'and then you can pop along to the brewery. I'm almost out of yeast.' She pressed pastry into the pie dish, trimmed it deftly and began to slice in the apples Sally had peeled.

Undeterred, Sally delivered her last broadside. 'And no grandchildren for you!' she said. 'How sad! When I wed I shall have lots of children and they'll have lots of —'

'Sally Lunn! Do stop!' cried Mistress Cooper. 'Your chatter makes my head spin! The cinnamon, *please*! You don't listen to a word I say. And bring the sugar while you're in the pantry.'

Five minutes later Sally was on her way to the brewery, brooding gloomily on the selfishness of certain parents, when a broadsheet was thrust into her hand by a scrawny youth with two missing front teeth.

'What's this?' she asked suspiciously.

'Read it and find out!' he told her cheekily and went

on his way, whistling, leaving Sally to examine the printed paper.

'A play bill!' she whispered and read on:

> 'By Subscription on the last day of May shall be presented a new history written by Francis Pettifer for the Benefit of Adam Sturry.

The Luckless Prince

Lord Welby	—	Mr Sturry
Lady Welby	—	Mrs Harrington
Duke of Byrne	—	Mr Farthing
Prince	—	Mr Siddell
Maidservant	—	Mrs Sturgis
Soldier	—	Mr Copely

> 'This same to be performed beneath the Guild Hall
> at Six O'Clock Precisely.
> Tickets available Nightly.'

'Strolling players!' she whispered and all thoughts of Ned Cooper were driven from her mind and replaced by an agonized longing to enjoy the heady delights offered by the broadsheet.

Her eyes shone with excitement as she drew a long slow breath and let it out again in a rush. Never, in all her life, had she attended a play and it suddenly became imperative that she should do so now. The adventures of the luckless prince must be revealed to her. And what of the Duke of Byrne? How did he figure in the tale? Even the names of the actors had a magical ring to them – Sturry! Sturgis! Copely!

But would her mistress allow it? Almost certainly

she would not. Strolling players were a strange breed, welcomed by some and despised by others. They moved from town to town, always on the verge of financial disaster and frequently refused permission to perform. Sally frowned. This band of players at least had won the authorities' approval thus far – maybe Mistress Cooper could be persuaded.

'The Luckless Prince!' breathed Sally. 'Oh, I must see it. I *must*!'

As she hurried home from the brewery she came to a decision. She would ask Mistress Cooper's permission to attend the play – but she would attend whether it was granted or not.

From his attic room in Walcot Street Barnaby looked across towards the drying racks and tutted morosely.

'Just my luck!' he grumbled. 'Stuck out here on the edge of the town! 'Tis miles to the Guild Hall. I shall get a drenching if it rains!'

His companion laughed, 'At least we haven't got Dame Harrington breathing down our necks. Look on the bright side, can't you.'

'You know I can't!'

Barnaby Copely was slim, tall, blond and handsome and convinced that one day he would end up on the London stage. At present, however, he was a member of an impoverished group of players. He was poor, overworked and harassed and on this particular night was feeling sorry for himself.

He threw himself on to the bed which creaked alarmingly and tossed a handful of spare playbills into the air. He watched them flutter to the floor and let them remain there. His handsome face wore a peevish expression as he regarded his friend.

'"For the Benefit of Adam Sturry",' he quoted bitterly. 'When do *I* get a benefit night? When do you? Never! That's when!'

Patiently his friend and fellow-actor collected up the bills and shuffled them neatly. Mark Siddell was shorter than Barnaby and less attractive but, having a less mercurial nature than his friend, was invariably cheerful.

'Sturry is twenty years older than you,' he observed mildly.

'And twenty times less sober!' retorted Barnaby.

'At least we've got a decent place.'

'A decent place! This hovel! It's too small to swing a cat and this bed sags like a beer belly! Lousy, too, I'll wager!'

'What do you expect for a shilling a week?' Mark asked, 'But I was referring to the venue at the Guild Hall, not to this room. We might do very well there.'

'My God, I hope so!' cried Barnaby. 'A square meal wouldn't come amiss. My stomach's rumbling like thunder.'

'You can always go back to your apprenticeship,' Mark told him, a trace of reproof in his voice. 'Nobody ever pretended that being an actor is a secure profession. Nobody asked you to run away in search of fame and fortune. You have no one to blame but yourself and you know it.'

Barnaby gave a melodramatic groan. 'Don't lecture me, Mark. I am in no mood for it. All I want is food in my belly! Is that too much to ask?' He sighed heavily and sat up. 'Go back to being a carpenter? Saints preserve me!'

'Your mother would thank Heaven if you did,' smiled Mark. 'She'd welcome you back with open arms and kill the fatted calf!'

'My mother might do so but not my father,' Barnaby told him. 'He would rejoice in my downfall. If ever there was an unforgiving man 'tis he.'

Barnaby sighed heavily then flung out one arm. 'I am cut off without a penny! A hostage to fate!'

He swung his legs to the ground and stood up. He and Mark began to gather up various props that stood around on the bare floor – a roll of canvas scenery, a selection of crowns tied together with string, two faded velvet cushions.

Barnaby's expression changed suddenly. 'My but she was bonny – that lass in Bristol. You will grant me that much, Mark. I do know how to pick a winner.'

Mark grinned. 'She was a peach,' he agreed. 'Pity she didn't fall for your artful patter.'

'Letitia,' mused Barnaby. 'What a heavenly name. And what a heavenly figure! I do like a woman to look like a woman.' He smiled appreciatively. 'Letitia Fullerton. There's a name to conjure with.'

Mark grinned. 'She had you sized up for a scoundrel, though,' he reminded his friend. 'You soon got your marching orders!'

'And rightly so!' Barnaby rolled expressive eyes. 'There's the rub, you see. I like a lively woman who has her wits about her. Bird brains do not interest me at all.'

'But the ones with their wits about them soon see you for what you are!'

Barnaby laughed, 'That's my problem in a nutshell. Still, they usually fall for me initially even if they do not stay the course. There's something about a scoundrel that appeals to women. I don't know what it is.' He shrugged, 'Ah, well. I wonder what luck we shall have in Bath?'

Mark picked up a bundle of papers and, waving them accusingly, asked his friend, 'So – are you word perfect?'

'Of course!'

Mark shook his head in mock desperation. 'You never learn, do you, Barnaby?' he scolded. 'No one knows their lines until an hour before the performance. If then! That way we keep old Farthing on tenterhooks. If we all knew our words he'd have nothing to fret about and no one to curse.'

Outside a clock struck the hour and with cries of disbelief they rushed out of the room and clattered down the stairs. The final rehearsal had now begun and they were going to be late.

As Sally had expected, Mistress Cooper flatly refused to allow her to attend the play, insisting that a playhouse was not a fit place for young ladies. Sally's suggestion that it would prove highly educational entirely failed to move her mistress and in desperation Sally approached Ned while his mother was spending the afternoon with her sister on the other side of the town.

'I would so dearly love to go,' she pleaded. 'I swear it would be the *greatest* thrill of my whole life and so *informative* being about dukes and princes and suchlike.'

193

Wide-eyed and breathless she regarded him hopefully as he washed his hands at the pump in the yard. 'If you were to say you would come with me your mother might agree. 'Twould be a bit of fun for you, too. Well, not fun exactly,' she amended hastily, 'but interesting. Oh, do say you'll come. I'm told that most of the town will be there to see it and if I miss it I shall be the most wretched girl in Bath.'

She handed him a towel for his hands and before he could speak rushed on.

'They say Mr Harrington, the troupe's manager, and Mr Sturry are come straight from the London stage. I was speaking to the butcher who heard it from one of the players. Mr Sturry, it seems, has played *Timon of Athens* at Drury Lane, no less! Just think of that!'

'*Timon of Athens*?'

'Certainly!'

'And who is this Timon of Athens?'

She stared at him blankly. 'He's – why, he's a great man. An *important* man.'

Without comment, Ned dried his hands on the towel and handed it back to her. As he headed for the kitchen door Sally was close behind him.

'There's to be music, too,' she told him, 'and painted scenery hired in London and they say the costumes would make your eyes start out of your very head! Oh!' She clasped her hands together in agonized appeal. 'Please say we might go together. Your mother would not refuse me if –'

He spoke up at last, his tone regretful. 'No, Sally,' he said, 'my mother is right on this matter. The players themselves may be of good repute – more likely they are not – but the audiences at such spectacles are an unruly lot. The players excite them and then there may well be trouble.'

He sat down on the kitchen stool and held out his foot and Sally knelt dutifully to pull off his boots.

'But surely if you were with me –' she began.

'I've said no, Sally.'

At that moment his foot slid free and Sally fell backwards with the boot clutched to her chest and her legs in the air. Her face was flushed with annoyance as she glared at him and hastily tidied her petticoats. His mouth twitched.

'And what are you laughing at?' she demanded.

'I'm not laughing.'

For a moment she regarded him suspiciously but then she set the boot aside and prepared to pull off the other one.

'I do believe you're frightened of that slip of a mother!' she told him crossly. 'And you a grown man! You could win her round if you tried. You know you could. Don't you want to see the play? Don't you want to help poor Mr Sturry?'

'Help Mr Sturry?' He looked at her without comprehension and desperately she seized what might prove to be her last chance.

'It's a benefit night, you see,' she explained. 'Mr Sturry who plays Lord Welby will be given half the night's takings. He's deep in debt, poor man, and needs every penny he can –'

'In debt?' Ned raised his eyebrows. 'How can he be in debt if he is so good an actor and has appeared at Drury Lane?'

Sally had no idea. 'He's been ailing,' she improvised, 'and has only just recovered.' Inspiration came to her. 'He probably came to Bath to take the waters and now he is cured! I dare say he needs the money to pay off his physician.'

'What a sad tale.'

Sally glanced at Ned's face but his expression told her nothing and she could not decide whether or not he was in earnest. She set the two boots side by side and knelt beside him praying for a miracle.

When the silence had lengthened unbearably she burst out, 'Oh, please say you will come.' She saw the collapse of all her hopes and searched frantically for an inducement he could not refuse. 'I'll do anything if you'll take me to the play,' she told him. 'Anything at all. I swear it!'

He raised his eyebrows. 'Anything?'

'Within reason,' she amended.

'Ah!' He put a wealth of meaning into the exclamation. 'Now I wonder –'

'Try me!' she said eagerly. 'I could clean your boots.'

'You clean them anyway.'

'Bake your favourite pie!'

'I'm not hungry.'

She searched her mind for something with which to tempt him, aware of his growing amusement.

'I could kiss you,' she offered, her cheeks reddening slightly.

'A kiss?' He hid his surprise. 'I'd enjoy that but I still would not take you to the play.'

'Why not?'

' 'Twould be bad for you.'

'Let me be the judge of that, Ned Cooper!'

Her face was flushed with determination. She really is quite attractive, he thought with surprise, and will one day be a handsome woman.

'As many kisses as you wish,' she offered in a low voice, 'and wherever you will!'

'Sally!' He struggled to keep his face straight but at the same time he could not help imagining how it would be to accept her offer. Perhaps, when she was older – but no! That would be impossible. He could not marry a servant and he would never compromise her. A pity.

'Ned! Didn't you hear what I said?' She was breathing rapidly and looked agitated. Whatever had she been saying?

'I said I would marry you!' she repeated. 'Not just yet but when I am older. I would make you a good wife, I swear it.'

'Marry me?' He leaned back in the chair, unable to believe his ears. Then he looked at Sally's face. 'Good Lord! The girl's serious!'

'Most certainly I'm serious,' she told him defiantly. 'I shall no doubt wed one day so it might as well be you as another. But only if you take me to the play, Ned. Not otherwise.'

She held her breath and he thought how very blue her eyes were and how bright her hair. For a long moment he was tempted to accept her impetuous offer but common sense came to his rescue, however, and he drew a deep breath.

'I do appreciate the offer –' he began and her face crumpled.

She jumped to her feet. 'But you won't!' she said. 'I can see it in your eyes. Oh, what a hateful man you are! Leading me on that way and then saying no. And don't you try to deny it −' Her lips trembled. 'Don't you dare laugh, Ned Cooper!'

He tried desperately to control himself but after a moment his laughter erupted and he was aware of Sally's furious face as she glared down at him.

'Then be damned with you!' she shouted. 'One of these days you'll end up lonely and wretched and that's no more than you deserve. No woman in her right mind would marry such a selfish man!'

She picked up his boots and threw them across the room, then flounced out, banging the door behind her.

Chapter Eight

A<small>T PRECISELY SIX</small> o'clock on the following day
Sally arrived breathless and panting at the Reys'
house and banged on the door. Louise came to
the door and stared at Sally in surprise.

'Whatever is it?' she asked as her future sister-in-law
tumbled into the hall. 'Is someone sick?'

Sally drew a deep breath. 'Not exactly,' she admitted,
'but I am in a fearful hurry and have a great favour to
ask of you. If you deny me I shall be the most
miserable wretch on earth.'

'A favour? Whatever can it be?'

Sally took another deep breath. 'I'm going to watch
the players at the Guild Hall, but I have told Mistress
Cooper that I am invited to spend the evening with
you. If she should ever ask you I want you to say 'twas
so.'

Louise began to stammer out a protest but Sally,
having anticipated this, now rushed on, 'If you don't
agree I shall lose my job. Surely you wouldn't wish
that upon me!'

Louise looked troubled. 'Indeed I would not but
nor do I wish to lie, Soli. In truth I doubt such an
occasion is suitable for you. I have never been to a play
and never expect to go. The audiences can be very

boisterous, rude even, and you might come to some harm. Why not spend the evening here with us,' she smiled, 'and make an honest woman of yourself! You would be most welcome.'

Sally shook her head. 'I am determined to go,' she told her. 'The play deals with princes and lords and such and will be most informative. Two of the cast are come straight from London!'

'That may be so but 'tis the audience that –'

Desperately Sally cried, 'Louise! Just say you will not betray me if you love me at all! For Jean's sake if not for mine. 'Tis little enough to ask when 'tis certain my mistress will never ask you.'

Louise regarded her helplessly for a moment, searching her mind for a more convincing argument but, finding none, at last nodded reluctantly.

'But only this once!' she warned, her kindly face troubled. 'I will never help you this way again for it goes against my conscience – as it should against yours!'

Ignoring this last reproof Sally flung both arms around Louise and hugged her gratefully and then was off, running along the road for fear of being late.

Half an hour later to her intense delight, she found herself in the allotted area below the Guild Hall, sitting in the thirteenth row on a hard wooden bench, jostled on either side by fellow playgoers and waiting impatiently for the performance to begin. The audience, about a hundred and fifty strong, were seated in rows in front of a makeshift stage which was partly concealed by a pair of faded velvet curtains which did not quite meet in the middle. Through this gap a tantalizing sliver of the set could be seen – a promise of forthcoming attractions. To entertain the restive audience a young man (no more than eleven years old and dressed in blue velvet) was playing lively music on his fiddle and good-naturedly ducking the strips of orange peel which were occasionally thrown in his direction. A row of candles burned fitfully along the edge of the stage, filling the air with a smell of burning tallow. The floor was covered with sawdust.

Sally amused herself by looking for a familiar face among the audience and was finally rewarded by a glimpse of the baker whom she had met at the baths. He was sitting among the privileged few in the first four rows, enjoying the luxury of individual chairs and a largely uninterrupted view of the stage. She also saw the butcher who called on Mistress Cooper and, in the back row, the knife grinder who had called at the house two days earlier. On her left a fat man with several chins was cracking nuts and dropping the shells on to the floor. On her right a young woman with a pockmarked face was fighting off an ardent admirer and Sally tried hard not to envy her. If only Ned Cooper had accompanied her she could have been resisting his advances but – so be it! It was his loss, she told herself with a determined toss of her head.

At last a head appeared from between the curtains and nodded to the musician, who suddenly began to play a different tune as the curtains slowly opened and a great sigh of excitement went up from the audience. The nuts and oranges were temporarily forgotten as the stage was revealed in all its glory, and a spontaneous burst of approval was given by way of stamping feet, loud cheers and whistles.

Sally gasped as her bemused eyes took in the scene – the interior of a grand house. Gilded furniture had been placed at strategic intervals and around the back of the stage a painted canvas depicted a wall hung with painted pictures and a painted door. Magically an improvised chandelier hung centre stage.

For a moment the stage remained empty but encouraging noises from the audience brought an actor on to the bare boards to give the introductory monologue. This, it appeared, was the Duke of Byrne and he explained that the play was set in London in the previous century and concerned the fate of a young prince who had fled from his native land of Boldavia to escape the murderous intentions of a wicked uncle.

From the very first moment Sally was spellbound, surrendering completely to the fantasy, transported to another world so that it mattered nothing if the players occasionally stumbled over their lines or the scenery swayed precariously. She identified totally with the characters and agonized with them over their problems. When Lady Welby tripped and almost fell, Sally was the only member of the audience who did not find it amusing; when the man sitting behind her jeered loudly during an amorous interlude she rounded on him furiously and, to his great astonishment, threatened to punch him.

The story-line was ragged and the acting far from polished but Sally revelled in every moment. The high spot of the evening for her was the appearance of Barnaby Copely in his role as the soldier. She was totally captivated by the swashbuckling character he portrayed and watched him with open-mouthed admiration as he strode to and fro across the stage, delivering his lines with more gusto than was necessary.

When finally the curtains closed at the end of the last act she was brought back to reality with a jolt of dismay and a sense of real loss. All around her the audience were rising to their feet, showing their appreciation with applause and catcalls (and a few boos from a drunken lout in the back row). Sally sprang up also and began to clap her hands with all the energy she could summon, unable to demonstrate the extent of her gratitude for the pleasure they had given her over the past two hours.

But the delights of the evening were not yet over, for as the cast lined up for the final bow the soldier caught her adoring eyes and to her immense surprise, winked broadly. Thunderstruck she watched him make his bow. Surely she had been mistaken. But no! When he straightened up again he looked at her directly and this time he jerked his head very slightly towards the rear of the building and Sally's senses swam as the full impact of his actions struck home. This incredibly handsome, wonderfully talented young actor was suggesting an assignation with a nobody by the name of Sally Lunn! As the actors vanished into the wings Sally's legs buckled with shock and she sat down again as all around her the clamorous audience began to disperse.

With an effort, she finally pulled herself together and made her way on trembling legs to stand in the cool night air trying to steady her racing pulse and calm her nerves. Presumably he would come in search of her – if he came at all. Time passed while she waited anxiously, racked by doubts. Just as she was about to give up and go home she saw him and her heart raced.

She was forced to admit that in his ordinary clothes Barnaby Copely looked less impressive than in his soldier's uniform, but she was in no mood to care and could only smile breathlessly at him as he moved towards her.

'Oh, Master Copely!' she began but to her surprise he took her right hand and bent his head to kiss it.

As she stared speechlessly at him he said, 'Sweet lady! You must forgive my forward ways but I could scarce take my eyes from you. I almost forgot my lines I was so entranced. With your looks you should be on the stage yourself.' She swallowed hard and tried to speak but for once words failed her and he went on, 'Tell me your name, I beg you. I am at your service.'

'Sally,' she stammered. 'Sally Lunn.'

'It has a fine ring to it. And you have a pleasant speaking voice. Let me take a better look at you. Turn around.' Obediently Sally made a slow turn, aware that his eyes did not leave her for a moment.

'Excellent!' he murmured. 'May I ask your age without seeming over forward?'

'I am sixteen, sir.'

He laughed. 'I pray you, do not call me "sir", or you will make me feel old! I am Barnaby to my friends. You must call me Barnaby. And you are sixteen, eh?'

'Yes, sir – I mean, Barnaby.'

'I knew it,' he murmured, as though to himself. 'I took one look and thought "that young woman will speak like an angel". And I was right.'

His gaze was steady and his tone earnest and Sally felt her cheeks burn.

'A—an angel?' she repeated.

He nodded solemnly. 'The stage is a cruel taskmaster,' he told her. 'Many have trod the boards with high hopes only to suffer the greatest disappointment. With you it would be different.' She stared at him, somewhat confused. Was he suggesting . . . No, that was nonsense.

But his next words confirmed her suspicion.

'Have you ever considered life upon the stage?'

'Me?' she gasped. 'A player?'

'An *actress*,' he corrected her, 'on the London stage. You have the looks and the voice. Mind you, 'tis a hard life with long hours but think of the glamour — the lights, the music, the *romance* of it all!'

She thought — and her senses swam deliciously.

'But I could never do it,' she told him reluctantly. 'I never could stand up there in front of an audience the way you did. Oh, sir — I mean, Barnaby — you were magnificent! You brought tears to my eyes with your speech.'

'Which one was that?' he asked eagerly.

'The one where you lay wounded after the duel.'

'Ah, yes.' He looked pleased.

'If you had died it would have broken my heart,' she told him.

He smiled, flattered. 'You enjoyed my performance, then.'

'Oh, yes I did. You were . . .' she searched for a suitable word '. . . you were unforgettable!'

He gave a little bow and said, 'My thanks, sweet lady.'

Sally became aware suddenly that the rest of the players had drifted away and that she and Barnaby Copely were alone in the darkness.

As though aware of her line of thought he said, 'Have no fear. You are quite safe with me. I may be only a humble player but I am a man of honour, nonetheless, and pride myself on my integrity.' Sally was charmed by these words, unaware that he was quoting some lines from another play.

'I did not doubt you . . .' she began, but he had taken her hands in his and was looking earnestly into her eyes.

'How would you like to go on the stage, Sally?' he asked. 'I am quite sincere. I might be able to help you.'

Before she could answer she saw his gaze slide past her and he muttered a low, 'Damnation!'

She turned to see another actor – a man whom she recognised as Master Siddell who had taken the part of the prince. He looked distinctly flustered and, with a muttered excuse to Sally, he took Barnaby by the arm and drew him to one side. She watched them curiously as they spoke at some length and was disturbed to see their expressions change.

Barnaby cried angrily, 'A pox on the man! I never did trust him! This is the very devil!'

Tentatively Sally moved towards them, disappointed that she was no longer the object of Barnaby's flattering interest and intrigued in spite of herself by the effect of Mr Siddell's news.

'Is something wrong?' she asked.

'No, no!' they told her as one voice, and Barnaby added, 'Nothing at all.'

Sally frowned at so patent a lie.

'If I could help –' she suggested, hoping to be taken into their confidence.

With a final shake of the head Mr Siddell bade her a brief goodnight, and hurried away. Left alone with Barnaby she looked at him eagerly to see if they had resolved their problem but saw by his expression that he was still worried.

'I have had some rather bad news,' he told her. 'I'm very much afraid I shall have to cut short our meeting.'

Sally's face fell. 'But – oh dear! I mean, will I see you again?' she asked. 'Tomorrow, perhaps?'

She wanted to weep with disappointment.

He was looking at her strangely. 'I dare say I *could* meet you tomorrow,' he said slowly. 'I would very much like to do so, in fact, to continue our discussion but I am at rather a disadvantage. I wonder if I dare trust you.'

'Trust me? Oh, most certainly you can!'

He hesitated again, then lowered his voice. 'My friend has just told me that a large sum of money due to us from our last engagement has been delayed – due to the incompetence of someone who shall be nameless. I find myself with no money, a temporary indisposition you understand, and wondered if – just until we meet tomorrow . . .'

Sally regarded him with dismay. 'Could I lend you some? Oh, Barnaby, I would judge it an honour but the truth is I am only a servant and have so little. But that I will lend with pleasure. I wish it could be more.' She thrust her hand into her purse and counted out two shillings and fourpence. 'Will that help you until your funds arrive?' she asked anxiously.

She was pleased to see his eyes light up as she let the coins fall into his hand.

'Sally Lunn, you are an angel!' he declared. 'I can never tell you how much this means to me. That you should trust me like this. A stranger. A simple player. It brings a lump to my throat.'

'And tomorrow?' she whispered. 'When shall we meet and where?'

'Ah!' He looked at her thoughtfully. 'Tomorrow . . . Let me see now. What about the riverside? We could take a stroll together beside the water and discuss your future.'

Sally wondered feverishly how she could possibly take time off to meet him. What further excuse could she invent? And suppose Mistress Cooper refused permission?

'Monkes Mill then,' she suggested. 'Beyond East Gate. Do you know it?'

He nodded.

'And what time?' she prompted.

'What? Oh, the time. About two o'clock? Would that suit?'

She nodded. Any time, she told herself. Anywhere. She *must* see him again, no matter what it cost.

He glanced round him cautiously. 'I must go now,' he told her. 'And bless you again for this.' He patted his pocket. 'I won't forget you, Sally Lunn.'

'Forget me?' The remark bothered her.

'Until tomorrow, I mean. I shall lie sleepless until the early hours, thinking about you. I believe I am in love with you.' He took off his cap and made an elaborate bow. 'At two o'clock at Monkes Mill.'

He replaced the cap with a flourish and said, 'Dare I steal a kiss from Sally Lunn? From my angel? From a possible future colleague?'

A kiss! She could refuse him nothing!

'Just one then,' she whispered and his lips brushed hers fleetingly.

He strode away without a backward glance and she watched him go with a happy heart. He loved her. She wondered how she would survive the long night without him.

Her mood of exultation lasted less than a half-mile for as she approached Mistress Cooper's house she became aware of a tall figure leaning against the wall. With a sinking heart she recognized Ned. Her footsteps faltered but then she remembered her carefully arranged alibi and approached him with a confidence which was dashed by his first words.

'And where have you been, Sally Lunn – as if I didn't know!'

Sally opened her eyes wide and said innocently, 'But your mother gave me permission to visit the Reys and –'

'I've just come from the Reys,' he told her grimly, 'and they have not seen you.'

Sally's face fell. So Louise had betrayed her after all. Her opinion of her sister-in-law plummeted.

'The horrid cat!' she cried angrily. 'She swore to help me. So much for loyalty!'

'You had no right to put her in such an awkward

position,' Ned told her. 'But in any case there was no way she could convince me you were there if you were not. My mother was concerned for your returning home in the dark alone and sent me to fetch you. Poor Louise could hardly conjure you from the air!'

Sally's face crumbled. 'Oh, Ned, I'm truly sorry but if you only knew how wonderful it was. If you had only been there! I wouldn't have missed it for the world – and no harm was done. See, here I am in one piece and none the worse for the adventure. I own the audience were noisy and a little boisterous but there was no malice in them.'

She longed to tell him about Barnaby and the possible change in her fortunes but common sense prevailed. If he told his mother she would certainly forbid the riverside meeting and Sally dared not risk such a calamity.

'Does my mistress know?' she asked soberly.

'Not yet,' said Ned. 'Why do you think I am skulking in the street like a ne'er-do-well? I am not enjoying myself, I can assure you.'

Hope flared suddenly as Sally realised the implications of what he was saying. He was waiting for her so that his mother need not know the truth!

'Oh, Ned! You dear man!' she cried and impetuously threw her arms around his neck.

Without a word he disentangled himself and regarded her steadily.

'You are such a child, Sally,' he said with a sigh. 'When will you learn that the world is full of traps for the unwary. You might have come to great harm and then how would we feel? We are responsible for you

210

while you are in our employ. You must understand that.'

She had the grace to hang her head and mutter an apology but inwardly she still rejoiced, and Barnaby's image glowed brighter than ever. Somehow, tomorrow she would have to find a way to slip out of the house and it seemed prudent to show proper remorse now in case Mistress Cooper confined her to the house as a punishment. The very idea sent a shiver of apprehension down her spine. Nothing must prevent her from learning more about life as an actress. She imagined Ned and his mother gazing at her in amazement as she broke the news about her departure to London. She felt sure that with Barnaby at her side she could achieve undreamed of heights.

'I truly am sorry,' she repeated, 'and I am so grateful to you for waiting for me. Will you forgive me, Ned?'

'Just this once,' he warned. 'Now calm yourself and we'll go in.'

Next morning the hours passed so slowly that Sally almost despaired but at last the clock on the Abbey church struck twelve. The sound both thrilled and dismayed her. Only two more hours until her meeting with Barnaby, yet she had so far been unable to think of an excuse to leave the house. Fortunately Ned was at the quarry so there was only her mistress to persuade – but what possible excuse could she provide?

Just before one, when she was becoming quite desperate, there was a knock at the front door and she opened it to admit Mistress Bayne, one of their neighbours. She was as tall as Mistress Cooper was small and she had (to put it politely) an enquiring nature and a runaway tongue which a century earlier would have landed her in the ducking stool. She settled herself at once on a chair in the parlour and her news came tumbling out in a flurry of words.

'Have you heard about the players? Oh, you haven't! 'Tis the most scandalous thing!'

'The players?' echoed Mistress Cooper, while Sally hovered within earshot. 'What have they done?'

'They have been deserted by their manager!' Mistress Bayne told them in scandalised tones. 'That's what they've done. Would you believe it? Mind you, one can hardly wonder at it. They are all such scoundrels. He ran off after the performance and not one of them has been paid their dues. Would you credit such a thing? And so none of the lodging keepers has received a penny in rent nor are likely to.'

Dismayed by this account Sally cried desperately, 'But where are the players? What of them?'

Mistress Cooper said, 'Sally! Mistress Bayne was speaking to *me*!'

Mistress Bayne shrugged. 'It seems they too have fled the town. What else could they do? They dare not wait around to be accused of debt or they would end up in the Bridewell. They say there's not one remaining in Bath.' She shook her head lugubriously.

'Oh, they're a wild and feckless breed. Players! Show me an actor and I'll show you a rogue!'

'That's not true!' cried Sally, whitefaced.

The two women turned to her in astonishment.

'I – I believe they are much maligned!' she stammered.

Mistress Cooper said tartly, 'And what would you know about such things? Since when were you an expert on the habits of strolling players?'

Sally stared at them with wild eyes, a prey to the most terrible doubts. She could not, *would* not, believe that Barnaby had fled with his fellow actors, taking her money with him. She could not countenance the idea that she would never see him again. Every word of the previous night's encounter came back to her including Mr Siddell's interruption. Was it possible he had been telling Barnaby about the manager's defection? If that were so then Barnaby's request for money . . . It was too terrible to contemplate.

Unable to hold back the words she burst out, 'He would not treat me so unkindly! I swear he meant well by me!'

'Who would not treat you unkindly?' asked Mistress Cooper, taken aback by Sally's obvious distress. 'What on earth are you talking about, child? Who meant well by you? You are making no sense at all.'

But Sally could only stare at her speechlessly as she tried to come to terms with what she had heard. Could it possibly be true? There was only one way to find out and that was to keep their arranged meeting. Barnaby would be there and he would confound all his detractors.

Mistress Cooper was looking at her suspiciously. 'Sally Lunn, have you met one of these rogues? Is that it? Answer me at once.' Her kindly face was stern and Sally realised with a sinking heart that she dare not confide in her. If Barnaby *had* taken all her money she would get no sympathy from her mistress. If she asked now for permission to go out it would almost certainly be refused in view of what had just passed between them. If only she had held her tongue, but it was too late for regrets. If she did not go to the river, however, she would never know the truth and she longed most desperately to believe in Barnaby Copely.

She opened her mouth and closed it again. No time for words. She darted out of the room before her astonished employer could call her back and ran along the passage to the front door. Once outside she ran down the street as fast as her legs would carry her. When she reached the river bank the clock had only just struck a quarter to two and she paced up and down in a fever of excitement, twisting her apron between anxious fingers and trying to silence the still small voice that warned her she had gone too far. This time there would be no Ned to ride gallantly to her rescue and the whole story would have to be told. She could not expect forgiveness and in her heart of hearts she knew that she did not deserve it.

The clock struck two and she stared hopefully towards the town, telling herself that at any moment she would see Barnaby walking jauntily towards her. He would explain everything to her entire satisfaction and they would be happy together.

By quarter past two she was feeling less confident and when the clock struck the half hour she was near to tears and feeling very sorry for herself.

'Please come!' she begged incoherently. 'Oh, please come, Barnaby. Take me away from here. I need you, Barnaby, I am in such trouble and all because of you.'

But her anguished prayers went unanswered. Barnaby

did not put in an appearance and by half past three Sally had finally admitted defeat.

He had used her and her thoughts were bitter in the extreme. His flowery compliments were no more than a ruse to rob her of the few shillings she possessed. He was a handsome thief who preyed on the gullible and she had been stupid enough to fall for his persuasive patter. Her earlier admiration for him turned to dislike and from dislike to hostility.

Afraid to go home and face her mistress she wandered aimlessly along the river bank coming slowly to the conclusion that men were her downfall. If Ned had agreed to escort her to the play none of this would have happened. If Jean had allowed her to live with the Reys she would never have been tempted from the straight and narrow. If Simon Petty had not compromised her Jean would perhaps have considered it. Even the luckless Jess came in for a share of her animosity for surely if he had truly loved her he would never have gone gallivanting off to join William's army. The more she thought about her past life the more convinced she became that men were sent into the world to bring grief to innocent women. She thought of poor Polly and her soldier and the hasty wedding that followed the seduction and wondered what might have happened between her and Barnaby. Perhaps Mr Siddell's interruption had saved her from disaster.

She sighed. Perhaps the promise of a new life in London had been pure invention on Barnaby's part – a ruse to win her confidence. Oh, how she loathed him! Tears sprang to her eyes and ran unchecked down her face.

'Men!' she sobbed. 'They are all the same! Nothing but trouble. Well, I'm done with them all! Who needs the wretches? I don't.'

At last she drew a long, gasping breath and blew her nose on her damp handkerchief. She raised her head and shouted, 'I hate you, Barnaby Copely! You wretch! You ingrate!'

For a moment she wondered if she should throw herself into the river but she couldn't swim and might drown. Perhaps not. She wiped her eyes on her sleeve and paused to survey her surroundings. She had wandered further than she intended and now found the Abbey garden between herself and the town.

'I hate you all!' she added wearily.

She reached the path that led to Ham Gate and turned her back on the river. She would lose her job and it was Barnaby's fault. It did not for one moment occur to her that her own wilful nature might be partly to blame.

'But it's no use crying over spilt milk,' she told herself.

She must return sometime and face her irate employer.

'It might as well be now,' she muttered.

Retribution would be swift, she was sure. She would lose her position in the Cooper household and she regretted that more than she would admit. Ned's part in the deception would come to light, of course, but she was in no mood to spare a thought for his predicament. He was a man. One of *them*. The enemy! She sniffed miserably.

'Men!' The very word had a poisonous ring to it.

Beyond the hedge she found a short cut and pushing her way through it she crossed a large garden and found herself in Segar's Alley, a narrow and unfamiliar street. A few newly-erected houses stood along the right-hand side but between these Sally spotted a small bakery.

As she lingered outside it the familiar smell of warm bread brought half-forgotten memories flooding back and fresh tears gathered as she considered how far short of her dreams her life in England had fallen. Eight years after her arrival in Appledore she now stood penniless, unemployed and without even a roof over her head.

She sobbed anew and was suddenly startled to hear a voice say, 'Hold on, child. It can't be as bad as that!'

Peering through her tears she saw a plump, middle-aged woman regarding her with a cheerful smile. The hands which rested on her ample hips were floury and there was an unmistakable smell of yeast about her person.

''Tis worse!' Sally informed her but somehow she managed a watery smile for this kindly soul.

'Worse is it?' The woman laughed. 'Well, 'pon my soul! You'd best come in with me. One of my son's tarts will soon put you to rights. You know what they say – feed a sorrow! What? Shaking your head? Then you've never tasted one of Toby Parker's tarts.'

And ignoring Sally's unconvincing protests, she led the way and Sally found herself in a homely kitchen. As Sally stared round the tiny room her tears dried up as if by magic. A ginger cat came forward to greet her, rubbing itself lovingly against her skirt and purring loudly. There was brown earthenware on the table and checked curtains hung at the window. A ham hung from the ceiling and branches of dried herbs scented the air. It was a warm and comforting place and Sally felt immediately at home there. She gulped down the last of her grief and smiled shakily. The worst was over.

'We were bakers,' Sally told her new friend five minutes later, when she had washed her face and was sitting at the table with a mug of small beer in front of her and a large crumbly fruit tart in her hand.

In between mouthfuls she poured out the story of their life in France and their flight to England and the unsuccessful search for her father. Then, with a little encouragement, she confessed to the trouble she was in, finding it easy to talk to this motherly woman who had introduced herself as Molly Parker, wife of Thomas and mother to Toby.

'Twenty-three years old, my son,' she told Sally, 'and as good a pastrycook as you'll find in this town.'

'I met a Mr Dalmer at the Baths,' Sally told her. 'He's a baker, too.'

'Dalmer!' Mistress Parker snorted. 'He's not half the baker my son is. My husband, now – he can bake a loaf as good as anyone but he's no hand with pastry. My Toby's game pie is a delight to behold and as for his fruit flan . . . !'

She kissed her fingertips and Sally grinned cheerfully.

'I would have worked in the bakery,' she explained, 'if it hadn't been for King Louis. He put an end to all that.' She swallowed the last mouthful of tart and said,

'Would you let me see the bakery before I go? It would be so good to see it all again.'

Molly Parker said, 'Maybe I could go one better than that. If you *have* lost your place we could maybe offer you a job here. Would you like that?'

'Like it?' Sally could hardly believe her ears.

'It would depend on my husband, of course,' Molly went on, 'but if he agrees you could start tomorrow. Mind you, it's not much to shout about. Just calling the bread in the streets and delivering pies and such to our few regulars. At present Toby does a bit but he's little enough time and we could do with an extra pair of hands. In time you might help out with the baking, if you say you're bred to it –' She laughed, '*Bread* to it! Hark at me!'

Sally laughed. 'It sounds good to me.'

'We couldn't pay you much but there's an attic room you could have and you'd eat well. Be nice to have another female about the place.' She chuckled, 'Even things up a bit!'

She brushed aside Sally's thanks and persuaded her to take another tart.

'When you've eaten that you'd best get round to your employer and confess all. Things may turn out better than you think, but if they don't you know where we are.'

With a quaking heart Sally made her way home. Although she knew she had another job if she needed it she enjoyed working for the old lady and hoped she would be allowed to stay.

One look at Mistress Cooper's face, however, convinced her that that was unlikely. The old lady was sitting bolt-upright in her favourite chair, her hands folded in her lap, her head very erect. Her expression was grim and uncompromising and Sally cursed Barnaby afresh.

'So, Sally, you ran off without a word of explanation and now you have condescended to return,' said Mistress Cooper icily. 'Perhaps you will now be kind enough to explain where you have been – and no lies! I want the whole truth and nothing less, so don't try to deceive me.'

Sally began, 'Oh, Mistress Cooper, do please –'

'And what is the matter with your face? Your eyes are all puffed up. You have been weeping unless I'm much mistaken.'

'Indeed I have,' Sally confessed. 'I have been sadly misled – cruelly treated.'

'Oh, you have, have you? Cruelly treated, you say. And by whom, may I ask?'

Her eyes did not leave Sally's face for a moment and the hands in her lap remained quite still.

'By Barnaby Copely, mistress. He vowed that he loved me and then –'

'Barnaby Copely? And who is he?'

Sally hesitated, reluctant to admit her attendance at the play.

Mistress Cooper raised her eyebrows. 'I'm waiting,' she remarked coldly.

'He – he's a player.'

The hands tightened involuntarily and the eyes narrowed.

'A player?' The tone was incredulous. 'You say a player has mistreated you? But how is that possible?

220

You do not know any players because I forbade you to attend the play. I did that because I know that players are no better than rogues and vagabonds and they are not suitable companions for decent citizens.'

Sally was silent, her head bowed.

'Well, Sally? Have you nothing more to tell me? Surely your tale of woe is not yet ended?'

With a sinking heart Sally realized that there would be no second chance for her here. When her mistress knew the whole truth she would undoubtedly tell her to leave.

'I did go to the play,' she said in a faltering voice. 'I know you forbade it but I *had* to go. I went and I met Barnaby and he . . .' Her voice trembled. 'And he swore he loved me — at least he thought he did.'

At last she had shaken the old lady out of her composure.

'He swore he loved you on so short an acquaintance? Oh, you silly, reckless child! How could you be taken in by such —' She broke off as a new thought struck her. 'I hope you didn't allow him any — privileges! Oh, surely you would not be that foolish!'

She looked genuinely concerned and Sally felt a fresh wave of guilt sweep through her. This old lady cared for her and she had defied her and betrayed her trust, all on account of a no-good rogue.

'No, indeed I didn't!' cried Sally, hastily erasing the memory of the kiss and wondering if she might somehow be forgiven even now. 'I was wrong to go to the play,' she cried, 'and I do most heartily regret it. I see now that he was a rogue —'

Just then Ned came into the room and his greeting

died on his lips as he looked from one to the other in dismay.

'Our girl has let us down!' his mother told him bluntly. 'She has defied my strict injunctions to stay away from the play and has been guilty of great foolishness.'

As Ned and Sally exchanged a guilty look it dawned on Mistress Cooper that Ned had also been part of the deceit since she had sent him to meet Sally and bring her home from the Reys' house. Before Ned could utter a word in his own defence (if that had been his intention) Sally rushed in.

' 'Twas all my fault, mistress!' she declared. 'I begged Ned not to tell. He wanted to – he was very angry with me –'

Ned looked at Sally and sat down. 'Tell me what has happened,' he said quietly.

Sally began the story again and this time she managed to tell it all.

Mistress Cooper could not hide her triumph.

'So!' she said. 'The wretch dangled fame before you like a carrot to a donkey and you fell for it! Then he ran off with your hard-earned money! What did I tell you? You should have paid me more heed. You young girls are all the same. You don't listen to those who know the world. Well, I can't pretend I'm sorry for you because I'm not. You deserved all you got – and more!'

'But I trusted him –' Sally began unwisely. 'And he said he loved me.'

Ned sighed and shook his head. 'Sally! How could you be so gullible!' he exclaimed. 'Why, you hardly knew the man!'

Sally swallowed miserably and wondered if Ned could persuade his mother to be lenient.

'I'll never be so foolish again,' she told them earnestly. 'I have truly learned my lesson.'

'Your sort never does!' snapped Mistress Cooper. 'Look at Polly and that young soldier.' She looked at Ned in exasperation. 'Servants! They are such a trial! I must admit I had thought Sally a cut above the rest of them till now.'

'You are right,' he said quickly. 'Sally is not like the others. True, she has made this one mistake –'

But Mistress Cooper was not to be so easily mollified.

'One mistake?' she cried indignantly. 'One, do you say? She has made a whole host of mistakes! She thought she could defy me and get away with it. She thought she knew better than I did about the nature of players. She fancied she could do as she pleased. She also thought this Barnaby wretch could fall in love with her at a moment's notice! One mistake, you say? And you would take her side against me. Really, Ned, I begin to think you are as foolish as she is!'

Ned said, 'I think we should give her another chance.'

His mother snorted angrily. 'Oh Ned, what fools men are! You are all taken in by fair curls and a pair of blue eyes. Well, I am not. I judge solely on merit and Sally's performance has disappointed me. I am not inclined to trust her again.'

She gave Sally a long, hard look and bit her lip in vexation.

The truth was that the old lady had grown very

fond of the girl and wanted to keep her but the thought of her own son aiding and abetting a servant rankled with her. They had conspired against her and she imagined them laughing together at her expense. It was quite unbearable. She could have forgiven the girl her stupidity but Ned's complicity in the deceit hurt more than she would admit. No doubt if she now allowed Ned to persuade her to keep Sally they would laugh together behind her back and crow over their victory. No, it was unthinkable. With a deep sigh she hardened her heart. Sally would have to go.

She spoke up quickly before she could weaken in her resolve.

'You had best pack your things,' she said to Sally. 'Your wages for this week are forfeit. I have no more to say.'

Sally gasped.

'Mother!' Ned looked at his mother in dismay. 'That is a little harsh. She has nowhere to go! Do you want her to sleep on the street or be arrested as a vagrant?'

Sally suddenly remembered that she did have somewhere to go and the knowledge gave her courage. She rose to her feet with as much dignity as she could muster and faced Ned.

'Pray don't trouble yourself on my account,' she told him. 'I do have somewhere to go. In spite of my foolishness there are still people who will give me another chance.'

'You are going to your brother?' he asked.

Mistress Cooper snorted. 'I doubt they will welcome you with open arms,' she said, 'when they hear of your wickedness.'

Sally shook her head. 'No, I am going to take up a new position,' she said and felt a small glow of satisfaction as they gazed at her in astonishment.

'A new position?' stammered Mistress Cooper. 'I don't believe it!'

Ned said, 'Is it true, Sally? I could not let you roam the streets.'

''Tis quite true,' she said. 'I shall work for the little baker in Segar's Alley. They have offered me a job. They will make me very welcome.'

There was a stunned silence.

At last Sally said, 'Well, I'll go now. And I am sorry – and grateful.'

There was a lump in her throat and she was afraid she would cry again so she hurried out of the room. She ran up the stairs, packed her few belongings and came back down again.

Mistress Cooper said uncertainly, 'Now Sally, wait . . .'

But Sally would not wait. She gave a courteous bob to Mistress Cooper and then looked at Ned.

'I won't forget you,' she told him and went out, closing the door quietly behind her.

By the time she had settled in at the bakery she had recovered her spirits and was beginning to thank the twist of fate that had brought her to this new home. Thomas Parker, Molly's husband, was bald, bluff and hearty. Toby, his son, was short and round and easygoing with ginger hair and a freckled face and a cheerful whistle. They all went out of their way to make her feel at home and when she went to bed that night in a small room at the top of the house, she knelt by her bed and thanked God for all his mercies and promised him earnestly that the rest of her life would be entirely blameless.

Chapter Nine

IT TOOK TOBY EXACTLY one week to fall hopelessly in love with Sally Lunn, but she resisted his amorous overtures kindly yet firmly. She was done with men, she informed him, and all that nonsense. In her experience men were a snare and a delusion and women were better off without them. When he insisted that he was not like other men in her life, she told him that he was 'baked in the same mould' and was doubtless no better and no worse. To his plea that she must surely yearn for children of her own, she replied that her limited experience of babies had not endeared them to her but that her brother and his wife would provide nephews and nieces over whom she could fuss if she felt so inclined. No, she told him, she did not crave a home of her own – she was perfectly content with her attic room and now had only two ambitions. One was to make a name for herself and the other was to find her father.

Fortunately for the harmony of the household Toby took his defeats with continued good humour and declared himself willing to bide his time until she should come to her senses.

Sally set out each morning with a basket of bread on her arm and her cries of 'New bread! Come and buy!'

soon became a familiar sound in the streets of Bath. Sally herself became a popular figure with her neat white cap and apron and the customers, who found her cheerful and unfailingly helpful, were quick to praise her to her employers. The little bakery, tucked away in its narrow alley, began to sell more bread and orders for pies and tarts followed until the turnover had almost doubled.

The Parkers' delight was short-lived, however, for on the first of June, Thomas's brother was taken with an apoplexy and word came that his condition was serious and he was not expected to live more than a few days. The Parkers, deeply saddened by this news, decided at once to travel to Bristol in the hope that they would be in time to see him before he died or at least to be there for the funeral. They closed the bakery, hired three horses and set off at once in a flurry of last-minute instructions to Sally who was to keep a small fire going during their absence.

Thus Sally found herself with time on her hands for an indefinite period and at first she relished her unexpected freedom. On the first day she threw herself wholeheartedly into the various household tasks which Mistress Parker had suggested in an effort to keep her usefully occupied. Sally polished the furniture, washed the curtains, cleaned the pewter and, with a long broom, ruthlessly sought out the many cobwebs which festooned the ceilings.

On the second day she found some writing materials and wrote a long and loving letter to her mother, telling her about her new job with the Parkers, but omitting the disastrous interlude with Barnaby Copely.

That done, she stitched some new lace round the neck of her Sunday blouse and went for a walk along the river.

By the third morning she was growing tired of her own company and the hours passed so slowly that she decided to wander the town in search of entertainment. She made enquiries after her father, with the usual lack of success, and then made her way to Mitre Green where a small crowd had gathered to watch the antics of a dancing bear. In spite of the animal's size it looked somehow defenceless as it lumbered clumsily about on the end of its chain and there was a dazed look in its small eyes that Sally found disquieting. When the bear's owner tied it to a nearby post and came round with his hat held out for pennies she shook her head and walked away.

She drifted aimlessly until she came to the King's Bath where she joined the spectators along the parapet. Among the bathers she recognized Mistress Cooper but that lady did not see her and Sally made no attempt to attract her attention. Seeing the old lady made Sally think fleetingly of Ned and she was surprised to find that, in spite of her newly-declared independence, she missed him. For a moment she toyed with the idea of waylaying him on his return from the quarry and pretending they had met accidentally, but she remembered in time that he had refused to accompany her to the players, for which omission she had still not forgiven him. She put him resolutely from her thoughts and returned her attention to the bathers.

Half an hour later she grew tired of watching them and moved on to discover a troupe of acrobats performing in the High Street. A feeling of restlessness had taken hold of her, however, and she soon grew tired of them also and made her way towards the stocks where a large, uncouth-looking man was making clumsy attempts to free himself. She watched his efforts dispassionately, feeling less pity for him than for the bear she had watched earlier. The bear, she reasoned, had done nothing to deserve its miserable fate, whereas a man was not put in the stocks without a good reason.

Mistaking her interest for compassion the man began to whine.

'Spare a thought for this unfortunate wretch,' he begged. 'I don't deserve this, mistress. I've done nothing wrong; as God is my witness!' He wriggled his hands and then his feet but could not draw them through the holes. 'They've all taken against me,' he went on bitterly. 'Won't give me a moment's peace, God rot them! Put me anywhere in the whole world and they're waiting for me – waiting to accuse me. Oh, I could tell you a tale or two would wipe the sneer from your pretty face!' He sighed heavily and shook his head. 'But you wouldn't listen. Wherever I go, whatever I do, I'm harried from pillar to post. Got a grudge against me, you might say.'

His words caught her waning interest. 'Anywhere in the world?' she echoed. 'Where have you been, then?'

To her surprise the man narrowed his eyes suspiciously.

'Now that would be telling, wouldn't it!' he said.

'Have you ever been to France?' she persisted. 'Have you ever met anyone from France? Do you know a man –'

He interrupted her angrily, 'That's my business. What right have you got to pry into a man's past, eh?'

'So you've never been out of England?'

He positively scowled now and began to mutter under his breath.

Sally gave up her line of enquiry and stepped forward to read the paper nailed to the stocks. 'It says here you were drunk and behaving in an improper manner to the alarm of the populace.'

He shook his head furiously. ''Tis a damnable lie! I never touched a drop.'

She wrinkled her nose. 'And yet you still reek of ale,' she said, beginning to lose interest in him.

'So you take their part, do you?' he cried. 'No milk of human kindness in the likes of you! A godbegotten prune, that's what you are. A heartless, inquisitive prune! A pox on your sort!'

He drew his cheeks together suddenly and spat at her. His aim was unerring and she stepped back just in time and surveyed him coldly, repelled by the shapeless beard, unkempt appearance and unsavoury smell. Matted blond hair framed his face, effectively concealing the small scar on his left temple.

'You're disgusting!' she told him and turned sharply on her heel. Impervious to the string of colourful epithets which he shouted after her, and with a shrug of her shoulders, she put him out of her mind.

As she walked back towards Segar's Alley it dawned on her for the first time that she now had the bakery all to herself and an idea began to take shape in her mind – an exciting idea that made her eyes gleam and the corners of her mouth turn up in happy anticipation.

She would try to recreate the *brioche* that Maman and Grandmère had so often baked in the far-off days in La Rochelle.

That same evening she put the idea into operation and soon after six she donned Mistress Parker's voluminous apron and, humming cheerfully, began to gather the ingredients under the inscrutable gaze of a large tortoiseshell cat. A bowl of eggs, brewer's yeast, unsalted butter, milk, flour, honey and salt. It was so many years since she had watched *brioche* made but she had grown up with the recipe and now it came back to her. It seemed only days ago instead of years that she had perched on that wobbly stool, a thumb in her mouth, watching the family at work and hoping for a few currants which occasionally came her way as a reward for good behaviour.

Now she warmed the milk and added the yeast to the tepid liquid. She mixed salt, honey and flour and then poured on the yeast mixture and stirred it carefully.

'*Brioche* from La Rochelle,' she informed the cat as she began to beat in the eggs. 'Tomorrow, if all goes well, we shall see how the English like our rich French bread.'

The cat broke into a loud, ragged purr and Sally grinned.

'Oh, you think they will appreciate it, do you? Then you are a most discerning creature! Here! Try it!'

She pinched a tiny scrap of dough and tossed it towards the cat who leaped down to investigate. After a moment's consideration, however, the animal stalked away disdainfully and sat pointedly in front of the oven.

Sally laughed, 'So, you don't like *brioche*! You pernickety creature! Rather have mouse, would you? But wait until it is finished. The butter still has to go in and you like butter. I'll wager you will like it better then.'

With eager hands she prepared the dough, handling the large amount with some difficulty but eventually mastering it.

'Now we cover it with a cloth and leave it for two hours,' she said, addressing her remarks to the cat's back, 'or was it three? I'm not certain. We shall have to keep an eye on it and see how it rises.'

Returning to the kitchen, Sally cut a few slices of bread and toasted them before the fire. She spread them with fat from Sunday's beef, and ate them hungrily.

Tomorrow, she decided, if her baking was successful, she would take some *brioches* to the Reys and would offer some to the other Huguenot families in the town. If there were any left she would sell them in the streets.

She waited with mounting excitement until the dough had risen to a spongy mass and then she worked it again, added the butter and put it in a fresh bowl. It was now nearly ten o'clock and Sally decided to leave it to rise for a second time overnight.

After locking up the house, she went to bed feeling happy and excited, and reflecting on her evening's work. In the bakery, surrounded by the familiar tools, she had felt comfortable and thoroughly at ease – as though she *belonged*. Cleaning out and preparing the oven and fetching and handling the ingredients had come as naturally as breathing and the creation of the dough had proved immensely satisfying. Without analysing her feelings too closely Sally was aware of a feeling of fulfilment.

She fell asleep that night impatient for the morning and her dreams were of her childhood in the bakery in La Rochelle.

Next morning she worked the risen dough for the third time, separated it into three dozen pieces and dropped them into round moulds. While the dough rose for the last time she built up the heat in the oven but by this time she was growing a little nervous. She had helped herself to the ingredients without permission and would have some explaining to do when the Parkers returned from the funeral. If her experiment failed and she could not sell her wares she would no doubt have to pay for everything she had used.

Later, with a fast-beating heart, she slid her pale creations into the glowing oven and crossed her fingers for luck. Once they were in the oven she tidied up and with an effort resisted the urge to open the oven door and take a quick look. She worried a lot, wondering if she had remembered the recipe correctly and if the proportions had been correct or if she had omitted anything. She talked to the cat and fiddled with her apron strings until after fifteen minutes a familiar smell filled the bakery.

'They smell good!' she told herself. After a further ten minutes she took a deep breath and opened the oven door. The *brioches* came out firm and risen, golden brown on top. At the sight of them, Sally burst into tears of relief. She longed to share the moment with one of the family – if only she could drop one into

Grandmère's approving hands or see Jean's face light up at the sight of them. But even the cat had disappeared and she must be content with her solitary triumph. Only when she had recovered her poise did it occur to her to taste one but instinct had told her that they were good – the deliciously buttery smell was all she needed by way of reassurance.

Proudly she transferred them to the table, and while they cooled she regarded them critically. There *was* one thing she had forgotten. 'The glaze!' she exclaimed and had a sudden vision of Grandmère brushing the tops of the *brioches*. A mixture of hot water, honey and eggs would make them shiny on top.

'Next time,' she consoled herself. 'Next time they'll be perfect!'

Without further delay she packed half of them in a basket, covered them with a blue checked cloth and set out to discover whether or not anyone would buy them.

'Try Sally Lunn's *brioches*!' she called, her tone triumphant. 'Fresh from the oven! Come and try them!'

To her delight she sold several on the way to the Reys who, kindly souls that they were, bought half a dozen to swell her sales. The Huguenot families, inspired by her industry, bought nine between them and half an hour later her basket was empty and she hurried back to Segar's Alley to collect the remainder.

To those who marvelled at the size, comparing them with the smaller Bath bun, she told them, 'One of mine will fill a hungry belly!' and advised serving it cut through with honey.

When the last one had been sold she counted out the

money she had made and dropped it all into an empty pot which she found on the shelf. She then sat back, determined to do better the following day.

Flushed with success she had a sudden longing to share her excitement with Ned Cooper but again she hesitated. She had seen him occasionally around the town but they had exchanged nothing more than pleasantries.

'No!' she told herself sternly. 'You don't need Ned Cooper or anyone else.'

With a sigh she shook her head, and reminded herself that that chapter of her life was closed forever.

The next day Sally increased the number of *brioches* to fifty and was gratified to find that all of them found a buyer within two hours. The day after she made sixty and by the end of a week she had increased her sales to six dozen.

She was cheerfully putting the last of these into her basket when the clatter of hooves outside made her pause. Then she recognized Toby's voice. The family had returned! She felt her stomach lurch with apprehension although she had almost convinced herself that they would be pleased with her achievement. Suppose, however, she was wrong? Her heart began to thump unsteadily. Suppose they resented her interference? Suppose – but, there was no time to panic. She just had time to arrange the *brioches* attractively in her basket before Thomas Parker walked in.

Sally turned to face him, her small chin jutting defiantly, prepared to defend her case if necessary, and saw his eyes move towards the oven door which was open and obviously cooling. Sally's brave words died in her throat as his brows contracted into a puzzled frown.

'What the deuce is going on here?' he demanded suspiciously.

With the air of a conjuror Sally threw back the cloth that covered her basket and held the contents out for his inspection.

'What the devil . . .' His mouth dropped open in surprise.

Molly Parker followed him into the kitchen.

'Look at this, Molly,' he said and there was a distinct edge to his voice.

She said, 'Sally?' before words failed her. She dumped her bag on the floor and gazed at the contents of the basket and then her husband's face.

Sally felt her throat grow dry but still could not speak. Toby was last in and he too stared speechlessly at the large golden *brioches* and his gaze took in all the evidence of her labours.

Quickly he said, 'Something smells good!'

'It does,' said Molly nervously.

Thomas said slowly, 'I asked you what was going on, Sally?'

She took a deep breath, and her words came out in a rush. 'I made them. 'Tis a French recipe. We call it *brioche*.'

'*Brioche*?' He glared at her. 'What the hell's *brioche*? In English, if you please.'

Three pairs of eyes watched the colour mount in Sally's face as she began haltingly to explain, ''Tis a kind of dough – a rich dough. Not quite a bread but made with eggs and honey.' She faltered but Toby winked encouragement, and she went on, 'A dough which is then enriched with butter. Lots of butter —'

Thomas snorted disapprovingly and said, '*Brioche!* Huh!'

Toby prompted softly, 'Go *on*, Sally.'

'My family have made it for generations and I have watched them since I was a child. In La Rochelle we sometimes baked them in a different shape — larger, perhaps, with a hole in the middle and then we added dried fruits and ate it at festival time.'

Seeing her discomfiture, Toby said loudly, 'Well, I'm damned! Our little Sally really is a baker. She has been hiding her light under a bushel.' He took one of the *brioches* and bit into it. 'Delicious!' he announced. 'Delicious and different. Try one, Father. See for yourself.'

Sally flashed him a glance of pure gratitude and held her breath.

Thomas walked forward, picked one of the buns from the basket and held it cautiously to his nose. He breathed deeply and said, 'I can smell butter. Lots of it.' He broke off a piece and examined it with a practised eye. 'And eggs.'

Sally said huskily, 'They sell well. Oh, Master Parker, please don't be angry.' She fell silent again as he put the sample into his mouth.

While he was eating it she ran to the shelf and took down the pot which was now full of money. 'Take it,' she said. 'This is for you. 'Tis what I earned. I promise you it covers the cost and leaves you a good profit.'

They all watched anxiously as Thomas chewed and

swallowed. At last he smiled, almost reluctantly. 'They're good!' he announced. 'They're very good!'

He handed his wife a sample and she too gave her approval.

Toby said, 'But what are they, Sally? I mean, what do you call them?'

''Tis *brioche* in France,' she said with a slight shrug. 'It doesn't have an English name.'

Thomas said, ''Tis not quite bread but nor is it cake . . . Perhaps we should call it a teacake.'

Sally's face broke into a broad smile as she realized what he had said. 'You mean you like it? We can make them again?'

His round face creased into a smile. 'I mean *you* can make them again,' he corrected her. 'These can be your speciality. I have my bread and Toby his pastry.'

Toby said thoughtfully, 'Sally Lunn's teacakes. Hmm? I wonder? 'Tis a bit of a mouthful – if you'll pardon the pun!'

They all groaned good-naturedly.

Sally said quickly, 'It sounds good to me. Sally Lunn's teacakes. Yes, I like it.'

Suddenly Toby cried, 'No! I've got it exactly! We'll simply call them "Sally Lunns" to rhyme with buns,' and he burst into delighted laughter.

'Sally Lunns?' Molly echoed, a little doubtfully.

They looked at each other but Toby was already convinced.

'Sally Lunns!' he repeated, and he took Sally by the hands and danced her round until they bumped into the trough and stumbled together, giggling like two children.

Thomas, ignoring their antics, began to count the money and now he turned to his wife and said, 'Cup your hands, Molly.' When she did so, he emptied the coins into them. Sally saw the look of surprise that flashed between them and relaxed.

Toby gave her a boisterous kiss and cried, 'Here's to Sally Lunn and her Sally Lunns!' and Sally experienced the sweet taste of success for the first time in her life.

As Ned made his solitary way down the hill from the quarry his thoughts, as usual, were on the various problems he had encountered throughout the day and he was feeling a trifle jaded. As he came within half a mile of the town he became aware of movement on the path ahead of him and instinctively he slowed his pace. He always carried a certain amount of money with him on Fridays and was conscious that he would present a very vulnerable target for footpads. He thought he could deal adequately with one assailant but if he were outnumbered his chances would be slim. He moved on cautiously and suddenly relaxed as the figure proved to be female and then, with a rush of pleasure, he identified Sally Lunn. She had obviously come out of her way to meet him and this knowledge warmed his heart in a most extraordinary way. His spirits soared and a broad smile of welcome lit up his rugged features.

Two years had passed since Sally's undignified departure from the Coopers' employ and she and Ned had met only once, accidentally, and then he had been in a hurry so they had exchanged only a few words. She had never come to look for him as she had now and he was inordinately flattered. His curiosity was aroused also.

'Sally Lunn!' he cried. 'By all that's wonderful! How good to see you again. But what brings you to this benighted spot?'

He thought she looked very well and had put on a little weight, which suited her, but more significantly he was aware that in the intervening years she had changed in subtle ways from a child to a young woman. She moved more decorously and with an unconscious dignity which he found appealing. He tried to remember how old she was – seventeen or eighteen, perhaps. And he was thirty. He sighed.

In answer to his question she said innocently, 'Oh, I just happened to be passing this way . . .' and they both laughed at this preposterous lie as she fell into step beside him.

A quick look at her face told him that she had news of some kind – good news, he guessed, by the sup pressed excitement in her blue eyes. For a moment, however, she kept it to herself.

'Are you pleased to see me?' she demanded.

'Most certainly I am.'

'You have not sought me out,' she said, a little reproachfully.

He was amused. 'Should I have?'

'Some men would have done so. Some would have missed me. It may surprise you to know that some men find me . . .'

He looked at her suspiciously but she kept her eyes on the path ahead and allowed the sentence to remain unfinished.

When he made no answer she said, 'Did you miss me?'

'I found the house very quiet!' he said, hiding a smile.

'You wretch!' She laughed. 'If you won't say something nice to me, Ned, then you shan't hear my news.'

'Let me guess it then,' he said. 'You have found your father.'

She shook her head.

'Then you have inherited a fortune.'

'No, more's the pity.'

A sudden unwelcome thought occurred to him. 'You are to be wed.'

'Wed? Certainly not!' She tossed her head in the old, familiar way. 'What would I want with a husband?'

'Most girls want a husband,' he remarked mildly.

'But not me!'

There was a pause and she glanced sideways at his face.

'I have news,' she told him.

'Am I to hear it?'

She touched his arm so that he stopped walking and faced her and now the news came in a flood of eager words.

'The Parkers are moving out of Segar's Alley. They are going to rent a larger house near the King's Bath, to share with Master Parker's father who is a widower and ailing and needs attention.'

Her eyes shone and Ned could not tear his gaze from her face.

'I shall stay on and will rent the room that was once their parlour.'

He looked at her blankly. 'Rent their parlour? But why?'

'To open as a coffee-house!' She took a step backwards, a look of triumph on her face. 'A coffee-house!' she repeated. 'Well, what do you say to that, Ned Cooper?'

'I don't know what to say,' he confessed, taken aback by her revelation. 'Are you sure 'tis wise, Sally? Are you certain?'

She tutted impatiently. 'Of course I am. I shall put six tables into the room and to each table four chairs. I shall serve my teacakes with coffee in winter and maybe with light cordials in summer. I shall call it Sally Lunn's and the people will flock to me!' Seeing his doubts, she leaned forward impulsively and took hold of his hands. 'I know what I'm doing, Ned. Truly I do. I have thought it all out most carefully. You need have no fear on my account.'

'But do you have the resources?' he asked, uncertain of the wisdom of her venture yet impressed by her confidence.

'Master Parker is lending me the money for the furniture and I shall buy good crockery and fine cutlery. I shall pay him back from my profits over the first year.'

'Does *he* think it a sound idea?'

'No,' she shrugged, 'but I do! He thinks we are in the wrong place but I have told him that is of no importance. There is nowhere else in Bath where you can eat Sally Lunns so they will have to come to Segar's Alley! And they *will* come, Ned. I know it.'

'You may be right,' he said dubiously. 'I hope so,

Sally, for your sake, but – forgive me, but I cannot imagine you as a business woman. You are still very young and –'

'Young? Pooh! What has age to do with it?' she demanded as they began to walk on. 'A good idea is good at any age! Suppose I was forty-five – would you then say it was a good idea? Most certainly you would. So why not now?'

He frowned, influenced by her argument in spite of his reservations.

She smiled up at him mischievously, 'Will you come and take coffee with us? Bring your mother. I will give you a good table by the window. My coffee will be the very best blend; my teacakes will melt in your mouth!'

'I'll try,' he said, 'but I doubt she will be persuaded. You are still "that naughty girl" as far as my mother is concerned.'

By this time they had reached the town and went their separate ways. He shook her hand and wished her luck with her new enterprise but his heart ached for her. Like Thomas Parker, Ned also believed the location to be most unsuitable and doubted she could succeed.

When he told his mother about it, later that evening, she threw up her hands in horror.

'A coffee-house in Segar's Alley? I never heard such nonsense!' She pointed an accusing finger at Ned. 'You should have talked her out of it.'

'Me?' He looked at her indignantly. 'Why should she listen to me?'

The old lady tutted despairingly. 'A coffee-house! Whatever next? I always thought the girl was feckless and now I'm sure of it.'

Chapter Ten

SEVEN YEARS LATER, almost to the day, Ned waited anxiously in the kitchen as the physician made his way carefully down the narrow stairs. As the old man entered the room Ned searched his face for reassurance but found none.

'I believe she is a little brighter today,' Ned prompted him. 'A little stronger, don't you think? The trouble is she has the appetite of a bird. Nothing I do or say will persuade her to eat more than a few mouthfuls. If only she would eat.'

He fell silent as the physician shook his head. 'I'm sorry, Master Cooper, but an appetite would make no difference. Your mother is failing, you see, and all the food in the world will not restore her. I will be blunt. She has a few weeks, perhaps a month or two. 'Tis unlikely –'

Ned stared at him in disbelief. 'A month or two! Oh, but that's impossible! She comes from a long-living family. Her own mother lived until she was seventy-two! Her sister until she was seventy-five! Her grandmother . . .'

He sat down suddenly, his face pale and drawn.

'Forgive me if I have been too blunt,' the old man was saying. He laid a hand gently on Ned's arm. ''Tis my way to be truthful despite popular opinion that a lie is kinder. Your mother's time has come – 'tis as simple as that.' He took a handkerchief from his pocket and flicked at his boots. 'Her heart is very tired and has been for a great many years. The fall she had recently has proved her undoing. Oh, I know there is no real damage – no broken bones – but it has been an ordeal and that wears out the heart quicker than anything. I always imagine anxiety eating into the muscles of the heart like a mouse at a lump of cheese.'

Ned stared at him, listening to the words but hearing nothing. There must be some mistake, he thought dazedly. His mother was frail – had grown noticeably frailer since her fall – but she would not die!

'You must be able to do something!' he stammered.

'I fear not.' The physician smiled as though to soften the unwelcome words. 'She cannot last much longer. Better to accept it gracefully. Death comes to us all –' He broke off, adjusting his wig and brushing an imaginary speck of dust from his coat. 'It comes to us all,' he repeated in what Ned called his religious voice. ''Tis only a separation from those we love.' He opened his bag and rummaged among its contents. Ned wanted to shout, 'Stop fidgeting, and tell me my mother will live!' The bag was closed again and now the physician fiddled with the strap.

'You and your mother will be reunited when your time comes.'

Ned stammered, 'I know you speak truly and mean to comfort me, but a few weeks? Such a little time! Are you sure?'

The physician laid a hand on Ned's shoulder. 'Indeed I am. When the good Lord calls . . .'

Ned covered his eyes in despair but opened them almost immediately.

'What can I do for her? How can I help? Have you changed her medicaments? I have told you that the green pills confuse her. Her mind wanders and –'

'The pills are not to blame,' the old man told him. 'Her mind is worn out and her memory plays tricks.' He frowned. 'Now where are my gloves?' He peered round the kitchen short-sightedly and promptly forgot about them. 'Now let me see, there was something else. Ah yes! Is Mistress Weller to your satisfaction? I have recommended her to several of my patients with good reports.'

The elderly widow came in twice a day to wash and dress Ned's mother and attended to her hair and other personal needs.

'She is an excellent nurse,' Ned agreed, 'very gentle and respectful. Even Mother can find no fault with her.'

'She will stay to the end,' said the physician and began to hum tunelessly to himself which was a sign that he was preparing to depart.

Ned saw no reason to detain him further and handed him his hat and gloves.

'She asks occasionally for my father,' Ned told him. 'She seems to imagine he is still alive.'

The physician smiled. 'Tell her the truth! But tell it gently. Say "Father died long ago. You have forgotten." She will accept it. If you pretend he is alive she will only fret at his absence.'

He stared down at his bag, his mind already on his next patient.

•

'Did I bring the liniment? Yes, I believe so.' He patted the bag affectionately. 'Poor Master Allyn has a gouty leg. Do you know him, I wonder? Used to be a butcher. Father of nine – all girls. A very nasty leg indeed. Bucketing has brought no relief so we must try the liniment – as a last resort, though in my opinion the stuff is only fit for horses.'

Ned saw him to the door and when he had gone, closed it and leaned back against it, trying to imagine life without his mother. Slowly he made his way back upstairs to her bedroom where she sat ensconced among numerous pillows. Her face was small and pinched but her eyes were fierce.

'That man is a fool!' she announced without preamble. 'If he thinks he can be rid of me that easily he has another think coming! Oh yes, Ned, he has told me his gloomy verdict – I insisted he did – but the man is a charlatan. I can see right through him. He thinks he will prophesy doom and then, if I do not oblige him by dying, he will claim that he has snatched me from the jaws of death and take all the credit upon himself! He must think me a gullible creature.'

For a moment Ned was almost persuaded that his mother meant what she said, but she did not meet his eyes and he realised that she was putting on an act for his benefit. Or maybe for her own? With the physician's words about honesty ringing in his ears he still did not know what to say.

'I want to see Sally!' she told him suddenly. 'Send her up to me. There is something we have to talk about. Something I intended to say to her before now.'

'Sally?' he echoed. 'Sally who?'

'Sally Lunn. Who else? And take that look off your face. I think she will understand. She is a good girl at heart although a little wilful but there is no malice in her.'

Ned sat down on the corner of the bed. 'Sally Lunn left us years ago, Mother,' he told her. 'She went to work for a baker in Segar's Alley and now she runs a coffee-house there. Have you forgotten?'

Thin fingers clutched at the blanket as his mother stared at him in astonishment.

'Runs a coffee-house?' she exclaimed. 'Our girl runs a coffee-house? What are you saying? Really Ned, I sometimes wonder . . .'

He smiled patiently. 'She is not our Sally now, Mother, and she is not our girl. She is living in Segar's Alley where she bakes teacakes. They are a kind of French bun and she calls them Sally Lunns. They are very popular.'

'French buns?' His mother frowned as vague memories slipped in and out of her head. 'Maybe I do recall –'

'I met her once and she told me the Parkers had moved out of the bakery to find better living accommodation –'

'The Parkers? I've never heard of them. 'Tis all double-Dutch to me!' his mother said irritably.

Ned said, 'Sally told me she was going to open one of the rooms as a coffee-house. Now do you recall? I told you about it and offered to take you there. I thought we might be her first customers to show there was no ill feeling. But you refused,' he added a little reproachfully. 'You said you thought it a most unsuitable idea.'

'And so it was!' his mother said with a sudden tightening of her lips. 'I recall she was a very deceitful girl! She went to that wretched play after I had expressly forbidden her to do so.' She sighed deeply. 'So that's where she ended up! In a coffee-house! Poor child! Still, she has only herself to blame.'

Ned hid a smile as he imagined how Sally would react to this wonderful distortion of the facts.

'She had a good position here with us,' his mother went on. 'And what are you smiling at, Ned? 'Tis the truth.' She sniffed disparagingly and muttered, 'One thing my mother taught me was never to allow a servant to get the better of me. I never have and I never will.'

Ned allowed this to pass without comment.

'Toby and his father still bake bread and . . .' he began, but now his mother's concentration was wavering.

'Toby? Really, Ned, you are making no kind of sense!' she grumbled wearily. 'All I want is to see Sally. That's not too much to ask, is it? Send the girl up to me at once.'

He counted silently to ten.

'Mama! I cannot do that,' he said. 'I have just explained. And Sally is no longer a girl. She is a grown woman, a business woman. Why, she must be twenty-five by now. If you seriously wish to speak to her I will call on her and explain the situation but I cannot promise she will come.'

Outwardly calm, almost reluctant, Ned suddenly discovered that the prospect of seeing Sally again gave him tremendous pleasure. After his mother's initial

250

refusal he had never visited the coffee-house although he could not say why he had stayed away. Now, however, he had a valid excuse and the thought of talking to her again excited him more than he chose to admit.

'I'll call on her tomorrow,' he said quickly, in case his mother changed her mind.

He had no idea what his mother could possibly have to say to her but he did not greatly care. Tomorrow he would see Sally Lunn and the thought was strangely comforting.

Sally hummed cheerfully under her breath as she rubbed beeswax into the table and polished it until it shone. A tapestry fireguard stood in front of the empty grate and Sally glanced at it proudly. Her first effort had produced a creditable (if somewhat uneven) design and grapes tumbled haphazardly from an earthenware bowl. Toby had described them as good enough to eat but then he was prejudiced.

The small room overlooked the street and today sunlight streamed in, reflecting from the whitewashed walls. A jug of yellow roses dropped their scented petals on the window ledge in one corner of which a tray of cutlery perched precariously. A shelf on the wall contained a row of small milk jugs. The aroma of roasting coffee beans drifted up from below mingled with the smell of warm, yeasty buns. These, fresh from the oven, were piled in a basket on the table by the door, covered with a clean blue cloth.

Sally glanced up as Toby thundered up the wooden stairs and poked his pink and perspiring face round the door.

251

'Fellow asking for Sally Lunn,' he told her breathlessly. 'I don't recognise him and I thought I knew all your admirers. Says he knows you.'

Sally looked at him blankly. 'And do I?'

'Tall as a bean pole and broad with it. Not your sort of man at all.'

She laughed. 'I know! I'm to wed a small fat man – you have told me so many times! Did he give his name, this bean pole?'

'I forget it,' he said with exaggerated innocence. 'You don't want to see him, do you?'

'Toby!'

'Calls himself Ned Cooper.'

She looked at him in surprise. 'Ned Cooper! Well I'm blowed! Please send him up, Toby. And don't look that way. He's not a rival. He's the son of the woman I worked for when I first came to Bath.'

As Toby retraced his steps Sally fussed with her appearance, tugging her curls into place and biting her lips to redden them a little, but when Ned entered the room she was apparently busy with the beeswax once more.

She looked up. 'Ned Cooper! 'Tis good to see you. I doubted you would ever come. Did your mother warn you to keep away?' Seeing that she had embarrassed him she added hastily, 'Forgive me! I forget my manners. I tease Toby so often it has become a habit.' As Ned still did not speak she said, 'You are a little early but you will take some coffee with me, I hope, and try one of my buns.'

'That would be very pleasant,' he answered.

For a moment neither spoke but then Sally waved a

hand towards the best table. 'Sit yourself by the window,' she told him. 'From there you will see all that goes on in Segar's Alley.'

He sat down obediently. 'I congratulate you, Sally. You have done very well. You must be very proud.'

'Pride comes before a fall,' she laughed, 'but yes! I confess I am pleased. I am carving a niche for myself. A small niche, possibly, but I hope to expand. I am very ambitious. In business one must never stand still. But I'll fetch some coffee. 'Tis the best that can be got and people speak well of it. They drink it by the gallon!'

He laughed and she remembered suddenly that she had once thought of him as a possible husband.

'It seems so long ago,' she said, amused, and he knew at once that she referred to her stay with them.

'You have changed!' he told her. He wanted to add something complimentary but she gave him no chance.

'Coffee!' she insisted and left him to his own devices. He stared out of the window, confused by the rush of feeling he felt towards her and inhibited by the knowledge that the round-faced Toby featured so largely in her life. Were they betrothed? They were both of an age to wed if they so desired. Toby looked no more than twenty-five or -six and they had a lot in common. He had a sudden vision of Sally and Toby with a family of red-haired children and the prospect did not appeal to him. Suddenly he felt that he must understand the relationship.

As soon as Sally reappeared he smiled casually. 'Gossip has it that you and Master Parker are to wed,' he told her untruthfully.

She laughed delightedly. 'Then gossip has it wrong,' she told him. 'Mind you, if Toby had his way we would have wed long since. He asks me every morning without fail!'

'You could do a lot worse,' Ned ventured. 'He seems a-a nice enough fellow.'

'But I am wed already!' She waved a hand expansively. 'To my work! I have no time for husbands or children. The coffee-house is my husband and those —' she pointed to the basket of buns, '— those are my children!'

He laughed with relief and watched as she selected one of the buns and slit it expertly through the middle.

'Try it!' she urged. 'Here, spread it with cinnamon butter. Cinnamon, butter and honey. If you can honestly say you have tasted anything better I shall take a pistol and shoot myself!'

Her large blue eyes watched him as he helped himself from the pot and spread the spicy concoction on to the bun.

'Your very first Sally Lunn!' she said. 'A momentous occasion. Perhaps you should make a wish!'

After a moment's hesitation he closed his eyes briefly then opened them again.

'Was that it?' she asked. 'Such a small wish!'

He nodded and bit into the bun and she watched him anxiously, waiting for his verdict. For a moment he pretended to consider.

'You can eat them with butter and jam,' she told him. 'Marmalade is good too — Oh, Ned! Do say you like it!'

'I like it!' he said, his voice suddenly husky, unable

to take his eyes from her face. 'Yes, 'tis quite superb. I like it very much.' He swallowed hard. 'Oh, Sally.'

Aware of his confusion, a faint colour rose in her cheeks. 'I meant the bun,' she said, disconcerted by her own emotions.

'I meant that, too,' he rallied with an effort and took another bite, then held the bun towards her. 'They are very good. Won't you share it with me?'

They ate in silence until only a few crumbs remained on the plate.

Annoyed with himself for his lack of composure, Ned stared out of the window while Sally sipped her coffee. Then she drew a long breath. 'Why did you come here, Ned?'

With a guilty start, he recalled the purpose of his errand and explained that his mother had asked to see her. Sally listened with her head on one side and made sympathetic noises.

'Is your mother still angry with me?' she asked warily.

'Who can tell? She is so confused.'

'I was a trial to her,' Sally confessed. 'I was a trial to my poor mother, too. And poor Henri.' She shrugged lightly. 'Even Jean found me exasperating.'

'How is he?'

'Father of five.' She hesitated. 'I fear the wool trade is not what it was five years ago but they manage.'

'And your father – did you ever find him?'

'No. But I haven't given up hope. He is around somewhere.'

He smiled. 'The same determined Sally! But will you visit my mother? She is determined to see you. Perhaps she feels she dealt too harshly with you and wishes to make her peace. Will you come, Sally?'

She nodded. 'Later today,' she promised, 'when we are not too busy. I could ask Toby to take my place – but only for a half hour.'

He finished his coffee and stood up. 'You are very kind. I shall – that is, my mother will look forward to seeing you again,' he said.

She held out her hand and he clasped it briefly.

'Until then,' she said and watched him go with regret.

As promised she arrived at number fourteen just after six o'clock and followed Ned up the familiar stairs.

'Mother! Sally is here,' Ned announced and went forward to the bed where the old lady dozed. Hearing him she roused herself and stared at Sally as Ned helped her to sit up and plumped the pillows around her.

'You look different,' she told Sally.

Sally smiled. 'I am much older.'

Mistress Cooper gave Ned a sharp look and said, 'What I have to say is private, Ned. Between Sally and me.'

Ned raised his eyebrows. 'Secrets, Mother?' He smiled at Sally. 'I'll wait downstairs. Call me when you are finished.'

As soon as the door closed behind him the old lady began to tug at a ring which she wore on her right hand.

'This is for you,' she told Sally. 'It belonged to my mother and she gave it to me on my wedding day. Marry Ned. He will be all alone when I –'

'Marry Ned?' cried Sally, both amused and embarrassed. 'I can't marry Ned!'

'Of course you can.' The old lady held out a hoop of emeralds set in gold. ''Tis high time you were wed. You cannot remain a spinster all your life. Every woman in her right mind wants a husband and Ned will suit you very well.'

Sally pushed away the gnarled hand, refusing to take the ring. 'Believe me, Mistress Cooper,' she said firmly, 'my experience with men has convinced me that marriage is not for me. They are more trouble than they are worth!' She thought fleetingly of Simon Pett and Barnaby Copely and her lips tightened. 'I shall never wed.'

'You will not always be young and healthy,' the old lady insisted. 'You too will get old and then you will need someone who cares for you. Ned would care for you. He would make you a good husband.'

'I tell you I shall not wed!'

'Take the ring. Try it for size. It will look well on your hand.'

'No, Mistress Cooper. I cannot wed your son.'

'But you love him, Sally. There was a time once – I recall you said as much. You reproached me when I wanted to keep him with me. You said he would be old and lonely. I can see it all so clearly now. He will need you, Sally. You must care for each other.'

Again she tried to thrust the ring into Sally's hand and again Sally drew back, out of reach.

'I was a child then,' she protested. 'I hardly knew what I was saying.'

'Then you haven't changed much!' the old lady

snapped. 'For you don't know what you are saying now! I tell you, you love my son and all you do is shake that pretty head of yours! Oh, Sally! Sally! What a very contrary girl you are!' Exhausted, she lay back on the pillow and sighed deeply.

Sally felt a rush of affection for her former employer – affection mingled with admiration.

'Forgive me,' she said gently, 'I cannot do as you wish but 'tis not because of some fault in Ned. I truly do respect him. He is a most honourable man and will make someone a good husband. Set your mind at ease on that score, Mistress Cooper. I doubt he will remain single but I shall never be his wife. I am too busy. My life is too full and I am happy as I am. Please, Mistress Cooper, put the ring back on your finger. 'Tis very beautiful but someone else must wear it. Someone else must wed your son.'

Stubbornly the old woman shook her head. 'He loves you, Sally. I can see it in his face. He hardly knows it himself but you are the right woman for him. Take the ring, I beg you and think it over. There is no hurry.' She closed her eyes briefly. 'I will last a while yet for all that physician's tomfoolery. You will see things more clearly in time.' She held the ring to the light, admiring it.

Sally said, 'Ned may not wish to marry. You cannot force a wife on him.'

'He will need someone to love, Sally.'

'Then let him find his own wife when he is ready.'

'You don't understand.' The old lady shook her head. 'You never would listen to reason. Always head-strong.'

She held out the ring but Sally rejected it once more. 'You must find someone else for your son,' she said firmly. 'What of your present girl?'

'She is a careless slut and much too young. Ned is thirty-five. No, no. She would never do.'

'The daughter of one of your friends, perhaps.'

'He will look at no one.' She sighed wearily.

Sally leaned over and took the frail hand in her own. 'Let him be,' she advised. 'Not all men are meant to wed. He will look after himself well enough. Put it out of your mind and think only about your own recovery.'

'So you refuse him?'

'I fear so,' Sally said gently.

'Poor Ned!'

To Sally's consternation two tears rolled slowly down Mistress Cooper's faded cheeks. 'My poor Ned! What have I done to him? I have been selfish. You were right all those years ago.'

'Oh, please don't cry!' Sally told her. 'You were – are – a good mother.'

Impulsively she moved closer so that she could offer a little comfort, patting the old lady's arm and murmuring words of reassurance. Outside the clock struck the hour and she wished Ned would reappear. She could not leave his mother in this tearful state but she must get back to Segar's Alley.

As though reading her mind Ned made his way up the stairs and as Sally turned towards the door, she felt the ring being pressed into her hand.

The old lady called out, 'Come in, Ned. We are done talking.' Sally looked at the ring which lay in her palm, winking green and gold.

'This is a little difficult.' she began. 'I don't know how to explain . . .'

Mistress Cooper brushed away her tears with a shaking hand. ''Tis not difficult at all,' she said. 'I have given Sally a ring. A little gift, nothing more.'

'Oh, but . . .' Sally looked appealingly at Ned and held out her hand to show him the emerald hoop.

'She is to keep it!' cried the old lady. 'Sally and I understand each other. Don't we, Sally?' Sally hesitated and she went on, 'I have no daughter so who else should I give it to? Sally will appreciate it. She is a good girl. There is no more to be said.'

To Sally Ned said, 'Do please keep it. 'Tis my mother's wish that you should have it. Here, put it on.'

Before she could protest, he had taken the ring and slipped it on to the middle finger of her right hand.

'Let me see,' cried the old lady and dutifully Sally held out her hand. The ring glinted on her well-shaped fingers and the old lady nodded with satisfaction.

'It looks well on her,' she told Ned, and to Sally she added, 'It fits you perfectly. I am right. You will see.'

'Right about what?' Ned asked but neither Sally nor his mother was prepared to explain the remark.

Sally tried to overcome the awkwardness with some general conversation and then it was time for her to go. As she made her farewells the old lady caught hold of her hand and kissed it.

'You will see,' she said again and sank back on the pillow with a faint smile on her face.

Ned led the way downstairs and then turned to her. 'What is troubling you?' he asked. 'Why are you so unwilling?'

Sally began to ease the ring from her finger but Ned's large hands closed over hers and he shook his head.

'My mother is right,' he told her. 'She has no one else to leave it to. Humour her, I beg you. It may be her last wish.'

'But – oh, this is so difficult!' Sally exclaimed. 'She wants me to –'

He put a finger to her lips so that the sentence remained unfinished.

'No arguments,' he said. 'Keep it in remembrance. I am pleased that it has found a good home and I shall like to think of it on your finger. You deserve pretty things.'

'Ned!' She looked at him with astonishment.

He lifted her hand and kissed the ring lightly. 'There! You have it with my blessing also. Now do you feel better about it?'

She looked at the ring in awe. Emeralds! She had never owned anything so costly. Overcome, she could only nod her head.

'Then wear it with pleasure,' he said.

Mistress Cooper died in the middle of October and Sally stood at the graveside, listening to the mournful words of the funeral service. From the corner of her eye she saw the grave-digger waiting, spade in hand, and to her surprise recognised the man whom she had seen so frequently in the stocks or the pillory. So, she thought with amusement, this was how he earned the money which paid for his ale.

He looked up and caught her eye and she hurriedly looked away.

The hollow voice of the vicar droned on, '. . . and as we commit our dearly beloved sister to her final resting place . . .'

There were very few mourners apart from Sally and Ned. Some neighbours had attended and the physician was there also. A young woman was sniffling into a grimy handkerchief and Sally supposed this to be their servant. Glancing across at Ned, Sally considered how he would fare with only the servant to look after him and wondered whether she dare suggest that he found himself a decent cook. But no, she reproved herself. It was none of her business.

Suddenly, as though he had grown tired of waiting, the grave-digger jumped out from behind the tree, spade in his hand and asked, 'Ready now, are you?'

All eyes turned towards him and the vicar, on the other side of the grave, glared across at him.

'No, we are not ready!' he said indignantly. 'Whatever are you thinking about? Get back at once!'

He waved a hand dismissively and the grave-digger retired behind his tree, grumbling under his breath. The vicar began to apologise to Ned for the man's lack of sensitivity but Ned motioned him to continue with the service.

'Ashes to ashes, dust to dust . . .'

Sally glanced down at her hands which were resplendent in the white chamois funeral gloves which Mistress Cooper had specified in her will. Beneath the right-hand glove she was aware of the emerald ring which still occasionally troubled her conscience in spite of Ned's earnest assurances. She looked across at him as he stooped to throw a sprig of rosemary into the grave. His eyes were dark and his expression inscrutable as he took up a handful of earth and sprinkled it after the rosemary.

As he straightened up his eyes caught hers and for a moment his control wavered. Sally saw briefly the misery and sensed the deep loss which he felt. She knew now that the old lady had forecast correctly the impact her death would have on him. Unconsciously she felt for the ring through the chamois leather and her sense of guilt returned. Ned was not a solitary man and he ought to marry and raise a family. The emerald ring should go to his wife; she, Sally, had no claim to it at all. For a moment her imagination took over and she saw herself as Ned's wife; saw herself in his arms; sharing his bed. A deep sigh escaped her and she hastily glanced away from Ned for fear he should guess her thoughts.

The thought of being Mrs Ned Cooper was not entirely unattractive, she had to admit that, but when the children came along, as they inevitably would, she would have no time for her coffee-house.

'Oh, Ned!' she whispered and wished with all her heart that life was not so complicated. If she was honest she was drawn to him and in other circumstances would be happy to be his wife. For a moment she almost wished away the coffee-house but then she shook her head, ashamed of such treachery.

With a jolt she realized that the service had come to an end and the mourners were moving away, leaving the sulky grave-digger to get on with his work.

Back at the house a small group of the town's poor had gathered outside to receive the twenty loaves of bread which Mistress Cooper had also specified in her will. A bough of rowan had been draped over the front door to repel evil spirits and the mourners ducked under this as they entered the house. They then made their way to the parlour which was exactly as Sally remembered it and she found it hard to believe how many years had passed since she had polished that same table under the old lady's eagle eye.

The maid served the simple funeral feast, a posset, stewed prunes, cheese and cake while Ned, obedient to his mother's wishes, went outside to distribute the bread.

When it was all over and the final respects had been paid Sally walked home in a thoughtful frame of mine. One day it would be her turn to die and her shrouded body would slip from the coffin into the waiting earth. Who would mourn for her, she wondered, and shivered involuntarily.

As her feet rang on the cobbles of Segar's Alley her spirits lifted a little at the thought of the warm hearth and welcoming cats that awaited her in the bakery. Once home she changed quickly into her working clothes and began at once to gather the ingredients for the night's baking.

There was no time for regrets, she told herself. No time for second thoughts. Ned had his row to hoe and she had hers. She had chosen her path and she was content.

Chapter Eleven

FOR SALLY THE next eight years passed in a whirl of frantic activity and deepening anxiety. Determined to prove herself as a woman of business she struggled single-mindedly to make the coffee-house prosper but, in spite of all her efforts, the success for which she yearned still eluded her. She made a living but that was all and for Sally that was not enough. She wanted Sally Lunn's to be *the* place to eat and exchange gossip; to be *known* and patronised by fashionable people. In short she was ambitious. She had renounced the chance of marriage and there was now nothing in her life that mattered so much to her as the coffee-house.

In the darkest moments she wondered whether perhaps Thomas Parker had been right after all. He had considered Sally Lunn's to be in the wrong place — too far from the centre of the town. But this thought was heresy; she thrust it to the back of her mind and plotted and schemed to achieve the recognition she craved.

Her mother wrote frequently, begging her to be satisfied with what she had already achieved and urging her to be sensible and find herself a husband before she was too old. Sally smiled as she read the letters and wrote back to say how happy she was and that there was, unfortunately, no room for men in her life. Jean reproached her from time to time, accusing her of neglecting her nephews and nieces and then, with an effort, she would put aside her worries and hurry round to visit, full of smiles and apologies and with armfuls of gifts for the children who so obviously adored her. Louise did her part, also. Thoroughly content with her own role as wife and mother she longed to see her sister-in-law similarly settled and never tired of recommending eligible men, of good Huguenot stock, who would like to make Sally's acquaintance. To please her, Sally met them but for one reason or another she managed to reject them all.

As the years passed, Sally grew older ('But not wiser!' her mother retorted despairingly on one occasion) and learned to hide her growing disappointment from her family and friends. Her coffee-house was often full but appearances were deceptive: many of the customers spent more time than money, sitting for an hour or more over one cup of coffee. Her ever-present nightmare was debt. Sally dreaded that one disastrous year might force her to give up the business and there were times when she felt that only a miracle would save her.

During these years the town of Bath survived, adapting to the deaths of Mary and then William and welcoming Anne as queen; accepting the various changes in government and shrugging off the apparently inevitable wars across the Channel. Sally gave the outside world little heed until Queen Anne paid the town a visit in 1702 to take the waters – a widely publicised event which gave Sally renewed hope. Although the visit proved most successful and revived waning interest in the town countrywide, it brought about no lasting improvement in the fortunes of the coffee-house and four years later, in 1706, Sally's concern for her business was as great as ever.

On a dull day in October of that year, she stood in the tiny work-room of Juliana Popjoy and turned slowly to the left while the dressmaker's deft fingers snatched disapprovingly at various pins and reinserted them in the lilac silk hem. Juliana sat back on her heels and regarded the dress critically while Sally waited abstractedly for the verdict. The actual fitting of the dress bored her but Juliana was a superb source of gossip and anything of interest was passed on to her clients at no extra charge.

'I think 'tis level now,' she told Sally. 'Take a look in the mirror and see for yourself.'

Reluctantly Sally inspected her reflection. At thirty-three she had put on a little more weight and her face was softly rounded. Her hair still curled but the pale straw colour had deepened into warm gold. Her blue eyes were a little wary now and her expression less tranquil. The difficulties of the past years had tested her natural confidence but had not soured her and she held her head as defiantly as ever.

Finally, she considered the dress and then nodded her approval.

'You agree?' asked Juliana. 'You think it level?'

'I think so.'

Juliana parted the skirt and lifted each side a little. 'You must imagine it over a flowered petticoat. See how well it drapes?'

Sally nodded. 'It looks very well. I was not sure that the colour would suit but I have come round to your way of thinking. With the dark coffee inserts —' She broke off and raised her arms slowly above her head, frowning slightly.

The dressmaker looked at her anxiously. 'Is the bodice too tight? I did wonder last week —'

'Possibly — but I don't want to spoil the line. It must hug the waist. What do you think?'

Juliana considered. 'I could ease it a little. It won't spoil it. You must be able to move comfortably.' She picked up the shears and began to release the tacking stitches.

'You were telling me about Master Nash,' Sally reminded her.

Juliana rolled her eyes expressively. 'A fine figure of a man! But you must have seen him around town. You can't mistake the hat he wears — a large white tricorne. Very striking. Perhaps he has been to your coffee-house?'

The question was an innocent one but Sally had to force a smile as she replied with a light laugh, 'I think not. I could hardly have missed a hat like that!'

'He wears a wonderfully curled wig and dresses in the finest satins with real French lace at his neck — such beautiful clothes!' She sighed, 'I do adore elegant men. A well-shaped calf and slim ankle will set my heart aflutter! Nash has dignity, too, and such a noble bearing.'

'And yet you say he has no wife?' Sally was curious.

'None that anyone has ever seen!' she laughed. 'If he has one he has left her behind in London. No, they say he is a bachelor. That is the beauty of it! Apparently he was a soldier at one time and then a lawyer.'

'And now what does he do?'

Juliana giggled. 'He gambles! And most successfully from all accounts. Mistress Swayle – you must have seen her around, poor foolish creature. She wears so many face patches one might think she had the plague! She heard in the strictest confidence that he will be the new Master of Ceremonies and is boasting that when that time comes he will "clean up the town" – whatever that might mean.'

'Let us hope he can do it,' said Sally tartly. 'I could give him a list as long as my arm! For a start the chairmen are nothing but rogues. He would sack them all if I had my way. The streets are full of litter and badly lit at night –'

'He could improve the roads, also,' said Juliana. 'One of my clients – Mistress Bignell, do you know her? Such broad shoulders – quite unseemly on a woman! 'Tis the very devil to disguise broad shoulders and she won't allow me to widen the sleeves. Anyway, she twisted her ankle only last week. Fell into a pothole large enough to drown in, so she said, although I confess she does like to exaggerate. Oh, they filled them all in for the Queen's visit! The Lord knows what they *didn't* do! Since then they have done nothing and the roads are now as bad as ever.' She set down the shears. 'You can lower your arms now. How does that seem? A little more roomy?'

Sally nodded and the dressmaker began to help her off with the dress, reverting immediately to her favourite topic.

'I passed Master Nash at the King's Bath the day before yesterday and he had two liveried servants with him. Two! Can you imagine! What ostentation! Everyone was looking at him but he affected to be unaware of it. Revelled in it, in fact. What a man!'

She sighed again and Sally said, 'He has impressed you, that is certain.'

'I stared as hard as any of them,' Juliana confessed, laying the new dress carefully over the back of a settee.

'But did he notice you? That is the question.'

Juliana looked at her earnestly. 'He did smile upon me and doffed his hat and I fancied his eyes held mine longer than was necessary for politeness' sake. I don't think I imagined it.'

'He has a way with the ladies then, this Master Nash?'

'Certainly he does.' She removed a number of pins from the front of her own bodice and returned them to the pin cushion. 'Any man that looks that fine and has money to burn is like a honey pot with women buzzing round.' She looked at herself in the mirror, running her hands over her curves approvingly, turning this way and that. 'I confess I would give my soul to have him notice me again, but then,' she shrugged, 'I am one of the crowd. He could snap his fingers and any woman would run to him! I wonder if he likes his women dark, passionate and experienced?' She laughed. 'Or fair and virginal, like you?'

'Virginal?' Sally, wriggling back into her petticoats, glanced up in amusement. 'Is it so obvious then?'

'To a woman, yes, I think so. Maybe not to a man. They can be so dense.'

She helped Sally back into her clothes and held out her gloves.

'Could you manage a little money on account?' she murmured and took the proffered coins gratefully. 'If you care to call back in three days from now it should be finished.'

'Three days it is,' said Sally. 'And I shall keep a sharp look-out for your Master Nash.'

'Master Beau Nash!' Juliana corrected her. 'Beau. That's what they call him, you know – but he's not mine, more's the pity.'

'Master-Beau-Nash,' Sally repeated slowly, with a smile. 'If I see him shall I give him your kind regards?'

The dressmaker rolled her eyes. 'Tell him Juliana Popjoy will give him more than kind regards!'

'I'll remember,' said Sally but as she left there was an excited gleam in her eye.

Sally had been somewhat mortified to learn about Beau Nash from the dressmaker and to realise that he had not found his way to her coffee-house since if he were to become Master of Ceremonies he would be in a strong position to help her. With patronage from such a man her business would surely flourish and all her worries would be at an end. If Sally Lunn's was ever to make a profit she must have customers who were rich and fashionable – customers like Master Nash and his friends.

With this aim in mind she went out the following morning, wearing her peacock blue jacket over a dark skirt, with the deliberate intention of contriving a meeting with him – accidentally, of course. It would never do for him to guess that their meeting had been carefully staged.

'Although that might flatter him,' she mused as she hurried through the streets.

Juliana had said he liked to gamble so where would he go at this time of day? To the cock pit, perhaps. There was plenty to gamble on there but it was not yet half past ten and the first fight was not due until noon. She put her head in at the door of various public houses but although cards were much in evidence in all of them Nash was not among the players.

'The bowling green, then,' she muttered, but he was not there, either, nor was he strolling in the shadow of the Abbey Church, admiring the architecture.

'He'll be watching the tennis!' she told herself. 'Probably making a bet on the outcome of a match.'

'Where are you, Master Nash?' she asked aloud.

She lingered beside the courts hoping to catch a glimpse of the famous white hat but the sight continued to elude her. Reminded of those other vain journeys she had undertaken in search of her father, for a moment her face clouded regretfully but, as she reached the King's Bath, her memories were suddenly swept away.

There ahead of her was the man she had been looking for. He was leaning over the parapet of the bath but today the two liveried servants were notable by their absence. As she drew nearer, Sally had to admit that Nash presented a very handsome figure. She could appreciate the elegant cut of his green silk coat which was heavily embroidered in white thread. His breeches were fashionably cut and fine silk hose complemented his well-shaped legs. He wore his white hat at a bold angle and Sally saw that it did indeed look well on him. When she stole another look at his face she saw with some surprise that he was much younger than she had imagined, about her own age, in fact, and she could easily understand Juliana's enthusiasm.

She made her way to the parapet and listened unashamedly to the conversation going on around her. From this she learned that one of the women bathers, possibly on the advice of her physician, had chosen to enter the water without the benefit of clothing. Her nakedness was exciting ribald comments from one or two of the male onlookers, in particular a foppish young man standing on Nash's right. Sally delayed the introduction she had planned and waited to see how the champion of decent behaviour would react.

'Puss! Puss! Come to Papa then!' shouted the man, almost falling over the parapet in his attempt to capture the woman's attention. He was slim, sallow complexioned and dressed in the height of fashion.

The woman below, realising at last that his remarks were intended for her, turned away in embarrassment and began to move off through the water.

Sally was surprised to see the colour mounting angrily in Nash's cheeks. The young man then whistled loudly and Nash turned angrily towards him.

'You have the manners of a goat, sir!' he said distinctly. The young man gave him an astonished look but, after a muttered discussion with his two friends, apparently decided to ignore the insult and, returning to his position on the parapet, continued his harassment.

With a provocative glance towards Nash he next cupped his hands to his mouth and shouted, 'I am on fire for you, mistress!' and there was loud laughter from those around him.

Nash turned to him and lowering his voice said levelly, 'Take warning, you young cub, or I swear I'll teach you better manners.'

The young man tossed his head. 'Oh, you will! And how will you do that, pray?'

For a moment the two men stared at each other and Sally saw the hesitation in the young man's eyes. His slack mouth twitched nervously and Sally crossed her fingers, hoping that he would have the sense to moderate his behaviour, but unfortunately his friends now urged him to 'ignore the impudent dog', and he was rash enough to take their advice.

Turning from Nash he again shouted down to the pool, 'Mistress, from where I stand you look like an angel! I would fain come closer to see for myself!'

All eyes were on Nash. To Sally's delight, he turned towards her. 'I fear he has gone too far, mistress. Would you oblige me?' And before she had time to answer she found herself holding the famous white tricorne hat.

'You will pardon me,' he murmured apologetically and without further preamble he took the young man's collar in his left hand and with the other hand seized hold of his breeches. The young man let out a scream of fear and began to babble an apology but his change of heart had come too late.

'So you would fain see the lady at close quarters!' growled Nash. 'Then you shall do just that!'

And in one smooth movement he swung the foolish young man off his feet and tossed him over the parapet into the bath.

With one accord the spectators leaned over to watch him and a ragged burst of applause broke out as he fell into the water with a tremendous splash. Even his friends enjoyed his predicament and jeered him as he surfaced, red-faced and spluttering, his velvet cap floating beside him in the water. He made his way to the edge of the water to the accompaniment of loud cheers and there the bath sergeant waited, stern and disapproving, to haul him out and march him away. The woman he had been insulting retrieved his sodden cap and threw it after him.

Sally's eyes shone as she returned Nash's hat. 'That was nobly done, sir!' she told him, unable to hide her admiration.

To her surprise he did not return her smile. Instead he said, 'That damned temper of mine! 'Twill mean a duel, if I am not mistaken, and I do so abhor the barbarous habit.'

'A duel!' She stared at him. 'Do men still fight duels?' He shrugged as he straightened his waistcoat and tugged his cuffs into place.

'Among right thinking people it is out of fashion,' he agreed, 'but that foolish young puppy scarcely fits into that category. He has lost face and will, I am certain, demand satisfaction. With such friends he can scarce avoid it and they will be only too willing to risk his neck for the spectacle.' He sighed heavily.

'Then allow me to second you,' Sally offered impetuously. 'What will it be? Pistols at dawn?' Seeing his startled expression she went on, 'I would be honoured to attend Master Beau Nash in that capacity.'

At last he smiled, 'A lady second? Now that would be most unconventional! I am almost tempted to accept your offer, but fear I must gratefully decline. May I ask though how you know my name, mistress? I don't think we have met before.'

'Your fame has preceded you,' she told him truthfully. 'My dressmaker has spoken of you most favourably.'

'And you trust the word of your dressmaker where men are concerned?' His eyes mocked her charmingly.

'Invariably,' she protested. 'Who else can one trust these days?'

He laughed. 'May I know your name?'

'I am Sally Lunn.'

She waited hopefully for a sign that her name was familiar to him but it was obvious he had never heard of her.

'I bake the finest buns in Bath,' she told him. 'Come to my coffee-house in Segar's Alley and I will be proud to serve you.'

'So you are a baker, Sally Lunn.' He looked at her with amusement. 'And what is so special about those buns of yours?'

'They are made from a secret recipe,' she replied. 'A Huguenot recipe. To be precise they are based on the *brioche* which my mother and grandmother baked many years ago.'

'Then you are of French origin?'

'From La Rochelle on the west coast.' She smiled. 'But England is my home now. I had to reinvent the recipe,' she told him. 'I was only a child when we left France.'

'And you bake *brioche* for the English. I am most impressed!'

Under the spell of his eyes she found herself chattering on to hide her confusion. 'Wild horses would not drag the recipe from me! Mr Dalmer has offered me a king's ransom for it but –'

'Mr Dalmer?'

'He is a baker from the other side of town. Whenever we meet he teases me about my buns . . .' She fell silent, annoyed with herself. He must think her a foolish, prattling girl and she had intended to impress him as a business woman.

'I hope his teasing is within the bounds of decency,' said Nash, 'or I might have to throw him into the baths as well as . . .'

He broke off abruptly, with a muttered curse, and Sally followed the direction of his gaze.

'As I feared,' he said as the dripping young man strode purposefully towards him accompanied by his friends who now wore expressions of concern mingled with outrage. His clothes had shrunk to his body and his wet hair clung to his head. He carried his cap which dripped water and he had removed one of his gloves.

To Sally, Nash whispered, 'What a sorry sight!' and shook his head regretfully.

The young man's face was pale with hate and his eyes glittered malevolently as he slapped the glove across Nash's face and tossed it at his feet.

'Sir, you have insulted Thomas Garner,' he announced through gritted teeth. 'I demand satisfaction. I challenge you to a duel – to the death! Tomorrow morning at seven of the clock!' he said with a snarl. 'Name your weapons.'

'Swords!' said Nash promptly. 'Name the place.'

In his rage the young man had forgotten this detail and he quickly conferred with his companions.

'The Old Abbey Orchard,' he said at last and Nash gave a slight nod.

'So be it,' he said coldly.

There was a sudden tension in the air as the two men faced each other. A duel to the death. The bizarre incident had taken an ominous turn and Sally did not find it funny any more.

Wreathed in an early morning mist, the old orchard presented a gloomy picture next morning and Sally shuddered as she drew nearer. The low-lying land, flooded whenever the river rose, was now swampy and the smell of stagnant water hung in the windless air. The few apple trees that remained were twisted and gaunt with age and neglect.

Sally, her skirts held high to avoid the damp reeds, peered hopefully through the mist as her feet squelched through the mud and at last she called out nervously, 'Is anyone there?'

Momentarily the words dissolved into the mist and she was about to assume herself alone when a man's voice called, 'Over here!'

She made her way thankfully towards the sound and suddenly found herself in a clearing where Nash and another man stood together. A third man stood nearby with a physician's bag on a small collapsible table and Sally saw with a shiver of alarm that a sheathed sword rested alongside the bag.

'Master Nash —' Sally began eagerly but he held up his hand. 'Please call me Richard,' he told her with a faint smile. 'This is hardly the time to stand on ceremony.' He introduced John Widden, his second, and Doctor Flock, the physician.

'I scarcely thought you would come,' Nash told Sally. ''Tis a gloomy place at the best of times and hardly the place one would choose to meet one's maker!'

'Oh, please don't talk that way!' she cried fearfully. 'I prayed most earnestly last night for your safety.'

The physician said, 'We must pray that no one is fatally wounded. 'Tis some years since I have had to officiate at such an unfortunate event and I rather hope it may prove to be the last.'

'I second that most heartily!' Nash told him.

For a moment they were all silent, their eyes straining through the mist to catch a glimpse of the opposition, but it was their ears that eventually warned them of the second party's approach. Thomas Garner, with his physician and second, materialized out of the gloom. Three of his friends followed immediately behind them, complaining loudly about the ruin of their fashionable shoes and apparently quite unaffected by the seriousness of the occasion. Sally recognized all three from the encounter at the baths. One, in a yellow waistcoat, she had already dubbed the Canary — he was a reed-like youth with a weak chin and pale blue eyes. The second man was older, probably in his twenties, and bore a

279

close resemblance to Thomas Garner, being perhaps his brother. The third, almost handsome, was nearer thirty, with a languid manner.

Sally whispered to Nash, 'Have you no other friends to support you?'

'I told no one,' he said, 'but you are here. What more could I ask?'

As soon as the preliminaries were under way Sally stepped back a little and watched as formal introductions were made between the two protagonists. A brief discussion between the two physicians followed and then a cursory inspection of the weapons was carried out by the seconds. She was aware that Thomas Garner's friends were regarding her with curiosity but she kept her head firmly averted from the tree beneath which they stood and looked steadfastly towards Nash.

Now a muttered conversation ensued between the duellists and their seconds and Sally drew her shawl more tightly around her shoulders and wished it was all over. Was it possible that within minutes one or both of the duellists would be dead or dying? It seemed incredible and yet, in her heightened state of anxiety, the atmosphere in the orchard seemed heavy with menace and anything was possible. Two grown men had agreed to cross swords and there was no way to stop them for, although duelling was less common now and was discouraged by the authorities, it was not yet illegal and there was no reason why the contest should not take place.

Helplessly she glanced around but there was no sign of any last-minute intervention. She stifled a cry of apprehension as Nash removed his coat and Thomas Garner immediately did likewise.

The seconds handed the swords to the duellists and one of them cried, 'Take your places!'

Nash and Garner placed themselves about three yards apart and each man, with his sword in his right hand, held his left hand behind his back. Sally noted that they were both right handed but did that make any difference? Was it to Nash's advantage or disadvantage? He was slightly taller than Garner but he carried more weight. And how good a swordsman was he? He had chosen swords instead of pistols so presumably he was suitably skilled. She wished she was more knowledgeable on the matter but was too proud to ask for information.

'Oh, please God!' she whispered. 'Keep him from harm. Keep them both from harm.'

Garner, she conceded, was an uncouth, insensitive youth but he did not deserve to die. She resisted the impulse to rush forward and try to stop them as neither of them would appreciate such interference. It would reflect on their courage. She would have to wait passively in the wings for the drama to be enacted.

'On guard!'

Both men sprang forward suddenly and steel rang against steel as their swords met for the first time in a brief parry. Both men drew back, swords raised defensively then lunged forward again on the attack – again that hideous sound as the blades found each other. There was another flurry of blows, another lunge, a longer parry and then the duellists fell back once more. Though breathing heavily, neither man showed signs of weakening. From the sidelines the seconds watched keenly for any signs of foul play or

unethical conduct, but both men were proving themselves not only proficient but masters of the art and
they could find no fault.

Sally stole a glance at Garner's friends and saw the
apprehension on their faces. From them she looked
towards the physicians. The face of one was expression-
less, the other was shaking his head unhappily.

A fresh clash of steel brought Sally's attention back
to the duellists and she watched fearfully as first one
and then the other appeared to gain control. To her
inexperienced eyes they appeared well matched, moving
with a practised grace that was almost pleasing to
watch.

'Dancing their way to death!' thought Sally, shocked
and disbelieving. She felt the press of tears behind her
eyelids. Then suddenly, without warning, came the
decisive stroke.

Nash had lowered his guard a fraction and the tip of
Garner's sword caught his upper arm. Blood spurted,
splashing the whiteness of his shirt. Sally's hands went
up to her face in dismay, but with a fierce flick of his
wrist Nash sent Garner's weapon spinning out of his
hand. Now the tip of his sword was at the young
man's throat.

There was a horrified murmur from Garner's friends
and a mutter of dismay from the seconds. Impetuously
Sally ran forward shouting, 'No! No! Oh, please don't
kill him!'

She stopped guiltily within yards of them and
covered her mouth with her hands, already regretting
her impulsive words, but the two men were unaware
of her as they stared fiercely into each other's eyes.

'Is honour satisfied?' Nash asked Garner.

Too choked to answer Garner gave a slight nod. Slowly Nash lowered his sword and handed it to his second, who now hurried forward and Garner's second hurried to retrieve his weapon. Ignoring the blood which was rapidly turning his sleeve deep red, Nash held out his hand and after a moment's hesitation Garner shook it briefly. Nash's physician, visibly relieved that the outcome had been no worse, ran forward to inspect the wound and Sally moved slowly to join them.

'I'm so sorry,' she told Nash. ''Twas foolish of me to interfere. I was so afraid for you and then for him. Do please forgive me.'

'There's no need for apologies,' he told her and she could see that he bore her no ill will. 'You can rest easy now. No one is going to die and this scratch will soon heal.' He turned to the physician and said lightly, ''Twas worth it, wouldn't you agree?'

'I would, sir,' replied the physician. 'You were very generous and the young puppy knows it.' He turned to Sally. 'Master Nash is undoubtedly the better swordsman and could easily have killed his opponent had he chosen, but if he had disarmed Garner without allowing the young fool a token strike honour would not have been satisfied.'

She looked at Nash who smiled and shrugged. 'I did throw him into the bath!' he reminded her and with a slight movement of his head he indicated his wound. 'This is the price I must pay for my own rash behaviour. But now it is over and done with. When the wound is bandaged I suggest you join me in a small celebration.'

Sally seized the opportunity. 'Why not join me in my coffee-house?' she asked.

After a brief hesitation he smiled again. 'A charming suggestion. I accept with pleasure. Shall you supply the teacakes? I will bring a bottle or two of my favourite wine.'

For a moment Sally was lost for words. Beau Nash was about to visit Segar's Alley. Reality was exceeding her wildest dreams.

'What do you say?' he prompted.

Her smile was radiant. 'I say you are a great man, Beau Nash, I am so glad we are going to be friends.'

An hour later a beam of weak sunshine had edged its way into Sally's front room where she and Nash were sitting companionably on opposite sides of one of the tables. A plate of teacakes and two bottles of Madeira stood on the table and glasses had already been raised in a variety of toasts – 'The Queen – God bless her!' 'Nash's survival!' 'Friendship!'

Nash refilled the glasses and said, 'To Sally Lunn's!'

The glasses clinked companionably and Sally regarded her visitor with something akin to adoration. She could not remember when she had felt so exhilarated – first the drama of the duel, then the relief at its outcome and now this cosy *tête-à-tête* with a man like Richard Nash. He had already eaten one of her teacakes and had started on a second (it seemed that duelling gave a man an appetite, she thought hazily).

She felt at peace with the whole world, and that world appeared to centre round Beau Nash.

Sally smiled at him and smothered a hiccup. She was

unused to wines and spirits and the Madeira was affecting her in the most delightful way. She felt positively pretty and the years seemed to roll away so that she felt like a girl again. Her body, as well as her mind, was behaving in an odd way and she found herself struggling with yearnings which for many years she had not allowed to surface. As she listened to Nash an image of Simon Pett rose uninvited in her mind and she felt again the excitement of that forbidden meeting. She sighed deeply and watched that image give way to another as Barnaby Copely rose up to remind her of what might have been.

She suddenly saw that she had been robbed of much that was pleasurable; of much that was a woman's due. Fate, she thought drowsily, had dealt unkindly with her and she would go to her grave unfulfilled, cheated of what should have been hers had circumstances not conspired against her so unkindly. Now Fate was giving her another chance, she told herself. Here was a charming man who admired her. Circumstances had thrown them together and who was she to resist what might prove to be her last chance?

She took another sip of wine and smiled at him seductively. 'I am told you are tipped by many to be the next Master of Ceremonies. Is that true?'

He shrugged modestly. 'In due course, maybe, but I doubt I shall step into those particular shoes just yet.'

Sally noticed with surprise that Nash appeared to be more handsome by the minute! His small mouth now seemed larger and his nose quite perfect. It was strange that she had not appreciated him fully until now.

'But when you do step into his shoes?' she asked.

To her surprise this question provoked an immediate and overwhelming response for she had inadvertently touched upon his favourite topic of conversation. He promptly launched into a vivid account of his plans should he ever attain that lofty office and Sally, slightly disconcerted, listened as attentively as the wine would allow. Later, she told herself, he would talk about her and matters would take their course.

It seemed that in Nash's opinion the town of Bath was a mere relic of medieval days. 'A piddling little wool town surrounded by munching sheep' was how he actually described it. Sally laughed at the unflattering description and, remembering her brother's trade, felt bound to protest.

''Tis the wool trade that has made the town what it is,' she told him. 'The wealth of the town comes from those racks of brightly-dyed wools drying in the sun beyond Broad Street. My brother, Jean –'

He interrupted her impatiently. 'It did come from that wool, I grant you, but now the revenue is scarcely worth bothering about and the total output dwindles each year. The weavers themselves know it. They can read the signs as easily as I can and some are already looking elsewhere to earn a living.' He leaned forward and wagged a finger at her. 'Bath will die on her feet if nothing is done to help her.'

'But how can you say that?' Sally demanded. 'Why, the Queen visited us not so many years ago.'

'Four years ago,' he told her, 'and that is my point. If Queen Anne –'

'And the wife of James II came towards the end of the last century!'

'Exactly so!' His eyes gleamed with enthusiasm. 'If Bath is good enough for royalty, it should also be good enough for their subjects. They should come to enjoy our hospitality in their hundreds. Their thousands, even! But do they?'

'Some people come.'

'Sick people come for the hot waters but –'

'Sixteen eighty-seven!' cried Sally. 'Mary of Modena. That was her name. James's queen.'

'Sally, don't you see my reasoning?' he implored her. 'It matters not who came or when. What matters is that Bath has so much more to offer than hot springs. I believe we can put Bath firmly on the map. I want people to say, "Oh, but *surely* you have visited Bath!"'

Sally nodded carefully. She was finding it very difficult to concentrate and shook her head to clear it. Then she took another sip of Madeira and gave her companion her full attention once more, admiring his forehead and the finely arched brows.

'We have to provide better amenities,' he was saying. 'We must build bigger and better lodging houses. Not within the walls. I own there is little enough room as it is, but outside the walls there are acres of land just waiting to be developed. Bath is a shoddy little place, Sally. You can't deny that.'

She had never thought of it that way but felt disinclined to say so. In fact she was reluctant to say anything at all. Words were not necessary. She felt wonderfully at peace with the whole world and if Nash wanted to change things, why stop him? Her eyes closed drowsily but at once his hand gripped her wrist and she tried to look more alert than she felt.

'What can Bath offer at present?' he asked but fortunately went on to answer his own question. 'Bearbaiting! A disgusting spectacle. Who wants to see a poor dumb animal being tormented? And who would pay good money to see a raggle-tailed group of strolling players?'

He did not notice her hastily averted eyes.

'And cockfighting. Oh, yes,' he adopted a mocking tone, 'take a walk to Timber Green, my lady, and you can see two gaming cocks tear each other to pieces! Oh, did they splash your fine dress with blood? How perfectly beastly!' He shook his head in disgust. ''Tis quite deplorable! In the name of God, this is the eighteenth century not the Middle Ages.' He sighed. 'At least there is talk now of abandoning the stocks and pillory. And not before time. What an abject sight – to see a poor wretch with his head through a piece of wood! I would chop them down and make a bonfire of them if I had my way. The sooner they go the better!' He took a gulp of wine. 'Where do you go for entertainments, Sally?'

She struggled to think clearly. Entertainments? Where *did* she go? 'I dance on the bowling green,' she told him. 'They have musicians . . .'

'Musicians! Huh!' His voice was scornful.

'A hautboy and a violin,' she protested, 'and I walk in the Orange Grove.'

This last made him snort in disgust. 'Orange Grove, my eye!' he exclaimed. 'There's not an orange tree in sight. They're all sycamores!'

'Oh no, Richard,' she began again, ready to explain that the row of sycamores and the column were a tribute to William of Orange, but he gave her no time.

'We need uplifting entertainments if we are to attract people of sensitivity and nobility. We need art galleries and museums. Why, all of Bath is a museum at present! 'Tis an outdated antiquity! All it lacks is a label!'

'Oh, Richard,' she said softly.

Unaware of her change of mood he reached for the last teacake, spread butter and honey on it and crammed it into his mouth. Sally began to giggle helplessly. Seeing her amusement he tried to say something but instead spat a few crumbs on to the table which sent them both into peals of laughter. Nash began to choke as a piece of cake went down the wrong way and Sally went round to pat him on the back. At once his arms went round her and she found herself sitting on his lap with her arms encircling his neck. Her body became a jumble of delightful sensations and it suddenly seemed a good idea to run her fingers lightly across his lips.

At that moment she thought him the most charming man in Bath, if not the whole of England, and it seemed only fair to tell him so.

'Richard,' she murmured, 'you are a most handsome fellow.' He was, however, in no mood to be diverted from his theme and appeared not to have heard so Sally, snuggled against him and with her head on his shoulder, tried very hard to follow the gist of his arguments. His face was alight with zeal and his words flowed effortlessly. Absentmindedly he kissed the top of her head.

''Tis all a matter of money,' he told her, 'and we have to offer investors an incentive. Oh, I know the people to approach, don't you fret! Not the landowners, nor the Tories. No, 'tis the Whigs who will make Bath famous. Once they see the way the wind's blowing they will fall over themselves to be part of the plan. They will all want a slice of the cake.'

The word 'cake' registered and Sally raised her head. 'There are plenty more,' she mumbled. 'At least I think so –'

This remark puzzled him and he frowned. 'You are not listening, Sally Lunn, my little currant bun!'

'I *am*!' she insisted. 'And there are no currants in –'

'Oh, go back to sleep!' he laughed. Her eyes closed but he no longer needed an audience.

Winding one of her curls around his finger he went on, 'We need men of vision, the finest architects, eminent doctors, first-class lawyers. Men with the courage of their convictions – or better still with the courage of *mine*!' He laughed. 'Men with the energy to get things done, who can cut through pettifogging rules and regulations.' He sighed deeply. 'Dear God, I'll do it if it takes every last breath in my body!'

He looked down on the woman who dozed in his lap, her fair curls tumbled against his chest.

'Oh, Sally!' he whispered. 'Little Sally Lunn!' He began to stroke her hair and as he did so his grand dreams for Bath slid away to be replaced by a more urgent need. He considered her affectionately. Would she be willing? He hardly knew her. Yet women, in his experience, were creatures of whim. She seemed to like him and he liked her.

'Sally!' he whispered and gave her a little shake.

She roused and looked up at him and he saw desire in her eyes also. Suddenly, he made up his mind. He must lie with her! A refusal on her part would be unacceptable.

He searched for the words but fortunately they were not necessary for she was awake and staring at him, with eyes full of longing.

'Richard!' she breathed. 'I think – Oh, Richard, after all these years, I think you are the one!'

His mouth fell open in astonishment. Had he heard aright? Was she . . .? He blinked, trying to think more clearly. Could she really be a virgin at her age? And with those charms? He was in luck!

A tiny spark of chivalry made him ask, 'Are you certain 'tis what you truly want?'

To his relief she nodded and pointed to the room above them.

'Sally!' With a whoop of joy he scooped her into his arms and began to stumble across the room and up the stairs . . .

Below them, Toby heard their uneven progress. He shook his head and cursed, wondering gloomily where it would all end.

Later, when Sally awoke, she found herself alone. At once memories flooded back and with a broad smile on her face she turned over and went back to sleep. When she woke again, she had sobered up and made her way slowly downstairs, one hand held to her aching head. One glance showed her that there were more customers than usual but a second glance confirmed that Nash was not among them.

She was not at all contrite, she told herself, as she continued down the stairs. She passed Toby and saw that his normally cheerful smile had deserted him but she met his eye as defiantly as she could. In the kitchen she sank down on a stool and rested her head in her hands. ''Tis none of Toby's business!' she muttered. She was a free woman and would award her favours where and when and upon whom she pleased.

Toby put his head round the door but before he could open his mouth she asked, 'Who's waiting on tables?'

'I got Jane in from along the way. I said for a few hours. I didn't know how long you would be "busy"!'

He laid a slight emphasis on the last word to let her know that he was under no misapprehension about her adventure. By his tone Sally understood that he did not approve.

'Very wise,' she told him. 'Jane is slow but sensible. One day we may be able to employ her full time.'

'When pigs fly!' he said, without enthusiasm.

She had hoped he would make her a tisane to cure her head as he often had in the past but it was clear he was obviously going to punish her for her sins. She sighed.

The church clock struck three and she looked genuinely startled. Three o'clock! Had she slept so long?

Catching her eye he said, 'You had a long sleep. Good wine, was it?'

'Very good.' She stared him straight in the eye.

'The "gentleman" left around noon,' he told her. 'He didn't say when he would be back – or even that he would be back!' he added unkindly.

Sally rubbed her eyes and gave a little moan of distress. Interpreting this correctly Toby banged a few pans as loudly as he could and Sally winced as the noises reverberated inside her skull.

'Must you?' she protested.

He gave her a spiteful look. 'Someone has to do some work around here,' he said. 'I'm sorry if it inconveniences you.' He rattled a handful of spoons together for good measure and before Sally could speak again he swung on his heel and went out, slamming the door loudly behind him.

She groaned aloud, 'Oh, Toby! Toby!'

But she understood. Toby was hurt by what he would consider her betrayal. Although she had never suggested in any way that she might one day agree to be his wife yet she knew he played a waiting game. But was she to blame for that? She did not think so yet still could not rid herself of a feeling of guilt.

She raised her head and said loudly, 'I shall do as I please and to hell with Toby Parker!' But the words had a hollow ring to them and she frowned and tried again. 'To hell with all of them! Except Richard!' A smile lit her face at the sound of his name.

She owed him so much, she told herself. He had unravelled the mystery; had taught her what love-making was all about. It was so simple. Now that she knew, she thought of all the wasted years when she had chosen to sleep alone. 'Richard-Beau-Nash!' she whispered. She loved Richard Beau Nash! She was certain of it. Her independence now meant nothing to her and from now on her world would revolve around Richard.

Suddenly her smile faded. Doubts filled her mind. One question loomed large in her thoughts – would he wed her? Had their time together meant anything to him or was she just another conquest? Juliana had said he had a way with ladies. Sally did not doubt it! As a lover he was practised, gentle, romantic.

She sighed, 'Oh, Richard! Do you love me?'

Her headache showed no improvement so she dragged herself to her feet and fetched a mug from the dresser. Into this she dropped caraway seeds and poured on hot water from the kettle on the hob nearby. Sipping the fragrant liquid she allowed her thoughts to dwell on her hazy recollections of the morning's revelations. She had most certainly enjoyed the experience, she told herself in surprise. The duties of a wife were distinctly more pleasurable than she had been led to expect.

If only she could guess at Nash's reaction. Had he already forgotten her? No, that was impossible. At this very moment he was most likely recalling their time together and planning another visit. For a moment she allowed her imagination to take flight and saw herself on his arm, making an appearance at the theatre; making a grand entrance at a ball – given in his honour, perhaps, by a grateful city! The women would whisper behind their fans, 'There goes Nash with Sally Lunn!' And how they would envy her. Richard Nash was going to take Bath by storm and she would be at his side.

A horrid thought occurred to her suddenly. Suppose Nash was married! He had no wife with him in Bath but he might have left one behind him in London. Worse still – she sat up in horror – he might be intending to send for her at some time to join him in Bath. Such a situation would be intolerable. She decided that at her next fitting she must ask Juliana for more information.

Toby reappeared in the doorway, a triumphant look on his face.

'Jane has gone home,' he announced. 'Will you serve tables or shall I do it?' His expression challenged her, daring her to refuse and her conscience pricked her.

'I'll do it,' she told him.

As she rose to her feet Toby cried, 'You won't see him again, Sally! I know the sort of man he is! You have thrown yourself away on a . . .' He hesitated as her mouth tightened.

'On a what?' she asked coldly.

'On a philanderer!'

Sally searched for a crushing rejoinder. 'On the contrary, I wager he'll be back before dark,' she said with a toss of her head, a movement which she immediately regretted. Before he could speak again she swept past him but the Madeira was taking its toll and, for the very first time, the coffee-house had lost its appeal.

That evening, soon after eight o'clock, there was a knock at the door and she opened it to find a young lad holding a linnet in a small gilded cage.

'For Sally Lunn,' he intoned, 'from an admirer!'

'For me?' she gasped.

She reached wonderingly for the cage but he withdrew it sharply so that it was slightly out of reach and thrust out a hopeful hand. She gave him a penny and he sped away leaving her to carry the bird into the bakery.

'From an admirer!' she repeated and her spirits

soared. So Richard had not forgotten her, she thought triumphantly. The pessimistic Toby Parker would have to eat his words.

Chapter Twelve

LESS THAN A WEEK later Ned made his way down the hill from the quarry, his thoughts as usual on Sally Lunn. He was only half aware of the path as he tried to avoid the worst of the mud – the result of two days' heavy rain – and he was quite unprepared for the sight of a huddled figure lying by the side of the track. With an exclamation of concern he leaned over the bundle of tattered clothing to investigate further but as soon as he recognized the man's face he straightened up in annoyance.

'You again! And in your cups, no doubt. Am I never to be rid of you?' he demanded. 'Get up, man, for heaven's sake!' The man struggled to a sitting position and did his best to look even more pathetic than he was.

'Just a few pence, Master Cooper,' he whined. 'I've not eaten for three days, as God is my witness. Not a bite of food has passed my lips since –'

Ned said sharply, 'What more do you want from me, Stubbs? I have done what I can for you and this is how you repay me. I found you a good job. What has become of that? A grave-digger does not earn a princely sum but certainly enough to keep body and soul together. You should not have to beg.'

'I know that, master, and I'm grateful but . . .' Stubbs scratched his matted head searching for a reason for his present predicament. 'I had a bit of ill luck and the reverend gentleman – God rot his soul! – took advantage of it and sent me packing. A very hard man, that reverend sir. So here I am, without a penny to my name. Without the wherewithal –'

'Enough of your nonsense!' said Ned contemptuously. 'I'll wager a drinking spree was your so-called ill luck!'

Suddenly the man let out a most realistic groan, screwed up his face and clutched at his stomach.

''Tis this griping,' he gasped, 'that's what done for me. Like a knife turning in my gut. Fair takes the wind out of my sails, and that's the godbegotten truth. Nothing will shift it but a drop of gin or a sip or two of brandy. Not much, you understand,' he added hastily. 'More as medicament, so to speak.'

Ned was still wary and only half-convinced by the man's behaviour. He had learned by bitter experience that Stubbs would stop at nothing to obtain money. No lie was too great for him; no trick too mean. He was his own worst enemy, with a shady past into which Ned had never dared to pry. Ned regarded him suspiciously. Was he pretending?

It was some time since he had found him slumped against his doorway in a drunken stupor and had taken pity on the wretch. Ned had rescued him from the stocks on several occasions and had persuaded the vicar to give him a trial period as grave-digger. Obviously this last attempt to help the man had also failed. Ned sighed. He would give him the benefit of the doubt.

'Give me your hands,' he said and hauled the disreputable creature to his feet.

'Just a penny,' cried Stubbs. 'I promise 'twill be the last you hear of me. I never will trouble you again. I'll turn over a new leaf. I'll –'

He doubled up again and this time Ned saw the perspiration beaded on his brow and knew the pain was genuine.

'Come along!' he said more kindly. 'We'll get you home and into bed. *Just* for tonight you shall sleep in our attic. The physician shall take a look at you. A bath and a shave would hardly come amiss, either.'

A look of horror came over Stubbs's face at the mention of the physician but he allowed himself to be helped down the track, murmuring meanwhile about his lack of faith in 'quacks and charlatans', and vowing to be completely recovered by the morning so that their unwelcome attentions would not be necessary.

By the time they reached Ned's home, however, he was no longer in a fit state to argue for the pain was very real and increasing with every step he took. His face was ashen and his breath came in agonized gasps. As soon as they entered the house Ned helped him out of his dirty clothes and into a hip bath full of warm water which he hoped might alleviate some of the pain, but Stubbs continued to cry and tremble as fresh cramps seized him. Ned washed him gently and soaped the matted hair, then tipped a bucket of rinsing water over him while Stubbs spluttered his protests.

'A drop of gin . . .?' he suggested hopefully.

'We must wait for the physician,' Ned told him. 'When you are in bed I will send a boy to fetch him. If he recommends brandy I have some that will do very well.'

He put Stubbs to bed and was about to leave the room when he heard him cry out. Stubbs was pointing towards the bottom of the bed.

'That stick!' he cried in a voice that shook with excitement. 'I'd know that stick anywhere. Hand it me, I beg you!'

Bewildered, Ned picked up Sally's stick from the chest. 'This one?' he asked.

In spite of his pain Stubbs managed a smile as he snatched it out of Ned's hand and examined it eagerly.

'Yes! Yes!' he murmured. 'The same duck's head – see the beak. I watched my father carve it, day after day. So slow, I thought – impatient brat that I was! I sat beside him and played with the shavings as they fell on to my knees. I was just so high! And see here, the notches he made – one for each of my birthdays!'

He pressed the stick to his lips and kissed it and two large tears rolled slowly down his face. Utterly confused, Ned could only watch in amazement.

At last he said, 'But that's impossible. That stick belongs to Sally, a Huguenot refugee. Brought it with her when she fled to England many years ago. She left it here.'

Before Stubbs could reply another cramp robbed him temporarily of speech but when he had recovered he said, 'Sally? The name means nothing to me.'

Ned tried to recall what Sally had told them of her escape.

'She came with a brother Jean – and her mother and grandmother.'

'Jean!' muttered Stubbs. He looked up at Ned. 'My son's name is Jean. Is my son here in England?'

Ned suddenly remembered with alarm that Sally's mother had remarried and he hesitated.

'Who are you?' he asked cautiously. 'You have changed your name – that much I do know. But what name were you *born* with? Are you English?'

But it seemed the man was now regretting his revelation. His lips closed stubbornly and he shook his head.

'Are you of French descent?' Ned persisted but now the man threw the stick on to the bed as though disgusted with it.

'Stubbs,' he muttered. 'Stubbs is good enough for me.' He cried out again and folded his arms protectively round his body.

'That brandy!' he whispered. 'A nip of brandy makes a world of difference!'

His words reminded Ned about the physician. 'What am I thinking of!' he chided himself and hurried downstairs to catch the eye of the first urchin that passed the house.

Having sent him off at a run he went back into his kitchen and sat down thoughtfully. Could this reprobate really be Sally's father who had disappeared all those years ago? And if so (and it seemed a distinct possibility) what impact would the discovery of his existence make on her family? He thought of Jean and his wife and children. And Marie, now happily married to another man. And Sally? Was this the father she had dreamed of for so long? If so, he would prove a bitter disappointment and a severe embarrassment, but was that a good enough reason for keeping his identity and whereabouts a secret?

301

He was still considering various aspects of the situation when the physician arrived and as soon as Ned had explained the problem they mounted the stairs together. The physician's examination was thorough; his diagnosis was precise.

'A large tumour in the bowel,' he told Ned, when they were outside the room, 'well-advanced and nigh on inoperable. Surgery would be expensive, possibly unsuccessful and might even hasten his demise. The kindest thing would be to let him go on his way. My advice to you is save your money and your pity for someone more worthwhile.'

Seeing Ned's dismay he added, 'The man is beyond help in more ways than one, Master Cooper. If you could save him now what good would it do? You know and I know that he would slowly and steadily drink himself into the grave. Why prolong his miserable existence?'

As Ned still did not speak, he said, 'I will give him something to ease the pain. Never fear. I will do what I can but you must see that it is God's will; his time is come. It happens to us all and he has little to live for.' He laid a hand on Ned's arm, 'I will send medicine before nightfall. Give him as much as he needs to ease the pain.'

Ned roused himself with difficulty from the turmoil of his thoughts.

'And you will call again?'

'As often as you wish.'

'Daily, then.'

The physician nodded, 'So be it.'

Ned closed the door behind him and drew a long, deep breath.

'In the name of God! What do I do now?' he whispered. And waited in vain for an answer.

The prescription arrived as promised and under the effect of the medicine, a strong opiate, Stubbs fell into a deep sleep.

However, in the room below him Ned was not so lucky. He lay wide eyed throughout the long hours of the night, considering various ways in which he could deal with the problem of Sally's father for he was no longer in any doubt about the man's true identity.

His first option was simply to tell Sally that her father was found but he could imagine her dismay on discovering who and what he was. Ned had no way of knowing what sort of man he had been before his move to England. He might have been an honest man, an upright citizen, although Ned found this rather hard to imagine. Sally would also have to be told that his death was imminent and that news would certainly cause her immeasurable distress. He might keep the man's identity a secret but suppose Sally discovered it after his death? How would she react to that? She might be very bitter and might blame Ned for preventing the longed-for reunion with her father.

A third possibility was to confide in another member of the family. Should he tell Marie that her husband was alive but dying? Or should he speak privately to Henri? From all he had gathered from Sally Henri was a sensible and humane man – but he had married Marie believing her to be a widow. The knowledge that her husband was still alive would be a terrible shock. He could approach Jean but he had married into a respectable family and the sudden appearance of Sally's father, in his present state, would shock and appall them all. Whichever way Ned looked at the problem it presented serious difficulties.

He tossed to and fro in search of a solution that would do least damage to those concerned. Most of all he wanted to save Sally from bitter disillusionment. Perhaps, after all, it would be better for the man to die under his chosen name. Stubbs would be buried without ceremony and Sally's cherished belief in her father would remain untarnished. She would never find him but did that really matter?

The early hours of the morning found him still awake but his weary brain had presented him with a possible way out of the maze. He could take one step at a time.

Firstly, he could persuade Stubbs to go into hospital and have the operation. If he survived it then at least he would be assured of a future. Ned could then decide whether or not to risk revealing the truth to Sally without involving the rest of the family who could, if she thought it wise, remain in blissful ignorance. Sally could also choose whether or not to confront her father. She might prefer to help him without disclosing who she was. She might even – and he was clutching at straws! – work the magic that would help her father make a new life for himself.

With a sigh, he turned on to his back and stared up at the ceiling. He nodded into the darkness, satisfied that perhaps he had finally produced a solution that would bear scrutiny in the cold light of day. Not that his worries were now over – far from it. He must investigate the cost of surgery and see whether or not his meagre savings would suffice. If not he would have to think again. There might be ways of raising some extra money but he would face that hurdle when he came to it. For the present he felt reasonably pleased with himself and could allow himself the luxury of a few hours of well-deserved sleep. He turned on to his side and settled his limbs more comfortably. As the dawn broke his eyelids closed and shortly after both body and mind were at rest.

Two days passed after the arrival of the linnet and Nash did not put in another appearance at Sally Lunn's. Toby found it difficult to hide his elation but Sally hid her disappointment and fussed constantly over the bird, praising its song whenever Toby was near enough to hear. She told herself that it was only a matter of time before Nash came back to her and that a man of his calibre had important affairs which demanded his attention and which must take priority over matters of the heart. She consoled herself with the knowledge that he thought highly of her – why else had he sent her such a wonderful gift?

On the third evening there was a prolonged rapping at the bakery door.

Toby said sourly, 'The wanderer returns!'

Ignoring this remark Sally rushed to the door, an eager smile on her face. She had prettied up the bedroom in preparation for Nash's next visit. New curtains now hung at the window and there was a bowl of late roses beside the bed; lavender had been sprinkled between the sheets and a new picture hung on the far wall.

With a cry of welcome she flung open the door and found herself staring at the empty step. Footsteps sounded and she saw a young lad running away, glancing back over his shoulder and laughing at her confusion.

Looking down she saw a small package tucked beside the step and her disappointment was tinged with sudden relief.

'Another gift!' she told Toby, her expression smug. He sniffed disparagingly but watched with curiosity as she unwrapped it with trembling fingers. A card dropped on to the table and she snatched it up.

'A little token of my esteem!' she read.

Toby snorted, 'Couldn't find the time to bring it himself, I suppose. Too busy flaunting himself around the town in his fine clothes and licking the shoes of his betters!' Sally gave him an icy look but she was becoming inured to his jibes and did not deign to answer.

A small velvet box was revealed and she opened it slowly, savouring the moment. In it, on a bed of white silk, lay a single pearl on a slim gold chain.

'Richard Beau Nash!' she breathed. 'Oh, what a gift! And what a man! A pearl! 'Tis quite perfect!' She held it up admiringly. 'What taste! What generosity! I shall wear it close to my heart.'

Toby said nothing. He was impressed by the gift and surprised, also, for he had heard rumours of Nash's penchant for pretty women and had genuinely believed Sally to be one of many. Perhaps he was wrong. It was certainly beginning to look as though the man was genuinely interested in her.

'A little token of my esteem,' she repeated.

Toby rallied, 'Little it certainly is! One solitary pearl. I wonder what became of the rest of the necklace?'

Flushed with pleasure Sally smiled at him with exaggerated sweetness, 'Is it so hard for you to believe that a man like Richard Nash should find me attractive? Am I so repulsive in your eyes then?'

'Oh, you are pretty enough,' he told her, 'but there are plenty prettier than you. Aye, and richer, too. Surely you can see that a wealthy woman would prove a much better match for a man like that.'

'Toby Parker, you're jealous!'

She moved to the small mirror that hung on the wall, and carefully fastened the chain round her neck. 'I think it becomes me very well!' she announced. Seeing his grim expression in the mirror she added crossly, 'And take that expression off your face! Oh, don't think I don't know what you are thinking. I have known you too long and can read you like a book. You hoped I should fall flat on my face! Admit it! You thought Richard had used me and would cast me off like an old shoe! Now that you see that he does care for me – enough to send me costly gifts – you cannot bear it! Fie on you, Toby Parker. You are so small-minded!'

Taken aback by her anger he could only mumble inaudibly but she was in no mood to listen. She went on recklessly. 'Well, if you no longer approve of my behaviour – if you think me a trollop – why not have the courage to say so?'

'I don't think you are a trollop . . .' he began, but added disastrously, '. . . at least, not exactly.'

She faced him, her hands on her hips, the pearl pendant almost lost against her white bodice.

'Not exactly!' she cried. 'And what does that mean?'

Abashed by her rage he floundered. He had not intended to provoke her to this extent and was reluctant to make matters worse, but his pride would not allow him to retract anything he had said. He stared into her furious face and could find no words. Suddenly he could bear it no longer and, turning on his heel, walked towards the door.

'Where are you going?' she demanded.

He fancied he heard anxiety in her voice.

'To find more cheerful company!' he growled and slammed the door so hard that a teacup was jerked from its hook on the dresser. It bounced to the stone floor and broke into pieces and Sally snatched another cup from its hook and threw it after him. She threw another and another until the row of hooks was empty, then she sank to her knees and burst into tears.

The pearl had restored her confidence in the man she now thought of as her lover for she could not believe that there were other women in his life who had lain with him so sweetly. Surely he must long to see her again as she longed for him. Toby, however, had voiced the question that still loomed large in her own mind. Why had Richard *sent* the gifts instead of bringing them in person?

She sat among the pieces of broken crockery, groping for them vaguely, blinded by her tears.

Oh, how she hated Toby Parker! 'Damn your eyes!' she told him. 'Richard loves me!'

She fingered the pearl and drew a long, choking breath. Toby's words rankled – she could never forgive him. It would serve him right if she walked out of his life forever but what would she do without her little coffee-house? It was all she had; it was her life's work and she could never willingly give it up.

'Oh, Richard! Come back to me!' she whispered. 'Prove him wrong.'

By the time she had cleared away the broken crockery she had made up her mind that she, too, could find more cheerful company. Tomorrow morning early, she would visit the Reys and tell them all about her first meeting with Richard Nash and about the duel that followed. She would also describe his visit to the coffee-house (omitting what had taken place in the bedroom) and would boast about the new customers he would be sending her. The Reys loved her. They would be impressed by Nash's interest in her and by the gifts he had sent. A visit to the Reys would reassure her. They were family and would restore her shattered confidence. Richard *did* care for her – and Toby, the scoffer, would soon be forced to eat his words! She would visit the Reys first thing in the morning

From the moment that Sally entered Jean's house the following morning she was conscious of a certain restraint on the part of her sister-in-law. Although they kissed as warmly as usual, Sally sensed in Louise a diffidence which immediately filled her with alarm.

'Come in, Solange,' Louise said with what Sally perceived as exaggerated cheerfulness. 'You are such a stranger to us these days. The children will be *so* excited. They have been asking for you but I told them you are very busy and will come as soon as you are able.'

Sally smiled. 'I hope they will forgive me. The time passes so quickly. I never intended to stay away so long. I am quite ashamed.' Nervously she tried to reassure herself that her imagination was playing tricks and that her own guilty feelings were making her over sensitive.

Louise chattered on as she led the way into the neat parlour but Sally fancied there was an unnatural intensity about the rush of words. Usually it was Sally who dominated the conversation – not from choice but because Louise was of a quieter disposition. She always insisted modestly that Sally's news was so much more interesting than her own which was mainly concerned with the children and their progress.

As the minutes passed, Sally became more convinced than ever that Louise was uneasy in her presence. There was something indefinable in her eyes, an unfamiliar tightness in her voice. She also clasped and unclasped her hands – a habit that Sally had never noticed before.

Sally said, ''Tis not lack of affection on my part which keeps me away. I hope you don't think that. I care for you all most sincerely.'

'Solange! Oh, my dear! We never thought such a thing – not for a moment!' cried Louise. She raised her voice and called, 'Children, I have a surprise for you. A visitor. Hurry down and see who it is.' To Sally she explained that the older ones were away at their lessons. 'But the little ones will be delighted to see you.'

From somewhere above them there was a patter of feet and then a clatter on the stairs and three children hurried into the room. There was no doubting the sincerity of their welcome, Sally thought gratefully, as they hurled themselves into her waiting arms. She hugged them long and hard, trying to fathom, meanwhile, the cause for the change she detected in her sister-in-law.

A terrible suspicion gripped her. Suppose they had heard gossip about herself and Richard Nash! She went hot and cold at the thought of such a disaster. Could Toby have told them? He might be jealous but he was not normally malicious although in his present mood it was just possible he had betrayed her. She felt a surge of anger. If he had she would throttle him with her bare hands! Another thought occurred, far worse than the first. Perhaps Richard himself had been indiscreet. She swallowed but her throat was dry with fright. Was it possible Richard himself had boasted of his conquest to all and sundry? No, no! Surely not. He respected her. He *admired* her. He had said so many wonderful things to her. Richard Nash was a gentleman and would never stoop so low. He could not do anything so unworthy of his high principles. She would never believe that of him.

She drew a shaky breath and tried to calm her nerves. She must be mistaken. Jean and Louise could know nothing of those events. The cause for Louise's diffidence must lie elsewhere. She smiled through trembling lips.

'Jean!' she asked. 'Is he well?'

As she said his name a fresh suspicion flared and relief gave way to a new fear.

'Is it Jean?' she burst out. 'Is that it? Something has happened to Jean and you don't want to tell me!'

311

Louise looked at her in astonishment, obviously surprised at the question. Sally cursed her own stupidity. Jean was safe. But almost at once fresh doubts assailed her.

'Maman?' she asked. 'Is Maman in good health?'

It was more than a year since she had last visited her mother and step-father. Henri had made her welcome and she had been civil towards him but the visits were never very successful; never more than duty calls. Marie had never forgiven her daughter for making Henri's life so difficult and for refusing to admit that Pierre was dead.

'Nothing has happened to anybody,' Louise assured her. 'Why are you so nervous, Soli? I have never seen you like this before.' She put an arm round her shoulder. 'Come into the kitchen and I will make a pot of lemon tea. That will calm you. You seem so agitated.'

The children, however, were clamouring for Sally's attention, tugging at her skirts in their eagerness. It appeared that she *must* inspect a new pet rabbit, *must* admire a new bonnet.

'Your aunt Soli will see everything later,' Louise chided them. 'For the moment she and I must talk.'

Sally's heart plummeted afresh at these ominous words and she wished desperately that she had stayed away, but it was too late now. Her thoughts raced anxiously. If Louise accused her of wantonness she could always deny it – unless Richard himself had been the source of the gossip. The thought made her cheeks burn with embarrassment. If Toby was right and Richard had already disregarded her she would die of mortification. And she would never forgive him! She would not forgive Toby, either, for being right!

As soon as she and Louise were alone and they each held a steaming cup of tea, her sister-in-law drew a deep breath and Sally tensed herself for the expected recriminations.

'Soli, I had not expected to have to tell you . . .' Louise began nervously, running an agitated finger round the edge of the cup. 'This is very difficult for me. Jean intended to call on you this evening. The fact is . . .'

Sally groaned silently. Richard *had* betrayed her. She must deny everything.

She said quickly, ''Tis not at all how it seems! Richard and I – that is, we are no more than friends. There was nothing . . .'

'I beg your pardon?' Louise looked puzzled.

A faint hope stirred in Sally's breast. 'Whatever you have heard . . .' she began, then something told her to say no more. When she did not continue Louise started again.

'We have some news for you, Soli. It concerns my uncle. You have most likely heard us speak of him. He left La Rochelle a year after us and went to America with his family.'

Sally nodded. She was weak with relief. Her secret was safe!

Louise's expression became more guarded. 'He has written to us constantly and now – well, now . . .' She drew a deep breath. 'We have agreed to join him in Williamsburg.'

For a moment Sally stared at her uncomprehendingly, then slowly but surely the meaning of Louise's words registered and she could only blink in disbelief. 'Williamsburg?' she echoed. 'America?'

America was the other side of the world. To go to America was like going to the moon.

Seeing her shocked expression Louise continued hurriedly and somewhat defensively, ''Tis no rash decision, Soli. Believe me. We have discussed it for months, wondering what to do for the best, but now we have made up our minds. We didn't speak to you before because we were undecided and didn't want to alarm you unnecessarily.'

'You are going to America? All of you?' Sally gazed at her wide-eyed. Her mind appeared to function in slow motion. Her beloved brother was going away and she would never see him again. 'Does Maman know?' she asked at last. Her mother would never allow such a thing.

Louise dashed her hopes at once. 'We have told her. My parents thought it best to invite you all to accompany us, if you wished. Oh, Solange, America is truly the land of opportunity. My uncle speaks of it in such glowing terms. We can all make a new life in Virginia you see. We have to assure a future for the children. We have to think of them. There is so little for them here. Williamsburg has many other English people there, and French, so we would not be among strangers. They will welcome us. It is a fine town with broad streets and the –'

'What did she say?'

Louise stared at her blankly. 'What did who say?'

'Maman.' Sally looked stricken. 'What did Maman say about you going away?'

Light dawned. 'Your mother? Oh, she said she was happy in England and was too old to uproot herself

314

and start again. I believe Henri would have come with us but your mother was adamant. But that need not prevent *you* from joining us, Soli. We want to take you with us. You would love America, I'm certain of it. The climate is very equable, apparently.'

Sally's thoughts were chaotic. First Richard Nash and now this. Everything was happening at once and she was out of her depth. She was being offered the chance to go to America!

'Do say you will at least think about it,' Louise implored her. 'We should hate to leave you behind and America is such a long way. We would never come back. We would never see each other again.' Louise looked so dismayed by this prospect that Sally reached out and clasped her hands.

'I don't know,' Sally said, ''tis so sudden. I must have time to think. I don't want to leave Bath but nor do I want to lose Jean – and you and the children,' she added hastily.

'Of course, you must have time to think,' Louise agreed soothingly. 'We shall not leave for several months. Probably early in the new year. The date is not yet fixed and there is so much to do.'

'But you do want me to come?' Sally asked humbly.

'Of course we do!' cried Louise.

Sally felt comforted by the warmth of her tone and the look of affection in her eyes but did she want to go to America? Sally tried to picture herself standing at the rail, while the ship moved away from the quayside. Toby and Richard were waving farewell and there were tears in their eyes. Perhaps in their mutual grief they would become friends! Sally's lips moved in a faint smile.

Would anyone else miss her, she wondered. Ned Cooper might. And she would miss him. She was surprised how much she would miss Ned. But as for Richard and Toby – it would be no more than they deserved. They would finally realize what they had lost. They would see quite clearly what a wonderful person she was when it was too late. She was almost tempted to go to America just to punish the pair of them, but was it worth giving up the coffee-house? Without realizing what she was doing she shook her head violently. Most definitely not. Reluctantly she let the picture fade from her mind.

She became aware that Louise was regarding her anxiously.

'You are shaking your head,' she said.

'I don't think I could go,' Sally told her. 'I have so much to lose.'

'You could start another coffee-house in Williamsburg,' Louise urged. ''Tis a bustling sea port with a growing population. You would do well there. Wait, I will give you some of my uncle's letters. Take them home with you and read them.'

She hurried to a dresser, pulled out a bundle of letters tied with tape and tossed them into Sally's lap.

'Williamsburg, Virginia, is on the east coast. My uncle is a silversmith with a little shop on Duke of Gloucester Street – a wide street such as we have never seen – with trees bordering the roadway. His oldest son, my cousin Will, is courting the milliner next door and his daughter is stepping out with the apothecary's son.' She laughed. 'But I have saved the best 'til last, Soli. My uncle's closest friend has opened a bakery behind a tavern and Jean is to be his partner. What is it called?' She frowned. 'Oh yes, the Raleigh Tavern. That is its name.

'So you see Jean will be returning to his old skill. With your permission he might introduce the people of Williamsburg to the delights of your famous teacakes. Just imagine Americans eating Sally Lunns! Oh, 'tis such a wonderful opportunity. You do see, don't you, that we must take it.' Sally could only stare at her, chilled by the prospect of her forthcoming loss and the suddenness of the news. Was there the slightest chance that they would change their minds, she wondered.

'I thought Jean was well set up here with the weaving trade,' she protested but even as she spoke Sally remembered Nash's words about Bath's failing wool trade.

'My father is aware that Bath is changing,' Louise told her regretfully. 'For some time now he has been worried about the business. Demand is falling. Nothing is as it was when we first came to England. Jean says we must be realistic. We have our whole lives ahead of us. Papa believes —' She broke off suddenly as for the first time she noticed the pearl Sally was wearing.

Her eyes widened. 'Solange! How beautiful!' She reached out and touched it delicately.

For Sally, however, the news of Jean's departure to foreign parts overshadowed the pleasure in her pearl.

Louise asked, 'Was it a gift or have you sold your soul to the devil for it?' She laughed as she said it but Sally did not meet her eyes.

''Twas Richard Nash gave it me,' she told her.

317

'Richard Nash? Not the man they call Beau Nash?' Louise made no attempt to hide her surprise.

'Yes.' In view of her family's imminent departure Sally's relationship with Richard no longer seemed of great consequence. 'It seems he has taken a fancy to me.'

She waited for her sister-in-law's reaction but Louise, dumbstruck by the news, said nothing. Sally continued airily, 'He visited my refreshment house and has promised to recommend me to his friends. I don't think I could have found a better patron, do you?'

Louise muttered, 'You and Beau Nash!'

Sally's smile was a little brittle. 'He gave me a linnet in a cage, also. He's a fascinating man – and most generous.'

Her tone defied Louise to ask just how generous Sally had been to merit such flattering tokens of attention and before Louise could comment further Sally had launched into an account of the episode at the bath and the duel that followed. When, breathlessly, she came to an end there was a long silence and she became aware that Louise was looking at her as though at a stranger. Sally jutted her chin defiantly. Now, no doubt, they would be only too glad to go to America without her. Well, let them go! Suddenly she felt tired and dispirited.

'Another cup of tea?' Louise suggested weakly.

But Sally was feeling the strain of the tensions of the past half-hour and announced that she would spend a few moments with the children and she must then fly. Ten minutes later she almost ran from the house.

Her beloved brother was deserting her, Richard was

playing a waiting game and she had forfeited Toby's friendship.

Bowed by this unexpected flurry of misfortune she walked home in a state of acute shock. Had she been able to foresee the next few weeks her discomfiture would have been complete.

Chapter Thirteen

NED MADE HIS way down the steep incline that led to the current working area, ducking his head frequently where the ceiling was low and narrowing his eyes as the daylight behind him gradually faded and he was forced to rely on his candle.

Eventually the passage widened into a large cavern where the men were working, their voices echoing eerily in the subterranean gloom. He had known most of the men for all their working lives and until recently would have trusted them completely. Men like John Speck, a picker, who had worked for him for nineteen years; Davy Wylie, a miserable man but hard-working; Henry Cripper, garrulous but strong as a horse, had worked the stone for seven years without a day's absence for illness – a record of which he was very proud.

Ned believed them to be honest but over the past months two men had left for various reasons and he had new workers to replace them. Now he had been faced with several small thefts which disturbed him greatly. One week a pickaxe had been unaccounted for; ten days later it was a crowbar that failed to appear at the end of the day. The tools belonged to the men and were left overnight in the store shed which was always locked. There were spare tools for use in emergencies but the men naturally preferred to work with implements with which they were familiar. Today Ned had decided to make an unexpected visit to the underground workings to see if he could discover anything untoward which might point to the culprit. Now, as he made his appearance, the men looked up, startled.

Speck quipped, 'You're a long way from home, master!' and Ned joined in the laughter.

'I've lost my way,' he told them. 'Thought I was on my way to Heaven!'

'Hell, more like!' said another man and there was more laughter.

Ned paused to watch the work in progress. A new wrist block was being worked and the picker was already reaching well into the gap with his pick. It was slow work and Ned, with a nod of approval for what he had seen, eventually moved on to find the new members of his team.

Sam Sturmer was younger than most of his fellow workers and wore a permanently sullen expression. He was employed to collect up the poorer quality stone that would be burnt in the lime kilns or used for filling walls. Hearing footsteps he glanced up and Ned fancied he saw a flash of alarm in the brown eyes which was quickly hidden.

'How are you getting on?' Ned asked. 'Is the work to your liking?'

Sturmer shrugged. ''Tis no worse than most work,' he said with a trace of resentment in his voice.

'Your six weeks are nearly up,' Ned reminded him. 'Are you hoping I shall take you on permanently?'

321

After a brief hesitation Sturmer said reluctantly, 'I reckon so.'

Ned regarded him uneasily. The man's manner was unforthcoming and Ned was well aware that one discontented worker could infect others. He had no intention of letting that happen but nor did he want to get rid of the man unjustly. He had an ailing mother, that much Ned knew, as well as a brother who was feeble-minded. Sturmer was the sole breadwinner and work was not easy to come by.

'I shall think on it,' Ned said and moved on to the other relative newcomer.

Jim Hawkes was a slack-mouthed, gangly man in his mid-twenties with a badly pock-marked face. He was one of four men hauling a slab of stone on a wooden trolley. It was newly cut and was being moved to its new position underground where it would be stored. Hawkes greeted Ned with a polite nod and carried on with his work.

Ned motioned the straining men to rest for a few moments and they relaxed thankfully, grateful for the unexpected respite. He beckoned the new man to one side.

'You look as though you are settling in,' he said conversationally. 'Any problems?'

'No, sir. None at all.'

'Getting along with the rest of the men?'

'Aye, reckon so.'

A man of few words, thought Ned wryly. Hawkes's wife had died in childbirth, he reflected, and his mother was now caring for the child, a girl, who was nearly a year old.

'No complaints, then?'

Hawkes shook his head determinedly.

''Tis well, then,' said Ned with a dismissive wave of his hand.

He retraced his steps thoughtfully. It was difficult, dangerous work and accidents were not infrequent. Once, long before Ned's time, a block of stone had overbalanced and a man had been crushed to death. Conscious of the dangers Ned was very strict about the enforcement of the regulations and his safety record was an enviable one.

He made his way back towards the light of day, no wiser than when he went down. Though he suspected Sturmer of the theft he was reluctant to dismiss him without evidence and so far his distrust of the man was purely intuitive.

As he approached his office he was surprised to see a man waiting for him outside. He was well dressed and rather portly and was out of breath from his climb.

'Good day to you!' said Ned. 'How can I help you?'

To Ned's surprise the newcomer did not acknowledge the greeting but instead drew a long thin parcel from behind his back and Ned knew immediately that his missing crowbar had returned.

'This was sold to my son at a very low price by one of your men,' the man told Ned. 'That's "walked" I told myself as soon as I set eyes on it.'

Ned unwrapped it, examined the end of it and recognized the mark. He eyed the man speculatively.

'You came all the way up here to bring it back?' Ned asked.

The man looked defiant. 'Sam Sturmer's no good!' he exclaimed. 'My daughter is taken with him and he with her but she's worth better. I've told her so but she can't or won't see it. Women are foolish creatures. They choose a man for all the wrong reasons. Blind as a bat to all my advice! Stubborn as a mule! I thought this might show her the error of her ways. I'll see her dead before I see her marry Sam Sturmer!'

'Ah!' Ned sighed.

'He's a surly wretch. Surly as they come,' the man continued. 'Well, there's your crowbar, Master Cooper, and I hope you'll see fit to bring charges against him. 'Twould do my heart good to see him safely behind bars, and that's the truth.'

Ned said, 'I'll deal with it as I see fit. Rest assured on that. And my thanks to you for the return of our property.' He almost added that there was a pickaxe still missing but thought better of it.

'Will you give me your name before you go?' Ned asked.

'Most certainly. 'Tis Jonathan Bessel. I'm a clerk at St John's Hospital. You will find me there five days a week should you need a statement.'

Ned thanked him for bringing the matter to his attention but he watched him leave with a heavy heart. He had no stomach for the unpleasant task that lay ahead and found no pleasure in the confirmation of his suspicions, but it had to be done. He would deal with it as promptly as possible.

At the end of the day Ned called Sturmer to him and challenged him with the evidence. To his surprise the man made no attempt to lie or to excuse his behaviour but replied simply that he had need of the money. When pressed he would say nothing more in his own defence but, without prompting, described Master Bessel in colourful and most unflattering terms.

Hardening his heart Ned told him bluntly that he was out of a job but that he would not press charges if the pickaxe was returned within twenty-four hours. Sturmer showed no gratitude for his leniency, however, and strode away down the path with a face like thunder, muttering ominously beneath his breath.

With an effort Ned put the matter out of his mind as he made his way home since he had a more pressing problem which needed his attention. Somehow he had to break the news to Stubbs about the seriousness of his condition and must persuade him to consider the operation. Ned had investigated the cost and had been to see a moneylender. All he needed now was Stubbs's acceptance of the plan.

Ned was so engrossed with this problem that he had almost reached his doorstep before he raised his head and saw Sally Lunn waiting for him. A smile lit up his face as he held out a hand in welcome but Sally's smile was less than radiant and was replaced immediately by a worried frown.

'I have just knocked at your door,' she told him. 'I must talk to you, Ned, if you will spare me a little time. I have so much on my mind – I hardly know if I am coming or going!'

At that moment the door opened in answer to her knock and Nan showed them in. She was a plump young woman with a discontented expression. Before

Ned had time to remove his coat she was grumbling about 'the lodger'.

'Sick he may be but he won't keep his hands to hisself!' she told him. 'I hardly dare go near the bed and that's a fact. And language! Well, he knows a sight more than my late departed father and *he* could turn the air blue when he wanted to.'

'I'm sorry, Nan,' said Ned. 'I'll speak to him about it.'

'Well, I don't know how long he's staying but . . .'

'Did the doctor call?' Ned interrupted.

'He did. No better, no worse. That's what he said. You should have heard what Stubbs called the physician after he'd gone! Talk about ears burning! I reckon his must have burst into flame, poor man!'

Ned hid a smile and told her to fetch some beer.

Sally indicated the basket and said, 'I brought you some teacakes.'

'We'll eat and talk at the same time,' said Ned. He handed the basket to Nan and she disappeared reluctantly.

'I didn't know you were taking in lodgers,' said Sally, rather surprised.

Ned said quickly, ''Tis a temporary measure, nothing more. A week maybe. But you haven't come here to talk about lodgers. You must make yourself comfortable and –'

'That Nan,' said Sally. 'Is she the best you can get? I wouldn't give her house room!'

'They come and go,' he said vaguely.

'If your mother was alive she'd soon send her packing. You need someone like our Jane. She does a few hours here and there when we need her.'

326

Sally settled herself into a chair and arranged her skirts. Ned noticed that she was wearing a smart skirt and jacket and a new hat.

'You look very grand,' he told her with a smile. 'But not too grand to need my advice. I'm pleased about that.'

Without preamble she said, 'Jean is going to America, Ned, and he wants me to go with him.'

Her eyes were downcast as she spoke and so she did not see the momentary anguish that flared in his. He recovered with an effort.

'America! That's a long way away,' he said. 'How do you feel about it? Do you think you will go?'

She looked up and his heart ached for her.

'I don't know what to do,' she confessed. 'I cannot bear the thought of all those miles separating us. Jean and Louise and the children are the only family I have – apart from Maman and Henri. I didn't know until now how much I need them all. They are all I have in the world to love.' She sighed deeply and went on, 'Oh, I know Maman thinks I should wed but there is no one – no man, that is – with whom I want to share my life. Poor Maman. She means it kindly, Ned, but she doesn't understand me. I have no secret yearnings for a man of my own and children to tug at my skirts. And why else should I marry, if not for love and children?'

Ned regarded her intently, longing to speak at last of his love for her but finally deciding that this was not the moment. She was frightened and confused and very vulnerable and he would not take advantage of her.

Instead he said gently, 'Perhaps in time you will regret your solitary state. My mother was always urging me to wed and now I know why.' He smiled suddenly. 'And so were you, at one time, Sally. And once, when you were in one of your tantrums you told me you were glad I was going to end up lonely and wretched.' But she stared at him blankly and he saw that she did not share his memories.

Suddenly she smiled. 'But I do recall your mother told me you were wedded to your quarry,' she told him, 'and loved the stone above all else!'

'Then more fool me,' he said, with a shake of the head. 'Stone must surely make a cold and heartless bedfellow!'

He hoped that this sly comment might nudge Sally into a consideration of the joys of marriage but she ignored the remark.

'The Reys have invited us all to accompany them,' she went on, 'but mercifully Maman and Henri have refused. I am between the devil and the deep blue sea! If I go I shall lose Maman and Henri. How could I bear it? But never to see my beloved brother again! Oh, Ned! What am I to do?'

Ned fought down an unreasonable pang of jealousy. Jean was her brother and entitled to her affection but he could not resist the thought that she might have expressed some regrets at the thought of parting with him. Did he figure so little in her life, he wondered. Could she go to America and not miss him? If she left England Ned would be desolate and even now his stomach churned at the prospect of losing her. She began to explain about Williamsburg, the bakery and Jean's partnership.

Ned nodded but his mind was racing. Would she stay if she knew about her father? Would a reprobate father compensate for the loss of her brother? Suppose he took her upstairs now and reunited father and daughter. What could he say? 'This wreck of a man is your father but he is fatally ill and likely to die!'

No, that would never do.

Sally said sharply, 'You are not listening, Ned!'

'Forgive me, I am very tired and have had problems at the quarry. Please go on.'

Nan appeared in the doorway with the tray. 'Can I go home now?' she asked.

He nodded and she went out, closing the door noisily behind her.

'She smells,' said Sally, wrinkling her nose, 'and her hair is dirty. You deserve better, Ned.'

''Tis of no account,' he said.

'America!' said Sally, reverting to her dilemma.

'I would miss you,' said Ned.

'Would you?'

He thought she sounded wistful.

'Most certainly. Bath would be a barren place without Sally Lunn!'

'Oh, Ned! You are such a dear!' She sighed and sipped her beer.

'I would like to persuade you to stay,' he went on carefully, 'but that would be selfish of me. I want what's best for you, Sally.'

She smiled. 'Your mother once said you were too soft-hearted. 'Tis a hard old world, Ned. Maybe you should begin to think about yourself and less about others.'

'I do think about myself,' he protested.

'I doubt it.' She pointed upwards, 'What of your so-called lodger − is he really paying you for the room? Or is he one of your lame ducks? Be honest now, Ned.'

He considered the question, his head on one side. 'He's an interesting project!' he told her. 'Yes, I think that describes him rather well.'

She smiled. 'You mean he's a scrounger and you haven't the heart to throw him out!'

'I thought we were going to talk about you.'

'Oh, dearest Ned!' she cried, her tone anguished. 'If only I could tell you everything! I am so dreadfully unhappy!'

'Then go to America with them,' he told her, 'if the prospect of a parting grieves you so much.'

''Tis not only the parting. There's something else but − Oh, how can I tell you? You are a man and will never understand!'

He looked at her in alarm. What else troubled her?

Seeing his anxious expression she said, 'Toby is angry with me because of this,' and held up the pearl which until that moment had escaped his notice.

'A pearl? But 'tis beautiful. Why should that anger him? Have you been too extravagant?'

She swallowed hard. ''Twas a gift,' she said, 'from Beau Nash.'

As the words sank in Ned stood up abruptly, unable to face her. He had heard rumours, of course, but had dismissed them as nonsense. Beau Nash and Sally Lunn! It was impossible.

She said, 'He is a good man, Ned, and he has such

plans for this town. He wants to make it a good place for people to live.'

'I heard rumours of a duel,' he said.

''Tis true, I was there. He was most chivalrous.'

'You were *there*?' He swung round, startled.

She explained the circumstances and he listened grimly. When she had finished he said, 'Oh, Sally!'

She told him how they had celebrated at the coffee-house but not what had occurred afterwards. She went on to speak of the new customers he had sent but as soon as she ran out of breath he asked quietly, 'And the pearl?'

She tried to lie but failed miserably, then fell silent and he guessed at once. For a long time neither spoke.

At last she said, 'I do believe he loves me, Ned.'

Ned shook his head. 'He is a man of the world, Sally. You do not understand.'

'He loves me!' she insisted.

'Do you love him?'

To her surprise she found herself stammering, 'Well I – I admire him very much. I could – I could make him a good wife.'

'Do you love him?' he repeated.

'I want to be with him,' she said. 'I think of him all the time!'

'Do you *love* him, Sally?'

'I long to see him again,' she cried. 'What more can I say? I want to lie with him again! Is that what you want to hear?'

''Tis not the same thing, Sally. Not necessarily.' His voice was gentle. 'There's gratitude, Sally. He has shown you another side of love. He has made you feel like a woman. A woman could love a man for that although she may not love the man himself. He may enjoy her body without loving her mind. 'Tis in a man's nature to be this way and no crime.'

His kindness undermined her and she began to cry softly. He crossed the room and pulled her to her feet and held her in his arms while she sobbed, but his heart was heavy with dread. She was such an innocent. Did she know what she had done? Did she understand the risk she had taken? Had it occurred to her that she might be with child?

Sally arrived home in a very thoughtful frame of mind. Being with Ned had comforted her a little but she still felt undecided about America. She had confessed to him that, all other reasons apart, part of her reluctance was the prospect of a long sea journey, the thought of which terrified her. Her memories of Grandmère's death were still vivid after all these years, and she dreaded the possibility of another tragedy. She now began to wonder whether, even at this late stage, Maman might bring pressure to bear and persuade the Reys to remain in England. Perhaps she would pay her a long overdue visit.

To her surprise she heard Toby whistling as she went into the bakery and found him weighing flour in readiness for the night's baking. Perhaps he had repented his surly behaviour, she thought with surprise.

'Home again, home again, jiggety-jig!' he said with a cheerful smile and Sally's spirits rose marginally. If Toby was going to be nice to her life would be more tolerable. She decided that now was a good time to tell him that she might be leaving England. That would surely bring him to his senses.

'I've been to see Ned Cooper,' she told him, daintily pulling off her gloves a finger at a time. 'I wanted to ask his advice. I might be going to –'

Toby said abruptly, 'A letter came for you. 'Tis on the table upstairs.'

At once her heart began to pound.

'Who brought it?' she asked as casually as she could.

'An urchin lad.'

Forgetting all about America she forced herself to appear calm as she made her way up the stairs but abandoned all pretence as she snatched it up and pressed it to her lips. She broke the seal and began to read:

My dear Mistress Lunn . . .

She laughed, 'Oh Richard! How formal!' and read on.

Our meeting was all too brief and the parting long . . .

'It has seemed an age!' Sally agreed.

I trust you will remember me when next we meet . . .

Remember him? How could she ever forget! 'You are much too modest!' she told him.

I have thought of you constantly and can wait no longer to see you again. I will take the liberty of calling on you at noon tomorrow in the hope that you will receive me. Your most sincere and ardent admirer.

He had not signed his name. Very wise, thought Sally. Very circumspect.

She kissed the letter again and somehow resisted the urge to shout aloud with joy. So he had *not* forgotten her. He had not used her unkindly and he did love her – he could not wait to see her again and had thought of her constantly!

'But not as constantly as I have thought of you!' she whispered. 'Oh, Richard! My love!' So much for Toby and Louise and Ned. The doubters were confounded.

Unable to keep the good news to herself a moment longer she rushed down to the bakery, the letter clutched firmly in her hand.

''Tis from Richard!' she told Toby. 'He insists he has missed me most dreadfully and can hardly wait to see me again. He will be calling tomorrow at noon so we must get Jane in to wait on tables.'

She watched to see the effect this had on him but he merely smiled.

'Master Nash, is it?' he said. 'Then we must kill the fatted calf!'

But he did not say it unkindly and did not appear at all put out. She looked at him suspiciously, then waved the letter in front of him.

'Nothing to say then, Toby?' she prompted.

He looked puzzled. 'Such as?'

She laughed aloud. 'Such as an apology?' she told him. 'Such as an admission that you were wrong about him?'

'No,' he said.

'But why not? Don't you believe me?'

Toby shrugged, 'I'll say it all tomorrow when he comes. *If* he comes.'

'But of course he'll come! At noon. 'Tis here, every word of it, in his own handwriting! Listen.' She read the letter to him. 'You see?'

He gave her a crooked smile and there was something in his eyes which bothered her.

She thrust the letter towards him. 'See for yourself!' she told him but he waved it away with floury hands.

Sally shook her head sadly. 'You disappoint me, Toby,' she told him. 'I never thought you a bad loser. Well, I shall go round at once and see Jane.' And she swept out with a disparaging toss of her head.

As the door closed behind her Toby put a thumb to his nose and wiggled his fingers in her direction.

'Master Nash, my arse!' he roared delightedly and his laughter filled the bakery.

After Sally had left him Ned went upstairs to tackle Stubbs where he found him reeking of brandy and in a maudlin frame of mind.

'Damnation!' muttered Ned and went downstairs to examine the brandy bottle. As he suspected it was empty. 'The wretch!' he exclaimed and went upstairs again. Either Nan had given it to keep him quiet or he had somehow discovered its whereabouts for himself. Well, he would ignore the matter. There was no more brandy so it could not happen again and there were more important things to be discussed.

He drew up a chair, greeted Stubbs cheerfully and enquired after his health.

'Well enough,' said Stubbs, his tone guarded. 'It comes and it goes. How I bear it I don't know. Fair knocks the breath from my body, and that's the god-begotten truth!'

Ned said quietly, 'Stubbs, the physician is very worried about you. Very worried indeed. You are a very sick man.'

'Don't I know it!' cried Stubbs. He was enjoying himself in Master Cooper's house. Being waited on hand and foot was a novelty; since he had no urgent business to attend to, he thought he might as well stay there as long as possible.

'The doctor tells me you need a little surgery,' Ned told him. 'Without it, you might . . .'

Stubbs sat up, his eyes popping. 'Surgery?' he cried. 'Me?'

Ned nodded and Stubbs began to shake his head.

'Never, never, never!' he cried. 'Not surgery! No, no!'

'But without it you have such a short time to live,' said Ned. 'You don't want to die, do you?'

'I don't want surgery, neither!' He shook his head again. 'Never! Oh no! No one's going to carve me up!'

''Tis hardly that,' Ned told him.

Patiently he began to explain that the surgeon was a very skilled man and that if Stubbs went into hospital every care would be taken of him.

Stubbs shook his head. 'I met a man once in an ale house,' he declared. 'His leg was broke by a kick from a horse and wouldn't mend. They talked him into surgery and what good did it do him? They sawed off his leg and gave him a wooden one. Pegleg, we called him, but his real name was Bunnit. George Bunnit.'

Ned said, 'A wooden leg is better than one that won't mend. He could walk again.'

'Much good it did him,' said Stubbs. 'A year later he was dead anyway. Choked himself to death on a fish bone.'

Ned decided against arguing the logic of Stubbs's example and continued to extol the virtues of the hospital until, worn down by Ned's persistence, Stubbs agreed cautiously to think it over. Ned's hopes rose and he jumped to his feet at once to fetch paper, quill and ink. He sat down beside the bed.

'The surgeon needs a few details,' he told Stubbs. ''Tis the normal procedure. Nothing to be alarmed about.'

But Stubbs obviously was alarmed.

'No details!' he announced firmly. 'I never have believed in them. No, no, no!'

He pressed his lips together as though to prevent the escape of any details. Ned pretended not to hear and dipped the quill into the ink.

'Name?' he began. At once Stubbs's alarm increased and he rubbed a hand over his face in agitation.

Ned smiled encouragingly. 'Shall we say Stubbs – or Warren or Smith? It makes little difference.'

Receiving no answer he wrote 'Stubbs'.

'Age?' he went on. 'Shall we say seventy?'

'Seventy?'

As Ned had hoped Stubbs was stung by the insult.

'I'm fifty-nine,' he said, 'not a day more. Seventy indeed!'

Ned wrote again.

'And where were you born?'

This last question proved too much. Stubbs leaned forward and snatched the paper from Ned's hands and tore it through.

'No details,' said Stubbs, 'and no hospital! And that's an end of it.'

'But why?' cried Ned.

'Because I say so, that's why!' Stubbs scowled. 'Details! Enough to ruin a man. A word on a paper can hang a man! Believe me, I know! I've learned a thing or two.'

The two men stared at each other and the silence lengthened. Ned waited.

At last Stubbs said, 'Look, Master Cooper, I know you mean well by me. Your sort always do. Always saving a man from his self without his permission. The point is . . .' He looked desperately round the room but finding no help there looked back at Ned. 'The point is I'm not altogether blameless, as you might say.'

'None of us are,' said Ned.

'Some of us are more blameless than others,' Stubbs told him. 'And I'm not one of them. You might say the law is interested in me – in the man I was, I mean.' His fingers plucked anxiously at the blanket. 'If they was to catch up with me it might go very badly for me. Very badly indeed. I might end up . . .' He drew a forefinger across his throat.

Ned suggested, 'But if it was a long time ago – whatever it was . . .'

Stubbs said, 'I killed a man, Master Cooper. They'll hang me if they catch me.'

'Dear God!' Ned closed his eyes despairingly.

Once started, however, Stubbs could not be stopped. The guilty secret he had carried for so long had proved such a burden that he now seized the opportunity to ease his conscience.

''Twas a brawl,' he confided, 'a drunken brawl. Nothing more than that. Two fools with too much ale inside them. He was bigger than me and he'd lost a shilling or two to me at brag. He followed me out and accused me of cheating and wanted his money back. I told him a few more home truths. He punched me in the gut and I saw red, Master Cooper. I hit him back and we fought a bit – too drunk to do much harm, if the truth be told. A crowd gathered the way they do and they was betting on who would go down first.'

He looked at Ned who merely nodded.

'I landed one to his jaw – just a jab. Nothing heavy, you know, but somehow he lost his balance. Went down on the cobbles like a sack of coals. The men were saying I'd won and asking each other to pay up but I waited for him to open his eyes. I was scared, Master Cooper, and that's the godbegotten truth! I thought he'd murder me when he did get up. You see, he'd never been downed before and he had his reputation to think of. A man has his pride.'

For a moment he appeared to have forgotten Ned as he relived those terrible moments.

'Then they began to think something was wrong. They tried to get him up and couldn't rouse him. They said he'd split his head open and he was dead, just like that.'

His eyes refocused on Ned's face and his own face puckered. 'It was an accident, Master Cooper, as God is my witness. I'm no murderer. A bad man, maybe. A weak man, yes, I daresay. But I'm no murderer.' He stared at Ned helplessly. 'I ran. What would you have done? What else could I do? Wait for the noose to go round my neck?' He clutched Ned's hand. 'Could have been the other way round. It could have been me killed – but it wasn't.'

He shook his head wearily.

Ned asked, 'And this happened in France?'

'Ah!' cried Stubbs. 'The stick! The duck-headed stick! Gave myself away, didn't I?'

'Yes, you did. You are French, then?'

He nodded. 'Pierre Luyon. That's my real name. I'm trusting you, Master Cooper. I don't know why. I came from La Rochelle. But no, I fled France for other reasons. I found a man in his cups and stole his purse. Someone saw me. I was a fool. I killed the man in Bideford, soon after I landed in England. I've been a fool. Marie was right. Marie was my wife.' He sighed. 'A damned fool! Her parents saw through me right from the start. They didn't want us to wed but Marie was . . .' He shrugged. 'She thought the world of me, Marie did and Jean, our firstborn, was on the way . . . So there I was, a wanted man. My so-called new start!' He laughed bitterly. 'How could I send to France for my family to join me? How could I tell them I was wanted for murder! I wrote once when I first arrived but then I daren't risk it. I changed my name. I kept on changing it. I had to.'

'So your family remained in France?' Ned asked carefully.

'They did, God help them! Times were bad over

there. That King Louis! Now there's your cold-blooded murderer. Thousands of Huguenots. Not that he soiled his own hands but he killed them nonetheless. Slaughter, that's what it was. I shall never know what became of my family. But what else could I do, Master Cooper? You tell me. I lost them all – a wife, son and daughter. I had a girl, Solange. She was just a child when I left. She'll be a woman now.'

Ned said nothing.

'My wife deserved better,' Stubbs said sadly. 'She was a good woman. Hard-working. But I never took up with another woman. How could I? Too much to hide, too many secrets. But 'tis lonely for a man without a family.'

'I'm so sorry,' said Ned.

Stubbs shrugged. 'So you can see why I say no details. You can see the sort of man I am and what I've become. How useless it all is.'

'At least I understand,' said Ned.

Stubbs stared fixedly at the handful of wool he had plucked from the blanket. 'But I've lost your respect, I dare say,' he said piteously.

'Not at all,' said Ned. But his heart ached.

The following day Sally woke early in a mood of wonderful excitement and leaped out of bed, unable to bear another moment's inactivity. Her eyes shone and her heart was full of gratitude as she pushed her feet into her slippers. Today her loyalty and faith were to be justified and those Jonahs who prophesied her downfall would be forced to acknowledge their mistake.

Today Richard was coming! She ran to the window and smiled. Even the weather had improved. Normally in November an early morning mist shrouded the roof tops but today it had not materialized. Instead a watery sun had risen over the hill beyond the river and the few clouds that she could see lay across the horizon to the north. The last of the leaves that clung to the bare trees were motionless and that meant a lack of wind.

She pushed open the window and leaned out. ''Tis going to be a fine day,' she whispered, 'and my love is coming to visit me. What more can I ask?' She determined to put all her cares aside. Nothing should be allowed to detract from the pleasure of Richard's visit.

Closing the window she crossed to the door and opening it a little, listened to the sounds from downstairs that told her Toby was still about. As soon as she went down he would go home and sleep for a few hours.

She poured cold water into the basin and washed from head to toe. Jane, her girl, would be in later and would bring up a jug of hot water but Sally could not wait that long. The cold water made her skin tingle and her face rosy and as she examined herself in the mirror she thought, without undue modesty, that, even sober, Richard would find no cause for complaint.

With reluctance, she then donned her working clothes for noon was still a long way off and there was plenty to be done before the clock struck twelve. She would have liked to spend the whole morning in blissful preparation, prettying herself and choosing her clothes and trying new ways to dress her hair, but instead she must attend to her baking, set the tables and see to a myriad of small tasks.

But never mind, she told herself. They would help to pass the time.

As she tied a clean apron round her waist she hoped Toby would still be feeling friendly towards her. His ill humour depressed her and today she wanted nothing to mar her joy. To her relief she found him relaxed and cheerful, sitting at the table eating one of his own tarts.

'You're up early,' he said. 'Too excited to sleep, I dare say.'

She glanced at him warily but his blue eyes met hers without blinking.

'I can't abear to lie in bed once I'm awake,' she said. 'Too much to do.'

'How very true,' he agreed.

She sat down opposite him and tried to appear calm and collected as though today was in no way special. He pushed the plate towards her and she chose a tart and bit into it hungrily. It was still warm from the oven.

'They're very hot!' he warned her, too late.

She sucked air into her mouth to cool her burnt tongue but was far too happy to let such a trifle bother her.

After Toby had gone home she prepared and baked the first batch of Sally Lunns and set the tables. Then the second batch went into the oven. Just before eleven the first few customers drifted in and they kept her busy until Jane arrived. Sally was then free to hurry upstairs and change her clothes.

The final minutes seemed interminable but at last the clock began to strike and she covered her face with her hands. She must remain calm, she reminded herself.

She must on no account upbraid Richard for staying away from her for so long. She must thank him prettily for the gifts and must never let him know how anxious and wretched she had been.

She had instructed Jane to show him into the kitchen (since her coffee-house was now filled with customers) and then to fetch her from the bedroom where she would be waiting his arrival. That way she would appear less eager and would be able to make an entrance.

As the clock finished striking Sally clasped her hands together and breathed deeply. Her gaze fell on the bed and with a smile she thought that before long she might find herself naked between the sheets with Richard's arms around her.

Jane's feet sounded suddenly on the stairs and a moment later she banged on the bedroom door.

'The gentleman's here, mistress!' she cried, unable to hide her excitement. 'And dressed so fine!'

'Thank you, Jane.' Sally told her, 'Tell him I shall be down in a moment or two and then you had better get back to the shop.'

'Will you be needing anything, mistress?'

'I think not but I shall send for you if we do.'

She waited until the girl had gone and then made her way demurely to the kitchen. She walked in with a smile of welcome on her face and a perfect stranger turned to greet her.

For a moment Sally's poise quite deserted her. Her mouth fell open with shock and she cried, 'Who in the name of . . .'

With an effort she bit back the rest of the discourteous question and struggled to recover her composure. Her thoughts raced as she forced a polite smile. Somehow this stranger had arrived at precisely the time Richard was due and Jane, the stupid girl, had assumed him to be Richard Nash. It really was most exasperating and she would have to get rid of him as soon as possible.

He moved towards her and she saw, with a shock, that he was looking at her with something amounting to adoration. There was no mistaking that expression. Her own reflection, earlier in the day, had shown her that same softening of the eyes when she thought of Richard. While she was still trying to puzzle out who her visitor was he took her hand and, bowing gracefully, raised her fingers to his lips and kissed them.

'Your humble and most devoted servant!' he said.

There was something vaguely familiar about him but Sally could not imagine where they might have met – if indeed they had. Certainly he had never visited the coffee-house.

'Your name, sir?' she stammered at last, hoping this might give her a clue.

'Oliver Meddows, at your service, mistress!' he replied.

She thought with a sudden spurt of anxiety that at any moment Richard would arrive. Would he be jealous? The idea was delightful. For a moment she toyed with the idea of detaining the young man so that Richard should find them together and see just how many admirers she had. But suppose he flew into a rage or departed in a huff? She dared not risk it. No, Oliver Meddows must state his business and be quick about it. Then she must hurry him away.

'And how can I be of service?' she asked.

She *had* seen him somewhere before. She was certain of it. The weak chin and those very pale blue eyes were vaguely familiar. He was exquisitely dressed in a claret-coloured coat and breeches. His hose was the finest and his shoes of kid leather matched his coat exactly. His waistcoat . . .

Sally's eyes widened as light dawned. Of course! The waistcoat! When they had last met he had worn a yellow waistcoat. Oliver Meddows was The Canary! He saw the dawn of recognition in her eyes and took courage from the smile that followed.

'Do you remember me?' he asked humbly.

'Now I do,' she told him and at the memory of the duel her smile grew a shade less warm. 'Whatever can you want of me?' she asked.

He gazed at her anxiously. 'I had hoped –' he began. 'That is, I thought we might forget the unfortunate circumstances under which we first met. The fact is you have captivated my heart, Mistress Lunn.' He shook his head dejectedly. 'When I saw you that morning at the duel I could scarce take my eyes off you. The fact that we supported rivals was a source of great regret. I longed to speak with you – to apologize for my own unworthy behaviour but in the circumstances –'

Sally said quickly, ''Tis of no account, Master Meddows, I assure you. I was scarcely aware of your existence. The circumstances *were* unfortunate, I agree. Let us say no more about it.'

'But I could not bear the thought of your disapproval,' he went on earnestly. 'I craved a kind word but knew I could expect nothing but coldness.'

346

'Please!' Sally held up a hand. 'The matter is closed as far as I am concerned. Master Nash's injury was not serious.'

'He is a generous man. A chivalrous man. We thought Thomas would be killed. He is very head-strong.'

Sally was tempted to say that his friends must take a share of the blame for encouraging him but she was in a hurry to be rid of him.

'Master Garner no longer interests me,' Sally told him. 'Now I am expecting a visitor and must ask you . . .'

But it appeared that Oliver Meddows was deter-mined to lay bare his soul and ask Sally's forgiveness and he was not to be thwarted.

'I was hoping that you might be willing to forget my foolishness at the Baths also,' he went on. 'I confess I was less than gallant but . . .' He shrugged helplessly. 'I have repented of my folly and beg you to overlook it.'

He was not unhandsome, she decided, and his com-plexion was good but such a boy! Perhaps he was twenty years old. Certainly no more. And he had come specifically to apologize for his uncouth behaviour at the Baths. She was flattered.

'Let us say no more about it,' she repeated gra-ciously. Now perhaps he would go away.

'And you forgive me?' he demanded.

'Certainly I do.'

'Then dare I ask a further favour?'

She was startled. 'A favour? What is it?'

'I am invited to a supper party on the twelfth,' he

told her eagerly, 'at the home of Master and Mistress Brayne. You have heard of them, perhaps?'

She had indeed, and was impressed. Joseph Brayne was one of the most influential men in the town; a friend of the mayor and a wealthy landowner.

'I would deem it an honour,' he went on, 'if you would accompany me.'

For once in her life words failed her. Meddows, dismayed by her silence, rushed on, almost stammering in his haste to persuade her.

'I can promise you a gathering of most proper and upright people – you need fear nothing untoward. I would be the happiest man alive if you would . . .'

He faltered to a stop as Sally spoke, 'You want me to come as your *guest*? As your *partner*?'

'Indeed I do. Oh, Mistress Lunn. I would be so proud!'

Completely at a loss she could only stare at him. This was exactly the opportunity she had been waiting for – the chance to meet the right people, *influential* people, whose patronage could make her little shop the best known in Bath. If only her own dear Richard had invited her instead of this comparative stranger. If only Richard had been invited. The thought occurred to her that perhaps he had received an invitation and had suggested today's meeting in order to invite her. How unbearable if she had already accepted the invitation of this young pipsqueak and was then forced to refuse Richard.

As she stood irresolute the clock struck the quarter. Richard was fifteen minutes late. He *must* come. The disappointment would be intolerable.

''Tis most generous of you,' she told Meddows. 'I wonder if I may consider your invitation – for a day or two perhaps? We hardly know each other.'

Even as she made the suggestion she realized it would not solve her problem. The only way she could turn him down in favour of Richard was by pretending that Richard had already invited her. Now it was too late to do so. Unless . . .

'I am so forgetful about dates,' she told him. 'The occasion you mention sounds familiar and I fear I may already have accepted an invitation. The letter is somewhere . . .' She looked around her for the non-existent letter. 'You must think me very foolish.'

'No, not at all,' he assured her. 'I am sure you must be greatly in demand. By all means give me your answer at a later time.' He took her hand. 'Such a pretty little hand!' He kissed it again. 'Oh, Mistress Lunn! Dare I think of you as Sally? Even your name –'

She interrupted him, 'I am expecting another visitor. If you give me your address I will send a message to you.' He fumbled in his pocket for a visiting card and handed it to her. Gilt edged, she noted with awe.

'I have offended you by my presumption,' he said miserably.

'Not at all, I am not offended. And you may call me Sally if you wish.'

He laid a hand on his heart. 'If you do agree to accompany me I swear to you my behaviour will be above reproach,' he told her. 'I am done with such infantile buffoonery and am ashamed that you saw me at my worst. Indeed, I am quite reformed. I will be all you ask of me, I promise you. Oh, Sally! My sweet, pretty Sally!'

His eye fell on the pearl and he smiled. 'I see you are wearing it. That gives me hope!'

'The pearl?'

'And the linnet pleased you also?' he asked with a smile. 'It has a pleasant song, I think.'

For a moment or two Sally did not understand the significance of his remarks. Then a suspicion flickered, wavered, and took a firm hold. Finally the truth burned itself into her consciousness and she felt numb with shock. As the truth dawned she could not repress a slight moan. Oliver Meddows had sent the linnet and the pearl! He had sent the letter also! *This* young whipper-snapper! God in Heaven! She felt her legs buckle and hastily groped her way to a chair.

He was immediately and genuinely concerned. 'My sweet Sally! You are so pale! Are you unwell?'

His pale eyes looked into hers with a warmth which at any other time would have charmed her. Now, however, her disillusionment was so great that tears pressed at her eyelids. She was never going to see Richard Nash again. He had abandoned her. Toby and Ned were right. Oh, how could she bear it? She felt like a leper, tainted with the ugliness of her own foolish pride. Shown up for what she really was — tawdry and cheap and a fool into the bargain!

She stared at her young admirer with a stricken expression. It was all so obvious. Richard Nash had used her and now had no further interest in her. No doubt he had already forgotten her. That was how little he had cared for her, or for her body! She screwed up her face in pain at the thought. She had given herself so willingly, so trustingly. Now it seemed that the only man who had ever known her intimately had found the event unmemorable. It was the ultimate humiliation, the final insult. She longed to run from the room and hide herself away and never be found again. She wanted to weep for a thousand years. She wanted to die!

Oliver Meddows knelt beside her. 'Sally? What ails you, my dear? What have I said or done?'

Those words, spoken by another, would have been balm to her wounded pride but instead they were an added source of irritation. At that moment she hated Oliver Meddows for being the wrong man.

'You must go now,' she told him bluntly through stiff lips that almost refused to function.

She saw the Adam's apple move convulsively in his throat and knew he was hurt but she did not care. Her own hurt, she thought, was so much greater than his.

'Just go!' she repeated, willing her tears not to fall until he had gone.

'But you *will* send me word? You will consider my invitation? You will . . .'

'Go! For pity's sake,' she cried desperately, as her fragile control wavered and the tears threatened to engulf her.

She heard the door close behind him and then his footsteps descended the stairs. When she was sure he had left the building she allowed her grief to submerge her.

It was hours later before she suddenly understood the reason for Toby's cheerfulness. Somehow he had known all along who her visitor would be.

It was the last straw.

Chapter Fourteen

THE FINAL FITTING for her new dress was arranged for the next morning and Sally knew she must attend since the worst thing she could do was hide herself away. If she was the subject of gossip in the town her reluctance to appear in public would be taken as a confession of guilt. She had lain awake for most of the night trying to come to terms with her unhappy situation and desperately seeking to minimize the damage to her pride. She had done some serious thinking and decided that Richard's neglect could only hurt her if she allowed it to do so, and she now tried hard to convince herself that she did not care a fig for the man. Richard Nash was a heartless philanderer and she was well rid of him. If he ever dared to call on her again she would send him packing in no uncertain terms and it would give her great pleasure to do so. He had, after all, merely confirmed what she had always suspected about men – that they were worthless, selfish creatures who considered no one but themselves.

The best way to treat a man like Nash (she would no longer think of him as Richard) was to ignore him. She resolved that his name would never again pass her lips and if anyone else spoke of him she would make it clear that she had never had any real interest in the man. In an effort to salvage her pride she decided to tell Juliana about Oliver Meddows' invitation. She would also wear the pearl and recount the romantic story of the unknown admirer and the linnet, and she would omit the fact that she had ever thought the gifts came from Nash.

She had made a few discreet enquiries about Oliver Meddows and had learned that he came from a wealthy family who lived in Bristol and had made their money in shipping. Oliver, their second son, had moved to Bath at an early age to live with a childless uncle and aunt and had been there ever since. The invitation to a private supper party was, Sally felt, a feather in her cap and something with which to impress the dressmaker.

Ten minutes early Sally waited at the door of Juliana's lodgings with her head held high. When the door was opened she managed a bright smile.

'Oh, my dear!' she began (before Juliana could comment on her pale face or slightly reddened eyes). 'What wouldn't I give for a good night's sleep. Life is so hectic and such fun! I have so much to tell you, I scarcely know where to begin.'

Juliana said, 'Oh, 'tis you. I wasn't expecting you so soon.'

Sally swept in and after a moment's hesitation Juliana helped her off with her coat. There was a faint blush to the dressmaker's cheeks which Sally did not notice as she held out the pearl between finger and thumb and waited for the dressmaker's comment. Juliana gasped with admiration.

'How perfect it is,' she said, 'and how well it looks against the blue of your dress.'

'A present from an unknown admirer!' Sally told her with a light laugh. 'A young admirer and such a sweet boy! A dear lamb!'

'But how can your admirer be unknown,' Juliana demanded 'if you know he is young and a lamb? You must also know who he is.'

Sally launched herself into the story, exaggerating wherever she thought it necessary and glossing over Toby's unpleasant behaviour. As the tale unfolded Sally thought Juliana looked suitably impressed and so far she had given no hint that she had heard any gossip that linked Sally's name with that of Nash. As Sally's dress was removed and the new one slipped over her head it seemed a good time to talk about the supper invitation.

'The young lamb has also invited me to a rather grand supper party,' she said lightly. 'I think this new dress will suit the occasion rather well. Perhaps I should wear it. What do you think?'

After the briefest pause Juliana said, 'I think it would suit admirably.'

Sally gave her a quick glance. She had the distinct impression that the dressmaker's attention was elsewhere. Slightly piqued she went on, 'His name is Oliver Meddows. You may have heard the name.'

'Meddows? Yes, I believe I have,' Juliana agreed. 'Are his family in Bristol?'

'They are.'

Abruptly Juliana excused herself and slipped out of the room. For a moment Sally thought she heard voices but then decided she had imagined it and while she waited for the dressmaker to reappear she admired herself in the mirror. The dress looked beautiful, flattering her figure and bringing out the colour of her eyes as Juliana had predicted. She wondered anxiously if the coffee lace was a shade too dark but then decided she was being too critical.

While she waited for Juliana's return she considered Meddows' invitation. Suppose she did accept – how well would this dress compare with the dresses the other women would be wearing? She imagined they would be wealthier than she was and could buy the best materials and employ the best dressmakers – but they might also be older than Sally. If so she would at least have youth on her side. But suppose she was wrong and they were all about Meddows' age? They might well be wealthier *and* younger and then she would feel horribly inferior and Meddows might make comparisons and regret inviting her. She tutted with vexation and became aware that Juliana still had not reappeared.

Now, from the other side of the door, there came the unmistakable sound of a smothered laugh and then Juliana came back into the room looking both flushed and flustered.

'Forgive me,' she said archly, 'I have a visitor.'

Sally's eyebrows rose. 'A visitor?' she repeated. 'So early in the morning?'

Juliana blushed and Sally realized that the visitor must be male and was annoyed with herself for falling into the trap. Better if she had let the comment pass as though it was of no interest to her.

'I'm not happy about the lace,' she said quickly. Anything, she thought, to take the simpering smile from Juliana's face. 'It's too dark. I thought so originally but you convinced me otherwise.'

Juliana said, 'I can take it off. It will take time but if you are in no hurry ...' She left the sentence unfinished.

Sally was wondering who Juliana's gentleman friend might be.

Juliana touched Sally's elbow. 'A penny for your thoughts!' she offered. 'You were miles away.'

Sally smiled, 'Forgive me. What did you say?'

'I want to know what to do about the lace.'

'Oh, let it be!' Sally told her. 'I really cannot face further alterations. These fittings take up so much of my time.' Juliana now checked the hem again and asked Sally if she had heard about the duel.

'Which one?' Sally asked, her tone casual.

'Why, between Garner and Nash,' cried Juliana. 'Everyone was talking about it.

'Oh, *that* duel,' Sally said with wonderful carelessness. 'Yes, I know all about it. So ridiculous! Grown men risking their lives for no good reason.'

'Nash was wounded in the arm.'

'Wounded?' cried Sally. 'My dear Juliana, you have been misinformed. 'Twas a scratch. Nothing serious.' As she spoke she watched the dressmaker's face in the mirror.

'They say he was defending a woman's honour,' Juliana told her.

'I dare say you could interpret it that way,' Sally conceded, 'but he admitted himself that he spoke out of turn and provoked the incident. He behaved quite outrageously in fact. Imagine throwing someone into the water from that height. The young man might have been – Ouch! Do be careful!'

Juliana had jabbed a pin into her ankle but Sally bit back the angry words, unsure whether or not it was deliberate.

'Someone told me you were present at the duel,' Juliana went on. 'You know how these foolish rumours start. I said surely not! A woman like Sally Lunn would have too much sense.'

Sally managed a light laugh. 'Curiosity!' she confessed. 'I could not resist seeing the farce played out to the bitter end. 'Twas more entertaining than any play! The sooner duelling is stamped out the better it will be, in my opinion.'

The dressmaker straightened up and Sally turned round slowly as instructed.

At that moment the door opened and a man stepped into the room. Fortunately Sally saw him first in the mirror and recognized him, and the few seconds' grace gave her time to recover from the shock before she had to face him.

It was Richard Nash.

He gave her a small bow and said, 'But how very elegant you look, Mistress Lunn.'

Sally tried to speak but her throat was dry and she could only nod her head, aware meanwhile of Juliana's look of triumph.

Nash then spoke to Juliana in a low voice. Then he kissed her hand. He turned to Sally and took hers before she could decide whether or not she should refuse him the privilege. He bent over her hand. 'Again my thanks for your hospitality,' he said loudly. 'I have recommended your coffee-house to several of my friends.' Then he whispered, 'Believe me, Sally, I am most discreet!'

Then he was gone.

When Toby came in that evening Sally knew that he had news which she might not wish to hear. His face was set in a nervous scowl and he tried not to catch her eye.

'If you have something to say,' she told him sharply, 'please get on with it. And don't pretend because I know you too well.'

He turned towards her slowly. ''Tis not what I want to say,' he told her, 'but what I must say.'

Still shaken from her encounter with Nash, Sally braced herself.

'I have to leave,' he blurted out. 'I'll be off in a week or two. I can see there's no hope. Nor ever will be.'

'No hope for what?' she asked although she knew in her heart what he meant.

'No hope for you and me. Not now. Not after that odious wretch . . .' He shook his head sadly. 'You know what I'm trying to say, Sally.'

She was silent, mortified by his changed opinion of her, sadder than she would ever admit. They had been good friends for so long – constant companions, in a way. He probably knew her better than anyone else did and had always wanted to marry her. But not now. What remained of her confidence ebbed slowly away and she waited dumbly for the rest of his speech.

'You know I loved you, Sally. I never pretended

otherwise. I thought it was just a matter of time until you'd love me in return but I see now you never will.'

'No,' she said. 'I wish I could but you can't force love, Toby. I know you would have made me a good husband but I would never have made you happy.' She sighed. 'I dare say I'm not the marrying sort. I told you many years ago.'

The ghost of a smile lit his face. 'You did tell me!' he reminded her. 'Every time I proposed you turned me down. I should have accepted what you said instead of hoping against hope.'

Sally said, 'You'll find someone else who will make you happy now that you know it won't be me.'

He shook his head. 'Never!' he declared. ''Tis you or no one.'

'Don't say that!' she cried. 'The town is full of young women who will jump at the chance to wed Toby Parker.'

His shoulders heaved in another sigh. 'I suppose I should thank Master Nash,' he said bitterly. 'At least he has made me face up to the truth at last. While there was no other man in your life I could pretend I stood a chance. Now I know better.'

Sally lowered her eyes. 'That's over. I was a fool.'

He smiled wanly. 'We all make mistakes,' he said. 'We're all human.'

'Some of us make more than others!' Sally whispered, half to herself.

'I still love you,' he said. 'I always will.'

'Even after . . .' She could not bring herself to mention Nash but he understood.

'Perhaps I should have done that,' he mused. 'Gotten

you drunk and rolled you into bed! Would you have wed me then?'

'No!' It was heartfelt. 'I doubt I shall ever wed.'

'Suppose Nash asked you tomorrow?'

He asked the question in all innocence, unaware of the debacle at Juliana's.

'No!' she cried passionately. 'Never! Never!' After a moment she added, 'I do sometimes learn from my mistakes.'

For a while they regarded each other unhappily.

'What will you do?' she asked him. 'Where will you go?' It did not occur to her that perhaps she should be the one to leave. She had made Sally Lunn's what it was but Toby's family owned it. Or held the lease – she had never thought to enquire.

'My mother's cousin is a gunsmith,' he told her. 'In Midsomer Norton, not far from here. His sons are gone – one to America, one dead of consumption. He wants someone to carry on the business. 'Tis a marvellous opportunity.'

'But you are not a gunsmith, Toby. What do you know about guns?'

He raised an imaginary gun. 'You load it and prime it and you pull the trigger. Bang!'

'Even I know that much!'

'I shall learn.'

'But you are such a good pastrycook. An excellent pastrycook. Will you ever be an excellent gunsmith?'

'Maybe not but I shall be a rich one!' He shrugged. 'People change from one job to another. Look at your brother – he became a fisherman, then a weaver. I shall be a gunsmith.'

She could not hide her dismay. 'So you, too, will be leaving Bath? It won't be the same without you, Toby.'

'Bath will survive!'

'And your parents? They will miss you.'

'We will all go.'

'Why does nothing stay the same?' she asked. 'I hate all these changes.'

'Perhaps you should change,' he suggested. 'Perhaps you should become Mistress Parker, wife of a wealthy gunsmith!' He gave a wry smile. 'I seem to have proposed again. It has become a habit! So – that was positively my last proposal.'

'You would still marry me, then?' She clung to the thought that in spite of her fall from grace he was still prepared to marry her.

'Apparently.'

'It was your heart speaking, not your head,' she told him gently. 'My answer must still be no, but I appreciate your offer. Forgive me.'

He shrugged again. ''Tis all over, then.'

An awkward silence fell and to break it Sally said, 'It seems everyone is leaving Bath! Soon the town will be deserted.' Her voice broke. 'Oh, Toby! Promise me we part as friends. These last few days – I have been so very confused and wretched and I have treated you badly.'

'I have been unkind to you also.'

'We must forgive each other, then!' She held out her hands and he grasped them so tightly she almost winced.

He asked, 'What will you do, Sally? You must not

die a lonely spinster.' His words sent a chill down her spine but before she could answer he went on. 'Perhaps you will wed young Meddows.'

'Oh no! He is too young – and too foolish,' she told him.

'Too young. Too old. Too rich. Too poor. Is there a man alive who you would take as a husband?'

She laughed with him. 'And I am too hard to please?' she said. 'Is that what you mean?'

He was suddenly serious, his eyes full of – was it pity? Sally felt that chill again.

'Don't wait too long,' he said softly. 'We all need someone to love. Even you.'

Then, for the first and last time he kissed her and she had never felt so alone in her life.

Toby was leaving at the end of the week and Sally set about finding a replacement. She decided that instead of selling bread, tarts and teacakes she would sell only bread and tea-cakes. That way she could employ someone part time simply to bake the bread, which would still form a staple part of the business.

She interviewed three applicants before finding a fourth whom she considered suitable. He was a middle-aged man, by the name of Andrew Wills, of a dour disposition but a good reputation as a baker of bread. He was also married with six children so Sally did not foresee any problems of a romantic nature developing between them, a fact which pleased her. She also took on a young lad who would come in for an hour at the end of each day as dogsbody.

Her personal life which had been calm for so long

had suddenly become a source of anxiety and unrest, for Nash had awakened in her desires which had previously lain dormant, and she now felt unsettled and vaguely dissatisfied with her lot and longed for a return to her old life when the coffee-house was all that she needed. She wanted to hate him for what had happened but found, to her annoyance, that she could not do so nor could she play the seduced woman because she had been a willing partner. She could not despise him for gossiping about her since he had promised discretion and she trusted him. She could not even fear the conception of a love child because her monthly cycle had not been interrupted. In a strange way, and greatly to her surprise, this had almost disappointed her although her common sense warned her against the upsurge of such ridiculous yearnings. Suddenly it seemed that her whole world was being turned upside-down and she was shaken and disorientated.

The day before Toby was due to leave, Sally was on her own at the end of a tiring day. She had closed the door on the last customer at six o'clock and had helped the lad with the washing up. He was slow and clumsy but he worked with a good will. He watched her anxiously as she made her rounds. She checked that he had filled and covered the two water buckets and had swept the floor of the bakery and finally stood with her hands on her hips, surveying her small kingdom with a critical eye. The crocks were in place, the oven door had been black leaded, the copper pans shone. She ran a finger along the shelf and could find no fault. The lad let out a sigh of relief.

'Mousetraps,' she muttered. Yes, they had been freshly baited.

To the boy's horror her gaze then moved ceilingwards and his fingers moved nervously to his mouth as her arm went up and she pointed accusingly.

'Cobwebs!' she announced and he nodded guiltily.

'Tomorrow you get them down!' she told him. 'You know where the long broom is.' He nodded again and swallowed hard as her eyes roamed the bakery once more. 'Scale pans?' She saw with satisfaction that they had been scoured clean. 'Good!' she said. 'You can go now.'

He held out his hand for the sixpence but when it was in his hand still made no move to go.

Sally laughed, 'Oh, you are still here? I wonder if I can guess why?'

His slow smile touched her heart.

'Here!' she said. She took two teacakes from the basket and wrapped them in a clean cloth. 'And don't nibble them on the way home!' she told him. As he scuttled out of the door she added, 'And ask your mother for a clean apron tomorrow!'

He murmured something in reply and then his footsteps clattered away on the cobbles and she closed the door.

Toby would not be in until later and she had the place to herself. Normally she would be looking forward to this time of the day but lately she had found it increasingly lonely. For a long moment she looked round the bakery with a bewildered mixture of affection and disenchantment. When a black cat appeared on the stairs she bent suddenly and scooped it up and held it against her chest, smothering its surprised head with kisses. It struggled so wildly in the unexpected embrace that she was finally forced to release it. It ran at once behind the faggot box with a loud and resentful 'miouw'.

'Go then!' Sally muttered. 'Stupid animal!'

Ten minutes later she was sitting at the kitchen table, trying to balance the day's takings and finding it harder than usual to concentrate. The figures danced before her eyes and her thoughts kept wandering to other matters – Jean's imminent departure to America, the supper party invitation, Andrew Wills the new baker.

Above her in its cage on the wall the linnet trilled and she glanced up briefly with a smile before returning once more to the page in front of her.

When a knock sounded at the door below she jumped to her feet gratefully, glad of the excuse to abandon her accounts, and hurried down to the bakery. To her surprise she found Ned Cooper standing on the doorstep and she was so pleased to see him that she only just refrained from throwing her arms around his neck.

'Come in!' she cried. 'We'll go up to the kitchen. 'Tis so good to see you, Ned.'

Seeing the open ledger on the table he said, 'I hope 'tis not an inconvenient time to call.'

But she interrupted him warmly, ''Tis always the right time for you to call, Ned. I am simply checking the accounts – or trying to do so! I see that I have paid too much for flour – the miller is a rogue and thinks me a fool! And eggs.' She pointed an accusing finger towards the pile of bills alongside the account book. 'I paid for three dozen, used twenty and have thirteen left! How does that add up? I was taught that twenty from thirty-six leaves sixteen.' She tossed her head indignantly. 'They think because I am a woman that I will turn a blind eye but I am not made that way. They should know me better by now. But don't let me chatter on about bills. Here I am with a visitor and I bore him with figures! Sit yourself down, Ned. Will you have a cup of tea or coffee, or something stronger? Madeira, maybe?'

'I think a glass of Madeira would go down well,' he told her as he sat down at the table. 'My news is – well, let us say 'tis good and bad, at the same time.'

Startled, she cried, 'Oh, Ned! Don't say that you are leaving Bath also? I could not bear it!'

'No, no,' he reassured her, 'nothing like that. It doesn't concern me at all – at least, only indirectly. It concerns you and – and someone else.'

She poured out the wine and they both raised their glasses.

'You are being most mysterious,' Sally told him. 'Do go on.'

He took a deep breath and then hesitated again. 'I have not known what to do for the best,' he told her. 'I have changed my mind a dozen times. Even now I may be making a mistake but you are a grown woman and I think – in fact I'm certain . . .'

His nervousness was infectious and she stared at him apprehensively.

'The fact is, Sally, that what I have to tell you may bring you heartache instead of joy.'

A dull ache spread through her. 'You are going to wed!' she said unsteadily.

'Going to wed? Me?' His astonishment was so great she almost laughed with relief. 'Indeed no! Nothing is farther from my mind. No, the fact is – God help me! Is this for the best? Oh, Sally, I wish I knew.'

His look was anguished and her apprehension deepened.

She set down her glass and reaching out, touched his hand. 'I am not a child,' she said. 'Tell me whatever it is, Ned, and put me out of my misery!'

' 'Tis your father, Sally,' he said. 'I have found him.'

Her surprise was total and for a moment she was unable to utter a word. Then a great elation seized her. Her faith was justified. Her father was found! Charity Becket had been right all along. She felt a twinge of guilt that her attempts to find him had lessened over the past few years and that there had been times when she had almost given up hope of ever seeing him again. She had never doubted that he was still alive but it had seemed improbable that he was still in Bath. And now Ned had found him!

'Oh Papa!' she whispered exultantly. Covering her face with her hands she murmured the words again and again.

Ned, watching her with a worried frown on his face, decided that he must tell it all before she became too excited. The disillusionment would be that much harder to bear.

'Sally,' he began. 'He is not how you imagine. He has had a wretched –'

'You have found him!' she cried. 'Oh, Ned! I can

hardly believe it after all these years. To see my father again! Not that I shall recognize him – or him me! I was such a child, just a baby really. Oh, Ned! I can scarce believe it even now.' She smiled at him radiantly. 'And it couldn't have come at a better time. Lately I have been so wretched, so empty. You can't imagine. I have felt so terribly alone!'

Reluctant to mar her happiness Ned sat watching her, and as he did so he saw the words he had spoken earlier sink suddenly into her consciousness. Abruptly her eyes darkened warily.

'What do you mean? He is not as I imagined?' she asked. 'I imagined nothing. How could I?'

Ned opened his mouth to explain but she was still not ready to listen.

Her voice was very low. 'I just long to be with him again and to know that he loves me. When I was a child I used to ask them about him and always they said that he loved me but I was never sure, you see. Never quite satisfied in my own mind. I wanted to hear it from his own lips. I wanted to see it in his eyes as he looked at me; to feel it in the tightness of his arms as he held me. Then I knew I would be sure.' She looked at Ned.

'Perhaps you think I am foolish.'

'No, I don't think that at all.'

She sighed. 'And then we came to England and Maman insisted he was dead I –' She stopped abruptly and her eyes widened. 'Maman!' she said. 'And Henri!'

He could only nod as the shock registered.

'Maman and Henri!' she repeated slowly. 'Dear God! What will this do to them?'

He waited, giving her mind time to grasp all the implications, not wanting to hurry her, sad that already her joy was diluted.

At last she said, 'They married in good faith, Ned. They won't be punished, will they?'

'Do they need to know?' he asked.

She put a hand to her head. 'You mean we shouldn't tell them? But Papa will want to see her – won't he? Oh, this is terrible!' She sprang to her feet and began to move restlessly about the room. She looked at him and smiled faintly. 'Poor Ned. You have had time to think of all this already. Of course you have. What a worry for you.'

''Tis of no account,' he told her. 'I merely wanted what's best for you, Sally.'

'You did right to tell me and I am longing to see him –' Again his words came back to her. 'What did you mean, Ned? You said Papa is not how I imagined him?'

He swallowed the last of the wine in one gulp seeking Dutch courage.

'I don't know how to describe him except to say he is a broken man, Sally. He has had a very hard life, full of trouble. He is sick –'

She picked up on the word immediately. 'Papa is sick? How sick?'

'Very sick, Sally,' he told her.

She jumped to her feet. 'I want to go to him! I must see him, Ned. After all these years! I cannot bear to waste another minute. Whatever he is like, I want to see him for myself.'

'Wait! Please!' he begged. 'You must hear me out.

You must understand fully. He does not know you are here in Bath. He has reconciled himself to the idea that either you are all still in La Rochelle or that you are all dead. I have not told him because of your mother and Henri. I thought perhaps you would want to talk to Jean and that between you, you would decide what to do.'

'Ah! Of course!' She sat down again and shook her head helplessly.

He saw the stricken look in her eyes and sensed that the tears were not far away.

'Is there any more, Ned?' she whispered. 'We have come this far. I must hear it all.'

'He has been dogged by misfortune,' he told her, choosing his words carefully so as to minimize the hurt. 'There was a fight – a terrible accident and a man died. They blamed your father. He –'

'Was it his fault?' she demanded.

'Indirectly. It was a drunken brawl.'

She whispered, 'A drunken brawl?' She swallowed.

'That was in Bideford. He changed his name and came to Bath.'

'He is *here* – in Bath?' She stared at him wide-eyed.

He nodded. 'At my house,' he told her. 'In your bed, in fact, but very sick. He is like to die unless he undergoes surgery and he refuses even to consider it. The physician has given him a few weeks to live. Your father is in great pain – 'tis pitiful to see him – but he will not allow me to help him. I have arranged everything but he will not consent. He believes he has nothing to live for but I thought if he knew about you – I wondered if we could keep it from your mother. I

370

didn't know what to do, Sally. You might persuade him.'

'Poor Papa! He is frightened of the knife,' she said, 'and the pain. I would be.'

'We all fear it,' said Ned. ''Tis natural enough.'

She nodded. After a moment or two she said wonderingly, 'So he has been in Bath all along?'

'Yes, he has.'

'Why didn't I find him?'

'You looked in the wrong places, perhaps. And asked after the wrong name. Does it matter now?'

He did not want to dwell on that particular aspect of her father's situation. If she saw him as an invalid she might not make the connection between him and the squalid wretch she had no doubt seen many times in the stocks. If possible she need never know the worst.

'I dare say not,' she said wearily.

Her face was haggard, he thought with a surge of compassion, and she looked years older.

'I just want to see him,' she said wistfully.

Ned stood up. 'I will take you to him.'

But she shook her head. 'No, not yet. I know we must decide what to tell him about Maman. I can wait a little longer. He is at your house, you say?' Her eyes narrowed. 'And you have arranged surgery for him. What is his complaint?'

'A tumour, very advanced.'

She cast her eyes heavenwards and cried, 'Oh, God! How could You do this?' To Ned she said, 'To give with one hand and take away with the other!'

'I wish with all my heart it had been otherwise,' he told her.

Suddenly a fresh thought struck her. 'And who was

going to pay for this surgery?' she asked. 'An operation is a costly affair.' Reluctantly he admitted that he intended to pay for it.

Sally stared at him in consternation. 'But why? And how? Are you such a rich man, Ned?'

'I have a little saved and there are other ways. I have spoken with a moneylender who is willing –'

'A moneylender? But Ned, they are such rogues. They are nothing more than leeches! They will suck you dry!'

He was silent.

'Ned, why?' she asked softly.

He shrugged, not meeting her eyes.

'Was it for me?' she insisted.

'For you, yes. For him, too. Maybe even for me,' he said. 'I don't know. Does it matter?'

'Most certainly it matters!' Sally told him. 'Oh, Ned, why are you so good to me? I don't deserve it.'

'You are too hard on yourself –' he began but she rushed on.

'I'm a selfish wretch. Oh yes, I am. A selfish, stubborn wretch! Poor Maman was right all those years ago. I am so wrapped up in my own affairs I neglect those who love me.' She frowned guiltily. 'I think only of my coffee-house! I don't deserve good friends and a loving family!'

Ned swallowed nervously. 'I would be more than a good friend, Sally, if only you would –'

Sally leaned forward and kissed his cheek. 'You are more than that already, Ned,' she assured him. 'You are my dearest friend in all the world!'

She thought this compliment did not excite him as

much as she expected so she added, 'I love you dearly.'

'Do you?' he whispered.

'Most certainly,' she said briskly, 'and I will never allow you to fall into the clutches of moneylenders. I, too, have a little money put by —'

But Ned was holding up his hand. 'This is all fruitless,' he pointed out. 'Stubbs refuses to go in to hospital.'

'I shall persuade him.' Her expression defied him to argue.

''Tis certainly his only hope,' he told her.

'And it will save him? You are certain?'

'No, Sally. It is a chance, no more than that.'

'And if you had not known he was my father — would you have tried to save him?'

Ned raised his hands in a helpless gesture, 'Maybe not. He would have had so little to live for. I doubt I would have put him through such an ordeal.'

Sally stood up abruptly. 'We'll go to him,' she said, 'and we'll save him in spite of himself! He'll survive. I know it — here!' She laid a hand on her heart and smiled up at him. 'He shall come and live with me. He's a baker by trade. He can help me. Between us we shall make Sally Lunn's a coffee-house to be reckoned with! The best in Bath! Oh, dearest Ned! You will never know how much this means to me.'

Ned stood up also and followed her to the door, secretly dismayed by her conviction that all would be well.

Sally paused for a moment to take a last look at the bakery. Once it had been all in all to her; now it would be nothing without her father.

*

As soon as Ned had left his house Nan took her shawl from behind the kitchen door and flung it round her shoulders. She was paid to stay another half-hour but saw no reason why she should play nursemaid to a nasty old man. Her master would be none the wiser unless Stubbs betrayed her. If he did that she would deny it and insist that she left on time and would say that Stubbs was lying to try and cause trouble. She had done it before and knew that her master always gave her the benefit of the doubt. She had given Stubbs the brandy bottle earlier to keep him quiet and, if necessary, would swear on her mother's grave that he had found it for himself.

She went upstairs and put her head round the door of the sickroom.

'I'm off now,' she declared. 'Got all you want, have you?' She did not look at him directly because he frightened her. His parchment-coloured skin was stretched across his face and somehow made his rheumy eyes appear larger than was natural. His bony hands reminded her of skeletons and when he laughed at one of his own vulgar jokes his voice rattled in his throat. She told her sister that when the pain was very bad and he groaned it was 'like a banshee wailing!'

Before he could answer her rhetorical question she quickly withdrew her head and went downstairs again.

From his sick bed Stubbs listened eagerly to her retreating footsteps and nodded with satisfaction at the sound of the street door closing behind her. He was in great pain and beads of perspiration stood out on his forehead. From beneath the blankets he drew the bottle of brandy and, holding it up to the light, examined it drunkenly. The last of his earthly pleasures, he thought hazily. The rest was up to God. Maybe He could do better: surely He could do no worse. One more mouthful, just one more swallow and then he was done with it all. He had promised himself that.

As the pain roared through him again he cried out and thrust the neck of the bottle between his teeth with a trembling hand so that some of the precious liquid splashed on to the coverlet and the rest went down his throat too quickly and made him choke.

'Be damned with it!' he moaned and threw the bottle into the corner of the room where it fell intact as though mocking his weakness.

'Be damned with it all!' he muttered. He pushed and tugged at the covers until he was free of them and then slid clumsily out of bed, and stood up on trembling legs.

'Now where has he put my godbegotten breeches?'

With an effort he lifted the lid of the chest but his own clothes were not there. Instead he saw one of Ned's coats and decided it would do as well as any other and pulled it on over his nightshirt. There were no breeches but he felt that decency was preserved. He could find no shoes but it hardly seemed to matter. What mattered most was that he should be gone from the house before Master Cooper returned. He must cling on to that idea.

His exertions had exhausted him and for a moment he swayed unsteadily and almost fell, but he leaned on the chest and slowly his strength returned.

'Let's see what God has to offer!' he mumbled with the ghost of a smile. 'Angels and suchlike! See if those canting black crows told us true!'

At the door of the room he hesitated, vaguely aware that he had forgotten something, and stared around him.

'Ah yes! Papa's stick!'

He stumbled back to the bed, fumbled beneath the pillow and pulled out the stick with the duck's-head handle. A sudden thought struck him and a smile lit up his face. Papa would be there – wherever *it* was! Papa would be waiting, arms outstretched to swing him into the air with that booming laugh of his! He smiled. Of course! He would not be among strangers.

'Papa!' he smiled lopsidedly. 'Papa! You see I have it still!' He held up the stick. 'I brought it with me . . .'

For a moment he closed his eyes and in his imagination saw the knife in his father's hands as he gently carved the stick. Suddenly his eyes snapped open in alarm. The knife! The surgeon's knife! He had almost forgotten his purpose.

He opened the door and half-fell down the stairs, clutching at the stair rope like a drowning man. His hands slipped and he fell the last few feet but when he reached the bottom he picked himself up and reached for the stick. Then, with some difficulty he opened the street door and let himself out of the house. A fresh spasm of pain caught and twisted him, reminding him of his carefully conceived plan. Even in his inebriated state he was aware that the purpose of this expedition must not escape him. He shook his head to clear his brain.

'South Gate!' he murmured thickly, with a glance to left and right to reassure himself that he was unobserved. 'I must get to the bridge.'

People were the problem, he knew that. People would interfere if he gave them half a chance. People like Master Cooper. Good, honest, interfering people who would not let a man die in peace but must needs threaten him with the surgeon's knife. Even now there were people who would stop him if they could. He must be cunning.

He made his way to the end of the road and then turned left. He knew all the short cuts and was soon in Abbey Lane where, to his dismay, he ran into a small group of women who stood gossiping together. They stared in disgust at the scrawny figure in its strange attire and drew back as he staggered past. He looked like a madman, brandishing a stick and muttering thickly to himself, but one of them, more caring than the others, called after him.

'Old man! Wait!'

But Stubbs laughed and lurched on. He was not going to be caught that easily! People! They couldn't be trusted not to meddle. He had no intention of being delayed by her or anyone else; nobody was going to persuade him to abandon his plan. He knew he must reach the bridge.

He left the women behind and stumbled on, weaving an erratic course, trying to avoid the worst of the litter, cursing the stray dogs that barked at him. His breath came painfully, his strength was almost spent and from time to time his legs buckled rebelliously beneath him, but at last he recognized Southgate and made his way thankfully under the arch.

The last stretch lay ahead – out through the gate, past the horse bath and on towards the bridge. A fresh wave of pain made him pause, doubled up in agony, then it was simply a matter of putting one foot in front of the other until at last the bridge came into sight.

He whispered, 'I'm coming as fast as I can, dammit!'

Two horsemen were crossing the bridge on their way into the city and Stubbs cowered back into the shadows to avoid being seen but one of the horses caught sight of him and shied in alarm. The horse's rider cursed and spurred the horse and rode on.

When they had gone Stubbs leant against the parapet of the bridge and smiled to himself. He had done it! Now he would be free of the pain and would be done with his burdensome life. With his remaining strength he pulled himself up on to the parapet and stared down into the swiftly flowing river. In the deepening gloom it looked inviting, smooth, peaceful. It seemed to beckon him, to offer him release.

Stubbs whispered, 'I'm coming!' and with the stick held firmly in his right hand, he gave a crooked grin and allowed himself to topple into the water.

Chapter Fifteen

SALLY AND NED arrived at the house and hurried up the stairs.

When they reached the door Ned put a restraining hand on her arm.

'Let me go in first,' he suggested. 'I'll tell him he has a visitor. Then I'll leave the two of you together. You can break the news to him – tell it in your own way.'

She nodded, breathlessly, her hands clasped nervously, her mouth closed to suppress her mounting excitement. She waited as he went into the room and heard his exclamation of incredulity.

'God's truth! He's not here!' cried Ned and Sally rushed into the room to stare at the empty, rumpled bed in shocked dismay.

'Damnation!' he cried.

'Oh, Ned!' Her lips trembled. The disappointment was almost more than she could bear.

He looked round the room in disbelief, noticed the chest with its raised lid and examined the contents.

'He's taken my coat,' he told her, 'but he can't be far. He was too sick to go far. Too sick, I would have thought, to even get down the stairs!'

They looked at each other, momentarily at a loss,

confused by the suddenness of this unexpected development. Sally clapped a hand to her mouth as a terrible thought occurred to her.

'Perhaps they've taken him into custody!' she cried. 'The authorities, I mean! You said he'd been in trouble.'

Ned shook his head, 'No, no. That's unlikely after so many years. He'd covered his tracks pretty well from all accounts. No, he must be in the house somewhere. Looking for the –' He stopped as his eyes fell on the brandy bottle in the corner of the room. 'Damnation!' he muttered.

'Oh!' said Sally following the direction of his gaze. She looked at Ned unhappily. 'Was that one of his problems?'

He shrugged, not meeting her eyes. 'We must search the house,' he said. 'He must be here.'

They searched the house from top to bottom before admitting defeat.

'He has gone out,' Ned admitted. 'I would have thought that impossible. Ah!' He snapped his fingers. 'We'll ask Nan what she knows. He might have said something – given her some clue as to his intentions.'

They went straight to the servant's home, a poor cottage near Timber Green, but Nan insisted, hand on heart, that she had left at the usual time and that the invalid had given no hint of his intentions.

'Fast asleep, he was,' she told them. 'Sleeping like a baby when I looked in to say I was going.'

'Did you know he had found the brandy?' Ned asked.

Her eyes widened innocently. 'The brandy? Never!

Now how did he get that, the sly old dog?' She shook her head in feigned amazement.

'And you are certain he said nothing untoward?' Ned persisted. 'He said nothing to make you suspicious?'

'Not a word. Bade me farewell, cheerful as a —'

'How could he bid you farewell if he was sleeping like a baby?' Sally demanded sharply.

Nan stared at her resentfully. 'That was before,' she said. 'Before he fell asleep.'

Ned thanked her and she went back indoors, banging the door behind her for Sally's benefit.

'She could be lying,' said Sally. 'Do you think she may have helped him? He may have bribed her.'

'He had no money,' said Ned. 'No, I think she's telling the truth. I doubt she knows anything of use. We're wasting time. We must start searching the streets.'

'But where could he be going?' Sally asked helplessly. 'An ale house, maybe? We don't know where to start looking.'

'We must ask as we go,' said Ned. 'He has no proper clothing and must be quite conspicuous in a nightshirt and coat! Poor Sally, don't look like that. We'll find him, I promise you. And I shall have something to say to him for frightening us this way.'

But behind these encouraging words he was deeply apprehensive. Knowing the old man's state of mind he now began to suspect the worst.

'We must search separately,' he told her. 'Ask everyone. Someone must have seen him.'

When they met again half an hour later, however, both were forced to admit defeat.

'I'm so sorry,' Ned told her, 'I can imagine your disappointment.'

Sally could not trust herself to speak but her pale face and anguished expression spoke for her.

'Will he come back, do you think?' she asked at last. 'When he sobers up, I mean?'

' 'Tis possible.'

'Did he have any friends? Could he be with them?'

Privately Ned thought it most unlikely but he didn't want to break her heart.

' 'Tis possible,' he said.

He cursed himself for not realizing that something of this kind might occur. With the benefit of hindsight he was beginning to fear a tragedy.

'Could he have gone to the hospital?' Sally suggested without much hope.

Ned shook his head. 'He was much too frightened. Wild horses wouldn't have dragged him there.'

'Even in his cups?'

'I think not.'

'Maybe he *has* been arrested. We could enquire.'

They made their way to the Bridewell at the top of Spurriers Lane and banged repeatedly at the door until a small window slid open revealing the gaoler – an unshaven, uncouth man with only one eye. When Ned described Stubbs the man shook his head.

'No mad men in tonight,' he told them with an emphatic shake of his head.

Sally's eyes flashed. 'He's not mad. He's sick!'

'Sick, mad, drunk – who cares?' he replied. 'There's been no one brought in since yesterday morning, and that's how I like it.'

He closed the window before they could bother him further and Ned and Sally stood irresolutely, wondering what to do next.

'We'll make one more tour of the town,' Ned suggested, 'and then we'll go home. If he does come home I want to be there – and you must have work to do for tomorrow.'

Sally agreed and they set off once more, asking everyone they met for news of an old, sick man. This time they were luckier. A man recalled that his horse had been frightened by a strange looking man.

'Just as we left the bridge on our way into the city,' he told them. 'A wild-looking man, barefooted as I recall, in a coat that was too big for him. Terrified my horse. Would that be your man?'

'Was he leaving town then?' asked Sally.

He shrugged, 'The wretch was heading that way, certainly. I was too busy controlling my mare to see what became of him. He could have had me off!'

They thanked him and walked to the bridge and for a moment they looked over into the swirling darkness.

Sally gave a sudden gasp. 'He wouldn't,' she whispered, 'would he? Oh, Ned!'

Ned thought it very likely but could not bring himself to confirm her fears.

'He's probably left town,' he told her. 'I'll get a horse and go after him before he gets too far.'

'He'll die of cold,' said Sally, 'if he stays out in this weather. I'll come with you.'

'No!' His tone was sharper than he intended. If he did find Stubbs he would be in a bad state and he wanted to spare Sally that ordeal.

'You've got work to do. You go back and get on with the baking. I've nothing to do. I'll go alone.'

'But Ned, I —'

'I swear I shall find him if any man can and as soon as I have him safely tucked up in bed you shall know of it. You trust me, don't you?'

'Certainly I do but —'

'No buts, Sally. Do as I ask. Keep busy and the time will pass more quickly.'

'Even if 'tis the middle of the night? You will still fetch me?'

'I swear it.'

A body was discovered the following day a few miles north of Keynsham and, because of the enquiries he had been making, Ned was informed and asked to attempt an identification.

Reluctantly he broke the news to Sally. She was broken-hearted but as he had feared, she insisted on accompanying him and they eventually rode out later the same day on their mournful errand. White-faced she stood beside Ned in the tiny room which served Keynsham as a morgue and stared into the crudely made coffin. Despite its immersion in the water the body was still recognizable and Ned nodded.

'That's Stubbs,' he said.

Sally stared at the figure with its gaunt, grey face. A farthing had been placed on each closed eye and a strip of linen bound the head to hold the jaw in place. She shuddered involuntarily but could not look away. He was carelessly covered with a linen sheet and his feet protruded comically. The fingers of one hand were spread despairingly but the other hand made a tight fist. Was this her father – this sad, lifeless old man? She swallowed hard and longed to weep but the tears refused to flow and she stared dry-eyed for a long time. She lifted a lock of the dead man's hair and saw the small scar.

The attendant coughed impatiently.

'That's Papa!' she said.

The attendant's expression changed at once.

'Your Pa, is he, mistress? Well, I am sorry. Still, these things happen.' He turned to Ned. 'Funniest thing I ever saw,' he confided. 'When they brought him in he was holding a stick. Clutching it real tight. Had a job to get it free. Imagine a corpse...' He glanced apologetically at Sally and amended his description. 'Imagine a dead man holding on to a stick! Never seen anything like it and I've worked here nigh on thirty years. Gave me quite a turn, in fact. Pretty little thing, too, with a duck's-head handle. I thought my grandson would like it but seeing as the lady here is the daughter, next of kin, as you might say . . .'

He crossed to a cupboard and drew out the stick and handed it to Sally, who took one look at it and began to cry.

As Ned made a move to comfort her the attendant gave him a warning glance. 'Best to let the tears come, sir,' he advised. 'Grief's a funny thing. It must *out*, sir, if you see what I mean. 'Tis the natural way. I had a neighbour once, lost her husband when she was only twenty and never shed a tear. Not one single, solitary tear. But,' he held up a stern finger, 'twenty-five years later, almost to the day, she started to cry and could not stop. Physician did what he could but she cried on and on, night and day. Pitiful to hear it, it was. Went into a decline and died. That's grief for you — very powerful grief is. Let it out, is my advice.'

Ned nodded distractedly, his eyes on Sally.

'Can you release the body?' he asked in a low voice. 'We'll hire a cart and take it back to Bath for burial.'

The man looked doubtful. 'Suicide, was it, or accident? Not foul play, I trust.'

'Accident,' Ned told him firmly.

'Ah, then I can release him. Papers to sign, of course. Always something to sign but then I can release him into your charge.'

He raised his voice a little and said, 'Should I close up the coffin, then?'

At his words Sally leaned forward and kissed her father's cold forehead, then gently wiped away the tears that had fallen on to his face. Still weeping, she nodded her head and Ned led her outside while the attendant hammered down the lid.

With an effort Sally controlled her tears. 'I wish I had seen him alive,' she said. 'Just once. I don't want to remember him like that.'

Ned hesitated. 'You did see him,' he told her.

She looked up at him. 'I did? But when? How?'

'At my mother's funeral,' he said gently. 'He was the grave-digger. Do you remember?'

'At your mother's funeral?' She was trying to remember. At last she said, 'Not the man with the spade? The one who jumped out and . . .' She smiled faintly. '*That* was Papa?'

He smiled. 'Yes. He called himself Warren at that

time, but that was your father. In some ways he was a splendid character,' he said. 'He had his ups and downs – more downs than ups, perhaps – but he had a way with him. He could be charming when he wanted and he had a sense of humour. He was resilient, too. In spite of all his problems there were times when I admired him.'

'You *admired* him?' Sally asked.

He nodded.

'But if he was a rogue –' she began.

Ned said firmly, 'There are good rogues and bad rogues. He wasn't so bad.'

'Oh, Ned!' she cried.

And then she was in his arms, laughing and crying and he never wanted to let her go.

Andrew Wills started Sunday evening and Sally, pale but composed, watched him surreptitiously to assure herself that he did in fact have all the experience he had promised. She was not disappointed. He worked quietly and efficiently, saying little, occasionally muttering to himself but otherwise silent. As different from Toby as chalk from cheese, she reflected. Whenever she spoke to him he answered briefly and respectfully but he did not look up from his work. He could hardly be described as a cheerful companion, and she missed Toby's cheerful whistling and friendly banter, but she could find no fault with Andrew's work and told herself that that was all that mattered. She thought hopefully that he might mellow with time. Under any other circumstances she might have cared more but the loss of her father and thoughts of his unhappy end had numbed her emotionally. Regrets for what might have been filled her mind to the exclusion of almost everything else. The knowledge that so small a margin of time had separated tragedy from triumph depressed her unutterably and without Ned's support her mental anguish would have been even greater.

Stubbs's body now rested at Ned's house and the funeral had been arranged for Monday afternoon. He had been decently laid out in a clean white gown and cap with flowers at his head, a candle at his feet and Grandpère's stick laid beside him, and the grim memory of his corpse had faded. Giving him the stick on which she had set such store was all Sally could ever do for the father she had never really known.

Monday morning found her busy in the bakery and she had just taken out the first batch of teacakes when there was a knock at the door. The boy opened it and Sally turned to see Oliver Meddows framed in the narrow doorway.

He looked agitated as he returned her greeting and followed her upstairs to the kitchen.

'My dear Mistress Lunn —' he began, ignoring her suggestion that he sit down.

She said at once, 'Mistress Lunn, is it now?'

'Oh!'

He looked guilty, she thought with surprise.

'That is, Sally,' he began again.

She waited, puzzled by his manner. He was so obviously ill at ease, not at all like the amorous young man he had been on his previous visit. With an effort she recalled his invitation to the supper party and the fact that she had not given him an answer. So much had happened that such frivolous considerations had entirely slipped her mind.

'Your invitation!' she said with a smile. 'Pray forgive me, Oliver. I promised to give you an answer and I –'

'I called here yesterday,' he told her, 'on three occasions.'

'I was called away,' she told him, 'but I will accept your kind invitation. If you will –'

'Ah!' he said and could not meet her gaze.

She watched him struggling for words.

'What is it?' she asked. 'You have something to say to me I can see. Is it so terrible?'

'I had to see you,' he stammered. 'I had to know from your own lips. I could not believe it!'

'Believe what?'

He stared at her miserably. 'Your father! Tell me 'tis not so, I beg you. I have heard such foolish rumours.'

Her eyes darkened. 'My father is dead. Yes, that is true. Poor Papa is – Oliver, what is the matter?'

He was shaking his head in disbelief. 'No, no! He was not your father. I won't believe it!'

'Papa was drowned,' she said. 'We went to Keynsham to bring back his body –'

She stopped as Oliver's eyes widened in horror.

Slowly she went on, 'We will bury him this afternoon.'

He had closed his eyes as though in pain and Sally mistook his reaction as shocked sympathy.

'He was very sick,' she began. 'In one way it has been a merciful release –'

Oliver's eyes snapped open. 'That drunken wretch was your father! Heavens! Then what they told me was true!'

The little colour Sally had in her face drained suddenly away as the gist of his questions became clear and for a moment she was shocked into silence. Then with the beginnings of anger the colour rushed back into her cheeks.

He was regarding her with something akin to distaste, she realized.

He stammered, 'When I heard – when they told me – never! I told them I would not believe it. You and that despicable object –' Sally's hand rose in one swift movement and struck him a fierce blow across the right side of his face.

'How dare you speak of my father in that way!' she shouted. 'Don't you dare speak ill of the dead! Why, he lies in his coffin little more than a mile from here and worth ten of the likes of you. You have the – the gall – the effrontery to . . .' Her eyes blazed as she took a step towards him, both hands clenched into fists.

He stepped back quickly, one hand on his face, which was already reddening, the other held out in front of him to ward off further blows.

'But you must see!' he began. 'You surely must understand that this puts me in a very difficult position. My aunt and uncle heard of the relationship and were horrified. I told them there was no truth in it but now . . .'

Somehow Sally restrained herself from hitting him again. During the ride back from Keynsham Ned had told her a lot about Stubbs's life and she had been able to view her father in a more compassionate light. Now this useless dolt – this addlepated fop! – had dared to speak disrespectfully of a man who in Sally's opinion had never had a proper chance in life.

'So!' she cried accusingly. 'You don't approve of my father! Well, so be it, Master Meddows. I doubt if he would have approved of you, born with a silver spoon in your stupid mouth! No need to earn an honest crust like the rest of us! Nothing to do all day but prance about in your fancy clothes and enjoy yourself.'

'Mistress Lunn!' he begged. 'That is, Sally, I –'

'Oh, I see it all,' she cried. 'Now that you know whose daughter I am you have decided that I am not a worthy companion. I'm not good enough for you now. You don't care to be seen with me in case your friends jeer behind your back! Oh yes, that's it exactly, you snivelling puppy! Well, I don't give that much for your invitation!' She snapped her fingers under his nose. 'Do you hear me? Have no fear, Master Meddows, I shall release you from your obligation. You will not have the embarrassment of escorting me. I have no wish to meet your friends if they are as narrow-minded as you are. Don't fret, Master Meddows! I would not accompany you to a vagrants' tea party! I would not be seen dead in your company!' She searched her mind wildly. 'I wouldn't be buried in the same graveyard,' she told him. 'Am I making myself clear?'

Awed by her anger he was backing away, glancing over his shoulder for a way of escape.

'You must understand,' he bleated plaintively. ''Tis not so much for myself but my aunt and uncle –'

'A pox on your aunt and uncle!' Sally tossed her head contemptuously. 'And a pox on you too! Now get out of here, before I kick you out!'

He turned and fled ignominiously from the room and Sally watched him go with a wildly beating heart.

'And don't ever come back!' she shouted as the door slammed behind him.

When he had gone she sank down on to the nearest chair and her anger gave way to hysterical laughter. She would return his pearl and the linnet, she decided. Perhaps she would return the latter *stuffed*! Briefly a wry smile twisted the corners of her mouth. But no, she could never do such a thing. The bird was innocent and she had grown fond of it.

'Oh, Papa!' she whispered. 'You are worth a dozen Oliver Meddows! To me if to no one else.'

As her anger cooled her sense of proportion returned. So she would not be going to the supper party. What a relief! How could she have borne the vain and stupid prattling of Oliver Meddows and his pea-brained friends? They were not her kind of people. They were scarcely real! No, she was well rid of them all. She was vexed that she had ever seriously considered attending such a tawdry event. Whatever had convinced her that an evening of brainless chatter among complacent, puffed-up nobodies might somehow prove enjoyable? She had had a lucky escape, she told herself. Thank goodness she had seen through Oliver Meddows before she had compromised herself by appearing in public with him.

She had just reached this happy state of mind when the boy appeared at the kitchen door to say that Master Wills had put the next batch of Sally Lunns into the oven for her and she was not to fret. He would keep an eye on them.

She nodded distractedly. 'Give him my thanks and I'll be down shortly,' she told the boy and he clattered away down the stairs.

Briefly her lips trembled and then she thought of her father and all that he had suffered. She took a deep breath and squared her shoulders resolutely. By nightfall her father would be in his grave but for her life must go on.

She took another deep breath and made her way slowly downstairs.

Christmas came at last but it was a subdued affair. Sally had turned down the invitation to go to America and they were all conscious that it would be their last Christmas together.

On the fifth of January, 1717, Jean and the Rey family left Bath. Sally, shivering and desolate, waved them farewell and watched through eyes blurred with tears as the wagon rolled away bearing her loved ones on the first part of their long journey to America.

For days afterwards she could not eat and for weeks she could not pass their house which now stood empty, awaiting new tenants. She rose each day and performed her various tasks but her heart was heavy, although Nash had kept his word and the coffee-house was welcoming a new class of customer. Her thoughts were always with Jean and his new family and she lived with the constant fear that the ship on which they sailed would go down with all souls.

She was caught up in a web of despondency from which she could not free herself and her sleep was spoiled by bad dreams. As the weeks passed she lost weight and became obsessed by the thought that she had made the wrong decision when she decided to stay in England.

One day in early March she stood beside her father's grave, a sprig of heather twisted nervously in her fingers.

'I should have gone with them, Papa,' she murmured. 'There is nothing for me here. Nothing and no one.'

There had been no letter from Jean but that was not to be wondered at for if they had made the journey safely they would only just have arrived. A letter could not be expected so soon. Sally, however, was impatient and irrational and inclined to expect the worst.

She looked at the wording on the small stone and smiled.

'P. L. STUBBS
Rest in Peace'

She had wanted her father's real name to somehow be indicated and Ned had suggested the initials.

'Pierre Luyon Stubbs!' she said. 'Do you like it, Papa? I think it has quite a ring to it. A certain elegance!'

With a sigh she knelt and placed the heather on the grave, then stood up and glanced around her for inspiration. She made weekly visits as though to compensate for the lack of contact during his life. If and when a letter came from Jean she had promised she would read it aloud to him.

A watery sun lit the church wall and fell across the grass in long shadows. The winter was past and spring would not be long. It was what Grandmère had called 'the thin time of the year'. A solitary thrush rustled about beneath the nearby myrtle tree and an invisible bird sang sporadically from deep within an ancient yew.

Her ears caught the sound of footsteps and she turned in their direction. To her surprise she saw Ned Cooper striding towards her.

He smiled at once and said, 'I thought I might find you here.'

She returned the smile. 'Don't tell me I am mad to come here so often. I know it but I still come, it comforts me a little.'

He glanced around the churchyard. ''Tis a gloomy place.'

'But spring is coming and then I shall bring flowers.' She looked at him curiously. 'What brings you here?'

'You,' he said simply. 'I've come to ask you to marry me.'

She smiled. 'I was wondering how long it would be before you did.'

'You knew I would?' His amazement was genuine. 'But I only knew myself an hour ago!'

'Dear Ned! You are so kind. I have become one of your lame dogs, haven't I? You see that I am pining and out of sorts and you . . .'

In spite of himself he laughed at her words.

'Not at all!' he protested. ''Tis simply that I woke up to the knowledge that we need one another.'

'A marriage of convenience, then?' Her eyes mocked him gently.

'Sally Lunn! What an awkward creature you are. My mother was right about you.' He took hold of her hand. 'Listen to me,' he begged. 'You choose to make fun of me but I mean what I say. I am surprised I didn't come to that conclusion years ago. We should be together, Sally. Don't you know that, in your heart? Somehow it was never the right moment. Somehow along the years we lost our way. Now it seems so obvious and I am angry with myself for all that wasted time. Will you marry me, Sally? I want to take care of you. I want to make you happy.'

She looked at him, and the teasing tone had vanished from her voice.

'I know, Ned, and I am very grateful for your concern but at the moment I feel I would be a burden to you – or to anyone I married.'

'I am used to burdens –' he began.

'But don't you see that if I ever marry I want it to be for a different reason,' she told him earnestly. 'I want it to be because I love someone and can't live without him. Call it romantic nonsense if you wish.'

''Tis romantic nonsense!'

'Ned!' She put his hand to her lips and kissed it. 'You are too good to me. You see that I am troubled and you want to help. You have a generous nature, too generous. Your mother told me years ago that people take advantage of your kind heart. Well, I won't do that.' Seeing his downcast expression she added, ''Tis not for lack of affection, either, Ned. Don't think that way. I am very fond of you but –' She broke off and spread her hands helplessly.

'But what?' he demanded. 'If we are fond of each other?'

''Tis not enough, Ned. Forgive me but I have been a spinster for a long time and would rather stay a spinster forever than marry a man for the wrong reasons.'

396

He sighed. 'Oh, Sally! Sally! I have said all the wrong things. I am such a fool. What woman in her right mind would accept such a blunt proposal? All I needed to say was that I love you! And indeed I do!'

She took his hand. 'No, Ned, you are wrong. Of course it matters that you love me but whatever you said I would still refuse. This is a difficult time for me. I am confused and unhappy and full of doubts. I don't know myself any more. Where is my confidence, my sense of purpose? I don't know what I want any more and that frightens me.' She released his hand and turned away, biting her lip. 'I need time to find myself again. Time to recapture that – that love of life I once had. Does that sound so unreasonable? Am I making any sense?'

'I could help you –'

'No!' she cried, suddenly impatient. 'Don't you see, Ned? I have to find my own salvation. Maybe with your help I would find it sooner but I have to do it alone. For my self-respect. Oh, Ned, dearest Ned. I feel so ungracious and yet I must make you understand how I feel.'

Gently he laid a hand on her shoulder. 'What you need is time. Is that what you are saying, Sally? Because if so, then I will wait.'

'Oh, Ned, I wish you would.'

'Forever, if I must –' He smiled. 'But I would rather it were sooner. My poor little Sally! I wish I could spirit away all your cares and make you happy again. I do so hate to see you so melancholy.'

He put his arms around her and kissed her and she returned the kiss dutifully.

397

'One day I shall be myself again!' she promised.

'I shall rely on it!'

She glanced at her father's grave. 'I wonder if Papa can see us?'

'I dare say he can.'

After a moment she said, 'Don't be alarmed, Ned, if I am away for a few days. I may ride over to Bideford to see my mother. It has been a long time since I saw her – and she may have had a letter from Jean.'

As they walked together out of the churchyard she wondered what had prompted her to say that for until that moment she had thought too little of her mother.

At the lych gate she stopped in surprise as she suddenly understood her motive. For the first time in her life she felt a longing to confide in Henri.

The journey back to Bideford lasted four days and proved entirely uneventful. The company in which she travelled bored her and they, finding her morose and uncommunicative, left her mainly to her own devices which suited her very well since she wanted time to think.

When at last they arrived her mother and Henri were delighted to see her and made her very welcome. Sally was surprised to see how much older Marie looked. Her hair was very grey now and she had put on weight; she appeared altogether less brisk than Sally remembered. It was obvious that her mother was now happy and contented. Life with Henri suited her, it seemed, and Sally was forced to admit (if only to herself) that the union had proved very satisfactory.

Henri's business was flourishing, the house was comfortably furnished and there was a live-in servant to do the heavy work as well as a cook who came in daily. They set a good table and Marie's clothes, though not truly fashionable, were certainly attractive and well cut and Sally was amused to see that her mother had grown a little vain with the passing years. Her temper also appeared to have improved and she no longer snapped at her daughter but listened to her attentively, which Sally found rather pleasant.

There had been no letter from Jean but Marie appeared untroubled by this.

'We shall hear all in good time,' she told Sally. 'America is a long way away – too far for carrier pigeons!'

Sally said reproachfully. 'I don't know how you could let them go like that, Maman. I thought you would certainly forbid it!'

Marie raised her eyebrows. 'Forbid it? What right have I to forbid them their chance? If that is what they wanted and Louise's parents were agreeable. If *they* had been against the idea I would have tried to persuade them to stay, but they were willing to go also.' She shrugged. 'But I shed a few tears. I don't deny it.'

Henri corrected her, 'You shed a great many tears, Marie!'

She smiled at him. 'Perhaps I did, but Jean has a good head on his shoulders. He is sensible. I don't fear for him and Louise the way I feared for Pierre when he left France for England.'

To Marie's surprise Sally allowed this reference to her father to go unremarked and did not meet her mother's gaze. Henri, too, seemed surprised at Sally's silence.

To change the subject he said quickly, 'You could have gone with them, Soli. Jean wanted you to go.'

'I was tempted,' she admitted, 'but I could not leave my coffee-house. I was pulled both ways and at the last I knew I had to stay.'

She forbore to mention the part Richard Nash had played in her decision. That chapter of her life, she had decided after much soul-searching, would remain firmly closed.

Marie said proudly, 'We met a man only last week who had been to Bath for his health – the poor man suffers from gout – and when we spoke of you he said he had visited you.'

At once Sally became the concerned business woman and leaning forward she asked eagerly for the man's verdict.

'He spoke highly of you,' Marie told her, 'and he liked the teacakes.'

Henri nodded. 'He was full of praise, too, for the company he shared there. A refined sort of person – they were his very words.'

Sally sat back, smiling with satisfaction. Though she could never entirely forgive Nash for his betrayal, over the past months her bitterness had faded into a dull ache of regret.

'And prompt service with a smile,' Marie added. 'He particularly mentioned that.'

Sally positively beamed. ''Tis hard work, Maman, but so rewarding, you see. I have even had an offer for it. A certain Mr Dalmer would love to own it. But how could I let it go? How could I leave it?'

Marie gave her a shrewd look. 'Is there nothing else

in your life then, Soli? Just hard work? No good man? No children? Not ever?'

'Now, Marie!' Henri chided. 'The girl knows what she wants. Don't press her.'

'Does she?' asked Marie, looking directly at Sally.

Sally said, 'If I stay alone 'tis not for want of offers. Your daughter, Maman, is not without suitors!'

'I should think not!' said Henri gallantly.

Sally laughed suddenly, 'I see it now, Maman! You allow Jean to take your grandchildren to America and then you look to me to replace them for you!'

'And you won't oblige me?'

Sally hesitated. 'Not yet', she said.

Marie wagged a finger at her. 'Don't leave it too long, Soli. The years slip by and you are not getting any younger. You will wake up one morning and find grey hairs, like mine! The girls of today are so different.' She tutted. 'When I was a girl all we wanted was a husband and children to care for. Now 'tis a coffee-shop! Well, that won't keep you warm in bed at night!'

They all laughed and Henri winked at Sally. 'Your mother is old-fashioned,' he told her. 'Take no heed. You must find your own way, Soli, whichever way that is.'

The following day was Monday and when Marie had gone to visit a sick neighbour Sally slipped downstairs to Henri's workroom. He was stitching a coat in heavy maroon satin, an eyeglass held firmly into his left eye. He looked up as she entered the room and smiled.

'I hoped you would seek me out,' he said. 'Come and sit beside me.'

Startled, she did as she was told and then, momentarily lost for words, looked about her with interest. There was cloth everywhere – on tables and shelves, draped over chairs, spilling negligently from drawers and chests. Silks, satins and serges filled the room with a cheerful profusion.

Henri waved a hand. 'I know how you feel about your coffee-house,' he told her, 'because I feel the same way about this. I could not leave it. 'Tis part of me, an extension of myself – of my soul, even!' He smiled. 'To tell the truth your mother was undecided about America. She thought very seriously about it, but for me there was no question. Bideford is my home now. I am known here, I have loyal customers. I have carved my niche, as they say, and I have friends. What else could America offer me?'

She nodded without comment and he held up the satin on which he was working. 'A Sunday coat for a man from the wealthy end of Appledore,' he told her. 'A man who owns three fishing boats but has never been to sea in his life. All left him by his father.' He pointed to a half-finished jacket in green silk which lay across the back of a chair. 'For a farmer just outside Bideford. His wife died last year and left him with seven children. He is to wed again. Wouldn't you, in his shoes!' He pointed again to a garment in dark blue serge. 'Sensible breeches for the local schoolmaster, a man singularly lacking in imagination. He has the same cut and cloth every year.' He laughed. 'Who am I to grumble? They are our bread and butter.'

'And jam?' Sally suggested.

'And a little jam.' His smile broadened. 'I'm not complaining.'

'Maman looks well,' said Sally. 'And happy.'

He gave her a long look but said nothing.

'In fact . . .' Sally began.

She watched as his needle resumed its course and studied his long thin fingers as they smoothed and eased the rich satin.

'In fact,' she repeated, 'I want to say something which is long overdue – something I should have said years ago. I want to . . .'

Henri glanced up and said gently, 'There is no need, Soli.'

'Oh, but there is!' she insisted. 'I have to tell you how sorry I am and how wrong I was to treat you the way I did. No!' She held up her hand. 'Let me finish, Henri. I want to apologize for my behaviour towards you. You were so good to us and I treated you unkindly. What would we have done without you? I shudder to think.' She looked at him appealingly. 'I want to ask your forgiveness, Henri. That is partly why I have come.'

'There is no need for forgiveness. You were only a child, Soli. I made allowances.' He was regarding her kindly, his needle poised over the satin. 'Believe me, I understood how you felt. Your own father was important to you. That's how it should be.'

'No,' she said flatly. 'I made you both miserable and it has been on my conscience all these years. Life was difficult enough and I made it worse. Now I can see more clearly I am so sorry. Please say you forgive me.'

'Of course I do. I understood. You were an unhappy child. If it had not been for Mistress Tidden . . .'

Sally smiled. 'I must visit her while I am here.'

403

He shook his head sadly. 'You are too late. She is gone from us, Soli. About three weeks ago. Twas very quick, very merciful.' Seeing her distress he added, 'You could visit her grave. Take a sprig of rosemary.'

She nodded. He produced a handkerchief and she wiped her eyes.

Suddenly, steeling herself, she cried out, 'Henri, I must tell you. I have found my father. At least I –' She swallowed. 'He is dead, Henri. He cannot come between you and Maman. I found him and lost him again – all in a day! Oh, dearest Henri, may I tell you about it? Can you bear it?' His hands had tensed but now he relaxed and nodded.

As Sally poured out her story he sat very still and listened intently to the details without once taking his eyes from her face.

'So you see he never knew that we were in England,' she told him. 'Never knew that poor Grandmère was drowned or that the rest of us were safe. Or that we cared about him.'

'Fate can be very cruel,' he said softly.

'I only wanted to be reunited with him,' Sally insisted. 'I would not have betrayed you and Maman. I would never have taken away what you have – do you see that, Henri? I meant no harm.'

'I see it all. Yes.' He had slipped the needle into the satin and now laid a hand on her arm. 'I am pleased for you, Soli. You now know what happened to him and will not spend the rest of your life wondering where he is or what has become of him. He had a sad life but he is at rest now. You know he had a kind friend and benefactor in this – what was his name?'

'Ned Cooper.'

'He must be a very good man.'

Sally nodded.

'Or else he is very fond of you?' Henri said slyly.

Sally let that pass.

'There was so much I wanted to say to him – to Papa, I mean. I wanted to say, "Here I am. Your not so little Solange!" To see his face light up with surprise. I wanted to tell you, Henri, and to ask you if you thought we should tell Maman. Now that he can cause no problem. Would she want to know, Henri? You know her better than I do.'

'I think she should be told.'

'All of it?'

He put his head on one side, considering. 'I think the truth is always best. As you say, he can pose no threat to her security now. Poor Pierre.'

She looked at him in surprise. 'You can say that?'

'He lost a loving family. Without them he was lost.'

She swallowed hard. 'I have done a lot of thinking on my way over to Bideford. I believe if he knew about you and Maman – that you have taken care of her and loved her – I think he might be grateful.'

'That's a comforting thought, Soll. I thank you.'

He resumed his stitching and Sally fell silent again.

Suddenly she said, 'Ned Cooper wants to marry me.'

'Do you love him?'

'I don't know,' she replied helplessly. 'I like and admire him but I don't feel the way I did over – over another man I once knew.'

'Love comes in many guises,' he said. 'Does he love you?'

'Oh, yes. He would make a good husband but –'

'But what?'

'We might not make each other happy.' She frowned unhappily. 'Perhaps I am too old to change my ways? I have always been alone with no one else to consider. I have always been independent. Made my way! Does that sound presumptuous? I don't mean it that way. He would want children –'

'And you do not?'

'I have never considered them. I have never had time to think about it.'

Henri gave a little sigh and looked at her thoughtfully.

'I have always regretted not having a family. Oh, you and Jean have been my children,' he smiled, 'whether you liked it or not!'

She laughed, 'I might make a terrible wife and mother! Who knows?'

'I think not. You have a lot to offer, Soli.' He smiled again and, removing the eyeglass, rubbed his eyes tiredly. 'Do you know what I think? I think you are afraid of failing. If you stay with Sally Lunn's coffee-house you know you will succeed. Marriage is an unopened book. You are reluctant to turn the first page.'

She stared at him in astonishment.

'Afraid?' she gasped. 'Me – afraid?'

'I think so.'

'Well!' She could only shake her head at what she considered a preposterous suggestion.

'Why don't you tell me about your Ned Cooper?' he suggested.

Sally eyed him doubtfully. 'There's little to tell,' she began. 'He is the son of Mistress Cooper who first employed me when I arrived in Bath. I wrote about her. He's tall, broad-shouldered, a heavily built man.'

'Stolid?' Henri suggested.

'No, not that exactly,' she amended, 'but *solid* as a rock. His eyes are brown – very dark and intense. His voice is low and – and somehow reassuring.' She stared ahead, trying to raise Ned's image. 'He's not an impulsive man. He thinks things through. Do you see what I mean?'

Henri nodded, watching her, his mouth curved into a faint smile.

'He's very kind, always helping people. And *so* gentle, Henri – he'd never willingly hurt a fly! He is not a moody man but very calm and thoughtful. A man you could trust. A loyal man. Steadfast. He works at one of the quarries above the town, supervising the men. He has his own office,' she said proudly. 'The owner is never there.'

'The owner trusts Ned to run the business?'

He looked impressed.

'Oh yes!' cried Soli, and her eyes met Henri's earnestly. 'Certainly he does. Ned Cooper is as straight as a die. Once he was betrothed to a girl called Rose but she died and his mother said he would never forget her or look at another woman. His mother didn't want to lose him, which was natural, I dare say, but I argued with her, of course. You know how awkward I could be. I said he would die a lonely old man.'

'But he *has* looked at another woman. He has looked at you.'

'Yes.'

'You must have made a rare impression on him.'

'I suppose so.' She sighed. 'He is not exactly romantic like – like another man I once knew.'

'Ah!' said Henri. 'This other man. Be very careful, Soli. Comparisons can be very dangerous.'

'Can they?'

He bit off a new length of thread and while he threaded it Sally waited impatiently for him to continue.

'Very dangerous indeed!' said Henri. 'If you want my advice, Soli, you will be very wary of comparisons.'

She stared down at her hands which were clasped restlessly in her lap. Henri inspected his work critically and then began to sew again.

'This other man – this romantic man – are you going to tell me his name?'

'I would rather not,' she said hastily.

'Did *he* propose marriage?'

'No.'

'But you hoped he would?'

'I thought he should!' Indignation made her indiscreet. 'After all we had . . .' She faltered and lowered her voice. 'After all we had been to each other.'

'Ah!'

There was a wealth of meaning in his sigh and Sally did not answer.

'Hardly a worthy man, then?' he continued. 'Hardly a Ned Cooper?'

His tone was so innocent that she laughed. 'Henri! I thought you said comparisons were dangerous?'

He rolled his eyes. 'So I did! I am hoist with my own petard! Forgive me.'

'Granted!' She laughed again. 'No, Ned would never behave that way. Ned is a gentleman while Richard –' She stopped herself just in time.

'We are none of us perfect,' Henri said softly. 'There is good in the worst of us and bad in the best of us. I like the sound of your Ned Cooper but have no fear on his account, Soli. If you do not take him for a husband another will. A man like that will not stay single once he has made up his mind to wed. I doubt very much he will die lonely.'

She gave him a level look. 'But I might! Is that what you mean?'

'Only from choice, Soli.'

'If I wed and had children I would have to give up my coffee-house.'

'Sell it to Mr Dalmer!'

Before she realised what she was doing Sally began to consider the idea, then stopped in confusion.

'Henri!' she cried. 'That was craftily done!'

She began to laugh and he joined her and Sally looked at him and thought how lucky her mother was to have such a man. Impulsively she leaned towards him and kissed his face, a light, fleeting, hesitant kiss. Slowly he slipped the needle into the satin and laid it out of harm's way. Then he said, 'Come here, my funny little Soli!' and held out his arms and, with a heartfelt sigh, Sally moved into them.

The next day she began her journey back to Bath in a jubilant mood. With Henri's help she had made up her mind to marry Ned Cooper.

Chapter Sixteen

THE WEATHER DURING her ride back to Bath was not as pleasant as it had been on the ride out. A cold wind blew into their faces for much of the time which chilled their spirits and made the horses fidgety. They were not waylaid, fortunately, but the best part of a day was lost by smaller mishaps – the loss of a horseshoe, the indisposition of one of the party and the breakdown of a wagon due to a loose rear wheel.

Eager to get home, Sally hid her frustration as well as she could but the delays irked her. By the time they reached the outskirts of Bath it was five o'clock in the evening and she was tired and out of temper. As soon as she had parted from her fellow travellers she went straight back to Segar's Alley and fell into bed.

She slept right through until the early hours of the next morning and then suddenly she was wide awake and could not bear to lie in bed a moment longer. She rose before the sun was properly up and went downstairs to light the fire and heat a kettle of water. While she waited for it to boil she wandered through the house, wondering how it would feel to know that someone else looked upon number four Segar's Alley as home.

Downstairs in the bakery she looked with affection at each and every item, from the trough to the smallest spoon, and tried to imagine someone – Mr Dalmer, perhaps – working here with his sleeves rolled up, making the Sally Lunns which had been her own creation. The thought posed a problem which she had considered, along with many other questions, during her journey home and about which she was still undecided. Should she sell the recipe for her Sally Lunns?

If she did not, then Sally Lunn's Coffee-House for which she had worked so hard would cease to exist. It would simply become a coffee-house like any other. No, she shook her head decidedly. If she wished her name to survive she must offer it as a going concern. In all probability she had no real choice in the matter because without her teacakes no baker worth his salt would be interested.

She sighed deeply and ran her fingers lovingly across the lid of the trough and thought at once of Toby, his round, good-natured face, ready smile and cheerful whistling. He had been so much a part of it and without him it could never be quite the same.

'*Plus ça change!*' Henri had said and he was probably right. Things changed for better or worse and perhaps, for her, the best years of Sally Lunn's were over. Change was all about her and she was preparing to turn a new page in her life. Perhaps the best was yet to come for life with Ned would provide a new challenge.

The tabby cat rubbed around her legs and she picked it up and kissed it. Soon she would have a husband and children to love and already the idea was not so alien to her. Henri had been an inspiration to her and she was so grateful that he and Marie had resisted the temptation to go to America. She smiled. She would give them a son-in-law they could love and respect and, hopefully, grandchildren to make up for the ones they might never see again.

She put the cat down and moved across to open the oven door. Inside it was warm and dark and she closed the door quickly. Later it would be glowing, the way she loved it. The faggot box was empty! She would have something to say to the boy when he arrived.

'Lackadaisical wretch!' she muttered but surprisingly this lapse did not bother her as much as it usually did and she realised with a start that already the heavy mantle of responsibility was slipping from her shoulders.

Upstairs in the kitchen she drank two cups of strong, sweet tea, which was rather a luxury, and by that time dawn had broken and a pale light illuminated the room. Later she would visit Andrew Wills and the boy and let them know she was back and that work would begin again that evening. The coffee-house would be open for business tomorrow.

Half an hour later she had washed and dressed and sat at the kitchen table composing a letter to Mr Dalmer.

My Dear Sir,
I shall shortly be affianced to Master Ned Cooper –

No, she did not like the word 'affianced' and began again:

My Dear Sir,
You may be interested to learn that before long
Sally Lunn's will be on the market –

It was too formal. She crumpled the paper and nibbled
the end of the quill thoughtfully.

Dear Mr Dalmer,
You have frequently teased me about Sally
Lunn's, professing a desire to buy the recipe for
my teacakes. I am now offering you the chance to
purchase that and my business also. I shall shortly
be wed to Master Ned Cooper and –'

Quill poised, she began to imagine Ned's face when
she told him she had changed her mind and was going
to accept his proposal. She thought she would meet
him on his way home from the quarry and she would
wear her heavy brown silk with the pale blue trim. Or
perhaps the dark green skirt and matching jacket.

Her new dress would do well for the wedding itself.
Mistress Ned Cooper!

A smile lit her face and she wondered if perhaps she
would go and tell him now, before he went to the
quarry. She could walk part of the way with him. She
finished her letter and decided she could wait no
longer to see Ned. She would deliver it to Mr Dalmer
on the way to Ned's house.

Just before seven, wearing her brown silk dress, she
threw a heavy shawl around her shoulders and set out.
As soon as the letter had been slipped under Dalmer's
door she hurried round to Ned's house rehearsing the
little speech she had prepared. To her surprise she had

to knock three times before the door was finally opened by Nan who, dressed in her nightgown, looked bleary-eyed and none too pleased by her early visitor.

'Good morrow,' said Sally, feeling ridiculously nervous. 'I have called to see your master. I hope he hasn't –'

'See the master?' answered Nan. She looked surprised. 'Why then, you haven't heard?'

Sally's heart contracted with a sudden premonition of disaster.

'Heard what?' she demanded urgently.

Nan rubbed her eyes sleepily. 'I thought everyone knew,' she said. 'I thought it was all over Bath. I thought –'

'Knew what?' Sally resisted the impulse to shake her. 'What should I know? Has something happened to him?'

The servant shivered a little and opened the door wider. 'I shall catch my death on this doorstep,' she grumbled. 'You'd best come inside.'

Sally stepped in to the small front room and said, 'What has happened? I've been away for more than a week. Tell me at once!'

Nan closed the door, refusing to be hurried. 'Why, he's only been half-murdered! That's what's happened.'

Sally stared at her in horror. 'Half-murdered!' she echoed dazedly. 'Ned has been half-murdered? But how? By whom? Oh God! How is he? He will recover, won't he?'

Nan shrugged. 'Who can say?' she replied unhelpfully. 'All I know is he was set upon at the quarry the day before yesterday and they found him with his head bashed in. Thought he was dead, they did. Gave them a rare old fright, from all accounts.'

'Gave who? The quarrymen?'

Nan nodded. 'Lying at the top of the slope, he was, with blood everywhere. Man named Sturmer. That's who they're looking for but it seems he's skipped the town.'

Sally put a trembling hand to her mouth. 'Where is he?' she whispered.

'No one knows. His mother and his brother have gone, too.'

'Not Sturmer!' cried Sally. 'Ned! Is he in the hospital? Or upstairs?'

'Upstairs. But you can't see him.'

'I take it he is in his own bedroom.'

'Yes, he is but the physician said he was – Here! Where do you think you're going?'

Sally had pushed past her and was hurrying up the stairs. Nan lumbered up after her, protesting that the patient was not to be disturbed.

At the top of the stairs Sally turned. 'For your information, Nan, your master and I are to be wed! In the meantime, while he is in this condition, I shall care for him and you will take your orders from me. Come back to me when you are washed and dressed.'

She left Nan with her mouth wide open and pushed open the door of Ned's bedroom. The state of the room made her curse under her breath. The fire was unlit and the room was very cold, Ned lay in bed with his head swathed in blood-soaked bandages. There was even dried blood on the pillow and a smell of stale urine pervaded the room. It was obvious that no one had attended to the man for a considerable length of time. The left side of Ned's face was chalk white but the other side was a mottled purple. His eyes were puffed and swollen and his lips were blue. She leaned over him, stunned by grief and fear.

'Ned! Can you hear me?' she whispered. ''Tis your own Sally. 'Tis Sally Lunn!'

He gave no indication that he had heard but his breath rattled suddenly in his throat, whether by chance or design she could not tell. She looked at him fearfully. He looked so terribly still. The thought of his desperate condition and Nan's neglect brought tears to her eyes but she brushed them away angrily. This was no time for tears. Somehow she must nurse him back to life. Picking up his hand she kissed it passionately.

'I won't let you die, Ned. I won't,' she told him.

She then went upstairs and threw open the door of the room where Nan was tugging her clothes on.

'I want hot water – you will light the kitchen fire before you do anything else. I shall light one in your master's bedroom. I want clean sheets – you will bring them to me. When did the doctor last call?'

The servant fumbled with the buttons of her dress. 'I don't know – the day before yesterday I think.'

'Weren't you here?'

'I went home for a bit,' she said evasively. 'I don't like being here on my own with him like that. I don't like sick folks, they give me the shivers.'

'You left your master and went home?' Sally asked incredulously. 'He lies at death's door and you left him alone?'

Nan scowled. 'He's not to know. He sleeps all the time.'

Sally fought down her rising anger. For the moment she needed the girl's help. She drew a long breath. 'On second thoughts I will see to the fires while you go for the physician,' she said evenly. 'Ask him to come at once. Tell him I am here and that we shall want fresh bandages. Oh, and medicaments. If the physician recommends anything go to the apothecary on the way home – here is some money.'

The girl eyed her sullenly as she thrust a purse into her hand.

'And, Nan!'

'What is it?'

'Hurry! You hear me? Straight to the physician – no dawdling.'

'I hear you,' said Nan through tight lips.

Sally kept her hands to herself with an effort. Later she would send the girl packing, she promised herself.

'Then go!' she said sharply.

The physician, when he arrived, could say nothing to reassure Sally that Ned would ultimately recover. He had done what he could, he told her, but the head wound was 'severe', and only a very strong man could be expected to survive such a blow. Sally told him firmly that Ned Cooper was one of the strongest men she knew and outwardly she was determinedly confident, but in her heart she was full of a most terrible anxiety. She had just lost her father and now it seemed she might also lose her husband-to-be.

She arranged for Andrew Wills and the boy to bake the bread but closed the coffee-house 'until further notice'. Then she moved into Ned's house and nursed him night and day. Nan, after a trial period of three days, was sent home and Jane came in daily in her stead.

Days passed without any sign of improvement in Ned's condition and the physician grew gloomier with each visit. Ned was, in fact, unconscious (not sleeping as Nan had assumed) and lay without moving a muscle, oblivious to his surroundings. Occasionally he uttered a sound that was half sigh, half groan and then Sally would fly to his side only to be disappointed as he relapsed once more into silence. He could not take any nourishment and grew painfully thin and Sally was forced to watch him grow steadily weaker with each day that passed. She washed him, changed his bandages and kept him warm but there was nothing more she could do except wait and pray and this last she did vehemently and with passion.

Master Dalmer finally discovered her whereabouts and came to express interest in her offer but she told him that for the present Sally Lunn's was closed and she had no idea when it would reopen. Nothing permanent could be settled until Ned Cooper was himself again. She knew, but did not say, that if Ned died she would return to Sally Lunn's and the business would no longer be on offer.

On January 25th one of her fears was laid to rest when the long-awaited letter from America finally arrived and she sat beside Ned's bed to read it.

My dearest Soli, [Jean had written in his untidy scrawl]
    You will see from this letter that we did arrive

safely in our new country. I will not dwell on the most arduous voyage which is best forgotten. You will understand if I say that I never intend to set foot on a ship again as long as I live.

The people of Williamsburg are very hospitable and in the past four days we have met with much kindness. For the present we shall share a rented house but in time we will move into a house of our own.

The town itself is younger than I imagined but bustling and energetic and growing fast. It is spread over a large area and the streets are wide with trees planted along the sidewalks. New fine buildings are going up everywhere and there is no poverty of which I am aware. One day it will be a fine city and we shall be proud to be part of it.

Louise sends her love and so do the little ones. The children were very ill on the voyage but made a rapid recovery the moment they set foot on dry land and are at this moment playing 'horseshoes' with the children of a neighbour.

Louise's parents are very homesick and subject to bouts of melancholy but I am hopeful the malaise will pass with time. 'Tis harder for people of their age to adapt to change.

The climate is less kind than I expected but I am assured the summer will be hot.

During the voyage we made friends with an apothecary and his wife by the name of Speke who come originally from Glastonbury and they also have settled in Williamsburg.

They have chosen a plot of land in North England Street so that their house, when it is built, will overlook a windmill as their previous house did in England. They say it will remind them of home but we will not think that way. For us Williamsburg is home and France and England are behind us.

If ever you change your mind, Soli, and want to join us you will be most welcome. *It will never be too late*.

His emphasis made Sally smile.

For the moment be happy and write to us often. We miss you very much and long for your letters but have no fear on our account. We are well content with our lot.

I will write again. Our prayers are for you always. Your loving brother, Jean.

PS I write also to Maman and Henri.

'Oh, Jean!' she whispered and closed her eyes and pressed the letter to her heart. Then she read it again, more slowly, savouring every word. She tried to imagine them in their new country, walking down those wide, tree-lined streets, but her imagination failed her. So they missed her! The thought was strangely comforting. And the Reys were homesick. Poor souls! The weather, too, was a disappointment. How tiresome. Reading between the lines she was reassured that she had made the right decision. She had been wise to stay in Bath!

She was pondering the game of horseshoes when

she glanced at Ned and suddenly saw his eyelids flicker.

'Ned!' she whispered, hardly daring to hope. For a moment nothing else happened.

Dear God! Had she imagined it?

They moved again and then, incredibly, they *opened* and he was staring at the ceiling.

'Ned!' she repeated, her heart racing with excitement. 'Oh, Ned, can you hear me? 'Tis your own Sally.'

He blinked and then he turned his head in her direction and she saw a glimmer of recognition in his brown eyes. He tried to speak but she laid a finger on his lips, fearful that he would overtire himself.

'No need to talk, Ned,' she told him, 'but oh, my dearest Ned! You are going to get well. My prayers have been answered.' In spite of her warning he again tried to speak and somehow his lips framed the word 'Sally' and her nightmare was almost over.

Less than an hour later Ned was able to swallow a few spoonfuls of gruel and after three days the astonished physician was boasting to his colleagues of his 'miracle cure'.

A month later Ned was sitting up in bed, the bandages had been removed and his hair was beginning to grow back over the wound. He was eating well and the natural colour had returned to his face.

'The bruising has gone.' Sally regarded him with satisfaction. 'You look like the Ned Cooper I remember. Here – see for yourself.'

He laughed as he took the small mirror from her and nodded approvingly at his reflection.

'As handsome as ever!' she said. 'And tomorrow the physician says you may get out of bed for the first time and sit in the chair. Before long we will have you on your feet again, as good as new, and then you will have no excuse to delay our wedding!'

He laughed. 'You have only yourself to blame. You could have made an honest man of me months ago had you not been so stubborn.'

'I have been well punished for my folly,' she replied, seating herself on the chair beside him and taking up her sewing. She stitched for a few moments and he waited. Something was troubling her but he knew better than to ask.

'No news?' he asked. 'I thought you had called in to Juliana Popjoy. You are usually bursting with titbits of gossip when you have been there.'

'News?' Sally paused to glance up. 'But of course. She hears good things of Dalmer. He has made a good start with Sally Lunn's. I knew he would, of course. It cannot fail now with Nash's recommendation.'

'Dalmer would be a fool to let such an opportunity slip through his fingers. But I am pleased for you, too, because Sally Lunn's will last – who knows how long?'

'I do hope so, Ned.'

He laughed. 'Kings may come and kings may go but you'll go on for ever!'

'Now you're teasing me!'

He reached out and took hold of her hand. 'Dalmer may grow rich on your reputation but I am richer by far for I have the real Sally Lunn.'

'Oh, Ned!'

He squeezed her hand and they exchanged a long look, full of love.

Suddenly she said, 'Nash was there.'

'At the coffee-house?' He watched her expression carefully.

'No, at Juliana's. She made no secret of their liaison. 'Tis the talk of the town, she tells me. For my part I wish them well.'

'Do you?'

'Most certainly. She is welcome to him. I know who has the better man!'

He smiled as she bent her head again, apparently intent on her needlework.

'You have some news,' he prompted at last. 'Something you don't want me to know. I can see it in your eyes. Won't you pluck up your courage and tell me?'

As she laid down the pillowslip her smile faded.

''Tis Sturmer,' she said. 'I heard it this morning. It seems he stole a horse and was later apprehended in Bridgewater. Three days later he was hanged for his pains.'

Ned was silent but Sally said, 'I cannot pity him, Ned. He left you to die. 'Twas unforgivable. Barbaric.'

When he did not speak she went on. 'If Sturmer had succeeded in his murderous attempts I would have two graves to tend now instead of one. 'Tis no thanks to him we are looking forward to our marriage.'

Ned sighed. 'And his mother and brother? What of them? Do you know?'

'They have gone into the workhouse in Bridgewater.'

He frowned at her words and Sally could see that

already his sympathies were aroused for the unfortunate mother and brother and she shook her head a little in fond exasperation. No doubt eventually he would find a way to relieve a little of their misery.

She thought suddenly of Henri's words, 'There is good in the worst of us and bad in the best of us.' He and Ned would have a lot in common, she reflected.

'You are an incorrigible champion of lost causes, Ned!' she said softly.

'Can you bear it?' he asked with a smile. 'My mother found it very tiresome!'

'The world is full of lame dogs,' she told him. 'Someone must help them. You have a generous heart. I think I can bear it. In fact, I love you the more for it.'

'And you still want to marry me?'

By way of answer she leaned over and kissed him full on the mouth.

Five weeks later they were man and wife and Sally was Sally Lunn no longer. For the rest of the world, however, the legend of Sally Lunn was just beginning.

All Sphere Books are available at your bookshop or newsagent, or can be ordered from the following address:

Sphere Books,
Cash Sales Department,
P.O. Box 11,
Falmouth,
Cornwall TR10 9EN.

Alternatively you may fax your order to the above address. Fax No. 0326 76423.

Payments can be made as follows: Cheque, postal order (payable to Macdonald & Co (Publishers) Ltd) or by credit cards, Visa/Access. Do not send cash or currency. UK customers: please send a cheque or postal order (no currency) and allow 80p for postage and packing for the first book plus 20p for each additional book up to a maximum charge of £2.00.

B.F.P.O. customers please allow 80p for the first book plus 20p for each additional book.

Overseas customers including Ireland, please allow £1.50 for postage and packing for the first book, £1.00 for the second book, and 30p for each additional book.

NAME (Block Letters) ....

ADDRESS ....

....

☐ I enclose my remittance for _____

☐ I wish to pay by Access/Visa Card

Number ☐☐☐☐☐☐☐☐☐☐☐☐☐☐☐☐☐

Card Expiry Date ☐☐☐☐